BROKEN

ELLIE MESSE

BROKEN

Second Edition

© 2017 L. E. Messenger

All rights reserved. This book or parts thereof may not be reproduced in any form, except for the inclusion of brief quotations in a review. This book or parts thereof may not be stored in any retrieval system, or transmitted in any form by any means—electronic, mechanical, photocopy, recording, or otherwise—without prior written permission of the publisher, except as provided by United States of America copyright law. For permission requests, write to the author, at "Attention: Permissions Coordinator," at the address elliemesse@gmail.com

This book is a work of fiction. Names, characters, establishments, organizations, and incidents are used fictitiously to give the sense of authenticity. Any resemblance to actual persons living or deceased, events, or locales is coincidental.

For information about special discounts for bulk purchases, please contact the author at, elliemesse@gmail.com

Cover art: © 2017 Messenger Art Gallery

ISBN-13: 978-1723269950

ISBN-10: 1723269956

BROKEN

To my amazing sister, Nae Nae.

My muse.

Thank you for the cuddles, the snuggles, and endless amount of encouragement.
As always, this is for you!

xxBug

BROKEN

"She seems so invisible.
But touch her and she'll wince.
She has secrets and trusts no one.
She's the perfect example of betrayal.
Because anyone she's ever trusted,
broke her."
-Unknown

BROKEN

NOTE FROM THE AUTHOR

Thank you, thank you, thank you for taking a chance on me.

I just wanted to mention a few points. When I started this, it was merely a challenge to entertain myself and my sister. I wanted to write extremes; extreme circumstances, extreme emotions, and personal extremes- like writing sex for the first time. I wanted to see just how far I could throw my mind and still be believable. It just so happened that I fell in love with the characters and couldn't keep them to myself.

This is also a HUGE book. I was given the option to break it down into two separate novels, but I couldn't do it, I wrote this start to finish with no breaks in between so in my mind this is one story, needing to be read in its entirety. Plus, I'm a very impatient reader, and in the event, you love it as much as I do, I didn't want to make anyone wait and be an asshole.

Side note, I'm a one-woman show with an army of supporters. This book is edited, formatted, proofread, etc. by nonprofessionals. If those things are important to you, this might not be the book for you.

So, without further ado- GO FORTH MY CHILDREN.

Love, Ellie

BROKEN

CHAPTER ONE

Mama didn't come home.
Daddy liked to hit.
Brothers followed suit.

My future was planned from birth; I'm aware I wasn't destined for good things. How I have an apartment that's located in a decent part of town is beyond me. The fact Derek, Joe, or Evan haven't hunted me down yet is a gift from God.

My brothers are ruthless and disgustingly loyal to my piece of shit father. My brother, Kaylan, was the only good thing I had in that awful house but just like everything good in my life, he left. He promised he'd take me with him, but he didn't; he disappeared in the middle of the night. The pain of his abandonment was worse than the physical pain of my father's fury, convinced I knew Kaylan's plans of running away; I endured his wrath until he was too tired to continue.

I was eight.

Just before my seventeenth birthday a 'house bunny' of my brothers, which roughly translates to; whores who sleep with my brothers for drugs or a few extra bucks, gave me an envelope that changed my life. Inside was twelve-hundred dollars in cash, a fake I.D and a note with one word scribbled across the surface, Run.

So, I ran.

Just like Kaylan.

I didn't ask questions, I shoved the envelope down my pants and walked down the hall.

That was a year and a half ago, but I can still feel the sticky air of the swamp cooler as I navigated through the cluttered house, the sour taste of whatever was brewing in the back bedroom. Derek had thrown a shoe at me demanding to know where I was going. I mumbled something about smoking and walked out. I remember thinking about how loud my shoes echoed against the sidewalk as I made my way to the street; the sound was deafening, mixed with the noise of blood rushing past my ears, I was confident they could hear me over the television. I lit up a cigarette and tried to walk as casually as I could down the driveway. My heart was trying to climb right out of my throat along with everything in my stomach when I turned off our walkway and kept moving, waiting for one of them to come barreling out of the house and drag me back by my hair, but they never came. I bought a bus ticket for the first available seat which lead me here to Phoenix.

Now, I don't know if you've ever been to Phoenix, but it's hot- like melt-your-face-off hot. I made a deal to work housekeeping for a discounted room at a shitty motel. It wasn't too bad if you could ignore the mice and roaches.

With my new I.D. making me old enough to legally drink, I was able to get a second job at a dive bar down the street that offered free meals after each shift and decent tips once I turned seventeen. Pretty sure the owners knew I wasn't twenty-one, but they never asked, and I never told.

After working there a few months my boss, Vinny, told me about his brother Josh needing help downtown at his nightclub. So now I work mornings as room service, happy hour at VIN's and nights at HEAT. Well, that's not entirely true; today was my last day working for Wanda's 'No-tell Motel' because today, I got the keys to my very own apartment. A surprisingly nice, one-bedroom apartment that's almost perfectly spaced between VIN's and HEAT. Sure, I'll have to work my ass off to furnish it, but it's mine. I don't have to share space with any six-legged creatures or sleep with mice, and I have faith I won't hear women crying out to our Lord and Savior in rush secession throughout the night, followed by the immediate argument that ends with slammed doors and colorful language thrown across the parking lot.

No, this place will be pest and prostitute free. The eighty-something-year-old woman living to my right is what I'm basing my faith on.

With a sharp 'click' the door opens into my living room. That's right; Ryan Carter Hale finally has a home.

CHAPTER TWO

"Haley!" Drew yells over the techno blasting through the speakers while flipping a bottle behind his back, the glass lands in his hand before he starts pouring the amber liquid across a row of shot glasses. "This heartthrob says I don't have game." He nods at the busty blonde leaning against the bar.

"That's cause you don't."

His whole body goes stiff as his smirk transforms into a deadpan, "Fucking rude."

"Bite me." I nod to the customer in front of me who holds up two fingers.

Pulling two long necks out of the cooler, I slide them to the guy as Drew continues, "I would, but you threatened to wear my balls for earrings."

"Sounds like me."

BROKEN

The strobe lights that line the ceiling flash in quick succession giving the illusion of flames across the club floor. Holding out his hand, Drew helps me climb on to the massive bar top before disappearing to assist Alice and Danica as the DJ plays an original song about heat and the flames of dancing or some bullshit as our three male bar-backs climb up behind us holding full shot glasses. The lights continue to flash before the spotlights land on the bar, painting us in a bluish glow.

Drew has been my partner since my first day; he pours the shot into his mouth, dips me so low I'm almost lying on the bar top before pretending to kiss me as the tequila slides from his mouth into mine. Just as the speakers blare "Feel the heat!" Someone lights Drew's alcohol-soaked fingers on fire as he yanks me upright, holding his flaming fingers in front of my face, I spray the alcohol across the surface, sending a cloud of flames above the crowd. As usual, the place explodes in drunken cheers. Drew does this flip thing off the bar with his usual flair before immediately leaning into the blonde's personal bubble, "How's that for game, sweetheart?"

Judging by the 'fuck me' eyes she's giving him, I assume I'll be hearing all about his sexcapades with her tomorrow.

I understand the attraction, Drew's well over six-foot-tall, short sandy brown hair that's lazily kept, ripped beyond belief and has a Georgian accent, all that with baby blue eyes? I have yet to meet a girl, apart from myself, that's immune to his charms. I had a moment of weakness during my first month that I considered dipping into that candy dish, but he's Josh's nephew, a womanizer, and despite what my I.D. says, I'm illegal. Well, I was at the time anyway.

Last call came and went leaving us lounging on the leather sofas while we wait for the others to get their side work done. Drew keeps throwing cherry stems at Danica, who pretends to be annoyed, while Simon huffs on about how Drew should have to sweep instead of him.

"Everything looks good, Y'all," Josh says exiting from behind the bar. "You're all free to clock out."

"Whahoo!" Drew uses the back of the couch as a launching pad, earning him a glare from Josh.

"Haley-" I look up to find Josh extending a folded envelope to me.

"Oh. Thanks!" I smile, pushing my paycheck into my bra.

BROKEN

"How come Haley gets cashed out, but we all have to wait for the bank to dish out our dues?" Alice asks in her usual bitchy tone.

"Because Hales is convinced the man is watching her," Drew answers for me, donning his leather riding jacket. He's so full of shit, but I appreciate the save.

"Because that's the way Haley and I have it arranged." Josh's answer is clipped. Furthering my earlier thought that they know I'm not twenty-one.

I fed him a crock story about how my bank account was locked down for identity theft and wouldn't be able to access it until the bank did their magic. After almost a year, neither Vinny nor Josh has mentioned it since; they just continue to pay me under the table. I know this because I didn't give them anything other than my fake ID when applying. No address, no social security number, nothing but a fake name on a piece of plastic.

"By the way-" his tone low enough that only I can hear as he hands me another envelope, this one bigger and more square than usual. "Go get yourself that couch."

As soon as the words were out of his mouth, everyone behind me starts singing,

BROKEN

Happy Birthday. I twist to see Drew holding a white and pink cupcake. Darkness crawls up my throat, threatening to choke me. I've never had someone sing me Happy Birthday before, thankfully the walls I've built inside my head are stronger than Fort Knox, so the tears stay in my throat rather than in my eyes. And so, what if my actual birthday was two months ago? According to my fake ID, Haley Carter's birthday is August seventeenth, and I'd rather be her than Ryan Hale any day.

Biting my lip, I close my eyes, wishing for this version of my life to last just a little while longer. As I blow the little blue candle out, I will the smoke to carry my wish to the heavens.

CHAPTER THREE

"Oh my God!" I sigh, sinking into the plush tan fabric.

"Seriously?" Drew huffs above me, "It's hideous."

"Shut up; it's like a cloud."

"Bullshit. Something that ugly can't be comfortable, move over."

Begrudgingly, I slide my legs off the side to make room for him.

He slams his weight down and groans. "Oh, no. You're right, this is nice."

"Don't you dare break my couch, douchebag." I glare at him.

He chuckles, sinking into the cushion. "Fuck, this is nice."

"I know!" I almost squeal.

BROKEN

Sleeping on the floor has been a bitch the last couple of days. I had to wait for Drew to borrow Josh's truck so I could bring this bad boy home.

"Go get the salesperson so we can load this up and by we, I mean you."

"Your couch, you go get 'em."

"Don't be a dick." I groan, pushing him with my foot.

"I'm the one who has to carry this into your apartment. You can get off your ass and find the person."

"I hate you." I smile, "Rock, paper, scissors?"

He opens one eye before smiling wickedly. "One, two," he winks, slamming his fist into the palm of his hand, "Three-"

I chuckle when he curses. With a loud grunt, he climbs to his feet, scanning the area for an attendant. "Just wave your arms above your head like a lunatic. I'm sure you'll get someone's attention."

"Lift up your shirt. I'm sure that'll work faster." He retorts, his eyes still scanning the store.

"Lift your shirt."

His hands grab the hem of his top, pulling it up to reveal the plains of his stomach, deep crevices run the length of him. A fit of laughter bubbles out of me when he begins jumping up and down, flailing his arms as his teeth hold his t-shirt up. He looks utterly ridiculous, but I can see the sparkle in the eyes of the women passing by.

When his tactics catch the eye of a thirty-something-year-old man with a beer gut, my laughter grows out of control. My sides are on fire, my face hurts, but I can't stop. The look on Drew's face will be forever burned into my mind. Little Miss D cup was mere seconds away from approaching when Tom the salesman nodded and came over to claim the sale. I can barely talk for the first few seconds as Drew is still staring in disbelief.

I give him a pat on the arm while I attempting to regain my composure, "That'll help with the inflamed ego, my friend."

Turning my attention to the male associate, I proceed to purchase my very own couch.

Drew ended up with Miss D cups phone number after all. I suppose watching him load the couch into the flatbed without the help of the two other attendants finally sealed the deal. She came out, claiming I'd forgotten my receipt and handed him a folded piece of paper. He wore a smug smile the entire drive to my complex.

Climbing out of the cab, he has an extra little hop to his step while collecting the couch out of the back. I lead him to my apartment, swing the door open and then step out of his way so he can get by.

"Jesus, Hales. Where the hell is all your stuff?"

I follow him into my empty apartment.

"I haven't picked it up yet." Somewhat true, more like I haven't bought it yet.

"How long have you been here?"

"Couple of days. Right there, please." I point to the center of the room, "Facing that wall."

He spins, setting the couch down where I asked. Stepping over, I nudge it forward with my hip until its back is lined up with the front door and hallway. Perfect.

A smile brightens my face before flopping down, "Thank you."

"Of course," He's still looking around at the empty walls, "Just let me know when you want to pick up the rest of your shit. I'll bring the trailer, and we can do it in one trip."

I don't want him to know that there's nothing to collect, so I go for a neutral response, "Cool, thanks."

"I'm gonna bounce, sunshine. Want a ride to VIN's?"

Pulling my burner phone out of my pocket, I check the time; I don't start for another hour and a half. "No, that's alright. Thanks though."

After flashing his boyish grin, he leaves me alone with my big fluffy sofa.

BROKEN

Oh man, this is nice, the fabric is like silk. The couch back home in Reno was crusty and stiff, plus it always smelled sour, no doubt had drugs and used condoms shoved into the cushions. Burying my face into the fabric, I inhale to clear the memory. Just smells like fabric- clean, new fabric, in my clean, new apartment.

An hour later, I'm at VIN's bar dressed in my usual uniform; a yellow t-shirt with the bar logo on the back, black pants, and my knock-off Chuck Taylors, tonight they're red. Walmart had them for ten bucks, so over time, I own just about every color they offer.

"Hello, Miss Carter. How are you tonight?" Vinny's thick frame asks from beneath the bar where he's stocking glasses.

"Good. Drew and I picked up my couch today."

"Is that right? Is it every bit as wonderful as you remembered?"

I may have mentioned the love I have for that piece of furniture once or twice. And by 'may' I mean I haven't shut up since I found it a few weeks ago. "And so much more."

He flashes his kind smile, "Dillon's getting ready to close the lunch menu, if you want to order food before your shift, I'd do it soon."

Oh, I want a turkey club something fierce. "Will do. Thank you."

Skirting behind him I push through the kitchen doors, scanning for Dillon; his hair is blue this week making him easy to spot. "Hey, Dillon."

"Hey! What will it be?"

"Turkey club, please."

"On it. You want seasoned or regular fries?"

"Whatever's older."

He nods without response, so I shuffle into the office to say hello to Vinny's wife, Jules, and clock in.

"Oh, good. You're here. I was just coming to find you." Her blonde hair cascades down her back in thick natural waves. She's a babe for being in her forties. "These are your tips from the jar." My eyes bulge at the wad in her hand.

"Holy crap."

She gives me a small laugh as I take the money from her. We get to keep the tips we're handed personally, but anything that gets put in the jar is divvied up evenly throughout the staff once a month.

"Must have been a good month."

"Well, Sarah got her degree and is moving to Charlotte, Andrew left, and Becca is only here on Friday and Saturdays, so, tips were split into four rather than seven."

My brow furrows, Becca's a single mom who can only get a sitter on Friday and Saturdays, so she's not able to work more than the two days. Quickly shifting through the money, I pull what looks to be about a hundred bucks and hand it to Jules, "For Becca."

Her eyes widen, "That's not-"

"No, really. She'd be here more than two days if she could."

"She gets tipped out after each shift rather than wait for the jar. Don't worry about it."

Well, alright. I pull my apron off the hook and settle the money into the center pocket before tying it around my waist.

"Happy belated Birthday, by the way."

My hands freeze behind my back. That's the second time I nearly choked on the shards of emotion inside my throat. "Thank you," I managed to squeeze out.

"I hear the HEAT crew surprised you."

"They did." I nod. The fact people remembered let alone care is still very new to me.

"How old does that make you now?" Make you now. See? Pretty sure they know.

Eighteen. "Twenty-two."

She nods with a knowing smile, "Ah, twenty-two. What I wouldn't give to be twenty-two again." Well, with a fancy little piece of plastic she could be. "How's the new apartment?"

"Amazing. I still have to get my stuff moved over." I lie.

"That's what Drew was saying earlier. Said he went with you to get your luxury sofa.

Claimed it was hideous but, and I quote, 'Comfortable as all hell.'" She chuckles softly.

"It's not hideous; it's beautiful. He's just a dude and doesn't appreciate it."

She laughs openly now. "Isn't that the truth. Are you-" We both turn when Dillon calls my order.

Without finishing her thought, she smiles and waves me away.

I made forty bucks at VIN's which is good considering it's just a dive bar, and HEAT is bloody packed tonight. Josh added two additional fire shows to appease the crowd, and we're making a killing. The usual banter between Drew and I has been on fire with all the people giving additional tips for funny bartenders.

Sliding three cocktails down the line, I spin to grab a clean towel when my freaking world comes to a halt.

"Hi, Ryan." Everything freezes.

Not just my body, but the blood in my veins, the heart in my chest, and the air in my lungs, they all freeze at that voice. The stillness is replaced by a vibration in my bones as I slowly turn around.

BROKEN

Messy, overgrown hair falls in blonde locks over familiar gray eyes. Jesus Christ.

"You were harder to find than I thought." What the fuck, how is it- this isn't- I don't. I don't know what's happening. "Especially since you're not blonde anymore."

I don't speak, all I'm capable of doing is staring. I examine his nose, which despite being broken countless times, remains straight. My eyes travel to his strong jaw that's lightly dusted with facial hair. Jesus Christ, it's him.

"You alright, Hales?" Drew's hand falls on my lower back, and despite my hate for being touched, he grounds me as I stare into the eyes of my long-lost brother. "Move along, friend."

Kaylan lets out a dark chuckle that isn't at all friendly, "How about you go back to work, friend. This is important."

"I'm sure it is, but this is a business, and she has work to do. So, I'm going to ask politely that you order your drink and move along."

"I'm not here to drink; I'm here to talk to Ryan." I shudder at the name.

Ryan's dead. She died in that hell hole a year and a half ago.

"Well, no one by that name works here. So, move along." Drew's tone deepens. His hand hasn't left my back, it's an odd thing to notice at a time like this, but it seems to be the only thing I can focus on.

"You don't need to protect her from me." Kaylan turns those startling gray eyes to me now, "You were always meant to survive, you know that?"

Funny since he left in the middle of the night, leaving behind a path of destruction and an eight-year-old with shattered promises and broken bones.

"Haley, do you know him?" Drew's tone is low and deadly.

I meet the eyes of my brother, the man who, at one point in my life, was my hero, he was my saving grace. Then he abandoned me and left me to collect the pieces.

"No." I say without an ounce of emotion, "I don't know him."

Drew nods and reaches forward pushing the button to call the bouncer.

"That's alright, Ry. I'll talk to you later." He slowly peels himself away from the counter as Drew speaks to the bouncer. "Maybe you can show me your fancy new apartment."

My eyes flutter shut as my body starts to shake harder.

BROKEN

Fuck.

"Hey?" Drew, who still has his hand on my back, whispers into my hair, "Hales, It's okay. We'll let Josh know not to let that guy in anymore, okay?"

"Won't help," I mutter, shaking his hand away.

God, I hate being touched.

Drew's eyes narrow in suspicion as I step around him, "I need a minute."

"I've got the bar. Use the VIP room; it's just Josh and my brother up there." I nod, not sure what else to do. I'm not going up there, but the suggestion was thoughtful.

Numb, I bum a cigarette from Danica and step into the employee's smoke area. Relishing the burn as it travels down my throat. Cigarettes taste like Reno, and I hate it, but the nicotine feels soothing under my skin. I can't stop shaking; I feel like I'm going to puke.

"Are you Haley?" A rich voice asks from the door behind me making me jump. I look over my shoulder to see a carbon copy of Drew standing there. I nod slightly, momentarily stunned by their likeness. "He asked me to take you home."

Um, no. "I'm fine. Thanks though."

BROKEN

Drew's twin steps out of the door, revealing his dark hair; Drew with black hair is hot. "I'm Parker, Drew's brother."

I nod again. Sweet baby Jesus, he's pretty. His jaw is a bit sharper than Drew's and covered with stubble, and his dark hair makes those blue eyes a beacon in the dim light.

Pulling in the final drag, I stamp the cherry out and push it into the plastic container. "Thanks, but I'm good."

I aim for a friendly smile, not entirely convinced I pull it off and step around him.

Ignoring the fact, I feel him enter behind me, I duck into the girl's bathroom to wash my hands. Peering into the mirror I notice I'm grossly pale, my gray eyes are still wide with panic, while my chest rises and falls in an irregular pattern. How the fuck did Kaylan find me? I stare at my reflection like it holds the answer. Kaylan of all people. If he can track me down, there's no doubt the rest of them can find me.

Drying my hands, I force myself to take steady breaths that hurt my chest before pushing through the doors. Parker is leaning against the wall with his hands in his pockets, staring at his shoes- cause that's not stalkerish or anything.

Continuing to ignore him, I enter behind the bar where Josh is drying a shot glass at my station.

"I've got it," I tell him, pulling the next glass out and running a towel over it.

"Go home, Haley. We've got this under control."

"It's no big deal." I force a casual tone, still drying glasses, "The guy was a creep, so what?"

Drew gives Josh a look that forces my eyebrows together, "What?"

Drew's mouth starts to open, but Josh cuts him off, "Go home."

Oh, shit. Am I in trouble? "I'm sorry," I say quickly.

Josh pulls back incredulously, "For what?"

"For freaking out before. I can do my job, I promise. He just caught me off guard-"

"Haley, you're not being punished. You didn't do anything wrong."

"Then why are you sending me home?" I don't want to go home. Kaylan knows where I live. FUCK, Kaylan knows where I live, and that bastard will most likely be waiting for me.

"Because you're uncomfortable. Go home, take a shower, then come back tomorrow." He offers me a lopsided grin. I guess he senses a 'Really, I'm fine.' coming cause he continues, "You've only got an hour left, go." He points to the exit. "Parker will take you home, so you don't have to walk."

I give him my best 'are-you-fucking-kidding' face, and he laughs. "Parker?" Tall, dark, and sexy leans over the bar towards us, my eyes follow the lines of his forearms as they support the weight of his chest. "Parker, Haley. Haley, Parker. Now you know each other."

Damn you, Joshua Hayes.

"Cute." I glare at him. I've denied rides from everyone except Drew. He knows that everyone knows that.

"Go on. I've got thirsty people here."

With an epic eye roll, I exit the bar and enter the employee break room, not surprised when my new shadow follows behind me.

"I don't need a ride, and I don't need a babysitter."

"There's a lot of people here, this way I can find you easily."

My back is to him, but I still roll my eyes as I slide my tips out of my apron and hang it up.

BROKEN

Shoving the cash into my bra, I walk past him again, heading to the front door when fingers vice around my wrist. Instinctively, I rip it free and glare at him.

The corner of his mouth tips up. "I'm parked out back."

"Good for you. You should probably go in that direction then." I turn away from him but the asshole steps in front of me, successfully cutting me off. His mouth curves up again before motioning to the back doors. "I'm not riding with you."

"I'm not trying to get laid, sweetheart. I'm just driving you from point A to point B."

"Like I said, Ken Doll. No, thank you. I'm fine taking the bus."

He chuckles a little, biting the corner of his lip. Oye, well that's pleasing to watch, isn't it? "That guy could follow you on the bus you know."

That gets my attention. Fuck, he has a point. Kaylan is probably counting on that; he would have me pinned without anyone around to know he's even a threat.

"Fine," I grumble turning around. I feel his eyes on me all the way outside.

BROKEN

"Over here." He nods, and I follow, my eyes skirting the area for the uninvited blonde abandoner. Thoughts of Kaylan vanish as I take in the panty dropping car Parker stops in front of, pretty sure my uterus just did a battle cry.

My exhale comes out raspy, "Holy shit." Fuck off, like you've never been turned on by a car before?

His eyebrows raise, "What?" He takes a look around the lot before resting back on me.

"'69 SS?"

He seems legitimately surprised, "Yeah, you're a fan of Camaros?"

"I'm fond of '69 Camaros, yes."

"See? Best friends already." He opens the door to reveal the heart-stopping interior; black leather seats, and the original steering wheel- shiny and spotless. The entire cab looks as if he drove it right off the lot. I sit quietly as he starts the car, but the purr of the engine has my mind screaming, Oh my God, Oh my God, Oh my God.

"Where to?"

"Basswood Apartments, it's a few blocks up."

"I know it." His mouth curves up on the right side again. Half smiles usually look like the person had a stroke but not on him. On him, it looks like weak knees and a broken heart.

We ride in silence, the closer we get, the more anxious I become. What if Kaylan's there? What if my other brothers are there? Holy fuck...what if he's there?

"You okay?" My head snaps out of the terrifying thought as I look at him.

"What?"

"Are you okay?" He nods at my hands that to my surprise are linked and threaded in a way that appears painful.

"Yeah." I unravel my fingers, laying my palms flat on my lap.

He pulls into the tenant covered parking and kills the engine. "Ummm..?"

"What?" He asks removing his keys and opening the door.

"Whatcha doing?" I ask slowly, trying to understand why stalker boy is getting out of the car.

"Walking you home, come on."

"That's okay." My voice is breathless as I try to climb out of the door without smacking it into the pole. "It's not necessary."

"Come on." He calls towards me at the hood of the car.

Clumsily climbing out, I slowly approach. "Not to be rude- but I don't exactly want you knowing where I live."

"4D. Come on." Whoa! What the fuck? Parker turns around when he realizes I haven't moved from the spot I've cemented to. "Drew told me. He wanted me to make sure you had peace of mind before going in by yourself."

Fucking Drew. We stare at each other, me in horrified shock, him slightly amused.

"Come on, sweetheart. I'm not a stalker." What's up with Hayes boys and the word, 'sweetheart'?

"If the tenant comes back, they'll tow your car."

"Duly noted. Let's go."

"No, seriously. You can't do that to your car."

Parker takes two steps in my direction before leaning down in my personal space, his breath dances across my cheek and I refuse to acknowledge that stir in my stomach, "It's my spot, sweetheart."

I go from hot to cold in a nanosecond. "What?"

Another half smile, "Come on."

BROKEN

He pulls away, heading in the direction of my apartment. If he lived here, surely, I would have noticed him. Well, maybe not him, what with my aversion to people and all, but the car. I definitely would have seen the car.

He stops in front of my apartment and waits for me to catch up, I begin fishing keys out of my pocket. "What apartment is yours?"

He seems so amused, and it bothers me that I don't know why. He nods across the courtyard. "Top left."

"How long have you lived here?"

"What's with the questions?" His amusement travels to his lips as they rise into a smile.

"Why not?"

He nods in a 'fair enough' way. "I moved in a few months ago."

"Never seen you."

"Been away on business. I got back yesterday; it's why I was at the club tonight."

"Drew never mentioned it."

"Good. Now, are you going to unlock the door or are we just going to stand out here playing twenty questions all night?"

"You're not coming inside."

"I didn't ask to."

BROKEN

Oh. Well, alright. Sliding the key into the deadbolt, the lock falls into the door with a satisfying thud. Pushing it open, I half expected to see Kaylan or Derek sitting on my couch, but the place is beautifully empty. "Alright. Well, thanks for the ride."

"Absolutely. If you need anything, I'm right over there." He offers another smile before walking across the grass to his building.

I stare after him before I realize I'm being nine shades of creepy and scurry into my apartment before he notices. The door clicks shut, and I quickly slip the chain on and slam the deadbolt across. It never bothered me to be alone until now. Now, the sting of loneliness sinks in as I stare at the only piece of furniture I own. Why the fuck did Kaylan have to come and ruin the one safe place I had? I don't want to move. I don't want to leave. But isn't that the curse I was born with? Good things don't happen to me, and when they do- they never last.

CHAPTER FOUR

I hate Kaylan.

I barely slept last night on my amazing couch. He ruined my freaking cloud, and I'm so pissed.

I took an angry shower, followed by the darkest eye makeup I think I've worn since I was in Reno. It's my artistic way of telling people to fuck off. My eyes are as dark as my mood as I stomp through the apartment getting ready. I don't work at VIN's today, so I still have hours until my shift at HEAT, but I can't stay here all day it feels like I'm inviting Kaylan to come here.

BROKEN

Scooping my keys off the nail by the door I decided to check out the clearance section at Furniture Warehouse. I am well aware I'm here on borrowed time, but it makes me feel better to pretend that I can stay.

Locking the deadbolt, I find myself peeking over my shoulder at Parker's apartment. Catching myself being creepy, yet again, I force my gaze away, focusing instead on the path towards the bus station when my shitty day grows shittier.

Kaylan.

"What the fuck are you doing here?" I snap.

"Rawr." He hisses, pulling upright from the bench. "Put the claws away, Kitten. I need to talk to-"

"Fuck you." I spit walking past him.

"I didn't expect you to be jumping with joy to see me, but I didn't expect you to hate me either."

"Yeah, well I didn't expect to wake up to an empty bedroom and get the shit beat out of me." He tries to speak, but I don't want his excuses. Rage grows inside me, twisting on the walkway I turn to face him, "You fucking left! In the middle of the night! You didn't even tell me goodbye! You just up and fucking disappeared leaving me to take the beating for both of us. You promised, but instead, you left me to pick up the pieces by myself, and you're surprised that I hate you?"

"Ryan, I was sixteen!" He roars.

"I WAS EIGHT!" I scream back.

Probably not the best idea in a crowded apartment complex that I'm trying to lay low in, but hey- I never claimed to be a bright girl. The pain is there on his face, but the fire inside of me is enough for me to overlook it.

"I was just a kid! What the fuck was I supposed to do with an eight-year-old?"

"You were supposed to keep me safe! You were supposed to get me out!"

"I did get you out!" He explodes, "What? You thought Caroline gave you the cash and I.D. out of the goodness of her heart?"

"Caroline?" Realization strikes the second I say her name, that house bunny, "You fucking asshole! You were there?!"

"Of course, I was there! Despite what you may think, I never left you!"

"Fuck you! Yes, you did!"

"Haley?" Kaylan and I both freeze, our eyes sliding to the six-foot god next to us.

BROKEN

"Parker- Hey." I try to tame my temper and internal hysteria enough to appear calm.

"You alright?" He asks, never taking his eyes off Kaylan.

"Yeah, I'm fine. He was just leaving."

"Was not. We're not done talking."

"Do you ever shut the hell up and listen? Get the fuck out of here." I snap.

"Ryan-"

"That's not my fucking name, Kaylan! Ryan bled out picking up the pieces you left behind!"

I turn away from both of them, walking towards the bus stop when I hear someone step forward which is quickly followed by a second pair.

"If you want your legs to remain a part of your body, I suggest you leave." Parker's voice is intimidating as he speaks to Kaylan.

"Fuck off, jock strap."

I'd love to see Kaylan get knocked the fuck out but he grew up in a house full of demons. He can take a hit and give one right back.

"I won't repeat myself."

"Look asshole, I appreciate that you're looking out for my sister, but this is between us. Ryan! I need to talk to you!"

BROKEN

I ignore him and keep walking, feeling both of their eyes burning into the back of my neck.

"Does Homecoming King know about Reno?"

That motherfucker! I spin around, "What the hell are you doing?!"

"Talk to me, or I talk to him."

Parker's face turns with confusion as his crossed arms slide down into his pockets. "What's he talking about, Haley?"

"Not her name, Quarterback."

"Kaylan," I point my finger in his directions as I stalk back towards them. "Keep your fucking mouth shut! You already destroyed my life once! Don't you dare do it again!"

"Then talk to me." He sounds defeated.

"You had ten years to talk to me. Nothing you have to say makes a damn bit of difference now. Go home, Kaylan."

"I found her."

Color me confused and damn my curiosity because instead of walking away I buy into his bullshit, "Who the fuck is her?"

"Mom."

I shrug, "Dead, I hope."

Parker's eyes snap to mine, and I wish he weren't here for this. His parents died when

BROKEN

Drew was twelve in a car accident, and I just hoped mine dead in front of him.

"Ry-" my death glare apparently reaches him because he chokes on the word, "Haley, that's who helped me-"

"Don't you dare finish that sentence." I seethe. "Don't you fucking tell me she got you out."

"She wanted to get you out too-"

"Fuck you, Kaylan." I push between clenched teeth, shoving the tears in my throat down. "Get out of my life and don't come back."

"You can't stay here."

"GO!" I point to the parking lot.

"If I could find you, how long until he does? You can't live your life off a fake name."

"KAYLAN!" I shriek, the panic growing up my throat. "That's my bosses' nephew!" I point to Parker, "BOTH of them!"

"You need to get out- keep moving." His eyes fall to Parker for a brief moment then return, the anger slips away as he continues, "Come with me."

"Yeah, cause that worked out so well the last time."

"I was just a kid." He shakes his head. "I'm sorry if I hurt you when I left, but I had to."

BROKEN

"If I could show you just how hurt I was, you'd never be able to look me in the eyes again."

"Yes, I could. Because you did the same thing, I did. You had an opportunity, and you took it." He shrugs, "You ran."

"I left. You ran."

"Sixteen isn't leaving." He shakes his head.

"Kaylan! Jesus Christ!"

"You're sixteen?!" Parker snaps, clearly still paying attention and pissed.

"No." I send daggers through Kaylan, "I left home when I was sixteen."

"A year ago." Kaylan clarifies.

"My foot's about to become a permanent part of your rectum, Kaylan!"

"Threats don't work on me, Kitten. You forget the devil was my father too."

"Yeah, well you've had ten years for the memories to fade."

"That shit doesn't fade, Ryan. You know it."

That's true. Those broken pieces poke and stab me every day. One cut heals, while another rips open.

"We're done talking. You've already fucked my life enough with your presence- I'm done. You want to run your mouth? Go for it."

"I didn't want to fuck everything up; I'm just trying to protect you."

"Congratulations. This is the second time you've managed to destroy everything by 'protecting' me."

"Ryan-" He pleads taking a step forward.

"My life was perfect here." I shake my head. "Guess that's the Hale way though, isn't it?"

I turn and walk away. Kaylan doesn't follow, he doesn't speak, and I'm completely fine with that.

CHAPTER FIVE

I missed the first bus and waved off the second. Have you ever hurt so bad that pain just turns to numbness? You're aware of the pain, but your brain can't process it, so you just stop existing? Phoenix was my heaven; I made a friend in Drew, and finally felt like I was holding all the right cards for once. Then Kaylan shows up and runs his mouth in front of Parker, successfully ripping my heart out in the process. My eyes look around, but I'm not comprehending anything. I didn't even notice the body next to me until it spoke.

"Your name's not Haley?"

I give him a weak shake of my head.

"It's Ryan?"

A weak nod.

An angry sigh escapes him, "How old are you, Ryan?"

"Don't call me that." My voice sounds like sandpaper feels.

"It's your name, isn't it?"

No answer.

"Are you sixteen?"

When I don't answer his tone grows more irritated, "Seventeen? Seriously, you need to tell me how old you are because both of my uncles are facing serious jail time if you're a minor."

"I'm not a minor."

"You're not twenty-two. So, don't feed me that bullshit."

"Never said I was."

"How old are you, Ryan?"

I stand up, surprised that my legs could support my weight. "I'll be gone in the morning, no need to worry about Vinny or Josh."

"I am worried about Vinny and Josh." He stands with me, "They knew you weren't twenty-one, but I can guarantee they thought you were at least of legal age to serve."

"I'm eighteen."

"Is that your real age or just what you're telling me?"

"I turned eighteen in July."

BROKEN

"July." He echoes, running his hands through his hair. "Jesus Christ. Any other lies I should know about?"

I step around him and keep walking until I've approached my apartment door. Parker's still by my side. "Where will you go?" His tone is gentle, but I can't seem to return the gesture.

"Don't worry about it." I step inside, shutting the door before Parker can respond. I guess it's a good thing I didn't get the place furnished after all.

Stepping into the closet, I grab the duffel I bought when I moved in, throwing in my collection of shoes, my bathroom supplies, and just enough clothes to get me by I haul it over my shoulder as I scan the kitchen, making sure nothing's out that will spoil. I write an apology to Josh, Vinny, and Drew. It was nice while it lasted at least. Flicking off the lights and locking up the apartment, I drop the keys into the envelope to Drew. He'll need them to get the couch I gave him.

After walking downtown to HEAT, I leave Drew and Josh's letters with the bouncer, before catching the bus to VIN's. I saved this one for last because I know it's going to be the harder of the two. Vinny immediately greets me with a warm smile as I enter the bar.

"Here on your day off? I thought kids these days were off being wild and ruthless?"

BROKEN

With a sad smile, I approached him, gripping the letter tight in my hands. Not even the tension of pulling the ends is enough to calm the shaking in my fingers. His eyes pull together at the sight of my duffel slung over my shoulder. I hand him the envelope, "My letter of resignation."

The hurt I see in his eyes is enough to cause the cracks to web across the surface of my soul. "Haley..."

"Please believe me when I say that I am so sorry." His hurt turns to confusion. Before he can speak and make this hurt more, I continue, "You have no idea how much you and Jules have helped me. You forever changed my life, thank you." Tears burned canyons down my throat as I walk away. He calls after me, but I'm too much of a coward to face him.

I haven't stepped foot in a Greyhound station for over a year, the smell of rubber and body odor assaults my senses, bringing back the memory of my arrival. Except when I arrived I had a feeling of hope, whereas now I feel nothing but heartache and guilt for not giving those who matter a proper goodbye.

Just like the first time I ran, I purchase a ticket for the first available seat. The bus doesn't leave for another four hours so I've managed to rearrange my duffle, putting my shoes on one side and my clothes on the other I'm able to form a relatively comfortable pillow.

Minutes feel like hours as they slowly tick by. My burner phone has been buzzing nonstop inside the bag, at this rate it'll be dead before I even board. Hopefully, I don't fall asleep and miss the bus.

The loud asshole that just slammed his weight into the seat above my head just guaranteed I won't fall asleep. The anger of his rudeness fades when it makes me think of how every time Drew sits down it's like a wrecking ball. Fresh pain slithers out of my pores. Note to self- don't make friends in, I look down at my ticket- Nebraska.

"Let me guess." I shoot upright at the sound of his voice, almost falling out of the chair. "L.A? No, New York." Drew leans over my bag, snatching the ticket out of my hand with ill-disguised disgust. "Norfolk... Nebraska" His disgust grows, "The fuck? Norfolk, really?" He shakes his head, flicking the ticket back into my lap. "What the hell is so damn important in Nebraska that I got a fucking letter over an actual goodbye?"

My tongue can't work past the lump in my throat, so I just shake my head.

"Called Parker. After Vinny got a hold of Josh, they rounded the cavalry to find you."

I don't know what sensation is stronger, the hurt or the fear.

BROKEN

"Heard your brother showed up." Fear. Fear is the stronger emotion.

I nod.

"From what Parker says, he sounds like the same prick we sent packing last night."

Another nod. The silence is painful.

"Heard your real name is manlier than mine."

If my body wasn't threatening to shatter across the terminal floor, I might have laughed.

The longer he waits to talk the harder it is to breathe.

"We knew." He finally says with a sigh. I risk glancing up, and his eyes burn into mine. "Not your real name or anything like that, but we knew you were a runner. That's why Vinny and Josh pay you under the table. Though, it was popular belief you were eighteen when you showed up, which would make you nineteen now and legally able to serve behind the bar." Another stretch of silence falls over us before he nods to himself. "I'm keeping the couch, by the way."

"Good." I mumble.

"It'll be my company chair."

"Gross."

"Wanna tell me why you're running?"

"No."

"Okay." He nods to himself once more, "Tell me why you're running."

"I can't stay here."

"Not an answer, try again. Why are you running?"

"Drew-"

"Don't pull that tone on me. I'm not the one who wrote you a half-assed letter of dismissal and then tried to book it to some godforsaken town that no one's heard of. You're my best friend, Hales. And if I'm going to lose my best friend, I deserve to know why."

Words just won't come. No matter how hard I try to force them out, they're stuck in my throat with no escape.

"Does it have anything to do with why you freak out whenever someone touches you? Or why you're always wearing long sleeves? 'Because you may think you have people fooled, but it's fucking Phoenix, dude."

I ignore his questions about the secrets I hide beneath my clothing. "It's just time to go."

"That's unfortunate." He takes in the station for a moment before standing up abruptly. "Come smoke with me?"

"You don't smoke."

"Yeah, well, you and your problems drove me to the disgusting habit." He offers his hand out to me. "Come on."

"I need to be in here in case they call my bus."

"Your bus doesn't leave for like three hours. I saw the ticket, dipshit. If you're dead set on leaving, then I'd like to at least hang out with you until then." 'He wiggles his fingers impatiently, beckoning me forward. Giving him my hand, he hoists me up before slinging my duffle over his shoulder.

"I can carry my bag, you know."

"Shut up, consider it payment for bumming a cigarette."

I scoff, pulling the pack out of my pocket as he holds the door open for me. Putting one between my lips, I barely flick the lighter before the purr of a Camaro grabs my attention. Drew walks around me and throws my duffel to Parker who catches it and tosses it in the open trunk.

"What the fuck?" I demand.

"Ryan Carter Hale." I flinched at my name while watching Josh push off the passenger door, reading something on his phone. "Born in Reno, Nevada. On, let's see-" He squints at the screen while my heart hammers painfully in my chest. "Wow, July second. So, not August seventeenth." He turns back to the phone as my heart threatens to beat out of my throat. "High School principal reported your disappearance, and according to the records online your dad said you went to live with your mom and brother in California." He looks up at me expectantly. Expecting what, I'm not sure.

"How do you know all of that?" I choke out.

"Google." He waves the phone at me, "Parker here caught parts of your name and hometown from your conversation with who we're assuming is your brother, knowing your real age, it wasn't hard to find you. It's nice to know the cops aren't after you by the way. Kudos on the name- Haley Rae Carter, Ryan Carter Hale- clever."

"Why 'Ryan' though?" Drew asks.

"Not appropriate." Parker scolds, though his lips are struggling to stay stern.

"Dad wanted boys," I say as if that wasn't obvious while lighting my cigarette.

"And Kaylan?" Parker speaks now.

"I don't know why that's his name."

"No," he chuckles, "I mean what about Kaylan?"

"I don't know what you're asking."

"I heard a lot during that conversation."

"You did." I agree, trying not give anything away.

"He said someone was looking for you."

Dammit. I shrug in response.

"Who's looking for you?" Josh asks, the kindness in his tone is sure to kill me.

I shrug again. "Can I have my bag back?"

"Fuck no." Drew scoffs, "Do you know how hard it was to find you? That's my insurance policy."

"Insurance on what?"

"That you'll stay."

I laugh without humor pulling in a long drag. "If you think holding my bag hostage is what's going to keep me here then you're sadly mistaken."

His brow furrows before glancing at each person in turn before coming back to me, "How can you leave without it?"

"I came here with an envelope of money and a fake I.D. I've still got the I.D. and four times the money I arrived with. I can always buy another toothbrush."

"What about your ticket?" Parker asks pulling it out of the front pocket of my duffle.

Blowing a cloud of smoke, I aim for nonchalance, "I can buy another one."

He looks at the ticket before coughing to cover his laugh, "To Norfolk, Nebraska?"

Josh makes a face before looking at me, "What's in Nebraska?"

I pull another drag into my lungs before answering. "Blue skies and country music?"

"You're eighteen," Josh starts, "Legal age to serve behind the bar is nineteen, but you can waitress. You still have a job at HEAT."

"I handed in my resignation."

"Thanking me and telling me you're sorry for leaving doesn't constitute a resignation."

"Then, I quit."

"Not without probable cause. Two-week minimum notice, it was in the employee packet you signed."

"With a fake name," I point out dryly, blowing the ash off my cigarette to avoid eye contact.

I don't need the bag- I may want the contents, but I could easily buy new things.

"Haley's your name. I'm not calling you a dude's name. My roommate would think I was gay if I started calling out 'Ryan!' in the middle of the night." Drew deadpans, earning a sad smile from me.

"God, I'm going to miss you." Dropping the cigarette to the sidewalk, I pressed my toe into the paper.

All humor vanishes from his face, "Hales, don't leave."

Tears slip down my throat, clogging my airway. "I can't stay."

"Because someone's looking for you?"

More like four someones. "I'm sorry."

"Do you actually think someone will fuck with you while we're around?"

Yeah but for how long? How long until I fuck up and they leave too? "I'm not destined for good things; it's not in my cards. Sooner or later you'd leave." I give him another sad smile.

He shakes his head, "Haven't left your ass once, sweetheart." Taking a step back, Drew steps forward, "Haley-"

"I'm good." I cut him off. He's still shaking his head; I can see him trying to think of a way to get me to stay, his efforts are confusing and painful. "I'll be fine. You're holding my burner hostage, so I'll have to call from the payphones along the way."

"You're still leaving?"

I nod, the burn in my eyes is foreign, becoming harder to push away the longer he stares at me.

"Let me drive you." Parker offers suddenly. Everyone turns to look at him at the same time

"To Nebraska?" Josh asked incredulously.

"To wherever she wants to go." He shrugs.

"I don't know you." I point out lamely.

"You don't know anyone on that bus either, or anyone in Nebraska for that matter."

True, but still not happening. "That's okay."

"Come on. I've got a full tank of gas and your bags already loaded." The right side of his mouth raises. He's too pretty to be real.

"If you leave, I'm sticking your couch in the men's bathroom at HEAT." Drew threatens.

I internally cringe, my poor couch.

I kiss my fingers and wave them at Drew before slipping into the station.

I know the footsteps behind me don't belong to customers, but I ignore the urge to turn around while approaching the counter.

"One for the first available seat please."

"I have one leaving at nine this evening for Washington."

"I'll take it."

"Don't do this." Parker's voice catches me by surprise.

I turn to see him drop a hip against the counter next to me. "What-"

"You can't blow up a bus."

"What?!" I shriek. Looking back to the attendant, "He's kidding."

"No, I'm not. I can't let you do this."

"What the fuck is wrong with you?" I stage whisper as horror snakes through me.

"Thank God, you found her before she could BLOW UP A BUS!" Drew screamed the last part. My eyes grow to the size of saucers.

"That's like a federal crime to say shit like that! Stop it, before we all get arrested because of your stupid mouths."

"Did you find her?" Josh rushes through the station door. "I got her note about the bus!"

I palm my face before laying my head on the counter. "Fuck my life. This isn't happening."

"Pretty sure she left to go call the cops." Parker laughs next to me.

"No shit!" I shoot my head up to glare at him. "What the fuck is wrong with you guys?"

"Guess you'll have to stay until things blow over." Parker shrugs.

"Yeah, or stay cause I'm a suspected terrorist, dumbass!"

"A win's a win, sweetheart."

BROKEN

I whip myself away from the counter, "Bunch of fucking idiots, I swear!"

"Has she always cursed this much?" Josh asks behind me as I stalk out of the terminal.

"Yeah. She also makes a lot of threats of bodily harm, too." Drew chirps.

"Keep running your mouth I'll make it a reality."

"See?"

Morons. Fingers brush my lower back, and my body tightens everywhere. I shoot out from the touch and glare. Parker half smiles and opens the Camaro door.

"Shotgun!" Drew calls out behind me. I glance over my shoulder to see Josh shove Drew sideways before climbing into his truck.

"After you." Parker holds the door open.

If I didn't have a deep love for his car, I would have whipped myself into the seat like an enraged preteen rather than the calm and collected manner I managed.

"On a scale of one to ten, how pissed are you?" He asks, pulling out of the Greyhound parking lot.

"Fourteen."

He lets out a whistle before putting two cigarettes between his lips and flipping open a Zippo. The muscle in his jaw flexes as he drags the flame into the tobacco. Snapping the lighter closed, he holds out a lit cigarette to me. Odd gesture- lighting it while it was in his mouth thing. Still, I accept.

"Thanks."

"Did that at least lower it to a thirteen?"

I scoff, blowing the smoke out the cracked window. "It would have, but the fact you smoke in this car just added to it so now I'm sitting at about fourteen point five."

He laughs, actually laughs. "I didn't think someone could love this car more than I do."

I watch smoke drift from the burning tobacco before sighing loudly.

"I didn't mention anything other than your name, where you lived, and the fact someone was looking for you."

"Okay." I draw slowly. I don't know where he's going with this.

"Figured if you wanted people to know the other stuff, you'd tell them."

"That my brother found my mom?"

"That, and the stuff that came before it."

I don't know what else was said. I remember he showed up as I was telling Kaylan to fuck off, but I don't remember saying anything incriminating. "Like?"

"Like you were eight when he left and what happened after that."

Oh shit. "How long were you standing there?"

"Not long. You guys were shouting at each other, wasn't hard to overhear. I made my presence known when I was close enough to get your attention."

"Oh. Thanks, I guess."

My mind is must be overheating from the blazing sun of Arizona because I'm not able to think of a single thing to say, so we drive the rest of the way in silence.

Josh pulls in behind us when we reach the apartment complex.

Climbing out of the car, I turn to see Drew jogging across the street towards me. "Go home, Drew!" I call out to him.

"Here to get my couch." He winks back.

"Whatever. For y'all's bullshit back at Greyhound, I'm taking it back. If S.W.A.T is gonna come busting through my windows, I'd like to be comfortable in my last few hours of freedom. Speaking of which- I need the key to my apartment."

"What?"

"The key, it was in the envelope."

"Oh shit. Yeah, it was. Hold on." He checks his pockets before a nervous laugh escapes his throat, "Dude, I think it's at HEAT."

"Seriously? Go get it!"

He laughs holding his hand out to Josh, who scoffs at the gesture then nods to the truck. "We'll be back. You guys want pizza?"

Before I can turn him down, Parker pipes up and accepts.

"You can hang out with me until they get back."

Peachy.

I sigh, moving to the rear of the car. "Can you pop the trunk, please?"

His eyebrows shoot to the sky. "Please, huh? Didn't think that word was in your vocabulary, what with all the threats and language you use."

The trunk pops. Just as I lift the door, Parker is next to me, hauling the bag up. "Yeah, the last time a Hayes boy took my bag, it was locked in a trunk. I can carry it."

He let out a 'pssht' noise and closes the trunk, still holding the duffel hostage, I might add.

Without a key to my apartment and the fact Parker is still holding onto my duffel, I'm forced to follow him up the stairs to his place and wait while he unlocks the door. He steps in first, and I hear his keys land into what sounds like a dish before stepping out of the way. Jeez! His place is out of a freaking magazine. Placed around a coffee table that matches the entertainment center and side tables sit black leather sofas. Three stools line up against the breakfast bar, which doesn't appear to be from the same living room set but still managed to match. Not one aspect of his place looks 'picked up'. Everything is dark and welcoming.

"Damn, your place is nice," I whisper, still gawking.

"Thanks."

"It looks like I stepped into a magazine."

He laughs under his breath, settling down on one of the sofas. "Your place isn't magazine worthy?"

"Sure, for an ad listing."

"What do you mean?"

"Mine's empty." I eye the wall decor and note that it too, matches the furniture.

"Why's that?"

"Didn't know how long I was staying and didn't want to get stuck trying to get rid of everything."

He nods like he understands, that or he's just polite.

"So, not to be a dark cloud or anything but what do I call you?" He asks after a few minutes of silence.

The corner of lip my twitches, "Haley."

He nods.

"You and Drew have a lot of the same mannerisms."

"Like what?"

"The way you both nod when you're done talking." I laugh when he nods.

"I nodded didn't I?"

"Yeah."

He shakes his head wearing a smile, showing just how perfect his teeth are. I internally roll my eyes. These boys are like Greek legends. "Now that you pointed it out, I want to nod."

"So, nod."

He does.

"Better?"

"Not really." He laughs. "Come on, sit down. Stop standing around like you're not welcome."

Closing the door, I take a seat on the edge of the couch opposite him; he stares at me. "It's not going to bite you, you know."

"Who's older? You or Drew?" I ask to draw his attention away from how awkward I'm being.

"I am, but only by ten months."

"Twenty-five?"

"Twenty-four."

"Drew's only twenty-three?"

He nods, and I laugh.

"Are you going to laugh every time I nod?"

"Probably."

With a shake of his head, he picks up the remote, "What kind of shows do you watch?"

"I haven't watched TV in like two years, so I don't even know what's relevant."

"What do you do in your free time if you don't watch TV?"

"Work." I shrug. "I used to read, but ran out of time."

"Then you better get ready, I'm about to educate you."

BROKEN

With his attention off me, I settle back into the couch. "Bring it."

We fall into a comfortable silence while he scrolls through Netflix.

After Parker learned I only got through three seasons of Sons of Anarchy, he demanded I finish it. We're two episodes in when Josh and Drew walk in carrying pizza boxes and soda.

"I've got good news and bad news. What do you want first?"

Parker said, 'Good' at the same time I said, 'bad,' so I threw a pillow at him.

"Good news- Parker you owe me twenty-seven fifty. Bad news- I lost your apartment key. Who wants what?"

"You what?!" I almost scream, throwing myself over the back of the couch to glare at him.

"Huh?" He feigns innocence.

"You lost the key to my apartment?"

"In my defense, I was in a rush to find you. Doesn't the office carry spare keys?"

"She's out til Monday." Parker pipes in while I glare at Drew. "You can crash here until then."

Uhh, that would be a no.

"Good luck with that," Drew mutters under his breath. Not quietly enough, though.

"What's that supposed to mean?" I demand.

"Are you going to stay here?"

"No."

"Point made."

"Point not made." I fire back.

"You don't trust anybody, Hales. You can crash at my house."

"I'm good." I scoff. "I'm fairly certain your place is a breeding ground for STDs."

"See? No trust."

"Not wanting to get the clap from sitting on your couch isn't the same thing as not trusting."

Josh and Parker seem to be amused by us, what with them giggling like schoolgirls and all.

"You think I'm bad? Josh is the owner of HEAT and unmarried. I'm willing to bet next month's rent that the couches on the main floor aren't just for sitting." I make a face while Josh's "Hey!" got a laugh out of both Hayes brothers. "And Parker sure as hell isn't a saint. That couch you're sitting on has seen more ass than a bar stool, sunshine."

Doubted.

BROKEN

"Not true. I haven't had any women over here since I moved in." Drew gives him an incredulous glare. "I'm serious. I go to their place."

The shit I've walked in on back in Reno was far worse than the things they're saying- except maybe Drew. He's had stories that made me question if I was somewhat prudish afterward.

"So, if you're not staying with Parker or me where are you going?"

I fall back on the couch with a loud sigh. "Well, seeing as you fucktards ruined my chances of sleeping on a bus, I have no idea, probably a hotel."

"You're staying here," Parker tells me, dropping a plate of pizza on the coffee table in front of me.

"I guess I'm staying here," I add in a sarcastic tone.

"Good. We can catch up on SOA." He can't be serious.

"Is that like a sex thing?" Drew asks with a full mouth. Josh slaps the back of his head. "Ah! What I do?"

"Sons of Anarchy, dummy."

"Oh. Sounds like a sex thing."

BROKEN

Parker throws the pillow I had initially thrown at him back at me with a wink before starting the show.

A year ago, getting on that bus was the most natural thing I ever did. An hour ago, it almost crushed me to do it again. Now, after they fought for me to stay- I don't know how I'll survive leaving.

CHAPTER SIX

After dinner, we watched another two episodes before Drew came up with the brilliant plan that Josh should give both of us the night off so the four of us could go out and party. I was not for the idea; Josh was.

Needless to say, I'm currently sliding on a pair of holy jeans I bought but have yet to wear. I couldn't resist them, they are the softest denim I've ever felt, and they're super stretchy, add the fact they were clearance? I was all over them. Shedding my black top, I throw on my skin-tight gray, long sleeve undershirt before sliding into my black and white knockoffs. Twisting, I realized I forgot to grab my over shirt, jeez I'm like boobs galore right now. This is my favorite undershirt because of how tight is, things don't have the room to move or ride up, but it's always under something. Currently, my girls are attempting to make the Great Escape through the opened buttons. Josh and Drew return while I am touching up my makeup. I finish quickly, collect things and make my exit.

A low whistle sounds as I step into the living room, "Holy curves, Batman!" Drew pipes up before Josh slaps the back of his head. "Gah! What I do!?"

With a roll of my eyes, I shove everything into my bag, searching for my black t-shirt to go over it.

"What are you doing?" Drew asks, rubbing the back of his head.

"Looking for my overshirt."

"What? No. Don't do that."

"I'm not going out like this; my boobs are falling out."

"Hence the reason I vetoed the shirt." Another slap. "Stop hitting me!" He whines. "Parker! A little help? Does she not look hot?" At the word hot he pulls away from Josh, expecting to get hit again, I'm sure.

Finding the t-shirt, I pull upright. Parker's leaning against the wall in a pair of dark jeans that hang off his hips and a black shirt that fits like a glove, fuck these boys look like Greek statues. While staring at him, I realized he's gawking just as hard.

"Tell me again how SOA isn't a sex thing?" Drew asks under his breath.

"It's like you want to get slapped again," I mumble, peeking back at Parker. He watches me before the corner of his lip tugs up. Acting as though I wasn't caught undressing him with my eyes, I raise my eyebrows, and I wave the shirt in my hand. He wrinkles his nose and shakes his head slightly. This will be a first; I toss the shirt back into the black duffel turning towards the door. "Let's go."

Drew twists his hat backward before clapping his hands together. "I'm with Josh. Hales, you're with Parker, not SOAing."

The satisfying slapping noise brings a smile to my face. Parker pulls away from the wall, following me out of the apartment and down to his car.

Twice, Josh has cursed Drew for convincing him to give us the night off seeing as HEAT is slammed. He also forgot I wasn't twenty-one until I turned Drew's shot down; I've never been a big fan of alcohol so staying blissfully sober isn't a night ruiner for me, everyone else drinks though. Drew's half gone when he drags me onto the dance floor, his fingers glide across my waist, pulling me closer as I give him a death glare.

"Calm down, sweetheart." He smiles at me, "We're dancing, not fucking."

He continues to hold his hand against my hip as we move to the music. Dare I say it- I'm having fun? Soon a busty blonde catches Drew's eye, and he goes to work grabbing her attention.

Parker replaces him almost immediately; he pulls my body against him, his hands resting low on my hips. I'm not fond of being touched, so the pressure of his hands makes my body tense, but as Drew had said, it's just dancing. Ordinary people like to be touched, swallowing the panic, I let him pull me into him further- this is much closer than Drew and I had been. Parker has his hips pressed against mine. He dances well, and it makes my head spin, though I refuse to think about why that is.

With a little-added pressure, he turns me around, so my ass is pressed into his...hips. Yes, this is definitely a first. One hand slides across my stomach while the other remains planted on my hip as he guides me closer until I'm grinding against him. Dancing, dry humping- the same thing nowadays, right?

When the techno number changes to Hozier's, *Take Me to Church*, I try to pull away, but his hands tighten against me. The hand resting on my stomach slides across to my elbow and gently guides my hand behind his neck, turning this into something far more intimate, and far more frightening. His warm fingers slide from my wrist back to my waist, and if I weren't so focused on the fact that I'm more or less sex-breathing, I would probably feel like Baby from Dirty Dancing right now.

Driving my fingers through his hair I lose myself to the music as his chin rests against my shoulder, shivers take hold of my body as his breath slides across my neck, whether that's a good or bad thing is debatable.

As the song picks up for the chorus, so do his hips. Keeping me pressed up against him I can feel the rise and fall of his chest, among other things, and my heart feels like it's going to beat out of my ears.

My carefree attitude vanishes when he fingers wrap around my left wrist and his lip press into my neck. My blood runs cold as hysteria fills my head. I jerk forward shoving his hands off me like they're on fire. His brow furrows, his lips move as he steps towards me, I think he asked what was wrong but the music's too loud, my heart is beating too hard, the memories are screaming in my head, and the fear is suffocating.

I shove through people, including Josh, Drew, and the blonde leech wrapped around his hips. I hear my name being called but I need air, I need my skin to stop burning, and I need the demons to go back to the hell buried in my head. Normal people don't panic like this because they were touched, but that's the thing about panic- you don't have the luxury of control.

Busting through the door leading to the outside patio, I suck in air. Not giving a damn my ragged breathing is causing people to stare at me.

A hand lands on my shoulder and I shriek, throwing my hands up to protect my face.

"Whoa- Hales! It's us, calm down. What happened?" Drew steps towards me, I catch Parker's worried expression over his shoulder.

Jesus Christ, I'm a nutcase.

"It was me," Parker says behind him pulling the attention off me.

I try to shake my head no, but Drew's looking at Parker and can't see.

"I kissed her on the dance floor then she bolted."

"I'm. Fine. It's. Not that." I huff, shoving the words out of my closed chest. "You. Grabbed me." I managed to get through the tiny gap in my throat.

"Oh, dude." Drew's eyes go wide, "Hales hates being touched, I thought you knew that."

Parker shakes his head, "We were touching long before I kissed her."

I shake my head again. Aren't they listening to me? He grabbed me. I've messed around with dudes before; kissing is whatever- it's the touching I can't handle, but they're in their own little world right now, and I can't pull in enough air to tell them to shut the hell up.

So, what do I do? I'm glad you asked.

I did what any rational person during a panic attack would do; I push past Drew, grab Parker's jaw and draw my lips to his.

Caught off guard, he doesn't have the reaction time to kiss me back when I pull away.

Drew woo's and bends over. "Oh, fuck!"

"Not.. cause you... kissed me." I force out. I wave my arm in front of his face, well at least I try to, he's like 6'2" or something and towers over my 5'5" frame "You... Touched me."

Parker doesn't even blink; he just stares at me, "Do that again."

My eyebrows pinch, "What?"

"That didn't count; I wasn't expecting it. Do it again."

"No... you guys-" I glared at them in turn, "Wouldn't... listen."

"I'm still not listening." He takes a step forward, smiling slyly.

"You're drunk." I managed to say that without wheezing. Yay, self-progress!

"I had a shot when we first got here and a beer. I'm not even close to drunk."

"So- wait," Drew pipes in, pushing between our bodies, "You didn't care that he kissed you?" I shake my head. "And you didn't care when y'all's sweaty bodies were pressed up against one another?"

"Jesus, Drew. We weren't fucking." Parker defends.

"Not yet. Give it another song I'm sure y'all would have moved onto the horizontal tango. Anyways, if that isn't what bothered you- what made you freak out?"

I roll my eyes. How many times do I have to tell them? "He grabbed me."

"On your left, huh?"

"What?" Parker and I ask at the same time.

"He grabbed you on your left?" He speaks each word slowly as if we're children.

I don't move as I try to understand the point of his observation. But then it dawns on me, oh shit, does he know?

"You don't care when someone touches you on the right." He adds.

"Not true," I shake my head, "I don't like being touched period."

"Yes, I know that. But when we work, I'm always on your right. Whenever I touch you, you get pissed, sure, but you don't freak out. Parker touched your left, and you booked it."

Parker pulls one of the two cigarettes in his mouth out and hands it to me. Nodding my thanks, I take it, drawing in a calming drag.

"What's your point?" Parker asks around his cigarette while pocketing his lighter.

BROKEN

Drew looks at me for a moment before his gaze falls to my sleeve, his brow pinches as his eyes draw a line from my shoulder to my wrist.

"Long sleeves," He mumbles low enough I don't think anyone but me heard. My breathing picks up again. Fuck- is he going to figure it out? Our eyes meet, and a sliver of sympathy crossed his gaze, "I'm drunk," he speaks louder so Parker can be privy to his thoughts, "I'm rambling. I've already lost my train of thought. Hey- remember when y'all kissed?"

I appreciate him deflecting the conversation, but a layer of ice still sits in the pit of my stomach. He is drunk, but he didn't lose his train of thought, I think he knows.

"Yeah, about that." Parker steps forward, "Let's do that again."

I shake my head, pulling another drag. My breathing is slowly returning to normal, the pressure in my chest easing. "That was to get your attention."

"You lost him, Hales. Get his attention again."

"Fuck off."

"There she is!" Drew yells, "I'd hug you, but I don't think that would help."

"You'd be correct."

"How about a hardy high-five?"

I crack a smile and slap his outstretched hand.

"Hey- there you guys are." Josh comes out with a pretty redhead on his arm.

"Needed a smoke break." Parker waves his cigarette.

"Shit will kill you, man."

"So will breathing. We all gotta go sometime."

Josh rolls his eyes, "It's last call."

I nod, stamping my cherry out. "We should go and beat the crowd."

Parker follows suit before leading us out of the club and into the parking lot.

"Are you good to drive?" I ask, stopping short of the opened door.

"I'd call us a cab if I wasn't."

"I'm with Josh. I'll see you losers tomorrow." Drew calls walking in the opposite direction. I flip him off in farewell before sliding into the comfortable leather seat.

CHAPTER SEVEN

Walking into Parker's apartment is nerve-racking. Apparently, it's 'too late' to get a hotel room, so I'm staying at Parker's, completely unaware of how any of this works. I've never slept at someone else's house before. I also haven't slept near another human being in almost ten years.

He strolls in, placing his keys on the side table near the door like it's just another day, I wish I could be that nonchalant about sleeping in the same space as a stranger.

Standing awkwardly in the door, I fidget with the sleeves of my shirt watching him meander through the living room and into the kitchen.

"Do you want anything to-" He pauses when he sees me still in the open door. A smile lifts the right side of his face. "Haley, come in. You're welcome here."

Embarrassment warms my cheeks as I step inside, closing the door behind me.

"Do you want a bottle of water or a soda or something?"

"No, thank you."

Opening the fridge, he pulls a bottle of water out for himself. "I have a bathroom in my bedroom so that one's yours." He points down the hall; I nod in response.

Not sure how to make this moment less awkward, I decide the best thing to do is lock myself in the bathroom- real mature, I know.

Approaching my bag; I pull out my shampoo, toothbrush, HEAT shorts and a loose long sleeve shirt before scurrying down the hall to the bathroom. I take my time setting each item down on the counter. Why I'm acting like I'm about to lose my virginity is beyond me.

A knock at the door sends my heart flying out of my chest as a yelp escapes my throat, I stare at the door with my hand over my heart while Parker chuckles from the outside. Opening the door, he wears a sexy half smile.

"Didn't mean to scare you. Here-" Parker holds out a folded towel, "There aren't any in there."

"Oh, thanks."

Oh my God, why isn't there a manual on how to spend the night at a guy's house?

He chuckles again and walks back to the living room. With a sigh of relief, I close the door.

The shower washed most of my nerves away. After collecting my damp hair at the nape of my neck, I exit the hall into the living room.

My stuff is gone.

Like gone, gone.

Releasing my makeshift ponytail, I check behind the couch, the island stools, even by the door. Where the hell is my stuff?

"Parker?" I call down the hall.

"Yeah?"

"Where's my shit?"

"Down here."

What? Why? I walk down the hall, and I freeze at the cracked door. "Why is it down here?"

The door pulls away, and Parker is standing in nothing but his jeans. Oh, mother mercy.

I can't tear my eyes away from his washboard stomach; the dips and curves slipping across his body- Jesus.

His tanned skin stretched tight over his muscles; he wasn't born I've decided, he was sculpted. No way he grew into this.

Blinking, the realization of my gawking hits me like a freaking mac truck. I quickly step back, mortified that I was caught staring at him like I wanted to eat him. Nervously, I peer up at his face, the bastard has his head tipped to the side like a puppy with a smug grin on his face, when our eyes met he wags his freaking eyebrows at me.

"You wear smug like an asshole."

His grin widens into a smile.

"You wear embarrassment well. The pink is pretty."

Oh my God! Am I blushing?

Clearing my throat, I pull a mask over my face, "Why's my stuff in here?"

"Figured you'd want easy access to it."

"Mhm? So, again- why's it in here?"

He pulls away from the door to reveal a massive bed with one of those super fluffy comforters on it. You know, the ones that leak air whenever you lay on them? Yeah, it's deep blue, and I'm fighting the urge to launch myself onto it like a five-year-old.

"For easy access."

"That doesn't make sense. If I'm sleeping in the living room-" Oh... "I'm not sleeping in the living room, am I?"

He shakes his head with a smile.

Oh. Well, then.

"Nice socks."

I glance down at my skeleton socks and wiggle my toes. "Thanks. So why am I sleeping here and not on the couch? Don't guest usually take the couch?"

"Do you want to be woken up at the crack of dawn by Drew complaining about how we let him drink too much?"

I'd stab him. "No."

"That's why. Kid's internal clock goes haywire whenever he drinks. Go on." He nods to the bed. "I'm gonna shower."

Without waiting for my response, he steps into the bathroom leaving me alone in his bedroom. Awkward. This is awkward, right?

Hesitantly, I pull the fluffy comforter down and climb into his bed. Holy shit on a cracker this is amazing. My body sinks into the mattress, I've died and become royalty.

A faint noise pulls me from my dreamless sleep, the lights are still on, and the bathroom door is cracked open, thick steam dances its way into the bedroom. I must have only been asleep for a few minutes. Damn. I remember climbing into his bed and marveling at how comfortable it was and then, BAM! I wake up; this fucking thing is magic, I don't think I've ever fallen asleep that fast before.

The closet door opens, and I snap my eyes shut. I haven't the slightest idea why I'm pretending to sleep, but here I am. Feeling how ridiculous I'm being, I open my eyes just to regret the decision instantly.

Parker is walking back into the bathroom with only a towel. A towel, that's loosely around his waist my eyes travel up his spine buried deep in the muscles of his back. He slowly closes the door, stopping it a few inches from the frame, probably to allow the steam to escape, giving me the perfect view of his clouded reflection in the mirror- of fucking course it does, why does life hate me? I should just roll over and go back to sleep. Yes, that's what I'll do.

I press my palms into the mattress to shift my body just as I catch a glimpse of him clearing the steam from the mirror. His sculpted chest and stomach paralyze me, the mirror ends just above his hips, and I'm not sure if I'm disappointed by that or not. I need to stop staring, I'm about twelve shades of creepy right now, yet I can't stop; I just lay back down. He runs his hands through his hair and then-then he looks at me.

Right. At. Me. Holding my eyes in the mirror, the smallest twitch of his lips curves into a smile. I'm dead. I can feel the heat of my face burning straight through the mattress. 'Stop staring!' I'm screaming at myself, but my eyes have deserted all communication with my brain because I don't look away, I don't break eye contact, I just stare back- like a fucking creep. He breaks first, returning to his routine. He doesn't care? What? Oh no- he's coming out.

Oh no, oh no, oh no. What the hell do I do? He walks casually out of the bathroom, wearing the towel around his waist and I'm still not looking away. Catching my eyes, he smiles again and winks, actually winks. I wish I would just die already. He opens a drawer, takes something out and walks back into the bathroom not bothering to shut the door behind him this time. He reaches low and, in the reflection, and I see the towel leave his hips. NOPE.

I shoot straight up and away from view. Oh my God, what the hell is wrong with me? I'm mortified with myself right now. I pull my knees to my chest and turn my face in the opposite direction of the bathroom. I suppose that's one way to make me stop staring. I cannot believe I did that, what a creep. I close my eyes and rest the back of my head on the wall behind me. Pervert. Grabbing the pillow, I bury my face in it, "Stupid, stupid, stupid." I chastise myself quietly.

The bathroom door closes, scaring me, I gasp and jump forward, the pillow against my face teeters on my lap before falling off the side of the bed. Parker's wearing a pair of black basketball shorts, barefoot, and is shirtless; he looks downright delicious. Meeting my eyes, he gives me another crooked smile while wandering over to opposite side of the bed, pulling the comforter down and climbs into the bed.

"Wait-" I pull my lips in, "You're-" I don't have words.

"Sleeping in my bed? Yes." I guess I'm wearing one hell of a face because he starts to laugh, "Don't be weird."

I'm not the one being weird- okay, well maybe a little, I was just caught being a peeping tom. But, I mean, the dude wants me to sleep in his bed! Never have I slept in a bed with a man. Sure, I would climb into Kaylan's when I was little, but that is entirely different.

"I'm not acting weird."

"Sure you are. It's just sleeping."

My body jerks in hesitation, what if my sleeves roll up?

"Haley?" My eyes snap from my sleeve to him, "Are you planning on seducing me?"

"What?!" I shriek, "No!"

He smiles like he doesn't believe me. In all fairness, I wouldn't believe me either after that. "Then you have nothing to worry about. Your virtue is safe with me."

I scoff. Yeah, my virtue is the least of my worries. I blow out a breath, settling down against the mattress, moving a few inches towards the edge in the process.

"Nice, right?" I appreciate the fact he's not talking about my little creeper moment.

"This is probably the most comfortable thing I've ever laid on. "

He chuckles, leaning over to kill the bedside lamp. "Night, Haley."

"Goodnight."

BROKEN

He's on his back beside me with one arm above his head, the other resting on his bare stomach. The light from outside casts blue light across his chest, making the dips and curves of his body deepen, my eyes follow the push and pull of the shadows as he breaths, fuck me he's pretty.

"Stop staring, sweetheart." My eyes snap up to his closed eyes, the right side of his mouth is turned up.

"I'm not staring."

"I'm not complaining." Gah, he's so- NOPE. Nope, not allowed to have those thoughts. "But if you want me to remain, gentlemen, you should stop."

"I'm not staring," I mumble like a child, settling further into the bed.

His chuckle sends goosebumps down my arms. Grabbing my sleeves, I roll the excess fabric in my hand, clenching it into my fists. Hopefully, I can hold onto it throughout the night.

"What's wrong?" His mumble breaks my internal dialog.

"Nothing."

"You're not sleeping."

"Because you're talking."

"You're stiff and fidgeting."

"Am not."

"So argumentative."

"So talkative."

BROKEN

The mattress pulses with his laughter. "Relax."

"I am relaxed. Now, shut up and go to sleep."

"Kay."

A few minutes tick by before his breathing evens out. I keep thinking about how I have to face him tomorrow, and my skin burns all over again. Burying my arm under the pillow, I take a deep breath and let the darkness claim me.

I'm roasting, my skin is sticky and the air feels thick around me. Pushing my sleeves up, I roll over and try to fall back asleep. That is until the realization hits me that I'm not on my couch. I yank my sleeves down, sitting up abruptly. The room is empty, the bathroom door is open, but the room door is closed. After a moment I notice the hushed voices trailing in from under the bedroom door. Thank God.

After climbing out of bed, shame squeezes my stomach reminding me that I was caught staring at him last night. Part of me wants to go hide under the covers but the other half knows there's no way to avoid this. Might as well get the humiliation over with sooner rather than later.

BROKEN

I run my fingers through my unruly hair as I scamper down the hall to the living room. Parker is still in his basketball shorts from last night, but he put on a t-shirt, unfortunately. He's sitting on the couch across from Drew, who looks fresh as a daisy for being shit faced the night before.

"Jesus, Hales. Are you trying to kill the guy?"

"What?" My voice is still heavy with sleep.

"That's just mean."

"What is?"

He nods to my legs. "You might as well be walking around in your underwear."

"These are the shorts from HEAT."

"I know what they are and I know what you look like in them."

"Shut up, they're just legs. If you haven't seen a pair before then it's not my problem."

"You're a grump in the morning." He huffs shaking his head.

His gaze has yet to leave my legs so I pop my hip against the kitchen island in annoyance, "If you're that uncomfortable, I can change."

"The only thing that's uncomfortable is the lack of room in my pants." My eyes roll to the heavens on their own accord. "Seriously bro, how the hell did you sleep next to that?"

'That' like I looked like a dog or something. "Gee, thanks."

"Not what I meant, Hales. You're hot and half naked, I'm just commending him on his efforts."

"Well, if y'all didn't fuck up my plans he wouldn't have had to make one." I realize we're talking about Parker like he's not here, but he hasn't decided to speak for himself yet, so fuck it.

"You would've slept with him?!"

"What? How did you even come to that conclusion right now?"

"You said he wouldn't have had to make an effort."

"Yeah, cause I would be hundreds of miles away."

"Oh, so you're not going to sleep with him?"

"Jesus. It's too early for this." I shake my head pulling away from the counter.

"So...? Not a no then?"

If I could light people on fire with a look, Drew would be a pile of ash right now.

Surrendering his hands, he lays back on the cushions. "Hey, wanna go swimming?"

"Where?" It's the first time Parker has spoken since I came out.

"I don't know, Josh's?"

Parker shrugs before looking over his shoulder at me, "Wanna go swimming?"

Parker wet and half naked? "Sure."

"Call Josh, see if he's cool with it." He tells Drew before turning back to me, those blue eyes are electric. "Do you have a bathing suit or do you want me to run you to the store?"

"I've got clothes I can wear."

"You're gonna wear clothes to go swimming?" Drew pipes in, holding the phone to his ear.

I shrug, "Why not?"

"Cause you're hot. Hot girls don't wear clothes in pools. That's for the deformed or ugly." Well, if the shoe fits.

"How shallow." Parker says sitting forward to rest his elbows on his knees.

"Clothes have like a ton of soap and shit in them. Josh might not want her in the pool without a suit. Hey- do you care if Parker, Hales, and I come over? We wanna go swimming." A smile tugs at my lips while Drew nods along with whatever Josh is saying. "Cool, thanks. Oh hey- Haley wants to wear clothes... Not in general asshole, in the pool... Yeah... Kay, see you soon." Hanging up the phone he shakes his head at me.

"No-go. Gotta wear a suit." Fuck. I can feel my chest tighten. "What's that store Lacy used to drag us to? The one where it's just swimwear?" Drew asks.

"The depot one?" Parker responds.

"Yeah."

"I don't remember what it's called but I know where it's at. You wanna take her over there?"

"If Lacy's picky-ass could find something, I'm sure Hales can."

"Who's Lacy?" I ask.

"Parker's ex. How soon can you be ready?" Drew asks before I could respond.

"Five minutes?"

Drew gives me an exaggerated scoff. "Bull. Shit. I've never met a woman who can go from waking up to out the door in five minutes."

"What do I get when I'm out the door five minutes from now?"

"I'll cut off my right testicle and give it to you on a silver platter."

"Deal."

"What do I get when you're not ready?"

BROKEN

"Whatever you want- but keep it to yourself, I like to be surprised."

"Alright then." He leans forward, opening an app on his phone, "Five minutes start- now."

With a smug smile of my own, I casually walked down the hall.

Once I'm in the safety of Parker's room, I switch gears and start moving like a mad woman. It doesn't take me long, but I don't want to be at the mercy of Drew. I pull out a pair of leggings and shirt along with my toothbrush and a hair tie. I brush my teeth in record time, quickly change, shoving some cash into my bra before throwing my feet into a pair of shoes and swiping on deodorant. I pull my hair into a messy bun as I walk back down the hall. Parker starts laughing immediately, I walk past them both, open the door and step outside.

"No fucking way." Drew mumbles staring at his phone.

"How long was I?"

"Four minutes, forty-seven seconds." He says shaking his head in disbelief. "Marry me."

Parker is still laughing while scooping up his keys to lock the door.

BROKEN

"Since I won, do I get a say in how the ball is removed? Oh, and can I pick out the platter?"

"That was some sorcery. I figured you'd be putting on makeup and shit."

"What's the point? We're going swimming."

"You're like every guy's dream girl."

"Hardly. Come on, slowpokes."

Drew grills me the entire way the car asking questions like, did you brush your teeth? Put on deodorant? Closing the Camaro door on him still wasn't enough to deter him. "But not like touched, you swiped it across? 'Cause I'm not interested in smelling your funk."

"Oh my God, drive!" I laugh-shout at Parker.

"Yes, ma'am." In exaggerated fashion, Parker takes off like a bullet.

CHAPTER EIGHT

"Oh! Hales, get this one!" Drew holds up a one piece made up entirely of hot pink floss.

"I think it would look better on you," I say, passing him.

He's like a damn kid in a candy store, every five seconds he's holding up a 'barely there' bathing suit telling me to get it. Peering down each aisle, I eventually find a woman wearing a purple polo sporting the depot logo.

"Excuse me?"

"Yes, what can I help you with?" I know Parker must have approached because the mousy brunette in front of me goes stiff and her cheeks start to pink.

"This is going to sound weird but do you have any bathing suits with long sleeves?"

"Mhm. They're over here next to the surfwear." Leading us a few aisles down she stops in front of a small section of long sleeved bathing suits. "What we have is here." She bounces her hand off the rod a couple of times, all the while unashamedly gawking at Parker. I don't know what she's waiting for but evidently, she gives up and retreats.

"Subtle," I mutter into the hangers.

"Jealous much?"

"Of the fact you have fans? No."

His mouth started to open, but Drew, the champion of interruption made his grand appearance. "You know, I should be mad that y'all ditched me, but I got this Betty's number, so it all worked out. What the hell are you holding?"

I look down at the black swim shirt. "A bathing suit."

"That's not a bathing suit it's a sweater."

"Shut up, Drew."

I shift through the measly rack placing the ones that look like they'll fit over my arm when Drew's low whistle steals my attention. "Ding, ding, ding, we have a winner." He holds up a black one piece, running navel to collarbone is a corset front.

"No." I shake my head.

"It's got sleeves."

"It's missing the entire front of it, Drew."

"Exactly," He shrugs. "Parker, yay or nay."

Parker tries to stifle the growing smirk. "It's pretty hot."

BROKEN

"So, yay?"

He nods, and my eyes fly to the ceiling. Boys.

Without a response, I take the four garments in my arms over to the dressing room.

My butt and boobs ruined the possibility of those. One, I might be able to pull off, but the girls are beyond squished, pulling the fabric of the top, I tug it down with a little shake trying to get all of my pieces to sit right when a bathing suit, hanger and all, slaps the wall above my head. "Jesus!" I yelp.

"Sorry!" Drew yells while laughing.

It's that corset one piece. With a sigh, I strip and slide it on, what I thought was a corset is just elastic strings, at least there wouldn't be fear of it untying. Wouldn't you know it- it fucking fits. Of course, it does. It's not that bad now that I look at it, it has cups like a bra built into it so it keeps the girls where they need to be and my ass is covered.

"Come on, Hales! You're acting like such a girl! What happened to the five-minute wonder?"

"I heard that was your name."

"What?"

Cracking the door open, I pop my head out, "I heard that was your name."

"One, rude. Two, not true. And three- hurry the hell up."

"You're the one who threw another one in so stop complaining."

"Oh, let me see!"

"Fuck no!"

He laughs as I change back into my clothes.

Parker and Drew are both leaning against the archway leading into the dressing rooms. Side by side I'm able to see the differences between them, they do look quite a bit alike, but it's hard to believe I thought they were twins at one point. Parker's frame is thicker and taller where Drew is leaner and more compact. His face is also squarer and lacks the hard angles of Drew's. Both of them stand when they hear the door shut behind me.

"Find one?"

"Yep. The one you picked out actually."

"For real?" He seems entirely too excited.

"The others didn't fit." Hanging the discarded items on the rack, we move to the checkout.

Twenty minutes and thirty dollars later we're driving up a private road with mansions on either side us.

"Josh is loaded, huh?"

"HEAT does well."

"Cheah- if you live in a neighborhood like this I'd say that was an understatement."

"He has four other clubs across the country."

BROKEN

"Really?"

He nods, "That's why we haven't met before. I moved back to Georgia a couple of years ago to help get the Savannah club up and running."

"Oh, that's cool," I start, but when we pull up to a massive electric gate, the words die in my throat.

Parker rolls down the window enters a pin, and the gates swing open. As we approach the massive structure, a small laugh bubbles out of me. "Oh my God. Josh lives here?"

He doesn't respond, but a smile graces his lips while he pulls up the half moon driveway to park next to Josh's pickup truck. Drew's bike slides next to my side just as Parker kills the engine.

"This isn't real." I shake my head. I might cry, I couldn't tell you why, but I've got the urge to.

Drew knocks on my window, "Cars are meant for two things; driving and fucking. Get naked or get out."

He barely misses the door when I swing it open, "The human body has over 95 billion nerves, and you're capable of getting on every single one of them." I hiss, closing the door behind me.

Drew glares at me while Parker laughs. I follow them up the steps to the massive front door, if that's what we're calling it. I'm willing to bet my savings you could drive a car through it with ease. Drew knocks twice before pushing it open.

Are you fucking kidding me?! Dark floors, white walls, chandeliers, massive staircase to the left, I've stepped into a fairy tale.

"Welcome to Casa de Hayes!" Drew exclaims, spreading out his open arms.

"More like Castle de Hayes."

Parker chuckles beside me before placing his hand on my lower back to lead me forward. I stiffen at the unexpected touch causing him to pull away immediately, "Shit. I'm sorry."

"What? No, you just startled me." I lie, following Drew through a large hallway to the right of the entrance that leads us into a kitchen the size of my apartment.

A massive island sits center where a beautiful brunette sits, flipping through a magazine. She looks up, and a smile brightens her face. She looks like the female version of Parker. If I didn't know better- I'd swear this was their mom.

"Hi, guys! How are you?" She slides off the stool to hug each brother in turn.

"Maria-" Josh says from beside me, making me jump. "This is Haley. Haley, Maria."

I give her a weak wave, "Hi."

"Haley works at HEAT with Drew."

"I hope he's been behaving himself." She gives me a kind smile that immediately pulls me in; she has a very maternal air about her.

"Yes, ma'am."

"So, what are you guys up to today?"

Drew hops up onto the counter grabbing something off a nearby plate and shoving it into his mouth, "Swimming."

"That sounds fun. I've gotta run, but I'll be back." She leans forward kissing both boys on the cheek. "Love you, boys." Both of them respond at the same time, and I'm not sure who said what.

"Pool's good to go, guys," Josh says while putting a bottle of some kind into the refrigerator that I'm confident he could climb into.

I find myself nodding, not entirely sure why. Drew must have caught it because he starts laughing. "I think Hales is a little star struck."

I give a weak smile when all three of them turn to stare at me. "I've never been in a house this big before."

"There's a bathroom down the hall you can change in," Parker tells me from his place against the wall. "Second door on the left."

Quickly shuffling down the hall to avoid any more of their attention, I change before shoving my clothes into the plastic shopping bag. With one final boob adjustment, I crack the door open- all of sudden incredibly aware of just how exposed I am right now. My usual, I-don't-give-a-fuck-about-my-appearance attitude has deserted me when I need it most.

Holding the bag close to my exposed body, I step out into the hall. Parker is leaning against the hall wall tapping his leg when I step into view. His leg stills as his eyes scan my body from head to toe and back up again, pausing longer in some areas than others.

"I don't know where to put my stuff," I tell him to avoid the silence all the while fidgeting with the plastic handle.

After a long pause, Parker clears his throat, "Uh, you can bring it outside, so you have it when we get done."

"Kay." I nod, wishing I had about six layers of clothing on. When neither of us move the awkward intensifies. "I'll follow you."

Lifting his gaze back to my face he turns sharply and walks through the kitchen and out a pair of floor to ceiling glass french doors. The patio is gigantic and overlooks a pool that could have its own zip code. Located on the other side of the chlorinated lake is another house, this one the size of a four, maybe five-car garage.

Parker pulls the shirt off his frame, and I about drool until Drew, being the reigning champion of lousy timing, whistles on the other side of him. "Fuck dude, do I have great taste or what?"

BROKEN

My anxiety level crawls another two points when Josh exits the house; his eyebrows shift heavenward when he sees me. "You changed your mind about the clothes."

My face turns to stone before fire rips out of my eyes. "You bastard!" I yell at Drew. "You said he wouldn't let me!"

"Don't be mad! You look great!"

I throw my bag at him, it smacks into his shoulder, "You owe me thirty bucks, jock strap!"

Parker wears a half amused, half sad expression. "That's fucked."

"Yeah, but look at her!" He waves at me, and I want to crawl into a hole as all three of them turn to do exactly that. "She would be in a shirt and jeans if she had it her way. You're welcome."

"Dick move." I fume.

"So was giving me a letter." He shrugs.

My tongue slides between my bottom teeth and lip while I laugh without humor.

"Whatever, dude." I huff.

"Low blow." Parker's voice is hushed while he shoots Drew a pointed look.

He walks past him, nodding at me to follow. We stepped out into the sun when a loud smacking sound echoes across the yard. "Gah! What the hell did I do?"

I choke on my giggle while trying to stifle my laugh. Drew follows rubbing the back of his head. "You think that's funny?"

BROKEN

"You deserved it." I throwback.

"Yeah? I deserved it?" He stalks forward making me step back until the pool is at my back.

"Don't you dare!" I point at him, "Drew, I'm serious-" I squeal when his hands land on my hips, launching me backward and into the water. The chill of the water is welcome on my heated skin. Breaking the surface, I laugh before screaming and covering my face. Drew cannon balls right next to me, sending a typhoon wave across the pool. After a moment he resurfaced shaking his head like a dog.

"Dick." I swim over until my feet can reach the bottom.

Parker had gotten in at some point and is in the process of dunking Drew.

"Play nice, boys!" Maria's angelic voice rings out from the patio. She wasn't gone long. Standing beside her, Jules and Vinny watch the commotion with smiles.

Both brothers call out their hellos at the same time, that's the second time they've done that today. To avoid their splashing, I tread over to the shallow area.

"Haley! Is that you, love?" Jules calls out, using her hand to shield her eyes from the sun.

"Yeah." I wave at her then shoot Vinny a wave as well.

"Oh, I'm so glad you stayed!" Her smile widens before pointing to my left.

BROKEN

I turned just in time to avoid Drew's incoming assault. "That's cheating!" He points to her.

"Do you trust me?" A rich voice comes over my shoulder, sending goose bumps racing across my skin from his proximity. Rotating my hips, I look back at him and nod. His hands come to rest on my hips, drawing me back, so I'm flush against with his chest. "One," his grip tightens, "Two," excitement ripples through me, "Three," On three he shoots me right out of the pool, sending me airborne before I crash back into the water.

"Keep her in the pool, Parker!" I heard Maria yell as I pop back up to the surface.

"Damn dude, how much do you weigh?" Drew yells out over Parker's shoulder.

"I don't know. One thirty?"

"Come here, my turn."

Treading back over, I let Drew launch me. I went a lot further this time than before.

"I call a redo!" Parker announces. "I wasn't aiming for distance the first time."

"You're going to break her!" Maria yells across the lawn with a laugh.

Swimming back to Parker, he winks at me. "Ready?"

"Better win."

"I don't lose, sweetheart."

BROKEN

On three I was airborne once again. I don't care how old you are; nothing is more fun than being launched across a pool like a rag doll.

"Bullshit!" Drew complains with a chuckle.

"Did you win?" I call to Parker who's grinning ear to ear.

"Of course."

"Alright, the next feat of strength. Hales, come here." Drew waves at me like Jack Nicholson in The Shining when he's telling Wendy to give him the bat and it makes me giggle.

"What am I doing?"

"I'm going to go underwater, you're going to put your feet on my shoulders, and when I stand- you jump."

"That sounds painful and likely to go wrong."

"Don't be a chicken shit."

"You just don't want to admit defeat." Parker teases.

"I'm not defeated. Hales, be a sweetheart and climb on my shoulders so I can put this douchebag to shame."

"Don't drown."

"Pssht. Please, you weigh next to nothing."

"Let me see your hands," Parker tells me holding his out to me.

I place mine inside his as Drew goes under the water. Helping me keep my balance, he holds me steady while I climb up Drew's back.

"As he stands, use his momentum to push you forward."

"'Cause this won't go wrong." I laugh as he lets go of my hands and places them in Drew's.

Without notice, Drew jumps off the ground. My body shoots forward, and I let out a shriek of surprise before the water swallows me whole.

I can hear cheers before my head breaks water. Holy crap. Drew and Parker are half a pool away from me. Parker shakes his head side to side in disbelief while Drew takes a bow.

Swimming over to them, Parker catches my hand and drags me towards him.

"Y'all want to stay for some grub?" Josh calls from the patio where he lifts the lid of a built-in grill.

"Hell yeah!" Drew answers enthusiastically before backflipping off the diving board at the other end.

"Haley, Parker?"

Looking at me, I shrug at Parker, "Sure."

"Yeah." He says absently while his fingers trace my hip bone.

"Haley, how do you like your meat?"

"Attached to Parker," Drew answers before I could even open my mouth.

"Andrew Mason Hayes!" Maria shrieks in a laughing scold, while my entire body burns. I can feel Parker's chest moving with silent laughter. I'm too mortified to speak.

"God, what is wrong with you?" Josh glares before turning back to me with an expected look.

I laugh nervously, trying to find my voice. "Um-"

"You can't answer cause I'm right, huh?"

"Medium-rare!" I yell at Josh, while splashing Drew in the face, "You're such an asshole."

He shrugs before dunking my head under water.

"Hey, Haley?" Josh's voice pulls me from my plate, "Drew mentioned you always wear long sleeves and I was wondering just how opposed are you to wearing a sleeveless dress?"

Taking my time to swallow, I feel the burn of everyone's eyes on me.

"I'd say pretty opposed." I nervously look up and meet his eyes. "Why do you ask?"

"Well, you're not old enough to be behind the bar. But you can be a cocktail waitress. If you were open to wearing a sleeveless dress, I have Abbey's old uniform, and you could go back to work tonight if you wanted to, but if not then you're going to have to wait for me to order a new one."

BROKEN

I don't know if I'm even staying, let alone if I'm going to go back to HEAT. "If it weren't for your ridiculous scheme, I'd be twelve-hundred miles east of here... I don't-" I cleared my throat feeling everyone's eyes on me. "I uh- I don't know how long I'm staying."

I feel Drew go stiff next to me; I refuse to look at him even when he speaks. "What the fuck do you mean, you don't know how long you're staying?" Still staring down, I play with my sleeve. "Forever, Haley. That's how long you're staying."

Little fissures spread across my heart. Wanting everyone's eyes off of me and this god awful burning behind my eyes to disappear, I blink rapidly and nod, "Yeah, maybe."

"No, not maybe. You're staying, say it."

"I'm staying."

"Promise."

"Drew." My body sags against the chair as I close my eyes.

"Promise me you'll stay."

"I can't promise that." Where the hell is a random sinkhole when you need one?

"Yes, you can. It's really easy, repeat after me; I promise I'll stay forever."

"Doesn't work like that."

"No... yes, it does."

"I promise I'll stay as long as I can."

"Fuck that. You could be gone tomorrow."

Everyone's staring at me; I can feel it, and I want to puke.

"I don't break promises, Drew. And I can't promise I'll be able to stay forever."

"You're eighteen, Hales. No one can drag you back to where you ran from."

"Drew!" I hiss, covering my face.

"Everyone here already knows." Maria doesn't. "What is it that you think will happen if you stay?"

I think he'll come for me; I think he'll take me and punish me for running. I think I'll lose them. My body starts to vibrate, and my muscles twitch without consent as my chest tightens. If he catches me, he'll go after them too.

"Drew, stop." Parker's voice is low and laced with concern.

Drew's mouth moves like he's going to speak but whatever he was going to say dies on his lips.

Forcing my lungs to expand, I try to pull in enough oxygen to respond when a voice whispers in my ear.

BROKEN

"I'm going to touch you," I hadn't even noticed Parker had stood up, let alone was right next to me. "Help me real quick?" He says loud enough for others to hear as his hands land on my ribs to help me stand.

My legs are jello. The embarrassment of causing a scene only adds to my panic. Jesus, I'm pathetic. Parker doesn't let go; even when we're in the kitchen, he leads me down the hall and into an office.

"Sit, sweetheart." He guides me to a chair waits until I'm seated before letting go.

"I'm fine," I whisper, cursing myself for not even being able to control my volume.

"No, you're not." He kneels down in front of me, so we're eye to eye. "I'm not going to ask what's wrong- not because I don't care but because I don't want you to have to relive it. I just want you to breathe, can you do that?"

His voice is painfully tender and grounding. I force air into my lungs and push it out.

"I want you to tell me five things you can see."

"You." Looking around Josh's home office, I list items as my eyes fall on them. "The desk, the rug, bookshelf, and the window."

"Good. Can you find four things to touch?"

BROKEN

Looking down I run my fingers over the surface of the red leather chair I'm sitting in, one. Gliding up the smooth sleeve of my bathing suit I pick up the ends of my hair before dropping my hands against my bare thigh.

"What are three things you can smell?"

"Um...furniture polish, chlorine, and..." I run out of options and look around.

"I'm going to touch you." He says gently reaching for my hand. I yank my wrist back but offer my right hand when he withdraws. Gently he takes my wrist and raises it to my face.

"Sunscreen."

"What are two things you can hear?"

"Your voice, and now mine."

He shakes his head. "Name two others."

"Um...I can hear you breathing and a rumbling, like an AC or something."

"Name something you can taste."

"You want me to lick something?"

The corner of his mouth raises, "No. What's something you can taste currently."

Moving my tongue around, I don't taste anything. "Me." I shrug.

He's very close to my face, and I can't help but watch his mouth as he speaks. "Pinpoint something specific."

BROKEN

In a rash, albeit ballsy as hell decision- I lean forward, running my fingers behind his neck and gently pull him forward until my lips graze his.

He doesn't blank this time. Leaning into me, his lips collide harder with mine. Our tongues meet, and a low, sexy groan escapes his throat as he leans forward against my mouth. He keeps moving until he's above me. Running his teeth against my bottom lip, a string of goosebumps race across my skin. Fuck, he's a good kisser.

"Jesus." He rests his forehead against mine, "I can't touch you, and it just might kill me." We're both breathing heavy as I meet his eyes.

Here's my dilemma- one: he's Parker. Two: he's my best friend's brother. And three: he's my boss' nephew. Ex-boss? Fuck who knows. If I give in and take the distraction, am I whoring myself out? I've known him for all of two minutes. My worries quickly become overpowered by my lack of willpower when my eyes fall to his lips. People fuck after talking to a stranger for two seconds so I can undoubtedly kiss one without judgment, right? I look back at his lips, fuck it.

BROKEN

"So, touch me," I whisper taking in his lower lip, I let it slide out from between my teeth.

The blue in his eyes darken before I feel his finger graze my jaw, I shiver when his rough fingers brush against the sensitive skin below my ear, and then tangle in my hair. His lips brush across mine, but he doesn't apply pressure. His breath tickles my skin as his lips slide up my jaw. His lips connect with my neck, causing me to inhale sharply as my knees press together. My fingers tangle in his hair while his mouth draws a line down my throat.

I'm on the verge of combustion when he finally reaches my mouth again. His lips are hungry and demanding as they consume me. I moan into his mouth and his body tenses, his grip tightening in my hair, steering my head where he wants me. Why haven't we been doing this from the start? Like all good things that happen to me- they end entirely too soon and completely unexpected.

The door opens.

CHAPTER NINE

My body jerks back, but the chair stops the motion abruptly while at the same time Parker quickly pulls away.

"Yes!" Drew throws both of his arms above his head in triumph. "Josh, you owe me twenty bucks!"

My fingers brush against my swollen lips as I stare at my lap feeling my face burn against the intrusion.

"Y'all better not have been having sex in my office!" Josh shouts as he approaches from down the hall. My hands fly over my face. "Parker you've got a damn bed upstairs." He finishes just outside of the door, "Everybody decent?"

"Oh my God." I groan into my hands.

"Is that a yes?"

"Yeah," Parker answers with a laugh. I spread my fingers so I can glare at him. This isn't funny. He's still crouched in front of the chair, one knee resting on the ground while the other supports his elbow. His thumb absently slides across his bottom lip.

"Why here?" Josh demands as he enters the room. His face is stern, but I can see him trying to fight a smile.

"We weren't doing anything," I say into my hands, completely mortified.

"Yeah right, that's why you're hiding behind your hands, and Parker has a shit-eating grin on his face?"

I crack my fingers again to see he's not lying. Parker's grinning ear to ear, he looks like he's trying not to laugh as he shakes his head at Josh.

"Oh my God! Tell him!" I push Parker's shoulder with my foot. His laughter finally breaks free, "Our clothes are still on!"

"Yeah, but for how long?" Drew asks from the hall.

"You're the worst friend in the world!" I groan, bending so I can bury my face in my lap. I've never wanted to vanish more than I do right now.

"I thought you had more class than this, Parker."

"Yeah, like using the desk," Drew adds, still standing in the hall.

"Fuck, just kill me now," I mumble, a hand lands on my knee followed by a gentle squeeze.

"It's so not what it looks like."

"What's that mumbler?" Josh asks.

Pulling my hands away from my face I repeat, "I said, it's so not what it looks like."

"Are you sure? Cause you're redder than that chair right now." I fucking bet. "I feel like I should give you the sex talk."

"For the love of God- do it!" Drew laughs from out in the hall.

"Please don't." I shake my head at Josh, before looking to Parker for help- "Stop laughing!" I push him again. "This isn't funny! He thinks we were hooking up in his office!"

Josh gives me a pointed look, "Oh my God, I'm going to cry!" I cover my face again. "We were just kissing, that's all- I swear."

"Not from where I was standing."

"Drew! You're five seconds away from becoming a eunuch!"

"Wouldn't be the first pair of balls you've touched in the last ten minutes."

Parker and Josh both break out in laughter.

"Jesus Christ!" I step over Parker's legs, who is now sitting on the ground and rush past Josh, trying to escape. Drew is leaning against the wall in front of the door. His hands cover his balls as I approach, giving me access to the back of his head. A satisfying 'slap' echoes off the walls of the gigantic house.

"Ow! Fuck!" He grabs the back of his head. "Ah!" He yells in my direction, but he's still smiling. "I might have deserved that."

"You think?!"

Avoiding every pair of eyes that fall on me. I rush outside to the patio, grab my bag of stuff and race back to the front door.

"Haley! We're just messing with you!" Drew calls after me, but I don't stop.

Pulling the massive door open, I rush outside without closing it behind me. Hopefully, Parker will get the message that I'm ready to go. I half walk, half run to his car. Throwing open the door, I rifle through the bag and pull out my jeans. I crave the safety of the vehicle, but I'm not an idiot. It's Phoenix, and he has leather seats. I'd prefer to keep my skin attached to my legs.

By the grace of God, I manage to get my shoes off and my legs through the jeans without touching any part of the car or scorching cement. Drew slowly approaches the car with his hands surrendered; I send him a death glare as I slide my jeans over my hips.

"Don't be mad, please?"

"I'm not mad, I'm horrified. You realize I see six of you every day, right?"

"That's why it was so funny. Look, Haley- they know you guys weren't bumping uglies, okay? We were just messing with you."

BROKEN

Running my hands through my hair, I twist it around my fist, just below my ear. My free hand absently rubs my forehead. "I'm so embarrassed."

"Why? Cause I walked in on you and Parker playing tonsil hockey."

He jumps back when I swipe my hand at him. "I hate you right now."

"Come back inside."

"Fuck. No."

"Come on. The joke's over. Plus, Maria made strawberry shortcake, you'll hurt her feelings if you leave without trying it."

"She looks like she could be your mom."

He shrugs, "Mom's sister. Moved in with Josh after my parents died. Helped raise us."

"Jeez, you've got a big family."

He shrugs again, "You coming in or are you going to leave and make us feel like a bunch of assholes?"

"You deserve to feel like a bunch of assholes."

"We do. I'm sorry."

"Your apology doesn't count when you're smiling."

"I know. I'm trying not to but- well come on, Hales! I walked in on you and my brother going at it; it's funny."

"No, it's not!" I whine, but the smile on my face cancels it out.

BROKEN

"So, you and Parker, huh?" He nudges me with his foot. "You know, people say we look alike."

I roll my eyes, shutting the car door and stepping around him. "Yeah, but Parker's better looking."

"One- rude. Two- not true. Three-" he pauses, "Rude."

"You said that one already."

"Yeah, well it deserved to be said twice."

Upon entering the house, the shit-hole known as Drew throws his arms out to the group of people in the kitchen while shouting, "She has returned!" in an accent.

Turning as red as my sneakers, I glare at the back of his head. "You're not allowed to speak for the next three minutes."

He twists suddenly, "What? Why?"

"We're fighting, now shut up."

With a child-like stomp of his foot, he stalks over and whips himself into a stool at the counter. Josh laughs before I turn on him, "You too!"

"Why me!"

"For putting me through that!"

"Is Parker in trouble?" Drew breaks his ten seconds of silence.

"No- shut the hell up. Neither of you is allowed to talk to me."

"I'm just saying; he's the-"

"Shh."

"Hold on. Hear me out; Parker's the one that didn't jump to the defense. He just sat there smiling. If anything, he instigated."

"Fine, the men in this house-" I looked over at Vinny who was sitting at the kitchen table chuckling, "Apart from Vinny, aren't allowed to talk to me for the next three minutes."

Parker's arms fly out in a 'what-the-hell' gesture, but his smile tells me he wasn't upset about it. Not like Parker talks a lot as it is.

Sitting down at the oversized table with Maria, Jules and Vinny, I jut out my chin in mock confidence.

"Parker and I kissed. But that's all. Despite the current accusations, I'd never disrespect Josh like that."

Maria, still wearing her warm smile, pats my hand, "We know."

Over the next three minutes, I had to shush Drew every twenty seconds until I eventually gave up.

"You can talk to me now. But I swear to God, Drew- if you make one more joke at my expense, I'll punch you in the face."

"Pshht, please! I'm sure you kiss harder than you hit."

"Dammit, Drew!" I stood up so fast; my vision turned white for a brief second.

"Ah! Poor choice of words! Poor choice of words! Don't hit me!"

"Now that my sentence is over," Josh starts while divvying up Maria's dessert, "About HEAT."

The words fall from my lips slowly, "What about it?"

"If you want the job- it's yours. It'll take a few days for your uniform to come in, so you have time to open a bank account. Oh, and you'll have to fill out an application with your real information."

"Okay."

"Okay?" He perks up at the counter.

I shrugged, "I promised I'd stay."

What the fuck am I doing? I shouldn't stay.

"YES!" Drew all but screams; jumping down, he wraps his thick arms around my waist, lifting me off the ground.

My chest squeezed shut, "Put me down, put me down, put me down." I rush out in a whisper.

"Sorry." He gives me an unapologetic smile.

"Alright then," Josh says handing out plates. "Come by the club tonight or tomorrow, and we'll get things settled."

"I don't want people to know."

Josh stops mid-step; his face contorts in confusion.

"My name, where I'm from, my age. Word of mouth travels fast, and there are things I left behind that I would like to remain there."

BROKEN

"I don't think we could call you anything but Haley," Josh starts, "As for the rest of your information, it's only for the legalities. And if anyone asked why you're not behind the bar, I'll tell them you asked for a different position. You have nothing to worry about."

I don't want him lying for me... "Hey, Josh?" He's already looking at me; a flush burns under my skin with how dumb I am. "I got harassed at the bar, and I'm not comfortable there. Do you have any openings on the floor?"

His brow pulls together, but he seems to catch up. "As a matter of fact- I do."

I nod, "Now, you don't have to lie."

The conversation turned easy after that. We laughed, ate, laughed some more. Good things don't last for me- I know that. Bad shit follows me wherever I go... but at least, for now, I'll enjoy it while it's here.

CHAPTER TEN

Quarter after ten, Parker drove me over to HEAT so I could fill out an application. Wasn't the most exciting thing I've ever done but with a smile, Josh congratulated me on being the newest cocktail waitress. Parker and him went up to the VIP room while I headed over to sit at the bar and keep Drew company. He wasn't overly thrilled to have Alice as his new bar-buddy.

All was going well until the filth of the earth sits down beside me. Wavy blonde hair pulled back into a clip, tight jeans, and a biker tank top. I knew who she was the second she ordered a drink; you never forget the voice of the person who chased the monsters away.

I dip my head, letting my hair create a screen between us. Slowly twisting, I try to escape unnoticed, that is until fucking Kaylan steps in front of me, leaning against the bar, doing a damn good job of trapping me. He raises his finger and Drew shoots a long neck to him and pulls the cash across the bar top before doing a double take. His eyes flash to mine and then to Kaylan, trying to place him.

"Kaylan showed up with this." She tells me. "He let me keep it."

Through the cracks in my hair, I see her fingers run across a photo. "I wanted to come get you." She says gently, laying the photo flat against the bar.

It's a photo of Kaylan and me. My grandfather, her father, came to visit a few weeks before Kaylan disappeared. It was the only time my father would ever pull his shit together. He'd hide the drugs, send the women away, and we'd play family for a weekend while my grandfather visited. I think he was the only thing my father feared. Grandpa used to tell Kaylan and me that it took a devil to kill a demon. I never really understood that but it's always stuck with me. The worst part in all of this is the fact the photo was taken when Kaylan and I had just gotten out of the pool; eleven purple scars run down my left arm.

She pulls the photo into her lap when I reach for it, "Don't." She hisses under her breath. "It's the only piece of you I have."

Glancing up, Drew's eyes are glued to the spot the photo laid a second before.

"Then take it and go." I say between gritted teeth. "You and your memories aren't welcome here."

"I just want to talk to my baby." Her voice cracks as she looks at me, the same grey eyes I see every morning staring back at me. She may have run out on us, but I remember enough to know this shit isn't real.

"Take your precious Kaylan and get the fuck out of my life. You died, and I don't talk to ghosts." Kaylan stiffens when I try to move past him, his body like a wall. I rear back and shoot my body weight into his side, he stumbles, giving me enough room to move past him. His hand snakes out, catching my forearm. Panic swells inside me until it feels like his grip is splitting my skin open.

"LET GO!"

He drops my hand immediately, looking shocked and regret filling his eyes, "I didn't mean-"

"If you ever fucking touch me again, I'll kill you."

"And if she doesn't, I will." A strong voice floats over my shoulder, soothing the tense muscles in my neck. I stepped back into Parker's chest, letting his body warmth form a protective shield around me.

"Who's this?" She asks Kaylan.

"Ryan's boyfriend." He mutters, his eyes never leaving mine.

BROKEN

Her hands come to rest on her smile. "Oh, honey. I'm so happy for you." Stepping forward she offers her hand to Parker, "I'm Susanna, Ryan's mom."

"My mom's dead. She went on a beer run and wrapped herself around a telephone phone." A hand glides across my hip, grounding me.

The hurt in her eyes doesn't reach me, the disappointment in Kaylan's barely registers.

Parker doesn't move to return the gesture. "And you were just leaving." I don't know how Drew managed to get out from the behind the bar so fast but here he is.

"Are these your friends, honey?" She asks with a smile despite the hurt in her eyes.

"How you keep getting in here is beyond me." Simon groans approaching behind Kaylan. He grips his arm, pulling him away from me.

I nod to her. "Take that with you."

"Mom," Kaylan calls, Simon stops to wait still holding onto Kaylan's arm.

"Baby, please don't throw me away. I didn't know what he was doing-"

"Stop," I warn.

"I swear I tried to get you out, too. Kaylan told me about-" She waved to my arm. "And I-"

"GET OUT." I lurch forward, but Parker's grip tightens, keeping me back.

Simon reaches forward, taking her by the elbow.

BROKEN

"Wait!" She cries, pulling away from him, reaching into her back pocket. She pulls out what looks like folded papers, and holds it out to me. "Please. I just want to talk to you."

When I don't move, Drew steps forward taking whatever it is out of her hands, then nods to Simon, who escorts them both to the exit.

Nervously approaching, he holds out a thick square of folded paper.

"I don't want that."

With a nod, he shoves it into his back pocket before looking over my shoulder at Parker. They do their silent conversation thing before he turns back to the bar.

"Walk with me?" Parker's mouth is close to my ear, his breath heating my neck. Nodding I let him guide me to the VIP room. Noticing only when I sit down that his hand never left my hip, even walking up to the second floor it remained. I watch as he pours what I think is bourbon into a small tumbler from the beverage cart before offering it to me.

I shake my head, "I'm not twenty-one."

"And?"

Taking the glass from him I throw the contents back. The amber liquid burns down my throat, an immediate heat coats my skin. Parker's eyebrows float to the heavens.

Wiping my mouth with the back of my hand, I set the glass down on the black coffee table in front of me. "That's twice my past has landed on your family's doorstep."

He shakes his head collecting the glass and setting it down on the tray. "That's not how we see it."

"I don't know how else you could see it."

"We've all got a past, Haley. It catches up to us all. Yours is just doing it in quick succession." He offers me a smile, but that comment did the opposite of his intent. If Kaylan and my mom were the worst of my past, I'd be able to handle that. Not the four men in Reno who want blood. "You're a natural blonde." It wasn't a question. I know he could see the similarities. Kaylan, Joe and I are all spitting images of her where Derek and Evan are carbon copies of my dad. I nod to answer his not-so-much-a-question, question.

"You probably don't want to hear this, but you look like her. So does your brother."

I nod again. "Joe, my other brother, looks like her too."

"How many siblings do you have?" This seems like a gateway conversation to a place I don't want to go.

Treading carefully, I answer honestly, "Four, all brothers."

"Older or younger?"

"Older."

"How old does that make your mom?"

"Forty-three, I think. Why?" I give him a teasing smile, trying to steer the conversation.

"Thinking about asking her out?" He doesn't bite.

"Forty-three with five kids? You guys must be close in age." He leans against the window overlooking the club with his arms crossed over his broad chest.

I shake my head. "Not really. Joe's four years older. Kaylan was eight when I was born, and Evan was ten. Derek was fourteen, but he's not my mom's son."

"How old was your mom when she had your brother?"

"Fifteen. Dad was twenty-five."

His face lifts with surprise. "That's young. Do you get along with any of your siblings?"

I find myself suddenly defensive with his constant questions. "Why do you care?"

"Just asking a question."

"A lot of questions." I point out.

He shrugs. "You were answering; thought I'd keep going."

"My family and this conversation are now dead."

"Can I ask a question unrelated to your family?"

"Maybe."

The right side of his mouth raises, "Why Phoenix?"

"I bought a bus ticket for the first available seat. The bus came here."

"So, if a bus landed you in Timbuktu, that's where you would have started your life?"

"Pretty hard to drive across the ocean, but I get what you're saying. Yes, as long as it was outside of Nevada's state lines, I would have stayed where it stopped."

"Wasn't there anywhere you dreamed of going?"

"If I wasn't praying for death to claim me it was a one-way ticket to anywhere but-" My eyes open at the realization at what I just said. Motherfucker. He wormed his way in despite my walls. My gaze turned deadly as he stands there, just freaking stands there while I try to light him on fire with my eyes. Then- then he motions for me to continue. "You did that on purpose." I seethe.

"Did what?" His face is clear of emotion.

"Tricked me into talking about Reno! Tricked me into talking about my-" I caught myself again. "Fuck." My fingers push into my hair, squeezing the strands until it causes pain.

"Why are you upset?" He asks calmly, fueling my temper. "Because you admitted to having a bad home life? Hate to break it to you, sweetheart, but I already knew that. What with the running away, and unwanted family reunions and all. You're acting like you gave up some major detail about your past, and maybe you did and I didn't catch it- but..." He trails off, shrugging. "Would it be that bad? Shit happens,

BROKEN

Haley. But you know what's worse? Keeping that shit buried inside of yourself; when you keep the bad in, it festers and bleeds, making it so you'll never be able to leave it behind. It's not the past if it's still haunting your present."

I stare at my knee, playing with imaginary lint and slightly nod. Minutes pass where neither of us speaks. The air is full of tension and unspoken words. I'm angry, and I'm hurt, but more than anything I'm annoyed that I want to kiss him for his words despite everything. A small knock interrupts our silence. I don't look up as Parker pulls away from the window to open the door. Feet enter, and I look up to see Josh and Drew- both looking incredibly uncomfortable.

Without speaking, Josh lays down a pack of papers in front of me. Four lines crease the pages. Resting on the cover is a document with two black and white images. The first is a license plate; the second is a photo of me boarding the bus out of Reno. And wouldn't you fucking know it- my unclothed arm is clear as fucking day.

CHAPTER ELEVEN

I stare at the dark lines marring my bare arm.

"I didn't open it- I swear. I threw it in the trash, and it just opened." Drew rushes out in one breath.

I remain silent; my leg bounces involuntarily as he continues in a pleading tone. "I didn't know what to do with it. I didn't want to show you and have you try to make a run for it, and I couldn't find Parker. Josh came up-" He trails off. My eyes don't leave the page. "Do you hate me?"

I shake my head, pushing it back towards Josh. "Shred it."

"Haley," He starts, "I think we need to talk about what's in there."

"We don't. Shred it."

"Haley." He sighs. "There are some things in there..." He trails off, looking at Drew and then Parker.

"It's either shit I already know or shit I don't want to know. I'm not kidding." I say standing, "Shred it."

I step around the table, making my way to the door.

"Haley, as your employer I legally have to ask you about this."

"Ask about what?" I spin around. "My mom showing up after twelve years wanting to catch up? Or my brother who just can't seem to leave me the hell alone?"

Picking up the packet of papers he holds the cover sheet forward. "I think we should talk privately."

My heart drops to my toes. "Why?"

"Because I have to ask you about what's in here."

Holding out my hand he offers the packet to me, I quickly flip through the pages, skimming over the words briefly. Apparently, she tried to get CPS involved right after she took Kaylan, too bad they never showed up. The fourth page has shit written about possible physical abuse, emotional abuse, and a doozy at the bottom, possible sexual assault.

"You want to know if I was raped?" I laugh without humor. Couldn't fucking stay or take me with her but she can scribble away what she thought might be happening to me.

Josh's gaze falls to the floor.

"Because you have to report any harm done either to me or by me, right? Legally?"

"Yes."

I laugh again and roll my eyes, tossing the papers like a frisbee to the coffee table.

"No, Josh. I wasn't raped." Truth. Sold? Well, that's a gray area. "Want to know if I was abused? No, Josh. I wasn't abused." Lie. "Want to know details of my childhood so you can report it and get me sent back to Nevada? Fuck you." I point to Parker, "This is why it would be bad if I talked about it. This exact moment right here."

Not waiting for a response, I throw the door open, taking the stairs two at a time, I shove through the crowd of dancers, briefly pausing to let incomers through before pushing out of the front doors into the hot Phoenix night.

I got two blocks before Drew's motorcycle pulls onto the shoulder. I should have stayed on the other side of the road. Removing his helmet, he climbs off, meeting me halfway.

"You running?"

"Nope, soul-searching." I step around him, continuing the walk to my apartment. I know I don't have a key so I can't get in but I can worry about that when I get there.

"Haley, please. I swear I didn't go through it." He says walking backward so we're facing each other.

"Kay." The hurt in his eyes makes me stop. "I'm not mad at you, even if you did open it and read it word for word I wouldn't be mad at you. A lot of that shit was speculation or what she thought was happening. Bitch hasn't been around for twelve years, but boy, she can write a list."

"So that stuff wasn't true?"

"Let it go, Drew." I sigh, walking forward again.

"I can't, Haley. I didn't know those were possibilities until you said them out loud. I'm not asking for details here; I'm just looking for a yes or no."

"Why?" I spin around. "Would it make you feel better to know I was a human ashtray? Would you sleep better at night knowing I was a piece of ass for some fuckboy to play with?" His face blanches, "Don't ask questions you don't want to know the answers to."

"I want to know."

"No, you don't."

"Haley. I'm not going to run back to Josh. He's not your employer outside of the club, believe me, he didn't want to do that."

"He hired me knowing I was underage and paid me under the table. I'm pretty sure he could bend the rules if he wanted to."

"Serving underage isn't the same thing as rape, Hales."

"I wasn't raped, anything I did was consensual. The manner it came about maybe not, but no one touched me without my say so."

"The manner?"

"Those are the details you claimed you weren't asking for. You wanted a yes or no, and I gave it to you."

He nods solemnly, "Can I ask you something else? It's super personal, and you're not gonna like it, but I'd like to ask anyway."

"What?"

"Do you wear sleeves because of those marks from the photo?"

My heart stalls, restarts, and stalls again before I answer, "Yes."

"That's why you're okay with your right side." He says more to himself than me. "Can I ask one more?"

"You want to know what happened?"

He nods.

"A few months before that picture was taken I ran through a sliding door." At least that's what the Reno General Hospital was told when I was brought in.

BROKEN

"The picture at the bus stop was a lot worse than the photo your mom had." He says softly, looking at anything but me.

Sure was; nine years worse.

I shrug. 'What are you asking?"

"I guess I'm not. I'm sorry that happened to you...running through the window I mean." The way he said running through the window implied he knew it wasn't a window that did the damage and an underlying tone that makes me feel like he thinks I did it to myself.

"Me too." I nod, feeling ashamed. "They aren't self-inflicted, just so you know."

His gaze lifts to mine, his brow falling over his eyes, "What isn't?"

"The glass window. Or the several other ones I fell through. They weren't self-inflicted."

"I don't know if that makes me feel better or worse, Hales."

I shrug. "Maybe you should take a page out of my book and don't feel anything at all. I left glass windows behind, Drew. And I'll keep running until there aren't any more to fall through."

CHAPTER TWELVE

I didn't accept his ride home, but that didn't deter him from following me. He'd pull forward and shoulder his bike until I caught up, rinse, and repeat. Pulling into the complex, he parks in guest parking, jogging to catch up with me.

"Where are you going?"

"My apartment."

"Did you find the key?"

"No."

"Then how are you going to get in?"

"I thought I'd try one of the windows." They're locked. I know they're locked because I checked and doubled check every night since Kaylan showed up.

"I've got a key to Parker's place, let's go raid his fridge. You can check your place after."

"Nice try. Once I'm in you'll keep me in until I eventually pass out."

"True. But A for effort, right?"

"I sniffed it out the moment you opened your mouth. C minus at best."

"Damn, Um...hey Parker is running around buck ass neked, let's go up and take a peek." The way he said naked manages to make laugh, despite my shitastic evening. "One- Neked? Two- That's your brother; so wanting to 'take a peek.' is twelve shades of gross and, three- If I wanted to see Parker naked, I'd ask."

"You're not doing it right." He whines in disapproval, "Number one is always 'rude.' If you're going to use my lines, at least do it right."

I don't respond because we've reached my apartment. I was here yesterday morning, but it still feels like forever. Trying the front window, it doesn't budge.

"I miss my couch," I gripe, walking to the dining room window and trying that one. Locked.

"Bedroom?"

I shake my head. "Not open. I'm never in there; I wouldn't have opened it."

"Well..." He slams his hands together so hard the clap echoes across the complex, we both know I won't be getting in, "Let's go raid Parker's fridge."

"Don't you have your own fridge to raid?" I ask falling into step with him.

BROKEN

"One- rude. Two- Parker has better food than me. Three- whose side are you on anyway?"

With a glorious eye roll meant for him to see, I walked the remaining distance in silence.

Upon entering, Drew immediately went into the kitchen. I shut the door, kicking off my sneakers and turned for the hall.

"Where are you going?" He yells down at me.

"To wait for Parker, buck ass neked in his bed."

I heard him choke, despite it being a dick move and shitty night, I start laughing.

"Well then-" I heard a male voice, loud and clear and it wasn't Drew's. My hands cover my face as my laughter gets stuck in my throat. "I guess I'm going to bed."

When the fuck did he come in? I take baby steps to the mouth of the hall and peer around the wall. Parker is dumping his keys as Drew cackles like an old hag in the kitchen to my right.

"A little warning, asshole!" I yell, throwing my shoe at him. He turns, taking the blow to his thigh, a chicken leg still in his hand.

"You are neither naked nor in my bed. I am incredibly disappointed right now."

"Blame Drew. He ruined it for you, and he's eating all your food." I tsk while shaking my head. "And to think of the stuff, we could have done if you put those two things together."

Quite satisfied with the shocked silence of both of them I sashay my proud little ass down the hall.

After my shower, I realize my only available clothing is dirty or inappropriate. Wrapping the towel tightly around myself, I slowly open the door, making sure the room is vacant before tiptoeing across Parker's bedroom to his closet, I want to snag a shirt, but they're Phoenix natives, and it appears he doesn't have a single long sleeve shirt. Cracking the bedroom door open, I press my face against the opening and call down the hall, "Parker?"

"Yeah?" I hear him get up from the couch.

"No, stay there. I was just wondering if you had a shirt I could borrow."

"Oh, yeah- anything in the closet."

I make a face, "With sleeves?"

"Oh shit, you know- I don't know. Maybe in one of the drawers? Do you want me to go out and get you something?"

"No. If not, I can wear what I wore last night, it's fine, thanks."

Shutting the door, I stepped over to his dresser and started pulling drawers open. Okay, seriously? What guy is this organized? Everything is folded and evenly spaced. Hmm, I wonder if he's got OCD. Closing the last drawer, I let out a sigh of defeat moving back to my bag in the bathroom. Maybe I just overlooked something. Dumping the contents onto the tile floor, I riffle through it.

Two problems, one: The only clean shirt left is skin tight and it's the red counterpart to my club attire. No way my boobs stay in there through the night. Two: my shirt from last night isn't in here. I could fucking cry. Where the hell would I put it? Looking around I try to remember what I did with it this morning in my rush to get out of the door in under five minutes but can't find it.

My options; dirty club shirt, dirty shirt from today that's a sports bra with sleeves or the red shirt. Those button-down tops can't contain my boobs overnight. So, I guess belly shirt it is. Throwing on my rainbow socks and HEAT shorts, I brush my teeth and finger through my hair before waltzing into the living room like my attire is done on purpose. I step over Drew's legs that are propped up on the coffee table, ignoring his open-mouthed stare, and sit on the same couch as Parker, leaving a buffer cushion between us. Pulling my knees up and under me, I look at the TV as if I was intrigued by whatever they were watching.

Feeling their eyes on me, I look at Drew and then at Parker. Parker's hand is frozen in front of his bottom lip, his eyes taking in my less-than-there outfit. Drew has an amused 'what-the-hell' expression.

I throw up my hands, "What?"

"I think you pissed her off, dude," Drew says staring at my boobs.

"Yes, Drew, I have a rack." His eyes snap to mine.

"Hey, if you're going to advertise, you can't get mad when I look."

"It's Phoenix. It's hot." It's a dumb excuse, but it was the first thing that came to mind.

"I'd offer to turn up the AC, but I think I just learned I'm a masochist," Parker admits next to me.

"Oh! That reminds me!" I lean over the couch, apparently not thinking, and click the lamp on and off a ton of times before turning to look at Parker expectantly. He's not paying attention to a damn thing I'm doing; his eyes are unashamedly glued to my ass where my shorts have ridden up.

"What the hell are you doing?" Drew is looking at me like I'm psychotic.

"Testing to see if Parker has OCD."

"Could have just asked, weirdo."

"Yeah, but people lie. His drawers are so organized I thought I'd test the theory."

"Well, I think the theory of those shorts was just proven."

Parker is unashamedly gawking. I pull the fabric lower, sitting back on my heels.

"Seriously?" I groan, grabbing a pillow I crush it to my stomach, "Better? Am I covered enough for you now?"

Parker leans on his elbow, his other arm reaching forward to grab the corner of the pillow, he tugs it out from under my arm. "If you're going to wear that, I want to be able to look." He laughs when I reach to snatch it back. He takes it and puts it behind his neck.

"If you want it, come get it. I can admire the view while you do it." Then he winks at me.

"Men are pigs," I mutter, sitting back and crossing my arms over my bare stomach, I try to watch whatever the hell is playing on the TV.

"Gah! I can feel your eyes on me, guys."

"You put a steak in front of a lion, is he not going to watch it?" Drew says with a smile. He's staring just to piss me off. Parker- well he's giving me goosebumps, and I don't want to focus on what that means.

"It was this or a shirt that my boobs would fall out of; I have no idea where the shirt I wore last night is. Since someone lost my key, I can't get anything else."

"Why didn't you just throw one of Parker's shirts on over it?"

I have never wanted to punch myself in the face more than I do at this moment.

"Cause I'm a fucking moron, that's why!"

"Dude!" Parker protests, throwing the pillow at Drew when I jump up from my seat. Hopping over Drew's legs, I rush down the hall.

Throwing the first shirt I touch on; it falls to my mid-thigh. Self-confidence goes up three points. I go back into the living room wearing a broad smile; Parker glares daggers at Drew.

"That's three things he's fucked up for you tonight, Parker." I laugh sitting back on the couch. "I wonder if he'll go for a fourth?"

"Better not." He grumbles. "What did you have in mind?"

"Well, I was thinking hot sex on the couch, but Drew's here, so-"

"Get out." Parker laughs pointing at the door. "Right now."

Drew flips him off. "Just go sit on his lap, Hales. That'll make his boo-boo feel all different kinds of better."

"I'm sure." I chuckle.

"I do have a boo-boo." Parker pouts, and it's kinda hot, and by 'kinda' I mean I kinda wanna sit on his face. Too blunt? My bad.

"Awe, do I need to kiss it and make it better?" I pout back, leaning towards him.

He nods. His eyes grow dark when I slip off the couch and approach him. Pressing my hand into the cushion, I lean forward, almost in breathing range. I watch his throat work as his gaze fall to my mouth. An evil smirk graces my lips as I pull away abruptly. "Kiss your big brother's boo-boo, Drew."

"The fuck?" He shrieks. "Hell no! You realize when we say boo-boo we're talking about his d-"

"I know what the reference is." I laugh, stepping away from Parker, my foot doesn't even leave the ground before his hands snake out, taking my hips and in one quick move, pulls me between his legs. He releases me the second I land- thank God.

"Rude." I glare over my shoulder.

"But so worth it."

"Telling you to touch me was a one-time deal." I breathe out.

He makes a noise of agreement against my skin, kissing the spot where my neck meets my shoulder. I wasn't expecting it and goosebumps ripple down my arms. "That's a neat trick." He whispers, kissing me again- higher this time. I tilt my head to give him better access allowing a new wave to dance down my legs; I drag his fingers across them.

"I like this."

"The goosebumps or my legs?" I smile to myself.

"Both." He reaches the soft patch just behind my ear, and it's enough to make me squirm. He chuckles against my skin; the sensation is going to make me combust. "What were you saying about touching?" His fingers blaze up my thighs.

"I don't remember." I breathe, resting back on his chest.

His thumb comes up, brushing against my cheek to turn my face towards him. His fingers finding their way into my hair. He lowers his face, pressing his forehead against mine, "Tell me to stop." he breathes, his voice raw and husky.

"No."

With a wicked smile, he twists his head, the distance closing quickly. Stop the world, let me live in this moment just a little while longer.

"I am right here!" Drew complains loudly. And by loudly, I mean I'm sure the neighbors across the courtyard heard him.

"That's four," I whisper against his mouth and then pull away.

"You're a dead man." He points to Drew as I flop down next to him. The hand he was holding out to Drew rests behind me.

I try to focus on the TV, I promise I do, but I am all too aware that his hand is less an inch away from me and for the first time in my life, I crave to be touched. Feeling like the need will split me open from the inside out, I lower myself, so I'm laying on my left side, resting my head on his thigh, folding my hands I tuck them under my chin.

BROKEN

Suddenly worried this might not be his scene, I roll my head so I can look up at him, "Does this bother you?"

His thumb brushes across my cheek, "Not even a little." Offering him a shy smile, I turn back to the TV. His hand slides off the back of the couch and rests on my hip, his thumb absently rubs circles.

I don't know when it happened, but I guess I fell asleep because I wake up to Parker saying he's going to touch me. I try to tell him not my left, but I don't know if it came out. Collecting me from the couch, he carries me down the hall, placing me gently on the mattress. I immediately miss his warmth when he pulls away.

Peeling my lids open, I catch sight of him taking his shirt off; and because he's Parker, everything he does makes my blood heat. Grabbing the fabric at the base of his neck, he pulls it over his head, the muscles in his back ripple, making my knees weak. Oh man, I've got it bad for the guy. He pops the button on his jeans, and I can't make myself look away- I should, it's creepy to watch, but I can't. His hip dimples deepen as his slide his pants and socks off. Leaving his boxers on, he pulls his shorts out of the drawer and slides them on before turning towards the bed; I don't have time to avert my eyes.

"Enjoying the show?"

"Irrevocably," I mumble.

A grin stretches across his face as he climbs in next to me.

The little voice in the back of my mind says I shouldn't. I'm well aware that I shouldn't, but I don't listen, I tell her to shut the hell up, and I curl up against Parker's ribs. He stiffens, holding his hands out like he isn't sure what to do them. Blindly reaching up, I find his hand and pull it around me. My left is underneath my body, so the darkness should, hopefully, stay at bay.

He hands curl around my ribs, "You're killing me." He groans.

"Why?" Insecurity blooms in my stomach.

"Because I don't know where I'm allowed to touch you, and God I want to touch you."

Pretty sure that's an innuendo. With a deep breath, the events of tonight replay. In a way, I clarified a few points with Drew, but Parker was left in that room thinking all those things. I'm not ready to tell him and I sure as hell don't want to relive it, so I offer him something small. "It's my left arm."

"What is?"

"It's what freaks me out. Being touched."

"Am I on your arm?"

He tries to move, but I stop him, tightening my grip on his ribs. "No, you're not touching me." I smile against his chest, "But if you wanted to-" I take a deep breath and swallow my fear, "If you wanted to touch me, just don't touch my left."

"I can do that."

I nod, smiling at myself. He doesn't push for information or bring up the scene at HEAT. My chest constricts and unwilling to think about what that means, I snuggle in closer, letting my eyes fall shut. The steady beat of his heart and the rise and fall of his chest lulls me to sleep.

CHAPTER THIRTEEN

The sensation of my flesh melting off my bones wakes me. Not willing to give in to consciousness just yet, I try readjusting my body for a more comfortable position when I notice something hard against my knee. What is that? I attempt to dislodge whatever is caught under the blanket by sliding my knee around it, all while trying to keep my mind in that purgatory stage of sleep and alertness.

A hand that is not mine, lands on my knee, stilling my movements and my eyes shoot open. I'm not only in Parker's bed, but I'm spun around him like freaking ivy. My shirt had ridden up in the night, exposing my stomach that's currently against his bare ribs. One leg is draped over his...well, his lower region; the other is tangled somewhere in the sheets. One of his arms is around my middle, his fingers splayed across the exposed skin as my head rests on his shoulder. His other hand, well...

"Not that I'm not flattered, sweetheart. But I don't think you realize what you're doing."

My cheeks burn as hot as the Phoenix sun, I pull my leg off his- well, off him and cover my face. "I'm so sorry."

Parker laughs, fucking laughs. Day two of doing something inappropriate with him and ending up embarrassed.

"Oh, trust me. I didn't mind." He laughs, his voice still thick from just waking up.

Oh God, he woke up because my leg was- and against his- oh God! I groan into my hands.

"There are worse ways for a man to wake up."

I roll onto my stomach so I can bury my face in the pillows. My face is burning so hot I'm positive I'm scorching his sheets and setting fire to the mattress. "I was asleep; I didn't know I was...you know."

His laughter deepens, his hand landing on the small of my back, I tense but don't pull away. He rubs my back in calming circles while chuckling.

"As I said, there are worse ways to wake up. I might suffer for the next half hour or so, but I'll recover."

BROKEN

Suffer? Oh, cause he's- Fuck. I shake my head in my hands. "You're not helping. Like I'm not already embarrassed enough, do you have to make it harder?"

"Well, I think you already know how hard it-"

My face skyrockets off the pillow, "Don't you dare finish that sentence!"

The bed dips with his laughter.

Grabbing the pillow my face was buried in, I slam it into his stomach. "Why are you so mean?!" Without wanting to, I laugh. "You're such a jerk."

His hands raise in surrender, "Hey- I could have let you continue, but I was a gentleman about it."

"A gentleman wouldn't have commented on it."

"I said I was a gentleman, not a saint." Hooded eyes roam down my body. "'Cause I am definitely not a saint."

The things he can accomplish with a look and a few little words. The atmosphere in the room changes as my blood runs hotter; my pulse beats harder.

My eyes follow him as he rolls over, putting his face only inches away from mine while he rests his weight on his forearms, his body pressing me into the mattress. His head dips lower, turning my face up with his nose. Before

BROKEN

I can respond or process a rational thought his mouth captures mine.

His lips are warm and soft; against my better judgment, I kiss him back. Then it changes; sweet turns to crushing, tender turns to fire as he consumes me. Both his hands tangle in my hair as he presses into me. Every thought, emotion, and worry is replaced by the desperate need for him. Holding his ribs, I pull him closer, opening my knees to allow more of his body to fall over mine. His mouth moves down my neck, and I can't control the moans that his lips trigger as they fall from my lips.

Greed overwhelms me, and I force his face back to mine. His hands slip under the hem of my shirt running over the plains of my stomach and up my ribs, lifting the fabric as he goes. My sanity is nowhere in sight as his lips return to my neck once again. I gasp, clutching his hair in my fingers when his teeth nip just behind my ear. He lets out a seductive chuckle, licking the sting away before his mouth is back on mine.

There's no turning back, even if I wanted to. I'm drunk off him; his scent, his mouth, everything about him is intoxicating. He pours liquor into my skin with every touch and I'm gone- I am so gone, and so lost that I never want to come back. His thumbs hook under the waistband of my shorts, inching them down with each kiss to my neck, collarbone, and down my stomach. I can't pull in enough air or keep my back from bowing to the pressure of his mouth. He works his way up, nipping at my throat when euphoria is lost.

Fucking cockblock master, Drew shows up.

Rapidly shaking my head, I pull his face back to mine, "He's not here." I say between kisses, "He'll go away."

Parker's fingers dig into my waist as I catch his bottom lip in my teeth. With a carnal growl, he presses me back into the mattress with his mouth.

The bedroom door opens.

I yelp, covering my waist with the blanket.

Parker drops his head to the mattress over my shoulder.

Drew laughs.

And just like that, it's over.

Still pissed about his little interruption I sit on the couch and glare at Drew for the duration of Parker's shower. After I ignored his laughed apologies, he finally figured out I was pissed and wisely shut his cake hole.

Parker comes out in jeans. I'm done talking. Jeans. Like I'm not frustrated enough as it is.

His jeans hang low on his hips, the fact that I don't see the band of his boxers, I'm half convinced he's going commando.

BROKEN

"Fuck, I hate you right now," I tell Drew, pushing up from the couch.

"I said I was sorry!"

Ignoring him I step into the kitchen where the gallon of milk is still sitting on the counter. Men.

"I'm bored." Drew whines, slumping deeper into the couch, "Let's go do something."

"Poolhall?" Parker asks Drew behind me while pouring himself a cup of coffee. I hear the smile in his tone.

"Fuck that." He fires back in a tone very unlike him. I don't know if you've noticed, but Drew is always happy.

"What? You don't like pool?" I ask, putting the milk back.

"No, he does." Parker chuckles, and I meet his eyes for the first time since he entered the living room. "He just doesn't like losing money."

"I don't know how the hell they do it." Drew tries to defend himself.

Drew's pout mixed with Parker's laugh leads me to think there's more to the story. "Am I missing something?"

"How much did they take last time?"

Take? What the hell?

"Shut up, Parker."

"How much?" Parker presses.

"Eight hundred." He grunts under his breath.

BROKEN

"DOLLARS?" I shriek, my palms smacking against the counter of their own accord.

Parker grabs his side while Drew drags a couch pillow over his face.

"You let yourself get hustled?!" I chastised. IDIOT.

"You say that like I knew what was happening!"

With a shake of my head, I point to the door. "Get changed, put on a hat. We're going to the pool hall."

"Why? You want to rub my face in it?"

"No, dumbass. We're gonna get your money back."

"Pray, tell." He throws his hands in annoyance.

I could tell him, probably should, but I'm far too annoyed. "I need thirty minutes."

With a grand and a half shoved into my bra, I pull my straightened hair over my chest to hide the outline of bills. Dressed in my red shirt, I pop the first two buttons to reveal more of my chest. With every breath, my cleavage is pushed forward.

Nodding at my reflection, I slide on my red knockoffs and meet the boys in the living room. My annoyance from earlier has ebbed with the challenge set in front of me.

"Fuck, Hales. You look good."

BROKEN

I give him a little twirl. I'm wearing the jeans I arrived from Reno in, I know there's a tear just below my right ass cheek, and the fabric is stretched to highlight every curve of my body, my favorite up-to-no-good jeans.

Drew's sitting in his usual spot on the couch, slack-jawed. Regaining his composure, he shakes his head, "Hell no." He points down the hall with an angry finger, "Change. You're not going to that place in those. Nope, not happening."

I scoff at his order, raising a defiant brow.

"Parker, a little help? Those dudes will be all over her! We'll be knocking heads together before we even get a table!"

I glance over my shoulder to Parker, who's leaning against the island with his arms crossed lazily over his chest. His brow slightly raised as he stares appreciatively at my ass. Not going to lie, I'm totally smiling.

I look back at Drew with a smug smile, "The jury has spoken."

"No, Haley. This isn't a place for a chick, let alone a chick who looks like you."

"Oh, come off it. We're gonna go play pool; I'm gonna distract them while you hustle back your money."

"I don't feel like getting arrested, Haley." His face is set in stone; it's weird to see him so serious.

My face scrunches up in response to his anger, "Why would you get arrested?"

"Cause I'm gonna kill anyone who looks at you."

I peek over my shoulder; Parker's gaze is still glued to my body.

"Parker hasn't stopped gawking, and he's still breathing."

He clears his throat and chuckles behind me.

"He doesn't count." Drew protests further.

"Whatever, I know what I'm doing. Come on."

Before he can speak, I throw open the door and take the stairs two at a time. The guys catch up with me quickly, Drew is still sulking about my attire but thankfully remains quiet.

We arrive at the pool hall, and I swear they all smell the same; furniture polish, cigarette smoke, and body odor. It's a nasty combination but oddly comforting. Reminds me of the few happy moments of my childhood when Kaylan and I would hustle the pool halls around Reno.

The John C. Reilly looking mother fucker at the entrance charges us twenty bucks a pop just for admission. The establishment itself is a hustle. Before I could pull out my money, Parker hands the guy three bills. Steering me to the back of the room, we find an empty table at the far end.

"Are they here?" I ask, admiring the stained-glass light over our table.

"Cowboys, three tables down."

Spinning around, I hop up onto the side of the pool table, glancing in their direction. Two guys are currently playing a couple; obviously winning.

"What's the plan little miss distraction?" Parker asks, stepping between my legs. Jesus, he hasn't even touched me yet, and I'm already breathing like a ravaged animal. The fire from earlier is still there, growing hotter the closer he gets.

"What are you doing?" I whisper, staring up at him. My thighs are a half centimeter away from his hips, I can feel his body heat through the denim, and it's driving me crazy. The urges it brings forward would get me arrested, but good God, it would be worth it.

"Asking you a question." His fingers graze my knees before both hands lower to the denim. So slowly I could scream, his hands slide up my legs until finally resting on my hips.

"Staking a claim?" I ask breathlessly.

I've never known a guy who could make me squirm, who makes me crave to be touched, a guy who I'm half tempted to let him fuck me on a billiards table in the middle of a packed pool hall.

He nods, his eyes hooded as they lock onto my mine. My heart is rolling over itself as he leans forward. He watches me for any signs of protest, but without a single reservation in me willing to speak up, I let him claim my mouth. It's not demanding or possessive, but knee breakingly sweet. My hands climb to the hem of his shirt and wrap around the fabric, pulling him closer, my knees tighten around his hips. He smiles against my mouth before giving me what I want.

One hand falls behind my neck and pulls me hard into his mouth. Fuck Drew's money at this point, I just want Parker's mouth on me, our clothes off in a corner somewhere, and a good rock song to set the mood.

Drew clears his throat loudly as he stares at us in disgust, "We gonna play pool or am I expected to watch my brother bend you over the table?"

"Is that an option?"

Parker laughs, kissing me chastely before pulling away.

I glare at Drew, "Could you be a bigger cockblock?"

Drew's arrogance knows no bounds when the bastard smiles and winks at me.

"What's the plan?" Parker asks again, grabbing two pool sticks from the rack.

BROKEN

"You guys are going to play for a while; I'm gonna watch them." I nod in the cowboy's direction. "Find their weaknesses."

"Alright, move your ass." I slide off the table allowing Drew to rack the balls.

Glancing over my shoulder at his handy work, I point out his mistake with a sweet smile, "There needs to be a stripe on one corner and a solid on the other." I point to where Drew has two solids on each end of the triangle. He glares but switches the solid three for the striped eleven.

Drew and Parker play behind me as I study the two men across the room. Blue shirt is left-handed; he takes all the easy shots suggesting he's the weaker player. His buddy in the cowboy hat obnoxiously snaps his gum while studying the table, he's aggressive in his technique and appears to only go for solids when given a choice. I watch for two more games before stepping around Parker and Drew.

"Put money down on the table. I'll be right back."

Ignoring Drew's objections, I approach Cowboy's table.

"Hi." I smile sweetly at them.

Cowboy pulls back, giving me a once-over. "Hey there, darlin'."

I hold my smile, twirling my hair around my finger, "I was with my friends over there," I nonchalantly point over my shoulder, his gaze follows. "And neither of them has gum." I give him a little pout, "Do you have any by chance?"

"Sure." He gives me a lopsided grin. Reaching into his back pocket, he pulls a pack of mint gum and holds it out to me.

"My favorite." Unwrapping it, I pop the piece into my mouth, "Thanks."

Exaggerating the natural sway of my hips, I sashay back to the guys and bend over the rail of our table.

"Without being obvious, tell me if he's looking."

"That's a dumb question, Hales. You're bent over the fucking table. Of course, the prick's looking."

"Good." Looking around I see two twenties on the table, "Twenty? Seriously?" I glare at both of them. "You're trying to get him to offer big bucks, not gas money." Reaching into my shirt, I pull the wad of bills out and sift through the money.

"Jesus Christ, Haley!" Drew hisses, "What the fuck are you doing pulling that kind of money out in this place?"

Ignoring him, I pull two hundred's out and lay it in front of me before folding up the cash and redepositing it in my bra.

"He's coming over," Parker mumbles without taking his gaze off his cue as he lines it up to sink the 8-ball.

BROKEN

"Act uninterested- not an asshole, just, uninterested," I whisper hastily.

Blowing a bubble, I pop it with my fingers, holding the string and twirling it around my finger. I smile sweetly at Cowboy when he stops at the corner of the table.

"How's it going, guys?" He asks, and with a wink to me "Ma'am."

"Good." Parker nods to him before sinking the winning shot.

"Not bad." Cowboy nods. "I see you're playing for cash. Care to play a round?"

Parker shrugs uncommitted, Drew makes a face, I try not to laugh at their lack of acting skills.

"I'll play." I volunteer.

"No offense, darlin', but I don't play for spare change, and it would be the peak of bad manners if I took your money."

"If you can beat me you mean." I smile, twisting my gum and then sucking it off my finger.

"Haley- you're decent, but I don't know if you need to be putting money down." What the fuck is Drew doing!?

"I beat you." I glare at him, silently telling him to shut his cake hole.

Cowboy laughs, "I beat him too."

"You guys are friends?" I perk up. The cute, little girl voice I'm using is annoying; even to me.

"I wouldn't say that, but we know each other."

"Come play with me; it could be fun." I give him the best bedroom eyes I can manage.

His eyes watch my mouth as my teeth press into my bottom lip. "Pretty please?"

"Hundred bucks." He says, not bothering to pull his eyes away from my mouth.

I flash a huge smile. "Aces! One on one or do I get a partner?"

"It's a hundred bucks a person- your call."

"Wanna play with me, Parker?" I twist to look at him and give him a subtle nod.

"Yeah, I'll play with you." His tone suggests it's not pool he's interested in playing and my blood heats. I'd be willing to go to jail to have that cocky ass smile between my legs. "You break, sweetheart."

My shitty break was half on purpose, half because I was distracted by Parker. I intentionally play like shit the first game, bending low to give cowboy an eyeful of cleavage or leaning on my toes to widen the tear in my jeans. I play a little less shitty the second and help Parker win the third. The first two games were for a hundred bucks; the third was double. We gave him four hundred then took four back.

"Yay, we won!" I clap. "I think I play better under the stress of big money."

BROKEN

The men around me politely smile, I know they all think I'm horrible at this- which is precisely what I'm aiming for.

During the second game, I learned that Cowboy has won over nine hundred today. It's just a bad idea to brag about things like that.

"I have an idea! Wanna double your daily winnings?"

"Haley- fuck no," Drew says standing from his place on the stool.

Ignoring him, I pull nine hundred dollars out of my stash and wave it in front of Cowboy. "Me and you, one on one."

He shakes his head, "As much as I'd love to take your money- I can't."

"You're not taking it; I'm betting it." I smile, bending over, so my chest swells against the fabric. I give him a pout, "Pretty please?"

After a minute his tongue slides across his bottom lip while he stares at the bills before he nods and pulls out his wallet, fishing out his money he lays it on the table next to mine.

"You're a moron," Drew tells me, sitting back down. Poor boy- maybe I should have mentioned I know what I'm doing beforehand...oh well.

"Can I break? I'm good at that."

"Of course. Ladies first."

With an evil grin, I chalk my cue. This time there is no nonsense. I take aim, striking the cue center apex, the balls explode outward, pocketing two solids and a stripe.

"Solids," I call, the little girl voice is gone.

One shot after another I sink every ball until only three remain. Cowboy is staring at the table with a blank expression as I line up and drop the orange five and then immediately after, the maroon seven. Only the eight ball remains, and he hasn't had a single turn. Adding salt to injury, I point to the bottom pocket next to my hip. Lining up the shot, I snap the stick forward; the cue smacks the eight in a kiss of death.

I stand straight and watch as the black ball blasts forward, bouncing off the cushion and races across the felt towards me, curves center table, sinking clean into the pocket. "Game."

Sauntering over to Cowboy I slide his money off the rail. "It's not nice to hustle."

Drew whoops loudly next to me as I stare into the eyes of a man who still has no idea what just happened. Pulling a twenty, I set it down on the red felt, giving Cowboy and his blue-shirted buddy one final look, "Drinks on me, boys." With that, I step past them and nod Parker and Drew to the exit.

Once outside, Drew starts shouting "Holy shit!" loud enough I'm sure all of Phoenix can hear. "Where the fuck did you learn to do that?!" He's flushed and breathless from all his screaming.

I shrug. I could tell them I used to hustle back in Reno but then that would lead to more questions and I don't want to relive having to pay the devil off to avoid a beating.

Parker approaches me, places both his hands on my cheeks and kisses me, "You're incredible." He shakes his head with a giant smile, "I thought you didn't know how to play."

Reminding me, I pull away from him and count out Drew's eight hundred and hand it forward.

"Stop getting hustled. That's twice now."

He shakes his head, "You hate being touched but you're just going to have to deal with it." His arms snake around my waist, lifting me off the ground. "Marry me, Haley Carter!"

I laugh as he sets me back on my feet and woo's like Ric Flair.

"Hot damn!" He smiles, "Come on, I'm buying Y'all dinner."

CHAPTER FOURTEEN

Parker and I follow Drew to a sports bar not far from the pool hall. The blonde waitress is all over Drew like denim on jeans. She struts to a booth, bending low to place the silverware, giving Drew a clear shot down her shirt, a move he is all too willing to appreciate with a gross stare.

"You propose to me and then hit on the waitress?!" I glare at Drew, throwing myself into the booth across from him. "It's our engagement party, asshole."

The waitress' cheeks turn a pretty shade of pink as she tucks a blonde lock behind her ear, refusing to make eye contact. "I'll be back to get you started on drinks."

BROKEN

She steps out of earshot, Drew kicks me under the table while Parker slides in next to me.

"What the fuck was that?! I almost had her number!"

"That's for your little interruption earlier," I tell him opening my menu. Score! First page, a Turkey Club!

"I walked in on accident. That shit right now was intentional."

"You also interrupted last night and at the pool hall. You may not be keeping score, but I am." I sing, setting my menu down.

"Dick move." He mumbles quickly watching her approach. "Well, maybe if you washed it once or twice you wouldn't have a yeast infection every other week, Hales."

"Or maybe if you didn't stick your dick in everything that'll hold still long enough, I'd be able to keep my snatch cleaner," I say without missing a beat before turning to the waitress, "Coke, please."

Parker has his head bowed, his hand covering the lower portion of his face.

"I wouldn't have to go looking if you put out."

"I'll put out when you can last the full eight seconds, cowboy."

Parker chokes on his laugh, playing it off as a cough. This poor waitress, we'll have to make up for our behavior with a fat tip.

"One- rude. Two- not true-" Parker and I both echo him, "Knock it, off. Three- stop lying, I'm the best sex you've ever had, and you know it."

"Putting it in and convulsing on top of me for five seconds doesn't constitute sex. It's a glorified seizure."

"We'll all have cokes," Parker tells her and she makes a quick escape. "Jeez, you guys." He laughs openly now, and my straight face finally breaks.

"Why'd you send her away?" Drew complains.

"She's probably going to quit after that."

"We'll give her a big fat tip for putting up with us," I add.

"A one-touch? Fucking really?" Drew glares at me but the smile tugging at his lips ruins his plans of being angry.

"That's your focus?" Parker laughs, "Not the fact she used the term 'snatch'?" He turns to me, "That's just nasty."

I shrug.

"Calling me a one-touch is worse than the word 'snatch.' Girls talk." He shakes his head, looking over his shoulder. "Pretty sure I won't be able to spit game here for the next six months."

"Like you don't get enough girls at HEAT," I tell him, eyeing the establishment.

BROKEN

"I'm a hungry man, Hales. You ruined my chances of picking up girls here. What if my soul mate shows up one day and I can't ask her out because of your mouth?"

"Then you'll come crying to me, and I'll tell you the same thing I'm going to tell you now- shouldn't have cockblocked me."

"Damn dude, can you go bend her over in the bathroom or something? She's moody."

Yes, please.

Parker's face curls in embarrassment before shaking his head slowly, "No."

Damn.

"She's moody as hell."

"You're just butthurt that I threw off your game, I'm not the one who's moody." I smile sweetly at him.

She comes back over and sets our drinks down, choosing only to make eye contact with Parker. A little spark of jealousy ignites in my stomach before I snuff it out. Apparently not quickly enough, Drew's lips curl into an evil smile,

"Jessica, right?" She turns when he says her name. "This is my best friend, Haley, and my brother, Parker. We apologize if we made you uncomfortable before."

She smiles, and it's a little warmer than before. "It's fine." She turns back to her pad.

"It's unfortunate timing. Hales and I started ragging on each other without realizing Parker had the intent of getting your number. I'm worried I might have hurt his chances."

Ice forms in my stomach and I try my best to ignore it. I have a crush, so what? I have no claim, and even though what he's saying is bullshit, that insecure little bitch in the back of my head is making me wonder if she's the type of girl Parker goes for. Drew made mention all the Hayes men are whores and Parker didn't object, if anything he agreed by saying he only goes to their house.

"I wouldn't say it's completely off the table." She smiles sweetly at Parker before taking our order and leaving to put our ticket in.

"What the hell?" Parker stage whispers when she's far enough away not to hear.

Drew has a smug smile that I'd like to smear across his perfectly shaved jaw. "Eye for an eye."

"What did I do?"

"You're just the bystander. That was for Haley."

Parker looks at me, and I shrug to hide the real emotion.

"Mhm." Drew gives me an incredulous look over the top of his glass.

"If you want to play with me, I'll play." I lean forward on my elbows.

Drew laughs it off, but it's forced. I raise my eyebrows and sit back. Sensing the change,

Parker steps in. "When do you want to get your new I.D.?"

Drew ignores him eyeing me, "You're scary when you want to be. Truce?"

"Swear you're done?"

"Pinky promise." He says with a cheeky grin. I hold my pinky out, and he stares at it. "For real?"

"Yup. Let's go."

Shaking his head, he wraps his thick pinky around mine.

"Now kiss your hand." He makes a face, "It seals the promise."

Without protest, he leans forward, and we kiss our fists.

"Break it, and I'll break you," I warn, but offer a smile to take the edge off our conversation.

"I.D.?" Parker asks again.

"Do I need one?"

"To work at HEAT, yes. Josh needs a copy on file."

An anvil lands in my stomach at the memory of me yelling at Josh. "If I still have a job, you mean."

His eyebrows pinch, "Of course you still have a job." he says at the same time Drew asks, "Why wouldn't you?"

"Told him to fuck off, remember."

Drew throws a dismissive hand at me.

"He doesn't care about that." Parker tells me, "It was a stressful situation, and he feels like he cornered you. He's not mad, and you still have a job."

"Pretty sure he'd fire me before he would you," Drew says, scoping out the restaurant.

"Doubt that." I tell him before turning to Parker, "I still have mine from Reno."

He shakes his head, "Not current. You've been out of state for over a year. He needs to have your current information."

Slumping down, I blow air out, "I'll catch a bus down sometime this week."

"I'll take you."

"You don't have to play chauffeur; I can take the bus."

"Do you have a driver's license?" Drew asks, genuinely curiosity colors his features.

I laugh at his expression, "Yes."

"Then why don't you drive?"

"Cars cost money."

"I watched you pull almost a grand out of your tits, dude. You've got the money."

"Well, I'm gonna need a lot more to convince Parker to sell me his Camaro."

Both boys laugh, "Not gonna happen, sweetheart."

"Parker and our Dad rebuilt that car. There's no way he'd sell it."

I snap my fingers in defeat. "Well, there goes that idea."

BROKEN

"But I'll drive you around in it all you want." He winks at me, "Including to the MVD. Just name the day."

"Don't you have a job or something?"

He nods, "My hours are flexible."

Drew laughs, "You make your own hours, prick."

"What do you do, anyway?" I ask taking a long pull from my coke.

He waits until after the approaching waitress sets our plates down to answer. "I'm an investor."

My eyebrows raise. "Wow, really?"

He nods. I laugh.

"That doesn't count, I was agreeing. I nodded with purpose." I pull my lips in trying to hide my smile. "What?"

"You're still nodding."

"Am not." He gently pokes my cheek with his finger, "You have dimples when you try not to smile."

I suck in my cheeks to hide them, "What do you invest in?"

"Mostly commercial property on the verge of going under. It's all very dry."

"He owns a percentage of HEAT, too."

The sip I was taking goes down the wrong tube, throwing me into a coughing fit. "Seriously?" I squeak against the burn.

"So does Drew."

BROKEN

Picking up my rolled straw wrapper, I throw it at him. "You never told me that!"

"I wanted you to love me for me, not my money."

I roll my eyes, turning back to Parker. "So, you just drive around looking for places that need financial help?"

"Not exactly. I pay people to do that for me. I just get to sit back and look pretty."

"You pay people?" He nods, "How?"

I know that was rude, but I can't get my head around the idea. I know Josh is loaded, but Drew has a roommate, and Parker lives in the same apartment complex I do.

"Usually with money."

"Ha. Ha. I don't get it."

"Well...someone applies and if I like the person I hire them. They work, I pay them for their time."

I shake my head, "I'm not an invalid. I mean how do you have the money to pay people?"

"Depending on the deal, I either buyout the company and claim the profits or I own a percentage and therefore receive a percentage of their profits."

"Are you fucking with me?"

"Not at all."

"You live in an apartment."

"Mhm."

"Mhm? That's it? So, you're telling me you're like this mega-rich business guy who chooses to slum it with us poor kids?"

"Hey now," He laughs, "I'm not slumming it, you said so yourself- I've got a great place."

"Well yeah- but even Drew has a house."

"Who says I don't have a house? Besides, being an investor means the majority of my money is tied into something."

"You live in an apartment!" I laugh to cover my embarrassment. I genuinely don't understand.

"That he owns," Drew adds.

"Wait, you own your apartment? That doesn't make sense. You can't own-" Realization dawns, "You own the complex?!"

The smallest smile graces his lips as I stare at him in shock. "So you could have gotten the spare to my apartment, but instead lied to play babysitter?"

His smile falls. "I didn't lie."

"Well, you didn't tell the truth."

"I said she wouldn't be back until Monday and that's the truth. I own the building, sure, but I don't manage it."

"Could you have gotten the key that night, yes or no?"

"Yes."

I throw my arms. "You both are a couple of jackasses."

"You didn't ask, and I didn't offer, but let's get one thing clear, sweetheart. I never lied to you."

"Lying by omission is still lying." I stir my drink with the straw.

"Maybe I just wanted you to sleep in my bed." He whispers in my ear, I try to shrug him off, but his teeth catch my ear, my knees instantly press together. "It wasn't my intent to be deceitful. Yes, I could have called and got you a key, but I didn't think about it. I was far too distracted for rational thought."

"Well, you're doing a good job handling it right now."

"I'm not distracted, in fact, I'm very, very focused at the moment."

"On what?" I glare at my drink.

"Watching you squirm." His hand falls to the inside of my thigh and squeezes.

I pull myself away from him with a glare, "I'm not squirming."

"Sure you are."

And like the very mature person I am, I reply with- wait for it. "Am not."

Chuckling he goes back to clean his plate; these boys can eat, my God.

After sticking the remains of my food in a styrofoam container, I throw an extra twenty on the table for the waitress. Parker looks on with a quizzical expression that I shrug off.

BROKEN

Drew gives us the one finger salute as his bike peels out of the parking lot towards HEAT.

I have an entire night with Parker, and I am suddenly very nervous to be alone with him.

CHAPTER FIFTEEN

Hands become vices around my limbs.

I'm trying to pull away, but they're too strong.

I try to scream, but something is shoved into my mouth.

A sour smell fills my nose as I drag in panicked breaths that hurt my chest.

Laughter fills my ears- not the I-heard-something-funny kind of laugh, but the kind that echoes out of the bowels of hell. The type that sinks into your bones, poisoning your blood with fear, and sending your heart beating so fast you think you'll pass out.

The damp carpet digs into my cheek.

I scream against the coarse strands, against the laughter, against their hands.

Filth and dirt carve into my flesh as I squirm to get free.

BROKEN

They like it when I struggle, it adds to their game of cat and mouse.

Slivers of light float between the golden strands of my hair.

Something pointed lands hard on the center of my spine when I thrash against their hold. I cry out in pain, the echoes of laughter growing with every whimper, with every tear.

I feel the harsh burn as something weaves around my ankles.

I didn't mean to. It was an accident. I was just scared.

They tie my feet together, I buck, but the knee in my back keeps me pinned down.

God, please make them stop. I beg you; please make them stop, I didn't mean to.

I hear metal click,

My heart falls so fast I wish it would make impact and kill me before the flames lick my skin.

I start to scream.

I scream against the filthy cloth in my mouth.

I scream against the floor.

I scream against their laughter.

I scream, but it doesn't stop them.

The flames are so hot it's cold.

I can't stand it; I can't handle the pain, I can't do anything but scream.

BROKEN

My heart races forward as my head fills with air.

Pain radiates across my temple, but it's nothing to the heat engulfing my arm.

Death claim me; please take me away, I'm yours.

Please.

Finally, the pain is enough to numb my mind.

It calls upon the darkness, letting it swoop in and take away the pain and fear leaving nothing but the cold abyss.

CHAPTER SIXTEEN

I rocket out of bed, sucking in air.

My arm tingles against the memory as I lay my hand on the sleeve telling myself it was just a dream. My heart is racing against my chest, and I can't catch my breath.

"What's wrong?" I nearly jumped out of my skin at the sound of Parker's voice. It's heavy with sleep as he sits up, he goes to touch me but pulls away when I flinch. "Are you okay?"

"I'm sorry." I shake my head; the demons are awake in my mind and it makes it hard to concentrate. "I'm fine. I didn't mean to wake you."

I forgot I was here. Which is dumb seeing as I don't have a bed or a man at my apartment.

His hand pulls the covers away from the middle of the bed as he lays back down, "Come here." I shake my head, closing my fists around the balled fabric of my sleeves, desperately trying to push the memory away. "I won't touch you, Haley. I promise." Slowly scooting over to the center of the bed, I lay down beside him. "Hold onto me, sweetheart."

I roll onto my side and bury my face into his chest; his scent fills my head. The muscles of his stomach flex when my hand trails across his skin, gripping his ribs.

Keeping his hands above his head as he promised, I snuggle in closer until my body is pressed tight against his.

"I can feel your heart pounding. You sure you're okay?"

I nod against his chest even though I'm far from being okay at the moment.

"Do you want to talk about it?"

"No," I whisper back. "I'm sorry I woke you, I didn't mean to."

"Don't apologize. I'd rather do this than sleep any day." I don't know what he means, but it feels like a compliment. "Do you feel better?"

In a daring move on my part, I reach above me, blindly searching for his arm. He hands it over, letting me guide it around my waist. "I do now."

I curl back into his chest, pressing my forehead against his pecs. His fingers absently run through my hair bringing an unexpected smile to my lips.

"Thank you," I whisper, kissing his chest. The muscles turn to stone under my lips, his grip tightening in my hair. "For everything."

He doesn't respond, but I feel the shift as he nods, his grip loosens as he continues to play with the strands.

"No one's ever played with my hair before."

His fingers still and I regret opening my mouth. "Do you want me to stop?"

"No." My fingers draw invisible designs against the deep canyons of his stomach.

I pretend to ignore the change in his breathing, I'm affecting him, and there's this part of me that's screaming with excitement with that knowledge.

His hips move a fraction of an inch before his opposite hand collects mine off his stomach. Shifting, I watch him bring it to his mouth, kissing the palm of my hand. Goosebumps run down my legs as our eyes meet. My heart stops. My breathing doubles. He knows he's getting to me too; I can see it in his eyes as he kisses my wrist.

Slowly, so slowly, he kisses down my arm, his breath hot through the fabric as my skin lights on fire, every nerve screams for more.

I trail my finger through the hair at the nape of his neck before steering his face down to mine.

His lips are soft- Jesus, they're so soft. A groan escapes his throat when my nails gently slide across his chest and travel down his abs to the waist of his shorts. Applying pressure to his hip, he lets me guide him until he's above me, raising my hips I grind against him.

He pulls back, brow furrowing before shaking his head, "Haley-" Covering his mouth with mine, I silence him.

My blood is boiling, and I want the distraction, I need the distraction. I need him to chase the demons away. His face ducks into the crook of my neck, sucking and biting down to my collarbone. He pushes the collar of my flannel to the side, biting my shoulder before licking and kissing the sting away. His hands squeeze my hips like he's trying to ground himself into me."Tell me to stop." He whispers against my skin.

"No." My voice is breathy and desperate.

He groans as his fingers slip under my shirt, lightly grazing my already burning skin.

"You're so soft." His fingers continue to explore my stomach while I slowly lose my mind. He feels good- too good. His forehead rests against my stomach as his hand curls around my ribs.

"If I don't stop now, I don't think I'm going to be able to."

I glance down at him, panting as I shake my head, "Then don't stop."

I don't know what's scarier, the fact he's unbuttoning my top or that I want him to. As each button opens, his mouth kisses a new section of exposed skin. I'm writhing against him, panting at his touch, if I weren't so caught up in the sensation of his mouth, I'd probably be embarrassed.

The last button gives and he lets the halves fall to my sides, exposing my chest and stomach. He leans back running both hands across my skin, starting at my collarbone, his fingers trail over my bare chest, down my ribs, and past my belly button before he bends, kissing and biting my hip. His mouth and tongue follow my waistband from one side to the other as his hands run from my knees, down my inner thighs. I buck when his mouth skirts across my underwear, his breath hot against the one place he's refusing to touch. I've never been so turned on in my life. TMI? Probably, but I'm too distracted to censor my thoughts at the moment.

His fingers hook into the waistband of my shorts, without a second thought I lift my hips so he can slide them off. Discarding them off to the side, he leans forward once again, kissing the inside of my knee, the scruff along his jaw trails a burning line to my hip. His tongue snakes out and meets that aching spot that throbs for him before settling closer. His breath is hot and my thighs shake in anticipation, then all teasing ends, his mouth presses into me, making the air catch in my lungs as my legs try to close around his head.

His hands hold my hips down, as I'm completely lost in sensation. I'm tasting colors and smelling sounds as I stifle a scream. Biting my lip to the point of pain as my body arches entirely off the bed; his hands tighten around my hips, keeping me pressed against him. I try to talk, or maybe beg, I don't know what the hell I'm trying to accomplish when the pressure grows so intense my toes curl on their own accord, and the air leaves my chest. Threading my fingers through his hair, I try to pull precious air into my lungs but that coil inside me snaps, and my body takes over. I don't possess the capacity at the moment to form the words necessary to describe what just happened, but I can tell you this- it was a first.

After my shaking limbs start to calm, he removes his mouth and slowly climbs the center of my stomach. Kissing his way through the valley between my chest, up my throat, then across my jaw until he captures my bottom lip between his teeth. I whimper and rock against him.

"Drew's down the hall." He whispers, not exactly what I wanted to think about at the moment but I know why he's saying it. He's telling me to be quiet.

"So?" I breathe as his knee falls between my legs, pushing them further apart. His hand drops to the waist of his shorts. "Are you a screamer?" I tease, meeting his hungry eyes. He smiles, lowering himself until our bare chests touch.

"No, but I'm about to make you one."

Before I can respond, I arch off the bed, his mouth catching my cry, kissing me with enough heat to light the world on fire.

CHAPTER SEVENTEEN

I slept with Parker.

Oh fuck, I slept with Parker. I sit up in bed, making sure my sleeves are pulled down as I stare at the red material. I forgot I was wearing Drew's shirt. I doubt he's going to want it back now. Looking over at the empty place next to me, "Fuck, I slept with Parker" and "Oh my GOD, I slept with Parker!" play who-can-be-louder in my head. Last night was incredible, and I don't know how to react to that. I'm caught between slamming my head against the wall and squealing with joy.

I remember falling asleep watching Sons of Anarchy with Parker. Drew showed up, giving me the flannel shirt to sleep in because all of my stuff is dirty, I went to bed. Parker came in at some point; my mind decided to take a trip down memory lane giving me a nightmare from my own personal hell, then I got naked with Parker.

The events of last night don't add up to sexy-time. I've known the dude for four days, and I slept with him. I drop my head into my hands, what the hell was I thinking?! Oh God, Parker said Drew was down the hall meaning he crashed on the couch- and I don't remember trying all that hard to be quiet... oh my God- and I'm going to have to face him shortly.

I fall back into the bed, squeezing my eyes shut. Just fall back asleep. I'll wake up, and nothing would have happened, nothing will be awkward, and nothing will change. Parker and I will be friends, Drew won't know what I sound like when I have sex, and I won't be mortified by that fact. Just. Fall. Asleep.

The door opens, and I curse internally. I open my eyes slowly as Parker enters, moving silently across the room to unplug his phone. He must feel my gaze because he looks at me, my body burns under his eyes. Awkward, why does it always have to end up being so awkward?!

"Good morning. Did I wake you up?"

I shake my head, scared that I've got a severe case of morning breath.

"Drew left to get donuts and coffee."

I nod, and he smiles; I curse myself again.

Crawling over the mattress, he lifts my chin and plants a tender kiss on my lips. I want to cry. I don't deserve this. I'm going to end up hurting him when I leave, and it's sure to destroy me. "You look sad."

"I'm not."

"Liar," He whispers against my lips. True. "What's wrong?"

"I don't want to hurt you."

He smiles, smiles. "What makes you think that's going to happen?"

"You don't want to get involved with me. The flirting was fun and last night was-" I shake my head debating if I should be completely honest or not, "Incredible, but I shouldn't have lead you on."

He smiles again before kissing me chastely. "You didn't lead me on."

"Nope, definitely did. Pretty sure we had sex last night."

"Pretty sure? Sweetheart, if you have to think about it, then I obviously need a second chance to prove myself."

"I'm not someone you want to get involved with. We can't do that again."

"If you don't want to, we won't. But tell me-" He leans over me once again, sealing his lips against mine and I melt, fucking melt. Jesus, he's too good at this. He smiles against my mouth. "Why do kiss me back if you don't want me?"

Awkward, awkward, awkward.

"It's you who doesn't want me."

Provocatively rocking against me, he shows me just how untrue that statement is.

"I'm broken, Parker... and there's just too many pieces missing. You'll bleed out before you can save me and I don't want that for you."

"You're not broken, sweetheart."

"Yes, I am," I say with certainty. "I'm not the girl for you."

"I disagree, but if that's the way you want it, then it's fine with me." He slides off the bed, readjusting parts of himself. "Just know, I'm not giving up. I'll convince you."

"Convince me of what?"

"Broken or not, that you're the girl for me." He smiles and turns to the door.

"That would be a stellar exit, I have to admit, but I have a question-" I take an embarrassed breath. "Did Drew say anything about last night?"

A huge smile consumes his face, "No. But I doubt he'll want that shirt back."

Drew came back with donuts, coffee, and a key to my apartment.

Things started to mellow out over the next few months. I took a bus to the MVD to avoid Parker and got an Arizona drivers license. A few days later I started working the floor at HEAT.

BROKEN

Tips were great but with all the added walking, not to mention in heels, I was dead on my feet by the time I got home at night.

I still hung out with Parker and Drew a few nights a week. Parker kept his promise, showing up to drive me home from work or stopping by with breakfast or a late dinner. They even hauled in a coffee table and a TV (that I am insisting is on loan) last week, claiming they were tired of me not understanding their TV references. Parker and I flirt, we've shared a few 'accidental' touches here and there, but I've forced distance.

The icing on the cake is that there have been zero sightings of Kaylan or her. I curse myself for thinking that as I round the corner, digging in my pocket for my keys. Now that I've thought it, Kaylan's going to jump out from behind the bushes, just watch.

Instead of Kaylan, it's Parker. And instead of bushes, it's my apartment door.

"Hey." I smile at him, sticking the key into the handle.

"Hi, sweetheart. How was work?"

"How domesticated," I laugh. "It was slow. Vinny told me to hit the bricks early."

A familiar voice makes Parker and I both turn, "Hey guys."

It's thirteen shades of weird to see Josh standing outside my complex right now. Parker and I greet him at the same time; he nudges me with his shoulder.

"Thanksgiving's on Thursday."

"Three?" Parker asks.

"Yup."

"Who's all coming?"

"So far- Vinny and Jules, Clark and Kelley plus the kids, Dillon, Drew- obviously, Maria, Claire said she'd try, and Lacy is Lacy so who knows what her plans are, which brings me to why I'm here." He turns his attention to me. Oh no. "The polite thing to do is ask what your plans are, but we both know you're going to make up a reason why you can't come, and I got shit to do. So, I'm here to tell you that you're riding with Parker to the house Thursday- don't make that face at me, you're coming, deal with it. It's not a black-tie event, come in jeans or a dress- you'll fit in either way."

Before I can get a word in Josh waves us goodbye and then just walks away. If I've ever wondered where Parker or Drew get their arrogance from- it's him.

"I could be going home for Thanksgiving," I mumble stepping into my apartment.

Parker smiles, "You are."

Emotions fill me like hot water in a balloon, but I refuse to acknowledge them or his pretty words.

He follows me in, and the all too familiar pull fills the atmosphere. Anytime we're alone I just want to pounce on him. This weird electricity fills the air, and the urges I get are almost nauseating.

Like right now for example- his hand runs through his hair, raising his shirt up, so a band of skin is visible, the hard muscle underneath ripples with his movements. This is how I'm going to die, in case you were wondering. His mouth curves up in the corner when he catches me staring.

"All you have to do is ask, sweetheart."

"I don't know what you're talking about." I play dumb, setting my leftover sandwich in the fridge. "What do you need, Parker? I have to get ready for work."

"Go out with me." He smiles. He's been asking me this since the day after I came back to my apartment.

"No." I smile sweetly back.

"Fine." He shrugs, "Spend the night with me."

My stomach drops, knots, then springs back into place. Fuck, if that doesn't make me want to launch myself at him right here and now. "No."

The corner of his lip raises in that panty-dropping half smile, "That wasn't very convincing, sweetheart."

Parker is a drug I want to OD on, and that is a very dangerous position to be in.

CHAPTER EIGHTEEN

Thursday morning Drew woke me by banging on my front door. After a small panic attack thinking, they found me; I got the courage to look through the peephole.

"I didn't realize you wanted to spend the holidays in a hospital bed," I grumble as he pushes past me.

"Brush your teeth, slap on some deodorant, and throw on your chucks. We've got a lot to do and not enough time to do it in."

"What the hell are you talking about?" I peak over the half wall to the stove; the little neon clock reads eight in the morning. "You have a fucking death wish to wake me up this early."

"Haley, I love you, but you need to get your ass moving."

"Why?"

"Because Lacy called and surprise she's coming to dinner."

"I have to be awake at eight because...?"

"Because she's Parker's ex. And I need to rub her face in your hotness."

Parker's ex? Seriously? "If she's his ex why is she coming?"

"Her family and my family are like super close and stuff. They normally come together for holidays, but the last couple of times she didn't show, claiming to be overseas or on a cruise or whatever it was with her boyfriend. They conveniently broke up when your name was added to the roster."

"Drew. Can we get to the point of why I need to be awake right now?"

"Because she's coming to dinner and she's gonna fuck with Parker's head, so I need you to get your hot little ass ready so that we can go."

"Go where? To Josh's?"

"Fuck no. We're gonna go get you clothes and shit."

"I have clothes, Drew." I shake my tired head at him.

"You're crazy hot Hales, you are. But I need you to be like out-of-this-world hot today, capisce?"

"Why?"

"Cause I need you to scare away Lacy."

"If Parker's still got a thing for her, shouldn't you just let him do this thing?"

"He's not into her; he's into you. Now, can you save your questions and just go get ready, pleeease?"

"Drew-"

"Haley. I'm basically begging at this point. Do me a solid? Please? I'm pulling the best friend card."

"Fine."

"Thank you! Now pull your five minutes to get ready magic so we can get the hell out of here."

Drew shoved me into some fancy named store with a personal shopper who paraded me around until Drew was finally happy. After finding a pair of heels that matched the cardigan she picked out, we were escorted to the checkout where Drew paid two hundred and seventy-three dollars for a bloody outfit. I swear to God I almost passed out. But apparently, that wasn't enough because we're now standing outside of a salon in downtown Phoenix.

"Why do I need my hair done? You know, I am capable of doing it myself. Your lack of faith in me is insulting."

"Haley- it's boxed dyed and faded. Why are you fighting me? Girls love this kind of shit."

"I'm not like other girls, I agreed to your ridiculously expensive clothes. I don't need this."

He groans, checking the time on his phone. "Look, I will owe you for the rest of my life. Just trust me and do it. You can get whatever you want, throw in your nails too if you want or you could-"

"Drew, stop. No. I don't do fancy; everyone knows this. I don't want to end up embarrassed."

"Why would you be embarrassed? You look hot, Haley."

"Then mission accomplished."

"Please?"

"Does it look that bad?" I pull my fingers through the dark strands; it looks fine to me.

"If I say yes will you shut up and go in?"

"Probably not. This is all too much."

"Why? Girls get all giddy about this kind of stuff."

"Because it looks like I'm trying too hard."

"Because you got your hair done and new outfit?"

"Yeah."

"That's seriously the stupidest thing you've ever said. I got my hair cut yesterday, and I'm picking up my shirt from the dry cleaners before dinner... and I'm a dude."

BROKEN

"What's everyone going to think when I come in looking like I stepped off a runway with my designer clothes and fancy hair? What's Parker gonna think? Cause I have a feeling he's going to think I did this because I felt threatened by his ex and that I'm pining for him."

"You can deny it all day long, but we both know you're into him. As for his ex- you could snap her in half with that glare of yours, as for everyone else, they're gonna think you look amazing."

"They're gonna know something's up."

"No, they won't." He gripes. "Please, just get your ass in there and do this."

I cross my arms over my chest, the cold chain of my layered necklace bites through the fabric on my sleeve.

We stare at each other a long moment before a huge grin spreads across his face.

"What?" I ask slowly, nervous about whatever plan he just thought of.

"I never got you a birthday present."

"So? I told you I'd gouge your eyes out if you did."

"Well-" His arms open wide. "There you go. You're worried about what people are gonna think, right? Well, I'll tell them I took you to get your hair done for your birthday. In reality, you're just doing me a solid, but there you go. They won't think twice about it."

I chew on my lip a minute before giving in. His stupid pleading face makes me weak and being my only friend; I can't bring myself to let him down.

My hair has been washed, dyed, and styled in loose waves. I told that woman I didn't care what she did as long as it stayed dark. She proceeded to add layers and then evened out my existing color before putting in a buttload of highlights and lightening the ends to a pretty caramel color. Not understanding personal boundaries, Drew paid to have my makeup done as well.

Stepping out and into the little lobby area, my stomach twists in nervous knots waiting for Drew to look up.

"Damn, Hales!" A slow smile crept up his face as he stood. Then he chuckles, "Holy shit."

"Good?"

"You're seriously the greatest human being on the face of the planet."

I run my fingers through the silky strands. I never realized hair could be this soft or smell this good.

"You like it, don't you?" He says with a smug grin.

"Kinda, yeah."

"So, you're in a good mood?"

"Yeah." I laugh.

"Good. So... I kinda need to call Parker and have him pick you up."

BROKEN

My smile drops as my eyes bulge. "What? Why?"

"Cause I brought you here on my bike."

"And?"

"And your ass is nearly falling out of that dress as it is. Plus, it's Phoenix, and you just got your hair and makeup done. Won't look good after sweating under a helmet for twenty minutes."

"Don't call him; I'll take a cab."

"Why? Cab's cost money, Parker's free."

"Parker is not my chauffeur."

Plus, if he gets me from my apartment there's a chance he won't notice, I'm kinda banking on the stereotype that men don't pay attention and I won't feel so awkward because I hate the fact that I'm nervous about his opinion.

I'm sure you can guess what two words I used when I hailed a cab and climbed in against Drew's wishes. Was it, "Fuck off?" If so, you're correct.

The cabbie pulled into the apartment complex a quarter to two, and I was a whole lot of nervous.

Handing the driver my fare I less than gracefully, climb out of the car and walk up the walkway. Coming around the corner my eyes immediately flash to Parker's apartment, a habit I haven't been able to quit, and I desperately wish I wouldn't have looked.

Parker is leaning over the railing of his balcony in nothing but his jeans, a cigarette between his lips. Our eyes meet for a brief moment before his slowly travel down my body. Guess that guys pay attention. Pretending not to notice I keep walking until I'm in the safety of my apartment.

Oh, my God. I don't know why, but I have the urge to buy box dye, scrub my face and change into my jeans and sneakers. My heart is beating so fast, pushing away from the door, I go down the hall and into the bathroom to look in the full-length mirror.

My gray eyes are luminous against the stark contrast of my dark burgundy makeup. My lips are stained a vibrant shade of maroon to match. I like my hair, it's the same dark brown, but it looks healthier and fuller. The crazy number of highlights creates this gorgeous ripple. I run my fingers through the silky waves; this can stay, I decide.

Stepping back, I take in the little black dress; it's simple, no design or patterns, it's snug around my chest and waist, but fans out in loose fabric that falls mid-thigh, it's pretty. A layered chain necklace falls to my belly button, bringing a sense of formal to the otherwise plain dress. The personal shopper paired it with a loose cardigan that's a deep maroon that matches my lipstick, as do my low Mary Jane heels. My legs are bare and pale, making them stand out against the dark colors.

Giving myself another once over I realize my face scrunched up without realizing it.

I should change.

I'm gonna change.

Stepping into the hall, I stop mid-step when a knock sounds against the front door. I glance at my bedroom and then at the door trying to decide which to choose. The latter won out. Opening the door, my breath is sucked right out of my body.

Parker stands in a black button-down, jeans, and black boots. His sleeves are rolled to his elbows, showing off his muscular forearms. Oh my GOD is he pretty.

"Hi." My voice is small, and I curse myself for being affected by him.

"Hi." His voice is low and breathy, making my stomach tingle. "Ready?"

"Oh." I bite my lip, "I was actually about to change real quick. I'll only be a second."

Catching my wrist, he turns me to face him, "Change? Why?"

"I feel ridiculous." I shrug.

With a slow shake of his head, he lets go of my wrist and steps back, looking over my attire. "You shouldn't, you look incredible."

My stomach does this weird flip-flutter thing like I was falling and my stomach couldn't keep up. "I feel stupid."

"The only thing that would be stupid is changing."

I play with my sleeve to distract myself from the argument ensuing inside my head.

"God, even your hair looks amazing." He picks up a lock from my shoulder; I watch as the strands pour over his fingers before falling back against my chest. "Did you get this done today?"

I nod, "Drew woke me up at eight this morning to go get it done. He got me the outfit too, claims it's a birthday gift, but really he just wants to stick it to your ex." His eyebrows knit together, "He pulled the best friend card, and I was obligated to go along with it."

"I guess that means Lacy's going."

"That's what he said."

"Well, sweetheart. I think his plan is going to work."

"Is anyone else going to be this dressed up?"

"Oh, yeah." The certainty in his tone ebbs some of the worry.

"I swear I'm not fishing for compliments; I just need peace of mind. A simple yes or no will suffice; I don't look stupid?"

His head shakes slowly while an almost pained expression crosses his face, "Not even a little."

My eyebrows knit together at the hurt I see, "You okay?"

"Yeah." His tone is still husky, and that pained look weighs heavy on his features.

"You look sad."

A small chuckle rocks his shoulder, "I'm not sad." He picks up another lock, twisting it around his finger. "Has your mind ever raged war with itself?"

All the time. I nod.

"Half of me is dying to kiss you where the other says I need to let you be."

"Which half is winning." Curse me for my breathy voice and double curse my stupid eyes for landing on his lips.

"The former at the moment."

I nod as he steps closer, "That's probably for the best."

His hands skirt around my neck and into my hair. Goosebumps break across my skin in a dance only he can call. "Am I going to ruin your makeup if I kiss you?"

Jesus, his mouth is so close to mine, I can smell his toothpaste and feel the heat of his breath as it sticks to my skin.

"I don't give a fuck about my makeup."

"Good." His lips brush mine, and I feel the heat all the way to my toes.

Not known for my patience- I lean forward closing the gap between us. His fingers tighten in my hair when a soft moan escapes my throat. Fuck, I missed this.

His kiss turns deadly as he steps into me, walking me backward until my back hits the wall. His hands are everywhere, squeezing my hip, then against my waist pushing me deeper into the curve of his body, before returning to my hair.

BROKEN

Fingers set fire as they graze my thigh, before curving around my hip to grab my ass. He groans into my mouth, pressing his hips against me before picking me up off the ground. I wrap my legs around his waist, while the wall supports most of my weight.

I can chew myself out for poor judgment later, this incurable need for him takes over as I reach between us, pulling his belt free and popping the button on his pants. He groans into my shoulder as my hand slides under the denim. Oh my God, he's going commando. His breathing turns heavy as his teeth sink into my shoulder, squeezing my thighs tighter against his hips.

"Fuck, Haley." He groans and rocks against my hand, one hand releases my hip and travels under my dress, engulfing my body in flames as the lace shifts to the side.

"How do you feel about being late?" I moan against his jaw. For the love of God, say yes, say yes.

To answer my question, his mouth captures mine. He doesn't put me down as he reaches between us, pulling himself out completely and lowering me onto him. Gasping, I cling to his shoulders tighter as he pushes himself inside me. Rational thought abandons me, replaced with the words, fuck, yes, and oh my God.

Lacing my fingers through his hair, he holds my hips, devouring my neck and shoulder while my body tightens and trembles around him.

"God damn," He grunts, his hands squeezing harder, he says something else, but I can't hear over my obnoxious breathing that at any other moment would embarrass me seven ways from Sunday, but I just can't seem to care. All I care about is him, me, and the friction between us as he pushes me to the edge.

My stomach hardens and I know I'm almost there, "Fuck." I moan throwing my head back, "God, don't stop. Please, don't stop."

He puts a hand on the wall above my shoulder, and I'm momentarily distracted by this stupid detail before I realize the significance; it stops my body from lifting with his, he hits me deeper, and I can't pull in enough oxygen, I can't do anything but feel.

In a blinding moment the coil inside me shatters, my entire body goes stiff and begins to spiral out of control. I swear to God, I lose my mind for a moment. My body takes over, and my throat can't keep up. I cry out something that is a cross between, 'Oh my God', 'Parker', and 'Fuck'. Can you imagine what that sounded like? Me either, and I was the one who said it.

My body writhes around him as he growls into my neck. His muscles turn stiff as his hands close around my hips while he pushes himself inside me one final time.

In case you haven't figured it out yet, Parker Hayes is an incredible fuck.

CHAPTER NINETEEN

We were half an hour late when we pulled up to Josh's house. Parker told me on the way up here that everyone gets together at three, but they don't eat until four or four thirty, so we're not really missing out on anything but small talk. Probably for the best. I would turn as red as my heels if we walked in while everyone had their mouths full of turkey and mashed potatoes.

Closing the car door, I accept Parker's hand and allow his fingers to slip between mine. Is this a bad idea? Probably. Do I stop him? Nope.

We walked hand in hand up the walkway and into the mansion. Voices and amazing aromas surround us the second we step in. Maria's the first to come into view.

"Kids are here!" She calls over her shoulder as she saunters forward in a lovely teal dress that makes the blue of her eyes electric. A matching sash around her waist highlights her curves, and her dark hair spills over one shoulder. She hugs Parker, oblivious to the fact he never lets go of my hand.

She must have had an early warning about my anti-touch policy because she holds her hand out to me, I place mine in hers, and she leans forward kissing each cheek in turn. "You look stunning."

"Thank you, so do you. Your dress is lovely."

"Flattery will get you everywhere." She always has the warmest smiles. "Everyone's out back watching the game."

We follow Maria down the hall; she turns into the kitchen while Parker continues forward with me in tow and out onto the covered patio. I take in more faces I don't know than ones I do.

Drew comes up behind Parker, clasping his shoulder. "'Bout time." His brow furrows as he looks us over then slides to the heavens. "Oh. Well, if you're gonna be late..." He shrugs. How the hell does he know?!

Leaning forward, he answers my unspoken question from across Parker's chest, "You've got bed head, sweetheart." I quickly run my fingers through the back of my hair and Drew laughs.

"I hear you were a busy boy today," Parker tells him as I continue to try and smooth my hair down.

"Every birthday girl deserves to be pampered."

"Planning my surprise party so soon?" A sultry female voice washes over their conversation. I look up to see, probably the prettiest human being I've ever seen.

Platinum blonde hair falls in thick sheets to her waist. She's my height but thinner and golden brown. She wears a quarter sleeve cream top with a neckline ending at the center of her stomach. The fabric is tucked into a black floral skirt that is maybe two inches below her crotch, and perfectly tan legs run for miles into black stilettos. Flawless makeup highlights delicate features, everything except the silver hoop in her nose screams royalty. Amber colored eyes land on me, "Oh, hi."

I offer her a smile, not sure how to respond to someone so flawless.

"I'm Lacy, a family friend."

"Haley." High five to me! I got a word out without tripping over myself. Parker's ex is as gorgeous as him, and I'm not gonna lie- I'm feeling a lot like the Devito to her Schwarzenegger right now.

"How are you doing, Parker? I haven't seen you in ages."

"Never better. How's life?" His bored tone makes me feel a little better.

"Good. Got a new place in San Diego."

"That's right. I forgot you moved out there, enjoying it?"

"Oh, I love it! Are you kidding?" Her laugh is angelic, and I kind of hate her for it. "I was meant for California." A moment of silence follows before she turns to me, "You work with Andrew, right?"

Andrew? Oh, I bet he loves that. "Yeah, over at HEAT."

"Fun, fun. I was just telling Josh he should open a club out in California." She turns back to Parker and Drew. "You guys would be able to come out and visit if you did."

"Hey, did you get work done?" Drew asks.

"No, why?"

His eyes squint as he leans towards her, "Your nose looks bigger."

"Grow up." She rolls her eyes, giving Parker a once over. Cocking her head to the side her full lips curl into a seductive smile, "You look good."

"He looks taken," Drew adds dryly.

Her eyes fall to our joined hands, and I swear to the man above that I watched her jaw clench as her body turns to steel.

"How long have you guys been together?" A plastic smile sits on her face, turning her soft features more angular and far less appealing.

"Oh man," Drew starts, "Haley moved in-" blowing out a breath, he mulls over his thought, "Two months ago?" I moved into the apartment two months ago, yeah. I nod. "So-" He trails off trying to pin his thought once again.

"Oh, wow." Her fake smile drops a fraction before raising again. Her eyes flash with jealousy as she looks us over. "No one told me. How rude I must seem." She turns to me, "I'm sorry if I upset you, I didn't know."

Not sure how to handle Drew's clear manipulation of the truth without lying myself, I offer her a polite smile.

"I think I left my phone in your car," I say absently, letting go of Parker's hand. "I'll be right back."

Stepping away from them, I sidestepped a man I've never met before and entered the kitchen; I make it four steps before Maria calls me over.

"I was just trying to find my phone; I think I left it in the car." I rush out in one breath.

Her eyebrows raise a moment while she nods, wearing a secret smile. "Do you need it now, or am I allowed to borrow you for a minute?"

Please! "I'm all yours."

With another warm smile, she pushes a cutting board and a stalk of celery in my direction as I approach the monster island.

"I need help dicing. Tedious process."

"Sure."

Placing a knife beside me, I go to work stripping the ribs while she settles down next to me. "I see you've met Lacy. I trust she was on her best behavior?"

"Yes, she seems very polite. Drew made a comment that might have pissed her off though."

She giggles, peeling a carrot. "They don't get along. What was it that he said?"

"Wasn't so much what he said but what he implied. He made it seem like Parker, and I were not only dating but living together."

Her giggle turns into a laugh that she quickly tries to cover. "That would do it. Did you correct him?"

I bite my lip, pretending to focus on chopping, "I didn't want to call him out, so I lied and said I had to get my phone."

She nods, "Good. I like your hair by the way, when did you get it done?"

"Drew took me earlier today for my birthday." I felt my face pinch together. I hate lying, "That's a lie. He wanted to drive her nuts and pulled the best friend card."

She laughs, covering her mouth with the back of her hand. "That didn't last long, did it?"

"What didn't?"

"That lie." She giggles.

"If you're going to lie it needs to be worth it."

"Worth it?"

"Worth losing the people in your life, losing their trust over."

She nods, "That's a good way to look at it. You could always take the tell-no-lies approach too." She smiles at me before dicing her row of peeled carrots.

"So, who's who?" I nod to the patio to change the subject.

The knife stills in her hand as she looks through the large windows overlooking the patio. "See that couple sitting at the table with Josh? That's Lacey's parents, Kelley and Clark. Their oldest son, Darren is talking to Vinny." She angles herself to get a better view, pointing to each person in turn as she continues, "The youngest of their brood is Tiffany, she's the pretty one in the red dress sitting by Dillon. The other one is Patricia, or Patty as we call her. I don't know where she ran off to, but she's as slippery as Lacy, so be mindful of that. That fat old man with the comb-over is my brother, Jack. And his wife is Angela; she's the one in the green skirt talking to Jules."

I see who she's talking about, but I don't at the same time because Lacy is currently sitting on the table with her legs crossed, her skirt is pinched at her hip, showing bare leg clear up to her ass. Parker is sitting in a chair across from her; she's positioned herself, so he's eye level with her legs.

I bite my lip and focus on the task of cutting when Maria's hand lands on mine, my body stiffens from the contact, but I don't pull away as she offers a gentle squeeze before going back to chopping as if nothing happened. Forcing the darkness down, I steady my hand and resume slicing while keeping my eyes cast down, refusing to look up. Jealousy is nasty and I don't want to feel that way. Parker may not be mine but that doesn't mean it hurts any less to think he's enjoying the view she's giving him. Yeah, yeah, yeah. I push him away and claim not to want him, but I then complain when a blonde leech is making an offer. Whatever, sue me for being indecisive, I blame it on the fact I have a vagina.

"God, she's gross." I jerk when Drew jumps up onto the counter next to me. My mind had re-imagined the celery rib as Lacy's glossy, perfectly tanned legs and he pops out of nowhere, landing like a damn anvil on the granite surface.

"What's she doing now?" Maria's soft tone is so maternal and warm; I wonder if she has kids of her own.

I bite back the urge to ask, asking questions just invites people to return the gesture.

"Haley walked away, and she all but flashed her crotch to him." He shudders at whatever mental image he concocted.

"Then why are you in here making him suffer alone?" She pins him with a stern look that makes my mouth twitch.

BROKEN

"Just checking on Haley, Bailey. Gotta say this was the last place I expected to find you, Hales."

"Just because I eat at VIN's doesn't mean I can't cook, thank you very much." I smile, sliding the chopped pieces into the colander that Maria extends to me.

"It's not that." He jumps down, landing next to me. "It's just that Maria doesn't let anyone help her cook. You must be pretty damn special to be in here right now."

Without permitting it, a smile steals over my face. I dipped my head to try and hide it.

"When you're finished there," Maria says from the sink, either pretending she didn't hear him or just unwilling to comment, "You can start shredding that monster to your left." I point to the cheese block next to me, and she nods. "Ever since the boys were little they demanded mac n' cheese for Thanksgiving." Her smile grows as I wipe the remains of the celery stalk into my hands and dump it into the trash.

"Hey, you want my help?" Drew asks, walking backward towards the patio doors.

"Hell no! Get out of my kitchen!" She swats playfully at him with a hand towel; he turns for the door giving me a told-you-so look.

After helping her grate the cheese and other odd jobs she boots me out with a smile. Drew sits next to Parker, and they're both currently speaking to a tall, golden-haired man who has the same dark tan as the human Barbie still sprawled out across from Parker. If I remember correctly, his name is Darren.

Moving tentatively towards them I debate whether I should join them or say hello to everyone else to by myself time. Though my plan is decided for me when Parker stretches back, his arm extending out to me. I take his outstretched hand and let him guide me forward. Without breaking conversation, he sits me down on his lap and pulls my back against his chest.

"Where'd you run off to?" Drew asks, loudly to catch attention but not loud enough to be obvious.

"Maria needed help in the kitchen." I watch Drew's teeth lock together to keep the smug smile from appearing.

"You cooked with Maria?" Lacy asks, half pretend polite- half snarky as hell.

"Yeah." I'm proud of myself for keeping a straight face while the others stare on. My tone was so nonchalant that I should win an award.

"Doing what?" She presses.

"Oh, just little stuff. Chopping and shredding mostly."

I felt Parker smile against my neck, before pressing a kiss to my hair.

"Oh, shit." Drew sits up straighter, "I'm sorry man. Darren, Haley. Haley, Darren."

"Hi," I smile at him, he returns in kind. "Nice to meet you."

"So, your best friend got with your brother?" He asks, slightly amused. "I didn't think you were capable of having female friends, man."

They both laugh. "It helps that I'm not a blonde. Seems to be his Achilles heel."

Drew nods in agreement, his gaze following something over my shoulder.

"There you are," Josh says behind us, I twist to look at him.

"Hey." I smile at him.

"Did you come willingly or did Parker have to drag into the car by your hair?" He asks with his friendly smile.

"Oh, I'm sure there was a little hair pulling." Drew mumbles next to me, I swat his arm.

"I came willingly."

"Bet you did." I turn and punch him this time.

"OW! What'd I do?"

I glare at him. He knows exactly what he was doing.

"Haley, have you met everyone yet?" Josh pulls my focus away from Drew who's doing his best not to laugh.

"Not yet, I got sidetracked my Maria."

"I saw." A smile I have yet to decipher touches his lips, "Follow me a minute? I'll introduce you."

"Sure." Parker releases me and watches on as I follow Josh to the table in front of the giant flat screen.

"Clark, Kelley- this is Haley. Haley, these are my oldest friends, Clark and Kelley Chancellor."

"It's nice to meet you," I tell them, playing with my sleeve.

"This gentleman over here is Maria's brother, Jack and his lovely wife, Angela." I smile and nod in greeting. "Little one there is Tiffany, she's Clark and Kelley's youngest. I see you've already met Darren and Lacy. Where'd Patty go?" He turns back to Clark.

"She left to pick up Eric and Kendall from the airport." His wife answers for him. "Said she'd try to make it back in time for pie."

"Ah, so I'll introduce you to her later." He takes a look around, "I think that's everyone."

"Haley's a darling," I hear Jules tell Angela. "She started working for us- Oh, two years ago I'd say."

She looks to me for confirmation, I offer her a nod, growing more and more uncomfortable. New people means questions, questions equals lies, and lies lead to trouble.

"Is that right?" Angela turns to me. "And you also work over at HEAT?"

"Yes, ma'am."

"Oomph. I have a hard-enough time convincing Celeste to get up for class every day.

I can't imagine trying to get her to take on a job, let alone two."

"Haley's very independent." Vinny adds, "Got herself an apartment over there at Basswood."

"Parker's new project?" Jack asks.

"That's the one."

"Wow. It's rare to see young people so driven and hard working these days. No wonder Parker and her get along so well." Jack smiles at me, and I see the family resemblance, they all share the same kind smile.

"Speaking of-" Josh says, pointing behind me. Not looking a gift horse in the mouth for the rescue, I smile at the group and basically run back over to the safety of Parker and Drew. I claim the seat between the two brothers rather than his lap while Parker and Darren talk about business using big words and even bigger hand gestures.

Drew nudges me, his fist resting in the palm of his hand, "One. Two.. Three-"

I take my fist and pop his fingers closed. "Rock beats scissors."

"Trickery! You always chose paper first!"

"What are you, twelve?" Lacy rolls her eyes, turning back to her brother and Parker, I don't miss the sweep her eyes do of his body. I wonder how she'd react if she knew that less than hour ago I was pressed against it.

I ignore her remark, getting in the ready position, "Best two out of three?"

He beat me the second, cheated trying to use fire in the third, so we rematched the fourth and I hit his rock with paper. He huffs, throwing his arms over his chest and dropped low into the seat. Tipping my head back, I laugh at his childlike reaction. After a second he starts laughing too, looks away and begins laughing harder. "Come here," He wheezes.

I lean into him; he pushes my hair off my shoulder as he laughs before pressing a spot where my neck meets my shoulder. A mild ache follows his touched and I recoil, placing my fingers on the sore spot.

"If it wasn't obvious why you were late before, it is now."

"What?"

"Hey, Parker?" He says, ignoring me.

Parker's attention turns to his brother, his gaze follows Drew's finger before pulling his lips in attempting to conceal a laugh. "Whoops."

No, he didn't! I stand up abruptly, pushing through the french doors, and speed walk into the hall bathroom. Throwing my hair away from my shoulder, I gasp. Oh, my God.

Parker Hayes gave me a fucking hickey.

CHAPTER TWENTY

I stare at my reflection. A quarter size bruise sits in the indention of my neck and shoulder. For whatever reason, I thought rubbing it would wipe it away- nope, just made it angrier. Movement in the mirror causes me to look up just as Parker steps into me, so my back is flush with his chest, his fingers skim the bare skin of my thighs. "Mad?" His lips close over the spot on my neck. Goosebumps storm across my skin.

"No." I'm breathy, and it's embarrassing. Our eyes are locked in the mirror as his fingers continue to move up my legs. "It'll just be a fun little game Drew plays called, *'Remember when Parker gave you a hickey on Thanksgiving'*."

He chuckles, "It wasn't intentional." He kisses me again.

"I'm sure Lacy finds it as funny as you do."

"I don't care what Lacy thinks." His fingers roam under the fabric of my dress, "All I can seem to focus on is the way your legs felt wrapped around my waist."

I can feel the blush burning under my makeup as butterflies rage war in my stomach. "The sounds you make," His lips press into my neck, "The way you feel." His fingers dig into my flesh. "I can't seem to think about anything else, no matter how hard I try."

"And exactly how hard are you trying?"

He smiles openly over my shoulder, "Not very."

A loud throat clearing separates us. "Told Maria I'd let you guys know that we're sitting for dinner." Lacy stands in the doorway.

Her gaze falls on my neck and then at Parker. "How juvenile."

"Princess, the position he had me in was far from being kid friendly." I shoulder-check her on the way out the door. Sure, all she's done is flirt with Parker, but Drew hates her, and the fact is, if Drew hates you- I hate you. Friend code.

"There you are." Drew nearly shouts when I enter the formal dining room, "I thought Parker was upstairs evening out the other side."

I bite my lip as curious eyes land on me. "I just might do it this time," I tell him moving quickly to the seat next to him.

"Do what?"

"Kill you."

Maria giggles as she sets down the bowl of macaroni and cheese in front of me. Parker is right behind me, taking the seat to my left.

"I'll let her too." He adds.

"Let her what?" Lacy invites herself into the conversation, sitting across from Parker.

"Fuck him seven ways from Sunday," Drew says without missing a beat.

Josh dropped the serving spoon.

I choked.

Maria laughed.

Lacy glared.

Dinner went without incident after that. All it took was Josh's death glare and Drew behaved himself.

"Can I have the whipped cream, Uncle Josh?" Lacy asks, holding her hands out towards him, she must have caught the look on my face because she stares right at me and continues, "I started calling him Uncle when Parker and I got engaged. Hard habit to break." She takes the glass bowl from his hands, "Thank you."

Drew blows out a huge breath, staring at his plate. I fight and win against the urge to shudder at the lump of ice that currently resides in my stomach. He was going to marry a woman, who apart from her conversational skills, is entirely flawless to messing around with me, a girl covered in flaws inside and out.

I master the act of nonchalance as I offer a small nod of understanding. Her eyes narrow at the three of us before a small angelic laugh crawls out of her throat, "You didn't know?" Her face brightens with the lack of denial on our part. "Well, then." She pulls herself straighter, a smug smile taking over her face. I'm so thankful the rest of the table is too enthralled in their conversations to pay any attention to ours. "I suppose all hope isn't lost then."

"There are a million other men out there, why does this bitch want to die going after mine?" I ask Drew. Okay, so he's not mine, but still.

Conversation slows around us. My adrenaline picks up as the blonde leech and I stare each other down.

"He hasn't spoken once." She points out, "Doesn't appear to me that he's all that invested in you. But please, continue with your petty little threats."

"Ladies," Josh warns from the other end of the table.

"Don't confuse my respect for this family as weakness, Princess. I'm a bad bitch when I need to be, and I can promise you, that's not a game you're willing to play." She scoffs with an incredulous smile. "I don't pull hair; I break teeth. Choose your next words wisely; I might be provoked to show you just how petty my threats are."

Her eye's narrow, but she doesn't speak. Parker leans over, his hand digging into my hair, his mouth crashes into mine with a possessive and ruthless kiss. Knocking the air out of my body and sending my heart flying into hyper speed. It's damn near impossible to force the moan back down my throat, but I manage it, he pulls away leaving me breathless and desperately wishing for walls or maybe even a broom closet. "Invested enough for you?" He asks with a glare that I don't ever want to be on the receiving end of.

The room is at a complete standstill, I don't think anyone is even breathing. I want to wring her fucking neck, but I also want to pull Parker into a quiet corner.

"Haley has a hickey." Drew basically shouts down the table.

"Drew's a eunuch." And because I'm me, my hand reaches between his legs and squeezes. He yelps, trying to pull away as I keep a sweet smile on my face.

"Devil woman!"

Drew and I continue our banter well into the evening. We continuously speak so Lacy doesn't have an opportunity to, that or Drew's trying to distract me from the blood bath I promised her. Either way, it's working.

CHAPTER TWENTY-ONE

Parker and Josh got into some kind of business discussion so I let Drew take me home on the bike.

Friday, I covered for Becca because her son was sick, so I worked a double. When I got home, I basically only had time to change and leave to make it to HEAT on time. Parker stopped by but with it being Black Friday I was far too busy serving discounted drinks to stop and chat. I was wrecked when I got home from the bus stop that I immediately passed out. Saturday was more or less the same thing, and Sunday I dedicated to sleep. I wasn't intentionally avoiding Parker, at least I don't think I was.

Sunday evening, I was pulled off my spot on the couch when a knock sounded on the door.

Creeping carefully across the floor, I looked through the peephole. Parker.

Judging by my hesitation and the idea to pretend to be out- There's a possibility that I might be avoiding him. Deciding I can't do this forever; I open the door.

"Hi, sweetheart." He wears his crooked smile that I both love and hate.

"Hey." I push the door open further, my silent invitation as I walk back over and collapse onto my couch.

He chuckles, closing the door behind him. "Lazy day?"

I nod, "I pretty much slept the day away and I'm still tired." I pull my knees to my chest, to give him room to sit.

"I should have told you about Lacy."

Oh, so we're just jumping right into the awkward, are we? Cool.

"Don't worry about it."

"No, I am. I haven't seen you in two days."

"Yeah. I'm sorry, Becca's little boy is sick, so I've been pulling doubles, mix that with HEAT- I've just been busy."

He nods. "The relationship ended a few months after we got engaged-"

"Parker, I don't need to know any of this."

"Yes, you do. If you didn't, I wouldn't feel so guilty about not telling you."

"I don't expect you to talk to me about stuff like this and I'm not mad. I was a little shocked

Drew didn't mention it, what with his big mouth and all, but I'm not mad. There's a lot you don't know about me, and I don't ask questions because I'm not willing to answer any of yours."

"I know." He smiles, easing some of the tension in the air. "What if I want you to know?"

I shrug, not really sure how to answer that.

"Lacy travels a lot. She's spoiled and her parents cater to her. We dated through high school, did the long-distance thing while I was off at school. I stayed faithful; she didn't."

"I'm sorry." She's a fucking moron is what I didn't say. Parker is gorgeous, like build a monument in his honor, gorgeous. And he's one of the sweetest human beings I've ever met. How you could stray from a guy like that- I'll never understand, nor do I care to.

"Not your fault."

"No, but it caused you pain. You shouldn't have been treated like that."

He cocks a barely-there smile. "I'm kind of glad she did it. I didn't cheat on her, but I didn't love her. I thought I did- that's why I proposed, but I was happier when we were off doing our own things. I felt like it was expected of me to marry her and I didn't want to hurt her, so I stayed."

"So, if she didn't cheat you probably would have married her?"

"No, I would have ended it. After having so much time apart, I could only handle her in low doses. Everything she did drove me crazy. I was just trying to find a way to end it without being the asshole."

"Well, on the bright side- you win at having the hottest ex." I nudge him with my foot.

He makes a face, "Yeah, I don't think she's that pretty. Shitty thing to say I know, but it's the truth."

I stare incredulously, "You're kidding, right? Name one flaw on that girl's body."

"Her personality is a glaring one."

"Not internal flaws. Name one thing that isn't perfect on her; I dare you."

"She has thin legs."

"By 'thin' do you mean long and perfectly tanned?"

"No, I mean thin as in thin. She also doesn't have an ass."

"I don't know; she seemed to be curved in all the right places to me."

His gaze drops to my waist for a brief second, creating a flurry of butterflies my stomach. "I've seen curves in all the right places, and she's not up to par."

I smile inwardly. Damn him and his pretty words.

"I'm sorry for not speaking up." I met his eyes with confusion. "I should have. What she said, about me not being invested," he shakes his head, "it's not true. You've got a quick tongue, and you're deadly. When she commented, I was waiting for you tell her to fuck off because I knew you could handle yourself."

"I don't need to be defended. So, I don't know why you're apologizing. We're not dating- even if we were, I still wouldn't need to be defended. I can take care of myself." I shrug. "And you sort of did step in, so don't feel bad."

"I do feel bad." He rushes out, reaching into his back pocket to pull out his ringing cell phone. He frowns at the screen before answer, "Hey...yeah, she's sitting right next to me, why?" The corner of his lip raises, "No, and if we were, I wouldn't stop to answer my phone." He laughs, and I can only assume Drew made a sex reference. "Yeah, hold on." He hands the phone to me, "Drew."

"What's up?"

"Why don't you answer your phone?"

I glance down at my lap and then at the coffee table, "I think it's still in my jeans. I forgot about it."

"Well, I've been blowing your phone up."

"I'll check it when I get off the phone with you." Parker nods at me before asking where it was. I mouthed bedroom, and before I could stop him, he went to get it; wasn't necessary.

"Don't worry about it. I know you're alive now which brings me to the here and now-come and keep me company. Oh! And bring tacos."

"It's my night off, and I'm lounging." I mock cry. "I don't wanna get up."

"Unless you're dying or naked you don't have an excuse."

"Maybe I am, you don't know."

"You're not. I already asked Parker."

Parker sits back down at my feet, dropping my burner on my stomach as I glare at him.

"I could be dying."

"Are you?"

"Yes."

"Of?"

"Irritation."

"Doesn't count."

"I could be in the process of getting naked."

"But you're not."

"I could be, dammit. You don't know!"

"Yes, I do. You're probably curled into the arm of the couch in long sleeves and sweatpants." All of that is true expect the sweatpants.

"Not true." They're leggings, so there.

"Prove it."

"Fine, smart ass."

I hold the phone between my cheek and shoulder while sliding my leggings off. Parker's eyebrows raise as he watches me lower them to my knees, taking my phone I snap a picture sticking my tongue and send it to Drew.

BROKEN

"Incoming." Getting them back up is a lot harder than getting them down. I put his phone on speaker, so I can use both hands to pull them over my hips.

"Did I just get a picture of you in your underwear?"

"See. Not decent. Can't come out."

"If you love me you'll bring me tacos."

"If you love me you'll let me lay here."

"Pleeeeeeease?"

"Didn't I just get done doing you a favor?"

"Yeah right! You certainly got more out of that than I did!"

"I seem to remember protesting the entire time."

"I doubt there was much protest when you were under my brother." My face scrunched together. "See! You got more out of it than me."

"If you're on the phone you're obviously on break. Go get some food or have it delivered."

"You're killing me."

Parker swatted my leg playfully, grabbing my attention. "I'll go."

Curse me for being disappointed by that statement, probably better this way though. I have a hard time not jumping his bones when we're alone. I nod.

"Parker said he'd do it."

"Best brother ever!"

"If you go out with me. "Parker interjects. There it is. I was waiting for that.

"No."

"What?! Hales you better not fuck this up for me."

Parker smile turned wicked. "What's it gonna be?"

"Still a no." I smile sweetly.

"Why not?"

"Yeah! Why not?" Drew is still on speaker.

"Because."

"Not an answer."

"How about a trade?" I offer.

"What's that?"

"Agree to get tacos, and I'll make it worthwhile."

"Go on a date with me."

"Yes or no, make the decision."

"What is it?"

My eyes roam down his chest. "Worth it."

"Mhm. You're tricky."

"Yes or no, Parker?"

His tongue swipes across the edges of his top teeth making my mouth go dry.

"I take it back. So, say no." I say quickly. Apparently, that wasn't the right thing to say.

"Deal. Drew, I'll be there shortly."

"SWEET! You rock, bro! Catch you later."

The line ends, and I'm still staring. Parker has a knowing smile as he patiently waits for me to speak. After a moment he waves his hand as if to say the floor was mine. "Let's see your version of 'worth it.'"

"I said I took it back." Fuck me; my breath is all husky and breathy. This is why he won't give up, dumbass. You say you don't want him and then go and give in. Showing him exactly how untrue those words are. He's not going to leave you alone until you leave him alone.

"I know what you said, but I'm intrigued by your idea of what worthwhile is and even more intrigued now that you don't want to."

"It would just encourage you, and I don't want to do that."

"Sure you do." He smiles, I shake my head. "You like the attention; you just don't want to admit it." I do like the attention, but it's wrong. If it were only my feelings on the line I'd have no reservations, but I don't want to hurt him- I don't want to lose him.

"I'll lose you sooner if we got together and I don't want that to happen."

"You're not going to lose me."

"I lose everyone, Parker. You may be here now, but sooner or later your number will be up and away you'll go."

"Or," He stands up from the couch, "I just might fall in love with you." He leans over, kissing my cheek, "and demand to keep you forever."

"Don't say that," I say quickly. "Don't joke about it and don't mean it. I'm not the kind of girl you fall in love with. You wanna mess around when you're lonely, I'm your girl, but don't trust me with your heart. I mean it."

"I don't know who hurt you so bad that you began to hate yourself, but you listen to me Haley Carter- despite what you may have done or what you might do, you're worth loving." He lowers himself, so I have no choice but to meet his eyes, " Hear me when I tell you that I plan to fill your life with so much happiness that it eventually heals those wounds inside you, fills you with so much light that the darkness ceases to exist because you're worth it. You can tell me no a thousand times, but I'm going to keep asking you out because you're worth it. I want you today, I want you tomorrow, I want you a week, a month, a year from now because you are worth it." He pulls away, heading for the door and I can't do anything but watch him leave. Words have slipped down my throat, turning my stomach sour. "You can try to protect me from yourself, but your attempts will fail at best because I know you. Not the girl who got on a bus when she was sixteen, but this girl right here, right now, I know you, Haley." He pulls the door open, pausing briefly in the threshold, "Just so you know, I didn't sleep with you because I was lonely. I slept you with you because you're the last thought I have before I fall asleep, and the first when I wake up. It's about time you realize you're worth a hell of a lot more than you think."

    The door shuts behind him as the first tear burns down my cheek. I don't know why I'm crying. Maybe it's because I wish his pretty words were real. Or perhaps it's because he can make me feel like I might actually matter to someone, that having him, Drew and Josh in my life has shown me that there is hope for more, that there's happiness and love in this world. I just have to decide how close to the sun I'm willing to fly because once my wings are burned, it's a long drop back to a very cold reality.

CHAPTER TWENTY-TWO

I've waited outside of Parker's house for over an hour. Sitting. I had a good cry, got angry for crying, got mad at Parker for making me cry, then stormed over here to give him hell. Though my anger drains as he approaches his stairs; he didn't do anything but say pretty things, I highly doubt he intended to make me cry. I picture him as one of those guys that gets uncomfortable around tears doing everything in his power to make them stop or he's the type to get the hell outta dodge. His eyes land on mine as he climbs the stairs, a look of confusion clouds his face when he stops a few steps below me.

"You okay?"

"I came over to yell at you," I admit, shifting to a more comfortable position.

"For what?"

"For what you said, but the longer I sat here, the less I found to be mad at."

He nods, pulling out two cigarettes before lighting them. He hands one to me, inhaling the smoke before speaking, "So you're not going to yell at me?"

I shake my head, pulling in a drag myself. "Not unless you want me to."

"Not even a little." He half smiles but I can see the trepidation in his eyes, "Why were you angry?"

I ignore his question, "For a man of few words, you sure say pretty things." I sigh, meeting his gaze, "Did you mean what you said?"

He nods, his throat working as he swallows. "Is that what made you mad? You thought I was lying?"

Again, I ignore his question. "Was that you declaring your love?" Say no. Say no. Say no. You don't love me. You can't. Please say no.

He fights against the smile growing on his face, "No."

I blow smoke across my shoes, watching the light catch the smooth edges before thinning and flying away.

"When and if I declare my love for you, it'll be much better than a bunch of words."

I shrugged looking at the cigarette in my hand, "I like your words."

"But you don't trust them. Everyone you've ever trusted has betrayed you in some way or another."

He's got me there. "I still like them."

"I still like you."

I smile, meeting his eyes. The blue is nonexistent in the dull light. The heavy shadows fall across his features, highlighting his cheekbones and the straight bridge of his nose, he really is gorgeous. "You better."

Taking a seat on the step below me, he presses his back against the rail and sighs, "Go out with me, Haley."

"Please stop asking. I can't."

"Because you'll hurt me?"

Or myself. "More or less."

He watches the cherry burn for a moment, "What if I'm not worried about that?"

"You don't have to be. I'm worried about it for you."

He laughs gently. "When's Josh's birthday?"

"June ninth, why?"

He shakes his head while inhaling, suggesting he was only curious. "Drew's?"

"Why?"

A thick band of smoke blows through his nose. "Just- answer."

"December fourth."

"Mine?"

"I don't know yours. I assume it's sometime in February though because you guys are only ten months apart."

He nods. "The nineteenth."

"Are you going to tell me why you're asking about birthdays?"

"Someone who didn't plan on staying wouldn't take the time to learn those details in a person's life."

"I never said I didn't want to stay." I do want to stay; I've never wanted anything so bad in my life, and I lived with the devil for sixteen years- that should prove just how bad that want is.

"But you're scared you'll hurt me by leaving, right?"

"Well, that's part of it."

"What's the other part?"

I sigh, taking the last available hit of tobacco. "Can't you just trust that I know what I'm talking about?"

"I could. But then I couldn't form an argument against it."

I stamp the cigarette out on the pebbled stairs. "You'll leave, and it won't just be you hurting."

"So, you're worried that I'll be the one hurting you?"

"No, I'm worried I'll hurt myself."

I didn't miss the quick flash of his eyes skirting my sleeve. "Why would I leave?"

I shrug. "I don't know. I'm never told just left behind. Something about me drives people away."

"Or it has everything to do with them and nothing to do with you."

Well, my own mom abandoned me. My brother left in the middle of the night. My father beat me for my existence, my brothers tortured me for a good time, and the one guy who I got close to, took one look at my arm and bolted. "Not the topic I want to be on."

"Well, we're here." He shrugs. When I continue to stare at my shoes trying to push the past out of my mind, he extinguishes his cigarette and sighs, "Go out with me."

"Why?"

"Why? You're fucking gorgeous. You have this amazing personality and an attitude from hell. You don't take shit from anybody, and you have this way of crawling under my skin and staying there. I think about you all the time. I've seen you when you first wake up, when you go off to work, and when you go balls out for a holiday." He takes a breath, and I meet his eyes, "I want to see how you look for a date- I want to see how you look when it's me who inspired it."

"You've seen me like that," I whisper.

"When?" I raise an eyebrow at him. "No, seriously. Cause I don't remember ever taking you out."

"No, but we did stay in, and that was far better than any date."

He closes his eyes and shakes his head. "You can't say shit like that." He laughs.

"Why not?" It's a real question.

"Because it triggers very detailed thoughts, and that's just not a nice thing to do."

"Like what?" I bit my lip to keep from smiling. I know what it triggers, but I like seeing him squirm.

"Like the way your body feels against mine. The way you move, the way you look, the sounds you make." His gaze travels over me and then stares straight ahead, readjusting areas through the denim, "As I said, it's not a very nice thing to do."

"I don't know," I start, pulling myself to my feet, stepping up onto the landing. "Maybe my memory is just better than yours."

His stands as well, "Why's that?"

"Cause I like mine."

I'm intentionally teasing him, it's probably not smart but fuck it. I need to redirect this conversation and sex seems to be the holy grail of distraction topics.

Grabbing my hand, he presses it against himself; Jesus. "I like mine too."

"I can see that. Guess it's not so mean after all, is it."

"This is what's mean." He presses into my palm. "It's a bitch to get rid of."

I close my fingers causing his breath to hiss between his teeth. "Too bad you don't have anyone to help out with that." I give him a sympathetic smile. "Shucks."

His hand falls to my waist, stepping into me. "Go out with me."

"No." But I do move my hand from the outside of the denim to the inside.

"Jesus." He groans, his face pressing into my neck. "You won't date me, fine. But good God, say you'll stay the night." His fingers dig into my hip as mine explore, "Fuck, please say yes."

If he keeps breathing like this and making those noises, I'll do anything he wants. His breath catches as my nails gently slide down his chest. "What are we gonna do if I stay?" I know what we're going to do- I just want to make him work for it.

"First and foremost, I'm going to fuck you on every available surface in my apartment." Dear, sweet, baby Jesus, I've never had butterflies rip through me so hard before. "After that, I don't care what we do. Dinner, movie, sleep, be your goddamn slave, name it, and it's yours."

I didn't expect him to be so forward. I try to cover my surprise, "Slave, huh?"

"Haley." His tone serious as his hooded eyes fall on mine. "You're killing me. I'm about three seconds away from pinning you against my door, if that isn't something you want- tell me now."

I shrug again, "Ask me again in the morning."

Alright, so it didn't come out how I wanted it to- whatever. I crush my mouth against his to clear any confusion. His hands steer me until my back slams against his door. I should have made him unlock it first cause now that I've started, I can't stop. He seems to be okay with that. One hand holds the back of my neck, keeping my face flush against his as his other deftly unlocks the door. I don't even care that it seemed like this is old hat to him. The door falls open, and we tumble inside. Catching the hem of his shirt, I pull it up and over his head as I run my tongue up the center of his chest. I've learned in my short time with him that his chest is his weakness. And one I'm all about exploiting. My nails scrape as my mouth kisses a hasty trail back to his lips. His arms snake under my ass, and I'm airborne. My hair falls forward over his shoulders as he consumes me. He sets me on the kitchen counter, angling me back so he can raise my top as he kisses a line from my navel to my bra. Pushing the fabric over my chest, he goes to lift it, and I sober immediately.

"No." The word rushes out as I hold the fabric to my chest and shake my head.

His brows pulled together for a second. "No, stop or no further?"

"I can't take my shirt off."

"But keep going?"

I nod. His tongue skims across his bottom lip almost like he's in deep thought, "Do you trust me?"

"Yes." I'm shocked by how easy that was to answer. I don't want to venture down that road at the moment but duly noted to return to that thought later.

His fingers hold the center of my top as he gently raises it, "Parker-"

"Trust me."

I keep the excess fabric clenched in my fists as his hands slip inside the shirt, exiting through the neck, he raises the hem over my head, hooking it behind my neck. My chest and stomach are exposed, but my arms and shoulders are still covered. His hands slide under my hair, gently pulling it out from the makeshift shirt he's created, kissing my exposed throat along the way. That's fine. My eyes fall closed, allowing his mouth to heat my blood. His fingers find my leggings, tugging them down my hips, as I unhook my bra, god bless the front clasp, while shimming the fabric under my butt so he can draw them down my legs. His mouth didn't leave my body once. Fingers trace my curves, and I'm on fucking fire.

We lose our remaining clothes, and he stays true to his word- well, for the most part. They're still some furniture for next time; cause

BROKEN

after that- there's undoubtedly going to be a next time.

CHAPTER TWENTY-THREE

"So why did you come over to yell at me?" He asks as his fingers run down the seam of my stomach.

"Nice try," I say sleepily. "You're going to put me to sleep if you keep doing that."

He plants a kiss just above my navel. "Tell me why you were mad."

"I wasn't, I was confused, and my go-to reaction was to get angry."

"Hmm." His lips travel up my torso as my fingers knot in his hair. "Because?"

"Because I was confused."

"Why?" He bites my jaw. I squirm under him, he's too good at this.

"It doesn't matter." I try to pull his face to mine, but he keeps his distance as he continues to tease me.

"It matters to me."

I shake my head, "Kiss me." He smiles, kissing me chastely, I groan when he pulls away. "Not what I meant."

"I know. Tell me why."

"You made me feel, and it's not something I'm familiar with. Now, kiss me."

"I hurt your feelings?"

"No. Now, kiss me."

His lips brush mine once, twice, then turns the heat up. Pulling away, he goes after my neck again. "What did you feel?"

"What?" I pant.

"What did you feel that made you angry."

I swallow the fear, "Hope."

Pulling away he searches my eyes before leaning forward and rewarding me with a heartbreaking kiss. He can be ruthless, possessive, heart melting, and heart-stopping- all with his mouth. Maybe that's the secret behind men of few words.

"Go out with me." He whispers against my mouth, his fingers trailing past my hips.

"No."

My back bows as his mouth swallows my cry.

"Go out with me." His voice is rough and seductive as his fingers move.

BROKEN

I pant while my head tips back. Digging my fingers into the sheet, "No."

His mouth closes around my neck. "You're going to say yes eventually."

I know I am- but it won't be an answer to his question.

"Parker-" My grip tightens as my knees begin to shake.

"Go out with me."

"Fuck- Please."

"Please what?"

I pant against his fingers, fuuuuck.

"Go out with me?"

I cry out, my muscles tensing, pulling me from the mattress, Parker doesn't stop, his mouth collides with mine, "Say, yes." Gripping his shoulder, I bury my face in his bicep. His voice is husky and seductive, "Baby, say yes."

And I almost do. "No," I whisper, but it's not very convincing.

His lips graze my neck as he lowers me back against the mattress, my fingers follow the line of his triceps, beckoning him forward until our chest touch. "I've got all night to change your mind, sweetheart." His lips find mine.

I heard birds and Drew- it's too fucking early for this shit. Parker groans, the bed dipping as he sits up. I hear the rustling of sheets before fabric slides up to cover my nakedness. He falls back into bed, pulling me against him. I can feel the pull of sleep just as the bedroom door opens.

"I'll fucking kill you if you wake us up," I mumble into the pillow.

"Oh fuck-" Drew sounds genuinely surprised. "Sorry, I didn't know you were here."

"Bye, Drew."

He chuckles but doesn't leave, "Parker, I've got Josh's truck."

"Fuck." He sighs next to me, rolling to the side.

"No, come back," I whine. I just wanna go back to sleep.

"I gotta help Drew really quick."

I mock cry, "Can't it wait a few more hours?"

"You're a clingy little thing, aren't you?" Drew says from the door.

I grab the pillow and chuck it at him. "Go away."

"And moody."

"I'm moody because you woke me up."

"Dude- it's almost ten." He laughs.

I groan and roll over. "We went to bed like four hours ago."

"Don't-" Parker warns. I can hear the smile in his tone; I imagine Drew was about to say something that would either piss me off or embarrass me, judging by my mood I'm going with pissed. "Go back to sleep." Parker kisses my hair. "I'll be back soon."

"I should get up; I gotta be at VIN's by two."

"Call in."

"Tempting, but I don't have anyone to cover for me."

"Go back to sleep. I'll get you there on time."

Not going to argue. "Kay."

"Hey- before I forget again," Drew starts, "Did I leave my spare key at your apartment?"

"Me?"

"Yeah, you."

"I don't know."

"I was supposed to give it Josh yesterday. Haven't you seen it? I remember having it in your kitchen."

"I don't know, Drew. Grab my keys out of my jeans and look. Just lock the deadbolt when you leave."

"Okay, sweet dreams."

"Sweet dreams," I mumble back.

Drew shuts the door before Parker climbs out of bed. I hear the sound of denim and fabric shifting while he dresses behind me. The bed dips as he leans over me kissing my temple. "I'll be back."

I mumble something that sounds like 'okay.'

He chuckles, sliding off the bed. The bedroom door opens, I don't remember hearing it shut.

BROKEN

CHAPTER TWENTY-FOUR

I woke up when Parker climbed back into bed; I pretended to sleep while he kissed up my neck. The smile gave me away, but I didn't open my eyes.

"Hi, gorgeous."

My smile deepens. Him and his pretty words.

"What time is it?"
"One."
"I gotta get up."
"Mhm."
"Did Drew find his spare?"
"I don't think so."

"That sucks." I pull myself upright, running my hands through my hair.

"I grabbed your clothes when we were there though; they're in the bathroom."

I smile at his sweetness. How thoughtful...fuck this is dangerous.

"We're playing with fire," I tell him, sitting up.

"Why's that?" He asks, moving my hair over my shoulder so he can kiss my neck.

"Because we're going to get burned."

"Not while I'm around. I'm all for fire safety."

I crack a smile and his warms.

"Any marks I need to worry about hiding?" I tilt my neck towards him.

He laughs, "No, but I can give you one if you're disappointed."

"That's alright." I hop off the bed in search of a hot shower.

Parker groans from his spot on the bed as the sheets fall away from my naked lower half, "Play hooky; I'll even make the call, so it's more convincing."

"They're short-staffed, I can't bail on them."

Entering the bathroom, I see the clothes he's laid out for me. Next to it is my white makeup bag and my toothbrush.

"This was sweet of you, getting all my stuff."

He doesn't speak, but I see him nod through the mirror.

Cocky bastard. I smile before shutting the door.

Parker got me to work on time; I was a little disappointed when he didn't stay. I guess Drew still needed his help. I mentally kick myself in the face for watching him drive away like some love-struck teenager. Shoving those heinous thoughts away, I pull the door open.

What. The. Fuck.

Kaylan sits at one of tables with a beer in his hand watching the flat screen against the wall. The blonde abandoner sits to his right, picking at her nails.

This is fucking ridiculous.

I stalk over to the counter, quickly passing Andrea and enter the kitchen. Dillon's fire red hair is spiked in every direction as he leans over the grill.

"Where's Vinny or Jules?" I ask when his eyes fall on mine.

"Uh, office or out back. You want anything?"

I almost say no, but then I remembered it's going to be a bitch of a night if I don't eat while I can. "Sure. Whatever you're trying to get rid of."

"On it." He calls as I push past the dishwasher's station to the office and peek inside. Jules's sweater is draped across the back of the office chair, her purse still resting on the desk but there is a pack of cigarettes thrown on the top, backing away I walk through the kitchen to the trash exit.

Stepping outside, I see Jules sitting at the little table watching Vinny talk on the phone, a cigarette resting between her fingers.

"We know." She speaks immediately, nodding to the seat next to her.

Vinny walks off the little platform and into the alley. I pull my pack out, lighting a smoke of my own as she continues. "The guy asked for you; only he didn't ask for Haley."

"That's my brother." I blow a lungful of smoke out.

"So that woman is your mom?"

"Unfortunately."

She nods, tapping on the filter to drop her ash into the little black tray. "She wants to talk to you."

"I'm so sorry that they're here. I keep telling them to go away but they won't. I'll do everything I can to get them to leave peacefully, I promise."

"Sweet girl, we're not angry." Her finger taps nervously against the iron table. "Maybe you should see what she has to say- Now, hold on before you say no, hear me out. Maybe if you bite the bullet and let her say her peace, she'll be done."

"She doesn't deserve to have peace."

"But you do." My chest tightens, no I don't. "Just give her-" She looks around aimlessly as she thinks, "Half an hour."

"I have a job to do."

"Half an hour won't kill us, Haley."

"She can have a minute for every year she was a part of my life."

"There you go. How long is that? Fifteen minutes?"

I laugh without humor, "Six."

Her face falls, she pushes the cigarette between her lips to buy herself time as she regains herself. "Two minutes per year. Give her that, when it's over tell her you gave her, her time and now she needs to give you yours."

I blow out a shaky breath, "I don't want to be anywhere near her."

"For me?"

Jesus, low blow, lady! Low blow. This damn family and getting what they want. Blowing my frustrations through my nose, I nod.

I stamp out my cigarette and take a deep breath. "The sooner you do it, the sooner it's over. "She offers me a kind smile as I pull myself to my feet. I sigh heavily, throwing my hair out of my face and walk back inside. Dillon is finishing two plates as I round the corner.

"Order up?"

"Yes, ma'am. Yours is done too."
"Where to?"
"Table fourteen." Peachy.
"I'm going over there anyway- I'll take them. Let Andrea finish her side work."

He hands me their plates, then adds mine to my forearm. "Thanks."

Stepping up to their table, I less than politely, slide their food to them. Plopping mine down in front Kaylan, I pull out a chair.

"What the hell do you want?" I stare at both of them.

"Hi, Kitten." Kaylan smiles at me, completely unfazed by my death glare.

"Ryan, you're going to eat with us?" Her hopeful tone and smile are nauseating.

"You have twelve minutes to say whatever it is that you have to say before I have you thrown to the curb. Eat fast, talk faster. Time started when I set the plates down. And stop calling me that."

"Haley?" She asks, and I nod, "I always wanted you to have a girl's name. When Kaylan was ordering your I.D., I thought it was fitting. You look like a Haley."

"Ten minutes."
"Can't we just eat and share small talk?"
"Like a family?" I ask.
Her smile brightens, "Exactly. Like a family."
"No. Nine and a half."

She gives me an exasperated breath, "I don't know where to start."

"Pick somewhere and do it fast. Clock's ticking."

"Ry, don't be like that. We're not attacking you." Kaylan chastises.

"You keep popping up at my work and making problems for me. It's not physical, but you're still attacking."

"I just want to talk to you, baby."

"Then talk!" I throw my hands out, beyond annoyed. Her face falls, and Kaylan coddles her. "She's a big girl; she can handle herself. Eight minutes."

"I tried to get you out." She starts. God, I could be having sex right now. Instead, I'm here. Good job, Haley. Good call. Aces. "I got Kaylan because he was older, it was easier to move him, and I didn't have to worry about him not remembering the lie or faking his name. After he left, your brothers were always with you. I was never able to get close, so I had Kaylan try. There were always people there. Kaylan thought to give that girl the stuff and then have you followed so we could meet up with you afterward. We weren't expecting you to hate us; we expected you to react like him, hurt and confused but not hate."

"I was here for over a year and a half before Kaylan showed up. That photo you left at my work with all your little speculations- which by the way thank you for. My boss had some fun questions that I'm not allowed to answer because of your little stunt. You can abandon me, save Kaylan, abandon me again, but boy can you write a list of the worst possibilities I might be experiencing. You couldn't take me because I was a liability but I could stay even though you thought I was being raped. I hope I end up with your award-winning maternal skills." I pull my phone out of my pocket to check the time, "Six minutes."

"Damn dude." Kaylan laughs. "Is that a flip phone?"

I twist it so he can get a better look while glaring at her.

"No way. Those are still a thing? Can I see?"

I slide it across the table, without thinking and he opens it, laughing. "It has actual buttons. This is wild."

"Sand's almost through the glass. Any parting words?"

"I tried everything. CPS, Private Investigators, everything-"

"Everything except the cops, right? Everything except being a parent, correct?"

"I didn't know what he was doing, he's a cruel man, but I never thought he would cut-"

"Stop," I warn. "Don't talk about that shit here. Not where I work, not where others can hear."

"I didn't know the extent of his actions until Kaylan was already out."

"Wow, yes, I can see how it takes ten years for that to sink in."

"We got you out." She shakes her head like I'm an ungrateful child.

"Ten years later."

"I saved you from four more marks." Her eyebrows raise like she's inviting me to push her.

Bitch! With pleasure!

"Thank you- you're right. You saved me from four more marks. Where the other nineteen were totally worth it."

"Ryan Carter-"

My eyebrows shoot up as I bust out laughing. "Oh man! Look at you!" I sit back with a huge smile, "Acting like a mom, middle naming me and everything." I laugh once before turning deadly, "Where the fuck were you when I was a human ashtray for ten years? Where the fuck were you when the blade bit into my arm because I was alive for another year? Acting like a mom? Fuck that. You're a glorified cum dumpster. Pushing out four kids just to up and leave to save your own ass. How's your black eye anyway? Seems to have healed okay; I'm so glad you got out when you did. It must be hell on earth only fearing his hands and not his pocket knife."

BROKEN

She throws the chair back as she stands to glare down at me, "Now you listen here. I get that I wasn't around, but you will not speak to me like this. Dammit, I am your mother!"

I stand before leaning over the table, Kaylan stands to protect Mommy dearest. "You're nothing but the dirty snatch I fell out of."

Her hand flies out; I pull back barely missing her palm. Fire rips through me as I catch her wrist, I stare at her in disbelief before pulling her arm. She stumbled forward, smacking into the table.

"Swing at me again, bitch! It'll be the last thing that arm ever does."

A hand snakes around my middle pulling me back in one fluid motion. Spinning around I catch Josh pulling a chair out from our table. What the fuck is he doing here?

"Everybody sit." His voice is not to be tested as he slams a folder against the table. I pull mine and sit a good four feet away from the blonde cunt in front of me.

"Susanna Carter?" He asks, looking at her while I try to calm my raging heart.

She pulls her angry eyes off of me and looks at Josh. "Yes."

"Legal name?"

"Yes."

"Not Hale?"

"No."

"Sit." He points to her chair. She crosses her arms like a child as he pulls a check from under a paper clip and flips it at her.

Her arms flail a moment while she tries to catch it. Her eyes pop out of her head as she looks at it. "What is this?"

"Sit."

She does.

He opens the folder in front of him, spinning it to face her. Producing a pen, he pops the cap setting it on top of the papers. What the hell is he doing? "Sign."

Her eyes are glued to the little rectangle in her hands.

"Mom?" Kaylan pulls her out of it, nodding to the folder.

Keeping the check in her hands she leans forward, shaking her head in confusion, "Ryan's eighteen."

"I'm well aware- sign."

Josh is kind of an asshole it turns out. I kind of like him more for it.

"I'm not signing this." What is it? What the hell is happening?

"You want that?" He nods to the check. "Then sign."

"She's eighteen; this is pointless." She pushes the folder back towards him.

He pulls a checkbook out of his back pocket, scribbles across the surface then rips it out and sets it on top of the folder, pushing it back once again. She stares at it. I'm so confused, but pride and anger keep me silent.

"You would need her father's signature too." Father? What?

"He's not listed on her birth certificate. Therefore, he would have to take me to court to protest it. I don't see that happening. Now- sign the documents so you can cash those checks." Court? And where the hell did he see my birth certificate?!

"Mom, don't-" Kaylan's tone is half disappointed, half disgusted as she picks up the pen.

Josh wastes no time telling her where to initial and where to sign. When she's finished, he takes the pen forcefully out of her hands, pulling the folder and sets them both in front of me. I look down at the Petition for Adoption then stare at him in shocked confusion.

The anger and malice he had are gone as he stares back. He gently nods to the papers, "Be a doll?"

"I don't know what this is." I mean I do- but I don't. I'm eighteen.

"He's trying to adopt you, Ryan," Kaylan says in stunned disbelief.

"I'm eighteen." I shake my head. I don't know what he's doing- Is he trying to make a point that I choose his family over my own? Because if that's the case- absolutely, where's the dotted line?

BROKEN

He gently nods to the papers again. I pick up the pen and sign where he tells me to; I'm surprised my hand is capable of completing the task. I'm so confused, like out-of-this-world confused.

Josh smiles, taking the pen. He scribbles his name here and there then offers the pen over my shoulder. I turn, unaware of anyone else's attendance. Of all people, Maria steps forward, also signing. Everything is happening so fast, and I still don't know what's going on. Josh stands, closing the folder.

"Haley." I look up and he nods for me to join him, I do.

"Now that that's all settled." He sighs a relieved breath before his face lights up with a huge smile. He turns to my mom, "Come near my kid again, and I'll have you arrested." My mouth falls open as I gawk at him. My kid. Josh just called me his kid. My mom huffs, looking as shocked as I am. "And if you ever raise your hand to her again, your ex won't be the only man you fear."

My mom's face scrunches in anger, Kaylan shakes his head looking heartbroken, "I hope that check was worth losing your daughter over." He growls.

"Ten thousand." She mumbles back, still glaring at Josh. My eyes are going to fall out of my head. Dollars?! Oh, my God. "That paper isn't legal. She's eighteen."

"Haley." Maria coos next to me. "Come with me?"

I kinda wanna know what's about to happen, but I let her take my hand because I'm not sure I'm capable of leading myself. She pulls me outside and around the building to the dumpsters, encouraging me to sit down.

"What just happened?" I have a voice! Praise the Lord! I pull a cigarette out of the pack and set it between my lips, Lordy, I'm shaky.

"You just became a Hayes." She smiles flicking my lighter for me. "Congratulations, you're dating your cousin."

CHAPTER TWENTY-FIVE

I choke, puffs of smoke project from my lungs with each hack. Maria starts to laugh, and not the polite kind, either. Heaves of laughter roll off her as I gasp for air. Tears stream down my face as I slowly pull in a painful breath. She collects herself, then loses it once more. It's infectious. Despite my shitastic encounter and the confusion muffling my thoughts, I manage to laugh with her.

"We're not dating."

This is apparently funnier than choking. She wipes her eyes, but can't look at me.

"Yes, that's what's important to take away from this." Her giggles turn back into laughter. "That was too funny."

"Is it safe to smoke?"

She nods trying to collect herself. After a moment silence falls over us as I slowly draw poison into my lungs.

"I'm eighteen." For whatever reason, I felt my well-known age was important to point out.

She nods. "He knows."

"So, was that just to prove a point?"

Her head pops to the side like a puppy as her brows pinch. When I don't continue, she shakes her head like she doesn't understand.

"I can't be adopted; I'm an adult. So, was that just a show to prove to her once and for all I don't want her around?"

"No. He legally adopted you. That was an adult adoption, in the state of Arizona, anyone between the ages of eighteen and twenty-one can still be adopted. Your parents don't need to be notified; I think that part was to prove a point. "

"Wait..." My heart drops like a bag of cement, "Josh just adopted me? Like, I mean adopted me. Now my dad, now his daughter adopted?"

"Yes."

"Oh, fuck."

Her brow creases, "What did you think he was doing?"

"I thought my boss was trying to get her leave. Why would he adopt me?"

"Because he doesn't look at you like an employee. Neither do Vinny and Jules."

"This is so...weird. How did he even know she was here and how did he get the papers? Was this a long thought out process? What? I- I don't-" I put my hands over my face. "I'm so confused, and I have a headache."

"Okay." She adjusts in her seat. "One at a time. He knew she was here because Vinny called when she showed up with your brother. I don't know if this was an existing plan, he printed the papers before we left the house."

"How? I thought adoption involved lawyers and court and a CPS worker."

"Child adoption can, yes. You're a legal, consenting adult. Really, with both parties signing without stipulations, all he has to do is file them."

"What happens now?"

"I'm not sure."

"So... Parker and I are now related?" My face twists in disgust before I can control it. Maria giggles.

"By a piece of paper, yes. It's not incest or anything."

Oh, this is fucked up.

I drop my cigarette into the ashtray before plowing my hands through my hair. "I have a headache."

I'm grateful for the silence that follows. My head is pounding.

"She okay?"

I look up to see Josh stepping onto the platform. Maria nods. "She's fine. Just got a headache."

"I bet." He tells her before nodding to me, "You good?"

I nod.

"Come on; I'm taking you home."

"I can't. They're understaffed; I'll be fine." I stand, and the cement pushes against the back of my eyes.

"They're the ones who are sending you home. The last hour's been rough on you; they can handle the bar."

"If I don't go home are you going to ground me?"

He laughs nervously while avoiding my eyes, "I might. Come on, kid." I follow behind him and Maria because I don't want to work today. I want to sleep and wake up this morning. When Parker tells me to play hooky, I'm going to say yes, and all this crazy shit won't happen. That's my plan.

As we near the car I watch Josh kiss the side of Maria's head, his hand low on her back as he opens the passenger side door of a shiny white car. He opens the back door for me as I approach. Climbing in, I'm even more confused than I was two minutes ago. Are they a thing? Parker's dad's brother is with Parker's mom's sister? Oh my God, my head hurts too bad for this shit. I don't want to sleep on my couch; I want Parker's big ass bed with his fluffy pillows and silk blankets.

"Oh crap! Kaylan still has my phone!"

"No, ma'am." Josh starts, reaching into his front pocket. He pulls out my burner and hands it back to me. "He gave it to me before they left. By the way- what the hell are you doing with a month to month flip phone?"

"It was cheap." A whole fifteen bucks.

He scoffs playfully, "I know how much you get paid. Aren't you kids supposed to be all about technology and apps and social media?"

"I don't have any social media accounts, and up until a few weeks ago I didn't have TV, so no."

"You didn't have a TV?" Maria asks, leaning over the center console to look at me. "What did you do for fun?"

"I work and sleep. Parker and Drew got tired of me not understanding their references, so they're loaning me a TV."

"Loaning?"

"Yeah, I'm giving it back when I get my own."

"Good luck." Josh chuckles

Opening my messages to text Parker, an incoming message vibrates.

BIG BROTHER: I take responsibility for my part in the past, but I had nothing to do with that shit right now. Don't hate me.

ME: Big brother? Seriously?? Did you programme your number on my phone?

My damn fault, shouldn't have let him touch it.

BIG BROTHER: Thought it was fitting. You're KITTEN in mine. ;)

ME: Because I'm so cute and fluffy? Fuck off.

BIG BROTHER: No cause your claws are always out, and you're feisty as hell.

ME: Can't imagine why. Lose my number.

BIG BROTHER: Not happening. Keep mine in case of an emergency.

BIG BROTHER: I want you in my life Ry. It's been a bitch living without you. I get that I can't force myself on you, but if you have my number, we can text. I'll stop showing up if you do.

ME: So, I just have to say hi, and you'll leave me alone?

BIG BROTHER: Yes. :) but I'd like it if we could progress from 'hi' to maybe a 'how are you?' And perhaps you answer when I ask you.

ME: Fine. But no more showing up at my work. I'll ensure you never reproduce if you do.

BIG BROTHER: Deal. I'm sorry mom did that.

ME: I'm not. I don't want her anywhere near me. I barely want you around.

BIG BROTHER: Barely is better than don't. I'll take it.

Rolling my eyes, I open a message to Parker,

BROKEN

ME: I have a terrible headache, I'm going home. My mom dropped by, and Josh dropped a bomb. Can I commandeer your bed??

The reply is immediate.

PARKER: The first text I ever get from you, and it's to ask to sleep in my bed? Best. Day. Ever. Of course. Everything ok?

ME: Yes and no. Wish I could explain, but I have no idea what just happened.

The phone vibrates, and I groan.

"It's Parker. He wants to know what's going on and I have no idea what to say."

"Start with hello," Josh says into the rearview mirror.

"Ha. Ha." I glare at him answering the call, "Hello?"

"Hey, what's going on?"

"I don't know."

"You're okay though?"

"Yeah, I think so. We're almost to the apartment. Are you home?"

"Drew and I are in the parking lot, are you on the bus?"

"No, Josh and Maria."

Silence.

"Okay, well we're at the stop light so I'll see you in a minute."

Silence fills the line. Awkward.

"Kay, Bye."

"Bye."

The line ends.

"Good job. That cleared things up." Josh chuckles, Maria gently shoves his arm.

"I don't even know what happened, can't explain something I don't understand myself. So, I volunteered you."

"How generous of you."

"I thought so. They're in the parking lot so try not run them over."

"No promises."

I smile a little as we pull through the gate.

Sure enough, Drew is sitting in the bed of Josh's truck; Parker leans against the back with his arms across his chest. Without missing a beat, Parker steps forward opening my door.

His eyes do a quick scan, before looking at Josh and Maria. "You guys good?"

"We're all wonderful." Maria moves around the hood to greet them.

"Is your apartment unlocked?"

He shakes his head while diving into his pockets to retrieve the keys.

"You dropped a bomb?" Drew asks from his place next to Parker.

"I sort of adopted Haley."

Parker's hand freezes mid-movement, Drew's face scrunches up. Fuck. I don't want to be here for this, too much. This is all way, way too much.

"I'll be at my place." I don't need his bed that bad. I step back, but Parker catches my wrist, twisting my hand over he presses the keys against my palm. His eyes search mine for a moment before he lets go. I try to smile at him but, I don't think it was very compelling.

"Can you do that?" Drew finally asks, "She's eighteen, right?"

My brain is throbbing. "I'm gonna go lay down."

Everyone lets me leave without protest. I'm so foggy and weirdly exhausted as I walk across the courtyard to Parker's apartment. The stairs are brutal, but I manage. Unlocking his door, I drop his keys inside and go straight to his bedroom.

Kicking my shoes off, I climb in. Jesus, I want his bed. Everything is so soft and fluffy and smells like him. My body sinks into the mattress as I settle my aching head against the cold pillow. I'm pretty sure I fall asleep before my eyes close.

CHAPTER TWENTY-SIX

I remember when Papa came to visit for Christmas. He got me a baby blue princess dress. I wore it night and day for the duration of his visit.

It had puffy white shoulders and clear sleeves covered in sparkles. The soft fabric fell to the top of my feet; I remember it tickled when I walked barefoot.

Evan said I wasn't pretty enough to be a Princess. He pushed me into the Christmas tree, Papa smacked his ear and then took Kaylan and me to the park.

He let Kaylan drive.

When I woke up the next day, Papa was gone, and Daddy was mad again.

BROKEN

The house smelled bitter, and the woman with the bloody lip slapped me when I walked into her. Derek laughed. Kaylan tried to hide me.

I didn't know why he was trying to push me into the closet, but then Daddy found us. A fat cigar, the one he only smoked with Mommy, was in his mouth and he pulled me out of the tight space.

The sleeve caught a nail and bit into my skin... he ripped my Princess dress.

I started crying, and Daddy shook me before throwing me against the floor. Pine needles dug into my hand. Daddy knocked Kaylan to the ground when he tried to help me. Everybody was yelling, Daddy was taking off his belt, but nothing registered except the fabric dangling off my shoulder.

Daddy hit Kaylan with his buckle until he stopped moving. Kaylan never cried, he would just go very still. He'd blink, and breath but nothing else would happen. He wouldn't talk or look at anything; he'd just stare straight ahead.

Daddy grabbed me and forced me to stand in front of the fireplace; he pulled down a picture of Mommy.

"Who is this?"

"Mommy."

Daddy hit me with the picture frame. "No. This is a whore! Who is this?"

Her name is Mommy; I don't know what to say.

He hit me again. "Say it. Tell me that's a whore! Who is this?"

"Whore."

"That's right. Where is the whore?"

I shook my head. Mommy went away a long time ago. Kaylan keeps saying she'll come back but she hasn't yet. Papa didn't talk about Mommy when he was here. Papa is Mommy's Daddy.

Daddy hit my ear, and I cried. "Where's the whore?"

"Where?" I echoed.

He shook me, and I cried harder. "You're a whore just like your mother! You know what happens to whores?"

I shook my head.

He pulled the cigar out of his mouth and held it in front of my face. The white smoke burned my eyes and stung my nose. He didn't let me pull away, even when I felt the heat on my nose. "Whore's get burned."

He pushed the glowing red part into the rip of my princess dress.

I started to scream.

I screamed and tried to get away, but Daddy wouldn't let me go until the smoke was gone. My shoulder screamed almost as loud as I was. I was bleeding, and my skin was gray from the ash.

"For every year that bitch stays gone you'll get treated like a whore."

BROKEN

Kaylan picked me up and tried to take me into the bathroom, but Daddy didn't tell him he could. Daddy pulled us back, even though Kaylan fell, I didn't get hurt. Kaylan always protects me.

Daddy punched Kaylan.

I remember Kaylan's blood was warm when it dripped onto my hand. Daddy ordered us to stand up; he ripped Kaylan's shirt off before getting his belt off the couch. I started crying harder. I hate the belt.

Kaylan grabbed my arm, and I screamed in pain. My shoulder was tight and ached and burned, but he didn't let go.

Daddy swung the belt, the sound of the metal buckle smacking into Kaylan's flesh made me shake. The leather struck forwards, hitting me behind the neck. I started to fall forward, but Kaylan's grip was so tight I would bruise; he knew if I fell I'd get it worse, so he held onto me.

Strike after strike after strike. Metal buckle to Kaylan, leather tip to me.

After a while, you stopped feeling it. But even as I went numb and my body ran out of tears he never let me go.

Kaylan never lets me go.

CHAPTER TWENTY-SEVEN

The throbbing isn't nearly as harsh when Parker gently wakes me.

"Here, sweetheart, take these." He places two pills in the palm of my hand before handing me a glass of water.

I toss the pills back before rolling onto my back. Cracking my eyes open, I notice the sun has begun to set.

"What time is it?"

"Little after six."

"Oh my God." I try to sit up but give up when my headache increases. "I should go home."

"No, you're fine." He takes a drink from the glass he handed me. I don't know why but the fact he's drinking after me gives me a flutter of unknown emotion. He's been far more intimate with his mouth, but for whatever reason, this tiny act sends a wave of ripples, tickling through my chest.

"I stayed last night."

"Oh, I haven't forgotten."

A smile tugs at my lips but it quickly vanishes. "It's been a day."

He nods. "I'm sorry about your mom."

"Ugh, I wanted to knock her ass out. Twelve years and she thinks she can hit me? Are you kidding." I sigh heavily, "Couldn't disrespect Vinny though."

"She what?" His tone turns from gentle to angry.

"When she tried to slap me..." I trail off watching his reaction. "You weren't apologizing for that part, were you?"

He slowly shakes his head.

"Oh. Well." I smile nervously. Awkward, awkward, awkward. "So, my mom tried to hit me. I moved before she could and then Josh showed up."

"Why did she try to hit you?"

"I pissed her off. She was pretending to be my mom, and I had enough. My mouth went off, and her hand went up." I laugh without humor. "If you didn't know about that, what were you apologizing for?"

"For her signing those papers for money."

BROKEN

"Oh- well, don't. I could care less about that. She's always been one who was easily paid off. I wish Josh didn't waste his money though."

He nods again, his eyes won't meet mine, and I have this sinking feeling that he's upset.

"Did Josh explain what happened?"

Another nod, the knots of paranoia tighten.

"Are you-" I pull my lips in, I don't want the answer, but now it's too late, "Are you mad?"

His brow furrows as he shakes his head, still looking at his lap. An intake of air in preparation to speak is cut short by none other than Drew, "Pull up your pants, kids! Dad's home." A loud pop sounds down the hall, "What I do?"

Parker gives me a tight-lipped smile, swats my thigh gently and goes to meet him down the hall.

Fuck. He's upset; I know he is.

"She up?" Josh asks.

"Yeah."

Noooooo. I don't want to do this right now.

"You mind if I talk to her?"

I don't hear Parker's reply- my monies on a head nod. A moment later there's a small rap against the open door.

"Hey." I force myself into a seated position. Resting my back on the headboard.

"How are you feeling?"

"Better."

"Can I talk to you for a minute?"

BROKEN

No, I'd prefer we just pretended today didn't happen. "Sure."

Josh moves to the foot of the bed and sits down. Sitting down means this isn't a quick conversation. Sitting down means feelings shall be shared, I've seen family TV.

"I sprang this whole adoption thing on you without asking what you wanted." He lets out a breath. "I didn't do it to distract your mom or prove a point; I printed them with the intent of making you a part of my family. I just didn't think it was going to be so soon. Vinny called me when she showed up, and I made the decision right then and there." A shake of his head and his brown eyes lock with mine, "I wasn't willing to share you. I knew at that moment that you're a member of this family and I wanted to prove to you that we weren't going anywhere. Whether a piece of paper establishes that or not, you're one of us. I can shred them as easily as I printed them- your mom doesn't have to know. We want you to be a member of this family, do you?"

Jesus, of course, I want a family. I wish I had that white picket fence and a dog and mundane problems. I want to matter, but my baggage is so heavy they'll drown trying to keep me above water.

"You don't want me; destruction follows me wherever I go. You have questions that I can't answer and a past I can't get away from. I'm not worth the hurt I'll bring."

"You couldn't be more wrong, kid." He smiles, "The only thing you've destroyed was the ties holding you back. You made such an impact on Vinny and Jules that they came to me looking to get you a better paying job. I thought he was an idiot." He laughs, "I was certain you were running from the cops, but then you showed up, and you were just a kid. I understood Vinny's need to help you. It was within the first two weeks when I realized how protective I was of you. Drew was being Drew and I wanted to ring his neck- turns out y'all were only friends, so no harm but, at that moment I knew whatever you were running from didn't matter, I knew you belonged. Your brother drops by and spills a few secrets and all of sudden you're on the run. At that moment, I knew I loved you. I didn't give a fuck that you were seventeen pretending to be twenty-one. I didn't care that I could lose my club because I'd rather lose that than you. I got your letter, and I swear the emotions I felt were the same if it were from Parker or Drew. I was scared you were gone forever. You're a part of my family whether you bring blood and destruction or sunshine and rainbows. I'm not asking if you think you should, I'm asking what you want."

Drew got his arrogance, but Parker got his pretty words. Hayes men- I swear. I don't want to acknowledge the twist in my chest or the sting behind my eyes. The voice in the back of my head is screaming this is a bad idea, telling me to run for the hills because I'll ruin everything...but she's the same voice that warned me against Parker, so I tell her to shut the hell up.

"I want a family." It's true. "But I don't know how to be in one." Again, true.

A smile tugs at his lips, he pulls them into his teeth. "You can start by coming to dinner tonight."

CHAPTER TWENTY-EIGHT

After a silent and awkward drive up here, we found Maria, Vinny, and Jules in the massive kitchen. Once hellos went out, everyone was booted from the kitchen- except me.

"I thought you didn't let people help you cook."

"I don't." Well, that clears everything up.

"Heard rumors of my impressive ramen skills?"

She giggles, stirring something in a steaming pot. Giggles but doesn't answer. Cool.

"So, are you, my mom, now?" I ask, turning on the faucet and plunging my hands into the stream of water.

BROKEN

She laughs outright, her eyes filled with warm affection as she pulls a clean hand towel out of a drawer and stands next to me. "I'm whatever you want me to be. According to the state, I'm just the witness-" Her sudden stop makes me look up. I follow her gaze, and that's when I see what made her freeze.

My sleeve had slipped just enough to reveal the tail ends of four purple gashes on the bones of my wrist. My heart seizes, and my body becomes paralyzed.

The towel falls gently across mangled skin. "Not today," She says so gently it's physically painful to hear, "but one day, I hope you'll be able to talk about what happened to you."

"Please don't tell anyone," I say softly, tears threaten to break the dam down. My chest vibrates with every breath as my panic tries to push past my eyes and up my throat.

"There isn't anything to tell."

"They can't know." I shake my head, almost violently. "No one can know." He'll punish anyone who knows. He can't find out.

Her brow falls low, but the kindness in her eyes remain. "I won't say anything. You have my word."

I nod, unable to speak. I fear the motion of opening my mouth will disintegrate the cement holding my walls upright, allowing years of unshed tears, hurt and pain to fall unchecked from my body and drown the world.

BROKEN

"What's the ETA for dinner?" Drew comes in through the large archway; I turn my face to hide the panic. "I'm starving."

"Boy, don't you know not to rush me? Come in here again; I'll bust your butt with that pot and have to start all over again."

I pull on a brave face while my hand fists around the fabric of my shirt. Drew gives me a wink before going back the way he came, beautifully unaware.

Maria silently lays salad items out on the counter, "Chop, peel and rinse." Her warm smile sits on her face as if the world as I know it didn't just come to a complete standstill.

With a deep breath, I welcome the distraction of preparing; it gives me uninterrupted time to pull my shit together.

My heart rate returns to normal as I help set the table. Josh and Drew are arguing over the TV while Vinny and Jules laugh and encourage them to continue. Parker is leaning against the wooden beam separating the dining room from the den, his eyes looking at everything but me.

Parker sits across from me tonight. Drew took my left next to Josh at the head. I appreciate the fact that Maria sat between Josh and Parker and not once did her eyes wander to my wrist. She carried on like it was all in my head. Vinny rests at the opposite end with Jules on his right, Josh and him are going back and forth about which end is the real head; Vinny believes it's his end because he's older. Josh says it's his end because it's his house.

Everything has been normal and lighthearted, except for the fact Parker hasn't so much as uttered a word to me since we left his place and that was only to ask if I needed to stop at my house. He's laughed and joked, so it's gotta be me that's causing this reaction, and I don't know where to start to try and fix it.

"So... does this adoption thing mean Haley's humping her cousin now?"

The popping noise following Josh's hand colliding with Drew's head doesn't even register. Parker has his eyes squeezed shut, slightly wrapping his head like he's trying to shove away an unwanted thought.

"Andrew Mason!" Maria tries to sound scolding but ends up laughing.

"What the hell is wrong with you?"

"I asked a legit question." He grumbles, rubbing his head.

I feel the first piece of my heart break off entirely and quickly stone my face to hide the heartbreak. He's bothered by this. He doesn't want me, I made things weird. That's why he's been silent and avoiding me.

I force a smile when people look at me for a reaction.

BROKEN

"I'll be right back." As gracefully as I can manage, I push away from the table. Staying collected in the hallway, I race down the tile floor locking myself in the bathroom as pain pushes past my eyes and shame drips off my chin.

This is stupid. Crying over a guy that I've been trying to push away from the start. This should be a good thing. He'll finally stop asking me out; we can carry on as friends. If this is a good thing why do I feel like my world is ending? Why is there this God-awful fucking ache in my chest?

I choke on my cry when someone knocks. I silently clear my throat and I try to come off fine, but I put on a shit performance, "Just a minute."

"Hales?"

"Hold on."

He doesn't. Drew pushes the door open, shutting it behind him. What the fuck, I locked it!

He doesn't speak as he grabs my shoulder and pulls me into his chest. Fun fact- being hugged when you're upset only makes you cry harder.

"I'm sorry." He whispers to the top of my head. "God, I'm so sorry."

"He doesn't want me anymore," I whisper back.

"What?"

"Parker. He doesn't want me anymore."

He pulls away just enough to look at me, "What are you talking about?"

"The papers. He's just not- he doesn't-" I suck in my lip as Drew pulls me back, squeezes me tighter than before.

"That's shitty, sweetheart. I'm sorry. You wanna get out of here?" I nod into his chest. "Okay, wait here. I'm gonna go get my keys."

He sneaks back out leaving me alone for a just a second. I let my hair fall over my shoulders to hide my red, tear-stained cheeks as we walk to the front door.

"Mama Mia!"

"Yeah?" Maria calls down the hall.

"Hales has a migraine. I'm taking her home, tell everyone bye for us?"

"Of course." She says approaching from the hall. "I'm sorry you're not feeling well." She hugs Drew as I continue to look at my feet.

"Love you." He tells her and then we're out the door.

The brick walkway feels uneven under my feet as we cross his bike. The edges of the brick feel piercing under my shoes.

"Long way or short way?" He asks handing me the helmet.

"I don't care."

Without another word, he climbs on waiting for me to throw my leg over before peeling out of the drive.

BROKEN

He took the long way, which is fine with me. Drew couldn't hear me cry over the wind, I could hug him without being weak, and the chill of the winter night helped distract me from the torment inside my chest.

The part that sucks the worst is that I didn't have to be with him to have my heart broken.

CHAPTER TWENTY-NINE

The first thing I did when he dropped me off was toe off my shoes and shed my pants. I kicked the denim across the room, on the way to the kitchen. Filling a mug with water, I shove it into the microwave. I've been home all of two minutes when a knock sounds. Of course- because Heaven forbids if I'm left alone to sulk. Looking through the peephole- who other than, Parker.

Why wouldn't Parker be here, right? I push the door open and go back into the kitchen without a word. The door closes, and I have to look up to see if he's still there.

BROKEN

His hands are in his pockets, the muscle in his forearm flexing. Fuck, he's pretty. I pull my eyes and watch the little cup spin inside the microwave. Ignoring the hurt rising in my throat.

"What happened?"

"With what?" Give me a mother fucking award! That was a beautiful delivery of complete nonchalance despite the hurricane of emotions rattling inside me.

"You just left."

"I've had a headache all day, Parker. I was tired, Drew said he'd bring me home."

"Something's wrong." Yeah, no shit.

"Yeah, my head is threatening to crack open." The microwave beeps, granting me a few seconds to try and ground myself.

Carefully removing the mug, I tear the top off a teabag and drop it into the cup, watching the water seep into the pores, filling it with its watery anchors before pulling it down. Huh- that's pretty much an exact representation of how my chest feels right now.

"You didn't tell anyone you were leaving- neither did Drew."

"So, is he expecting a house call too?"

Ignoring my question, his voice turns very serious. "What are you doing?"

"Making tea."

"Not that, I mean why are acting like this?" Just trying to keep my shit together is all.

BROKEN

"Like what?" I dunk the tea bag into the water a little harder than necessary, watching as the rich color poisons the water in thick clouds.

"Distant." I don't answer; I don't know how. I'm trying not to show him that I'm hurting. "What happened? You seemed fine at dinner and then just bolted."

"I didn't bolt. I had a headache, Drew offered to take me home. You and Josh were somewhere in that maze of a house, so we left. We told Maria to let you know. It's not like I hoped on a bus for state lines, I came home."

"That's not it. Something happened. Either I did something, or you climbed back into your head and ran because of Drew's mouth. Either way, it's not a headache. What freaked you out?"

"I'm not freaked out. I'm tired. I've had a hell of a day; I just want to go to bed."

I catch his head shake out of the corner of my eye. "You're closing yourself off again."

"I am not. I think I'm quite forthcoming." In bullshit. I avoid his eyes, opening cabinets looking for the little packets of sugar I shoved somewhere.

"Look at me."

"What?" I heard him just fine; I just don't have a way out of that request yet.

"Look at me, Haley."

"Hold on; I'm trying to find the sugar." I climb up the counter to look in the back of the cabinets. In reality, I'm considering climbing in there and hiding from the world.

"I did something." His voice is much closer than it was before. Fuck. No, no. Close proximity is a bad idea.

"No, you didn't. Do you have sugar at your place?" Say yes. Go get it. I can come up with a plan while you're gone. Say yes.

"Baby, get off the counter."

Don't call me that, fissures spread across the surface of my already bleeding heart. "Sugar, yes or no?"

"You're not looking for sugar; you're looking for an escape. Get down."

If I climbed in here, I think he might have me committed, so I slowly climb down looking through the empty drawers.

"You're trying to push me away, why?"

"Don't be ridiculous."

"You think you're so tricky, but I know what you're doing. You're sacrificing your happiness for mine. When are you going to realize you are my happiness?"

It's like being hit with the buckle, but instead of my ribs, it's my chest. It's like when he was with Lacy, he wanted out, but he didn't want to be the asshole...and he shouldn't be the asshole in this. I'm the one who made it weird- go figure Ryan went and fucked up another good thing.

"I'm not sacrificing anything." Just that thing in my chest that keeps me alive.

"Either I did something, or you're having one of yourself sacrificing moments. Spill."

"Fine. Look, it was fun, now it's over." I shrug like it's no big deal even though I can feel the stiffness in my ribs every time I inhale.

"Bullshit."

"Parker- we're basically related now, it's weird." For you.

"If we were related, I'm pretty sure I could go to jail for the things I've done to your body."

"I don't know what you're looking for, Parker. I'm not the one with the problem. Now answer my earlier question, do you have sugar? Cause I'd like to drink this and go to bed."

He grabs my arm, twisting me to face him, I avoid his eyes and look at the floor. I've been crying, and I don't want him to know. His thumb raises my chin before skirting my tear stained cheeks, "Who said I had a problem?"

I step back waving at him, "You're obviously bothered! You wouldn't hold eye contact; you're not talking, not touching, nothing. The second the adoption is brought up you go silent. But it's fine, cause whatever it was we were doing is done. No worries."

You don't want to be the asshole, remember? Just take the out, Parker. Go home.

"You think I'm upset? Haley-" He shakes his head, "No. Surprised? Yes. Shocked that you agreed to it? Fuck yeah, but I'm not upset, I could never be upset about that. And not touching you? You hate being touched, especially when you're upset. I was just giving you room."

"What about your lack of conversational skills and avoiding eye contact?" Shut uuuuuuuuup, Haley. Just stick with repeating how it's over. My heart squeezes at that word. Over.

"I don't know- maybe because anytime I look at you I want to shove you up against the wall? Maybe because you chose my family over your own, so in this selfish way I know I can keep you and that makes my first observation that much stronger?"

"I've been upset before, and that didn't stop you." It was out before I could stop it- I swear.

"For someone claiming not to be interested, you sure are observant. Do you want me to touch you, Haley?" He takes a step forward, and my heart does this flip and flutter thing.

"No," I say quickly. "I don't want you to touch me. I was just making an observation."

"About my hands and how they weren't on your body."

Didn't I point this out before? Sex- the Holy grail to topic jumping.

BROKEN

"Not just your hands but everything else, you're bothered, and I know."

"Do you want everything else to touch you?" His eyes darken, and I realize my mistake.

"No." Damn you, voice! Your breathy ass voice isn't helping sell this shit at all. "I misspoke. I'm saying I wasn't paying attention to your hands; I noticed all those other things too."

"Mhm. You noticed them because you've decided we're done?"

Fuck. He's asking questions too fast; I can't keep the lies straight. "No. I noticed them because you're being obvious. And I'm just not interested in fucking my cousin- so there's that."

Parker takes another step, closing the distance between us. My breath comes in heavier as his hand slides behind my neck the other grabs the sink behind me; he backs me up, so his body is pressed against mine. His mouth skims mine as he speaks, "Tell me you don't want me and I'll leave."

Every breath he takes pushes into my chest. He slides his lips across my jaw, and my heart threatens to beat out of my chest.

I force my eyes to open and try to control my breathing, "I don't want you." Liar, liar, liar.

"I don't believe you." He brushes his lips under my ear and down my neck.

BROKEN

I fight every urge not to arch my back at his touch. This is wrong, his uncle is now my, what- Dad? That, and I think I might be in love with him.

He releases the sink to run his hand up my bare thighs, "Tell me to stop," the sensation sends goosebumps across my body.

I don't want him to stop, I never, ever want him to stop. My throat makes a noise I didn't grant permission for as his teeth graze my throat. My self-restraint threatens to collapse. I know I shouldn't- I should stop this, but he's poisoning my blood, filling my head with high thoughts.

So, instead, I take the moron route and run my fingers through his dark hair, pulling his face to mine. His lips are soft and just as eager as mine as I wrap my arms around his neck. In one swift move, he lifts me and sets me on the edge of the sink, the metal is ice against my burning skin. My body pulses and breathes him in like a drug.

I pull away, grabbing the neck of his shirt and pull it over his head. Shadows fill every contour of his muscular frame as my reservations fly out the window and into oncoming traffic. Grabbing the waist of his jeans, I pull him back into me, his lips find mine until they feel swollen and my lungs constrict.

He moves back to my neck as I pant, pulling precious air into my burning lungs, trying to extinguish the fire he's created. His hands dig into the fabric against my waist, without thinking, I raise my arms, allowing him to lift the t-shirt over my head. His fingers slide up my bare back leaving a trail of fire behind them, the heat of his body presses through the thin material of my sleeves. He kisses a line from my collarbone, up my neck and then follows my jaw until he consumes my mouth once again.

I'm still holding the waist of his jeans, and I pull him even closer. He groans, kissing me harder, his hands tightening around me as he pulls me from the sink.

Wrap my legs around his waist; he steps back holding me against him; we don't break contact until I realize he's going towards my bedroom, "No bed." I pant.

He smiles against my mouth before claiming it once again, he keeps moving down the hall, and I don't think he heard me until I feel the soft down of a comforter on my back, his body pressing me deeper into the mattress. My eyes widen as I take in the gigantic white, four poster bed.

"What the hell- when did you- how did you?"

"Drew never lost his spare." He takes my bottom lip, and I groan.

Fuck the bed; I can ask questions later. His mouth runs a line of flames from my ear, down my neck, his breath pushes through the fabric of my long sleeve before his lips press into my stomach, all the way to the waistband of my shorts, his mouth making me certifiably insane.

His knee falls between my legs pushing them apart.

Every sense, nerve, and thought is consumed by him, gone is the girl who was scared and running, gone are the worries and the rational thoughts. All I can focus on is his hands and his mouth and how there's still too much space between us.

CHAPTER THIRTY

I've figured out the best way to make Parker stop asking questions.

We're both laying on our sides, facing each other in my massive new bed. Every time he starts to ask a question I cut him off by kissing him. His fingers have been threaded through my hair for the last half hour.

I plan on kissing him to exhaustion. If he tries to pull away, all I have to do is rake my nails across his chest. It's as if his chest is a match and my fingers create the friction necessary to light him on fire.

"Why were you-" Closing the gap I cut him off, at this point, it's more of a game than anything else. "No, ma'am." He pulls away. "Talk to me." He's put distance between our bodies- crap. My fingers slide down his sternum, "You're trying to distract me."

"Am not." I smile inwardly when he closes his eyes.

"Are too" His hand collects mine off his chest, he brings it to his lips, kissing my palm. "You're a sneaky little thing."

"If I wanted to distract you, I'd succeed."

"Mhm." His playful doubt makes me smile.

Sitting up, I unhook my bra, sliding the straps down my sleeves before pulling it out from under my shirt, Parker watches with mild amusement.

"As I said, if I wanted to distract you," I start, crawling over to him, "I'd succeed." I slip one leg over his waist, his hands automatically slide up my thighs, resting on my hips as I straddle him. He pulls his bottom lip watching his thumbs circle my hip bone.

Grabbing the hem of my shirt, I inch it slowly up my stomach, stealing his genius idea, I hook the hem behind my neck before pulling my hair through. His chest is rising and falling rapidly as his fingers glide across my skin, exploring the new boundaries drawn.

"How's this for distracting?" I rock my hips against him; his grip tightens, the muscle in his jaw flexing.

Blue eyes land on mine. "You aren't going to talk about what happened are you?" Running my fingers through my hair, I slowly rock against him again. "Fuck."

BROKEN

Sitting up he makes it, so we're nose to nose, his lips pushing mine apart. Lifting me up on my knees, there's a brief moment of heavy breathing between us as he pushes inside me. Swallowing my gasp, his arms twist around me, one keeping me pressed against his chest, the other knots in my hair as we lose ourselves once again. This is where I want to be.

"Don't run." He breathes against my mouth.

"I won't."

"Promise me." His fingers dig deeper into my hip.

"I promise." I pant as the coil inside me tightens, "God, I promise."

With snake-like movement, he presses me onto my back, driving deeper inside me. God, Fuck, and Parker fall from my lips as he buries himself deeper until that coil snaps. I'm ripped from the mattress as my body seizes around him. His hand grasps the back of my neck as his teeth dig into my shoulder. He slams into me one last time before his hand vises around my hip.

I don't want to be anywhere but here. Only here. Only him.

Falling asleep with Parker is probably my favorite thing at this point. The way he moves my hair so he can kiss my shoulder or neck. The way my body molds so perfectly with his, the way his fingers draw absently across my skin.

BROKEN

The steady beat of his heart against my shoulder blades, the rise, and fall of his chest, all of it is like a little piece of heaven created just for me.

When he slides out of bed, my happy place breaks a little. He grabs his buzzing phone out of his pants pocket, "Hold on." he whispers.

I hear the denim ruffle against his skin as he slips them on. When he passes my feet, I watch him slip out of my room, closing the door silently behind him. His voice is a low muffle from the living room. I roll over and find that my shirt is still slipped behind my sore neck. I sit up, correcting the fabric, but it's still tight and uncomfortable.

Pulling the covers down, I slide out of bed and grab a zip up hoodie from the pile in the corner of my closet. In lightening speed, I pull my shirt off, immediately replacing it with my hoodie, and climb back into bed. I was just wishing for a bed like Parker's, and here I am laying in a giant white four post bed. And it smells like him now too, the icing on the cake.

Footsteps approach the door, a second later the doorknobs twists and his bare chest greets me before those blue eyes land on mine.

"Morning, gorgeous."

"Mornin'." I mimic his slight Georgian accent.

He smiles climbing up the foot of the bed; he lowers himself giving me a sweet kiss, "You're cute."

"How come Drew's twangier than you?"

He chuckles, laying down beside me. "Twangy, huh?"

"It's a word."

"Is it?" He chuckles playing with my zipper.

"It's got letters doesn't it?"

He laughs openly, "Point made. And I don't know why his stuck."

"Yours stuck too."

His nose scrunches as he shakes his head, oh my god he's adorable. "Nope, I speak twang-less."

I laugh, "That's not a word."

"It's got letters doesn't it?" He smiles down at me.

"I wouldn't know, it's hard to spell noises."

"Noises? I'll show you noises." His fingers tickle down my ribs.

"No!" I laugh, pulling my knees up, trying to stifle his assault. "Parker!"

"Say it."

"Ah! Say what?" Another heave of laughter bubbles out.

"Twang-less is a word."

"Twang-less is a word! It's a word."

His fingers still, "Are you sure? It doesn't sound like it is." My mouth falls open in mock offense, "Use it in a sentence."

"It's your word! You make a sentence."

"I," he leans down kissing me, "speak twang-less."

"No, you don't. But it's sexy."

"Hmm," his lips fall over mine once again, "Alright, maybe I have a little twang." He holds his finger and thumb apart, demonstrating the tiny sliver in between.

I nod with a smile. "Then we're agreed." His lips close against mine, heating my blood. I moan as his fingers pull the zipper down, I didn't think people actually had sex as much as we do. I thought that was all made up to stroke egos, but hot damn if I don't want to all the time. He kisses me once chastely before pulling the zipper back up.

"Wha- why is that happening?"

He chuckles as he sits up, "We have to behave. Josh is dropping by for a sec."

"How come?"

He shrugs. "I don't know. He tried to call you, but I think your phone's still out in the living room, so he called me to see if I was with you. Said he needed to drop something off for you."

I wonder if it's something I have to do for the adoption? A pit forms in my stomach the second the thought crosses my mind, I'm glad I didn't ask that out loud. My happiness starts to thin as reality comes crashing down, taking hold with its icy grip. The adoption makes Parker weird, the ignoring, the argument, the hot makeup sex, though I don't think we made up...if he wanted out would he have slept with me? Doesn't really seem his style to string me along.

Forcing an air of confidence, I sit up, "Does the adoption make things weird?"

He pauses at the foot of the bed, turns slowly and leans against the bedpost, "Not even a little, at least for me. Is it weird for you?"

"Are you sure?"

"Is it weird for you?" He repeats.

"Not in the way it could be weird for you."

"Explain."

"It's weird to be wanted." I shrug, drawing my sleeve into my hand. "It's weird to be chosen and not seen as a nuisance. But it's not weird being with you."

"That's what last night was about." It's not a question, more like he was simply speaking his thought process as he studies the ground, "You thought I was going to end it, so you tried to do it first." His eyes meet mine, "Why did you think that?"

I shrug, "Just did."

"Not an answer. Try again."

"You just seemed really distant."

"So, distance means I want to end this?" Nothing about his body language or tone is angry, but my heart still picks up speed. I shrug.

"No, sweetheart. Walk me through this."

BROKEN

"When you were with Lacy, you wanted out, but you didn't want to be the asshole. Last night I was giving you your out."

A pained expression crosses his face as he shakes his head. "Baby, that's the last thing I want." Coming around, he sits down at my feet, "I was waiting for you to freak out and bolt. Everything seemed too good to be true, and I was fully expecting to wake up this morning with a note taped to my door, and a million missed calls from Drew."

"Then why were you so distant?"

"It wasn't intentional. I couldn't pull the nightmare out of my head and was obsessing over ways to get you to stay if you tried to leave."

"But when Drew asked if I was fucking my cousin you made this face like it was the nastiest thing that ever crossed your mind."

His hand pushes the hair behind my ear before pulling me forward. His lips brush my jaw then softly across my lips, "I thought his constant jokes were going to be the nail in the coffin. I made Drew go apologize after you left the table, then you were gone, and I was scared I wasn't going to get here in time."

"So, you were weird because you thought I was going to run, not because a piece of paper says we're related?"

"Correct."

"So, you're fine having sex with your cousin?" His laughter shakes the bed as he rests his forehead against my shoulder.

Pulling back he tries to slow it enough to talk, "I feel like this is one of those Catch-22 situations, so I'll say this- I like having sex with you. Like is putting it incredibly lightly but there's your answer."

My heart does this little dance inside my chest, and I force myself not to cry. "I thought I lost you last night," I whisper.

"Oh, sweet girl." He smiles at me, "You're going to need so much more than a piece of paper to make me even consider that."

"Like what?" I ask because apparently, I love pain and awful conversations.

"Having a dick might do it."

I snort-laugh, "What?"

"If you had a dick, I might consider it."

"Might?"

"Well it's hard to picture that situation, I'm well acquainted with the area in question. But if you did, there are a lot of things that we would have to sort out." How is he doing this with a straight face? "Like, would you be willing to lop it off? Is it bigger than mine?" I laugh harder, "It would all depend on your answers."

I can't talk through the giggles, so I simply shake my head at him.

"Now that we're talking about it," He starts pulling the covers away from my waist, "I feel like I should inspect the area again."

"What about Josh?"

"It's cool that Y'all are close, but I can assure you he isn't needed for this part."

My eyes bulge as I push his shoulder, "Gross!"

He laughs, taking my face in his hands, he kisses me while lowering me to the mattress. Unzipping my hoodie as his mouth slides down the center of my body.

"Thought you said he was coming over." I pant as he gets closer and closer.

"I should probably make this a quick observation and perform a detailed inspection later."

I nod against the pillow too caught up in how close he is and the hands that are wrapping around my thighs. My hips buck, "Pretty sure you're stuck with me, love."

I'm not able to answer after that.

Pulling my hair into a half-assed bun, I race down the hall to open the door.

Josh gives me a warm smile as he holds a little white box. My brows pinch, "Catch." Stepping back, I catch the little rectangle and then glare at him. He chuckles stepping inside.

Rolling the box over, I see the logo. "What is this?"

"What do you think? Hey, Parker."

It's a fucking brand spanking new iPhone. There's a number that follows that, but I don't pay attention to that part. Popping the lid off I look at the pearl white face. Jesus, it's beautiful.

"She's got a flip phone for fuck's sake," Josh tells Parker who smiles. "You have a new number, hope you weren't attached to old one."

"How much do I owe you?" I ask turning it on. When he doesn't answer I look up; brown eyes glare back at me. "What?"

"Nothing. You owe me nothing. Perks to being one of my kids."

I make a face, "I can't-"

"Where the hell is all your stuff?" He looks around at my bare apartment.

"Don't trash my place. I like it this way."

"Convenient?"

"Very." I throw back in the same bitter tone.

"For running?"

I look up with a glare of my own. "This whole Brady Bunch thing is new to me. Give me time; I'll put stuff in here. I lived in a motel before this. Baby steps."

His glare vanishes as his features smooth, "You ever had one of those before?"

He nods to the phone in my hands that I'm currently button smashing on.

"Nope. Flip phone was my one and only. But I talked to Drew on Parker's the other day."

Josh chuckles, "Do you have an email?" I shake my head, and he laughs. "You're eighteen and don't even have an email. You are disproving every teenage stereotype."

Pulling his phone out of his pocket he proceeds to create all the necessary accounts to get the phone on.

"This is cool. I'm scared I'm going to break it though."

Josh shrugs, shrugs. "We'll get you a protective case. What are your plans today?"

"Don't have any," I say over my shoulder, sitting on the couch. "How do I put phone numbers in?"

"How do you-? Seriously?" Josh chuckles, "Help her will ya?"

Parker smiles in response, approaching the couch. I expected him to sit at my feet like he usually does but instead his arms snake under my legs and behind my back, lifting me and then sitting me in his lap, so my back is against his chest.

"See that?" He points to a little green button, I nod. "Press it." A white screen opens.

"Alright kids, I got shit to do, I'll see you guys later. Haley, you good to work tonight?"

"Yeah, why wouldn't I?"

"Just checking." He pulls his sunglasses from his shirt before waving. "Bye."

He slips out the front door as I twist back around and snuggle up under Parker,

"Where's the camera?"

"Push this." I do, "Now scroll over...right there." Opening the app, I lift the phone which Parker immediately lowers.

He presses a button so I can see myself on the screen- that's fucking cool. Raising the phone again he presses his face into my neck and blows air against my skin just as the shutter sounds.

"Behave!" I swat at him. He smiles pulling me in and kissing my cheek. "Okay, take another one." He's got this shit down to a science, this one he pulled my face against his in a panty dropping kiss- I nearly dropped my damn phone.

"You're bad." I scold with a smile.

"In a really hot way though, right? Girls love bad boys."

"In a very hot way." He kisses my nose before wrapping his arms around my waist and smiling for the photo. It's heartbreakingly sweet, and I abso-fucking-lutely made it my wallpaper. After our little photo shoot, I leaned back and let him teach me all about the wonders of the iPhone.

CHAPTER THIRTY-ONE

We played with my phone then ended up playing with each other before Parker needed to do some birthday shopping for Drew that evidently required my attendance, so I'm standing in a store dedicated solely to sports as he fills a basket.

"I thought Drew was a diehard Cardinals fan?"

"He is." He answers, dropping a Steelers mug into the basket.

"Then who's that for?"

"Josh."

"Umm...?" I laugh uneasy, "But Josh likes the Cardinals, too."

"I know."

"Not to hurt your male ego or anything but that's Pittsburgh."

BROKEN

The right side of his mouth raises, "I know. He hates the Steelers. I do this every year, twice a year."

I scoff-laugh, "Why?"

"Because it drives him crazy. Got him footed pajamas for his birthday."

"That's so mean! Why would you buy him something he hates?"

"To drive him crazy. I've been doing it so long; I think he might get offended if I stopped."

I shake my head, fingering a football helmet chess board.

"What are you going to get him?"

"For Christmas?" He nods and my stomach drops, I forgot that I was going to have to attend the Hayes family holidays now, "I don't know. '#1 Dad' cup?" I laugh awkwardly.

"He'd actually like that. What are you getting Drew?"

"A swift kick in the ass." I got him a blow-up doll from the novelty shop for his birthday this weekend.

"What am I getting?" He wags his eyebrows at me.

"Me." I smile sweetly.

Humor slips from his face when I look back at him, "If you're kidding, that's a mean joke."

I roll my eyes, putting the little helmets back on their designated squares. A hand finds my hip, twisting me to face him. "Go out with me. It can be my Christmas present."

"What a shitty gift that would be."

His face scrunched up, "For who? Cause I can assure you, that's at the top of my list."

"You get sex, and that's better than a date."

"Let's put that theory to the test. Go out with me, and we can compare the two."

"We're out right now."

"I'm talking about a good old-fashioned date not keeping me company at a mall."

"It's just the two of us; we're talking, you're spending money- sounds like it's more or less the same thing."

He slowly shakes his head with a small smile playing across his lips, "What kind of fucked updates have you been on?"

I haven't, but I've seen them on TV. "Are you done yet?"

"I am if you'll go out with me."

"Parker! No, stop asking."

He laughs, bending forward to brush a kiss against my lips, "Say yes and I will."

"I have to work tonight, and your shenanigans are going to make me late."

"If I had it my way my shenanigans would keep you from going to work."

"Due to my family's shenanigans, I've gotta step my game up if I want to keep my income."

"If we keep using the word 'shenanigans' I'm going to have to learn how to spell it. Come on; you're taking forever."

I scoff as he turns for the counter. "Yes, because I was the one who was taking forever."

"I know. You're lucky I'm a patient man."

The urge to roll my eyes is cut short when Parker reaches down to take my hand, gently bringing it to his lips and kissing my palm. How can such a tiny thing make my chest ache this much? Seriously, it's like I see the hole I'm digging, but I just keep throwing shovelfuls over my shoulder like it's my job.

I'm an idiot, and I realize that but my brain has cut off the ability to amend that. His fingers fall between mine, linking our hands together before pulling me forward, so we're chest to chest. Leaning down he tips my face up with his nose and kisses me with one of his knee-bustingly sweet kisses. I'm aware 'bustingly' isn't a word, but his lips are on mine, and my brain is deprived of oxygen as his mouth floods my mind with naked thoughts. Walls- I'd like some right now.

He pays for his gag gifts, reclaiming my hand before escorting me to the car. Hand holding- how can that possibly be a turn on? I'm convinced Parker is killing off my brain cells.

"What the fuck?" I lean forward looking out the windshield. I see Vinny and Drew carrying a big ass table covered in plastic over the courtyard from my seat in the Camaro while Parker pulls into his spot.

Climbing out of the car, I'm able to see Josh's truck is connected to a flatbed trailer that's packed with shit. "What's happening?"

Parker doesn't respond as he steps around the car, reaching for my hand. I let him take it and lead me to where Josh is leaning over the bed of his truck, unstrapping a neon yellow belt.

"What the hell is happening?" I demand.

"Oh good. You're here; you can unlock the door."

"What?"

"Door. That big piece of wood that allows you to enter your house. Unlock the metal part."

"I know what a door is. What is all of this?"

"Housewarming party. Door, please."

Wait, no. This isn't for me. No fucking way am I letting him furnish my house. They have to know I'd never be okay with this. "For who?"

Josh rolls his eyes, his hands still unhooking the straps. "Seriously? Who do you think?"

"It's not for me, so who?"

"Why do you make everything so difficult? Just say thank you and open the door."

"You got me a phone. I'm good. Thank you."

"You're not living in an empty apartment. I've got shit to do-" He points towards my apartment building, "Open the door."

BROKEN

"How did you even-" Parker. I twist in his grip, so we're facing each other, "YOU."

He shrugs, shrugs.

I give him a scorching glare before turning back to Josh, "I can't. Take it back."

"You can't open a door?" Josh's incredulous tone is starting to annoy me.

"No, jackass. I can't accept this stuff. A phone was more than enough. I don't need all of this."

"You know what the funnest part about being me is?"

I glare at him without answering.

"Not giving a shit if you want something or not. It's here; it's for you. Unless you want to haul all this inside yourself, open the door so the guys can do it for you."

I huff, grabbing my hair. The feeling of awkwardness blooms inside my stomach sending its pollen to invest my body. "Josh-" I sigh. "Shit like this makes me feel uncomfortable. I told you I'd get stuff-"

"Again, funnest part of being me. You're not getting any special treatment here, Haley. I got Parker and Drew started off too. Bonus for being my kid." The belt finally gives, and he wraps it in his hand before placing it in the metal box connected to the bed of his truck.

Exasperated by his dismissal, I turn to Parker seeking backup.

"Don't just stand there! Help me."

"You want to get the smaller boxes, and I'll get the good stuff?"

I huff and shove his shoulder. "Ugh, men! Josh, stop ignoring me. Take. It. Back."

He leans against the truck and smiles, "No."

"Why not?!"

"Because this is what I do and I enjoy it."

"Pissing me off? Cause that's what's happening." I'm not actually mad, more like this awkward noose is around my neck, and I'd do anything at this point to make it disappear.

"Fine. Merry Christmas, Santa came early."

"Buy me a pen for Christmas, not a house full of stuff!"

Parker and him share the same scrunched up expression, "A pen?" Josh asks not bothering to smooth his appearance.

I shrug with a slight nod, "Yeah."

"Like a regular writing pen?" Parker asks, "Does it have to be basic blue or black ink or can we go all out and get a fun color?"

"Fuck off. This is too much, and you know it, or you would have asked or given me some sort of heads up rather than have Parker go out and distract me."

"Whoa-" Parker pipes up, almost offended. "I didn't even know about this."

"Well, you don't exactly look surprised."

"It's Josh." He states this like its common knowledge that he goes out and spends what I can only imagine is thousands of dollars on someone at the drop of a hat.

"Hey, sunshine. Look! New shit!" Drew hugs me from behind, his bicep pushing into my arm.

It becomes incredibly hard to breathe. "Let go, let go, let go."

His embrace falls away immediately, "Shit. Sorry. Hardy high five?"

I slap his outstretched hand, ignoring the curious slash worried expressions that are on me.

"Hi, Vinny."

"Miss Carter," He dips his head, "Or should I say, Hayes?"

Oye, that's a heavy dose of awkward, isn't it? "Uhh..."

"She wants us to load it all back up." Josh says lazily, "Doesn't want it."

"Well have fun. I'm not reloading the trailer. You don't want it. You load it, sunshine."

Open and closing my fist; I try to push the darkness back. "Want to go inside?"

I didn't even realize Parker had moved behind me. I nod and let him lead me to what I initially thought was going to be his apartment, but instead, he steered me left at the fork and up to my door. A shit ton of stuff sits covered in plastic.

"This is too much," I whisper.

"This is what family does. It's strange to you because you've never had one. He's looking out for you. Let him." Parker has this stupid way of getting me to do shit, and it's starting to piss me off.

I dig into my pocket and slap the key into his hand. He smiles, knowing he won and opens the door. I wiggle my arms while pacing as I watch the men trickle in with more and more and more shit. Fuck, I'm going to be busy. I can't watch this. My entire living and dining room area is packed with stuff, and they're still making trips.

I decide the perfect escape is just to get ready for work. I slip in the shower, brush out my hair, brush my teeth and change into my VIN's uniform. Throwing on my blue knockoffs, I exit to thankfully, empty apartment.

"Oy vey."

CHAPTER THIRTY-TWO

Apparently, because I signed those damn papers it gave Josh the right to drive me fucking insane. I finished my shift at VIN's, got to HEAT and he fucking sent me home. But of course, the fun doesn't end there, after storming off like a child I went outside where Parker and his Camaro waited because I was apparently the only one unaware of this grand scheme. Not three seconds after pulling into the apartment complex Drew pulled into guest parking.

"I find it endlessly annoying that I'm always the last to know." I huff as I climb out. I don't have the heart to slam the car door but dammit if I don't have the urge to.

"Sup', sunshine!"

BROKEN

I roll my eyes and walk past him. I'm not in the mood for this shit.

"What's up with you?"

"Unlike you guys, I need to work but apparently I can't because my apartment is full of a bunch of shit I didn't ask for. So, apparently that's reason enough for Josh to keep me from earning the money I need if I want to continue to live here, but whatever, you know?"

Do I sound ungrateful? Yes. Am I? Probably a little. It's not my fault; I'm not used to kindness. Everything I've ever received always came with a price. I prefer to do shit on my own for a reason.

"Hales, you've got like a grand stuffed in your bra, and we both know it. Plus, Parker kinda owns this place. I think he'll let it slide if you're ever short."

I throw my arms, spinning on him. "That's not okay, Drew! Just because I'm sleeping with him doesn't give me the right to take advantage of that!"

He steps forward and tries to take in my shoulders; I immediately withdraw from his reach. "And that's why he'd let it slide. You're not the type to take advantage."

I look at Parker who, as usual, is completely silent watching on. Damn it if it doesn't piss me off sometimes. "Nothing?"

"What?" He asks.

I blow out an angry burst of air and stomp on my door.

"Are you like on your period or something?"

Closing my eyes, I count to ten and slowly blow out a breath. Gently reminding myself that he's my best friend and I don't actually want to kill him. Unlocking the door, I slip inside beyond annoyed.

I leave the door open and go straight to my room, pulling off my heels I toss them into the corner of the closet before grabbing a pair of yoga pants and a zip-up hoodie from the pile of clothes on the opposite side.

"Not in the mood for any more banter, Drew."

"Not Drew." I turn to see Parker leaning against the doorframe with his arms crossed over his chest. "What's wrong?"

"Nothing."

"Something. I know it's not what Drew suggested, so what is it?"

I exhale loudly looking at the clothes in my hand before meeting his expectant gaze. "Nobody listens." I shrug. "I keep saying all of this is too much and no one listens. I swear I'm one panic attack away from checking myself into the psych ward. I'm not used to any of this, and it's just too much."

He steps forward with hands extended; I allow him to pull me against his chest. I don't care who you are- anything can feel better with a good hug.

"People care about you now, sweetheart. They want to make you feel it."

"I felt it before all of this extravagance; I don't need it."

"Well, some of it you do."

I stiffen in his arms, and he chuckles.

"Sweetheart, you don't have dishes or even silverware."

"So? I do just fine without it. Plus, I never have to do dishes."

"What about when you want cereal?"

"I go to your place." I smile into his chest.

"If y'all are getting naked, I'm gonna be so pissed!" Drew yells down the hall, and I roll my eyes.

"I'm going to kill him one day."

He chuckles, kissing my hair. "How about if I tell them to back off with all of the- what did you call it? Extravagance?" I nod. "Okay, how about I tell them to stop, and you accept what's already in your possession?"

"Including Christmas?"

"If you want."

"Fine. If you tell them to stop buying me shit, I'll stop being bitchy."

"Gah, you're getting freaky, aren't you?"

"Ugh! Your balls are about to be the star on my tree if you don't knock it off!" I yell back.

"On second thought, maybe it'd be best if you were. It would fix your mood!"

"I'm seriously going to kill him."

Parker chuckles before kissing my cheek and letting me go. He nods to the bathroom before retreating down the hall.

I change quickly, pulling my hair up into a messy bun. The guys have pulled almost all of the plastic off the furniture and have opened all of the boxes to reveal their contents. Framed landscapes, decorative bowls, one with nothing but sheets of black wood.

"God, there's so much."

"That's why we're here." Drew smiles up from where he's kneeling. "We men. We build." He says in a caveman's voice while pounding on his chest.

"You're an idiot." I laugh. "What's that?" I nod to the box he's currently opening.

"Don't know yet."

"How did he manage to get all of this on such short notice?"

Drew laughs, "He more or less just ordered everything out of the sample rooms."

My eyes grow, "What?"

"Yeah, you know how they have mock rooms, we went in, and he pointed, bought whatever was available. If it wasn't, he just got the closest thing."

Jesus, the men in this family, have more money than sense. A computer startup sends me spinning around to the kitchen. Parker is leaning over a slim white laptop.

"What the fuck is that?" I shriek.

He gives me a gentle smile, "We need some jams."

"That better be yours."

"He wishes! Josh hooked you up."

I glare at Drew for a moment before turning back to Parker. He holds out his hand; I slide mine against him before it's pulled it to his lips, he speaks against my palm. "It's okay."

"What the hell are these?" Drew asks behind me, I turn to see him holding my stash of Mike and Ike's, "Is this a gallon bag of candy?"

I try to grab it from him, but he pulls it away.

"Why do you have so much?"

"I only like the pink ones," I shrug.

Reaching for the bag again, he lets me take it.

"So why do you have a giant bag of candy you don't like?"

A small ache forms in my chest, but I push it to the side. "I used to give them to Kaylan. I stopped eating them when I realized he wasn't coming home." I notice the candies bounce a little harder than necessary as they land back in the drawer, "I've had this ever since."

"You keep a giant bag of candy?"

"Don't be a dick, Drew. I just do, okay?"

BROKEN

"Why don't you give it to him? Bet it would make him feel like a total doucher."

Probably would. Speaking of Kaylan, I haven't texted him, probably should before he shows up again. "I don't feel like seeing him," I say while unlocking my phone and opening my contacts,

"So? Let me do it. I think it'd be hilarious."

"It would be mean," I say absently while texting,

ME: Hey, It's Haley. This is my new number. Daily text. You're welcome.

Drew's eyebrows are pinched when I put the phone into my pocket, "Who are you texting?"

"Kaylan. We have an agreement. If I send him a text a day, he'll stop dropping by."

"Did you tell him to come over?"

"Nope. Point of the text is not to see him."

"I'm serious, Hales. Let me give him the bag of old ass candy."

I look over Parker's shoulder and watch as he sets up the laptop as I speak, "No. You don't know the whole story. I appreciate you hating him because I do, but there's a lot more to it."

"Like what?" He huffs, I hear his heavy ass land on my counter.

"You sit like a wrecking ball." I shake my head, "Kaylan did more good than bad that's all you need to know."

"If that's true why do you hate him?"

"He left me. He promised he'd take me with him and he didn't."

"That's shitty. How old were you?"

"Eight."

He lets out a low whistle, "Damn. How old was he?"

"Sixteen."

"Did he ever tell you why he didn't take you?"

"My mom came back and got him out. Said I was a liability, so she took him and left."

"So, why are you mad at him if she's the reason Y'all weren't together?"

"He was sixteen. He could have taken me when he left- damn the consequences, but he didn't. He waited eight years to come for me."

"What do you mean?"

I sigh loudly, turning to give him my full attention. "Why are you asking so many questions?"

"Cause you're my best friend and I barely know you. I'm not bothering you for information that sends you into a shaking mess; I'm just curious about you and your brother."

"If I tell you about Kaylan will you stop with the questions?"

"For tonight, yeah."

I roll my eyes, "Kaylan gave a house bunny an envelope with cash, an I.D. and a note that said 'run.' I stuffed it down my pants and left. Got on a bus and ended up here."

"What's a house bunny?" Parker asks to my right.

"That's what we called the girls that came over for drugs or cash. They'd sleep with my brothers or dad in exchange for it."

"Drugs?" Drew's face is so shocked I almost laugh.

"Yep, family business."

"Wait, do you sell?"

I can only imagine the look of horror painted on my face, "What the- Fuck no!"

He throws his hands up in surrender, "I'm just asking! You walk around with a shit ton of cash. It was an honest question. So, back to you and Kaylan, how did you know it was from him?"

"The day Parker found out my real name was the same day Kaylan dropped that it was him that brought it."

"So, he got you out?"

"No, he sent a skank in to deliver it, then waited two years to approach me."

"Hold up, two years? But I thought they were trailing the bus? That shit your mom left at HEAT had a ton of info on your whereabouts between Nevada and here."

I shrug. "I don't know, don't care. But there you go."

"But I still don't understand. It doesn't sound like he had a lot of control over things until recently."

"Whose side are you on?"

"Yours, obviously. Just trying to look at it from all sides."

"Doesn't sound like you're on my side," I mumble turning back into Parker; his hand casually falls to my lower back as the other continues drawing patterns on the little black square.

"I'm always on your side, Hales. So, why hold on to the candy?"

"I don't know. Just did and I don't have the heart to throw it away. It's too good of a reminder."

"Reminder of what?"

"That the people you love never stay." Parker's hand tightens around my middle before he faces me.

"We're not them, sweetheart."

"I never said you were."

He leans in and kisses my cheek, "We're keeping you forever whether you like it or not."

"Everyone hates Lacy, and that bitch is still around." Drew points out. Not sure that's helpful. "Hey! Let's hook her and Kaylan up together!"

"No!" Parker and I say in unison. "Kaylan fucked up, but he doesn't deserve that."

"If I'm your best friend you'll text Kaylan and tell him to come over so I can give him the bag."

"Why? What good will that do?"

BROKEN

"Do you love him?"

"What kind of question is that?"

"An easy one, yes or no?"

I shrug. "Yeah, I guess."

"So, give him the bag. You've held onto it for what- ten years?"

"Something like that."

"Give him the candy, Hales. Not only will it be a kick in the balls but it shows you still care."

"I don't care."

"What the fuck ever! Yes, you do and you should. He fucked up; I get it. But he's your brother; if Parker fucked up, I'd do it."

"If Parker left in the middle of the night and let you take the beatings that followed for eight years and then popped up, you'd be all buddy-buddy with him?"

"Not ignoring the fact you said 'beatings' right now BTdubs, but if he showed up, I'd hear him out, figure out how long he deserved to suffer, and then move on."

I shake my head. "He just needs to leave me alone. He died the night he left."

"Did he die or did you?" Pain spikes my chest, and I feel the sting behind my eyes. I quickly blink to rid the moisture. "Just do it, Hales. Trust me."

I pull my phone out, mainly to just avoid eye contact and unlock it.

BIG BROTHER: Hey, Kitten. Glad I was included in the number swap. How was your day?

ME: I need to give you something.

ME: When are you free?

BIG BROTHER: Now. Where?

ME: My apartment.

ME: Come alone, or I'll have Drew and Parker hold you down while I beat the shit out of you.

BIG BROTHER: Deal. See you in 5.

Five? What, five minutes?

"Says he'll be here in five. I'm handing it to him and telling him to fuck off."

"Fine by me, not unless Parker wants to throw a few back with him?"

"Absolutely not." He mumbles under his hand. "Do you have a YouTube account?"

I laugh, "No."

I'm rewarded with a sexy half smile. A few seconds later music starts to pour from the speakers. "Everything's ready to go."

"Thanks. Don't know what I'll use it for."

"You'll find something, I'm sure." He winks before taking in the furniture, "Tell us where you want stuff."

I sigh and look around, "I have no idea. Just stick shit in places, I guess."

He chuckles motioning for Drew to help him with the weird triangle cabinet thing. Drew and Parker pick it up with ease, moving it to the corner in the dining room. Oh, now the triangle makes sense, it fits into the corner perfectly.

There's so much stuff. With the music blaring I don't think I'll hear the door, so I open it, propping it open with one of the new dining room chairs. I step around Drew who's currently pushing a fluffy recliner into the living room and enter the kitchen to start putting cups and plates into the cabinets. Hands snake around my hips followed by warm breath along my neck. I smile, leaning into his touch.

"Are you sure you want to do this with Kaylan?"

"No."

"You don't have to."

"It's stupid to give them to him; I should have just thrown them away."

"It's not dumb, sweetheart. It's all you had of him."

Jesus- is that why I never got rid of them? Fuck, that's pathetic.

A knock sounds behind me, Parker and I both turn to see a Kaylan in a hoodie and jeans standing awkwardly in the doorway. His blonde hair falls over his gray eyes.

"Hey brother, I'm Drew." Drew stretches his hand out to Kaylan who pulls his from his pocket and accepts. Fucking turn coat.

"Kaylan."

"Hurt her again, and I'll rip your face off."

Kaylan's face falls a second before he catches himself. "Understood."

"Good. This fine piece of man groping your baby sister is my brother, Parker."

A smile hits my face even though I tried to fight it. Drew is doing all of this with a smile though the threat in his voice is very real, I've decided this is my favorite version of Drew.

Kaylan nods to Parker when he refused to take his hands off my waist. "Hey, Kitten."

"Hey."

"You've got a nice place."

"Thanks." I look around, in a few short minutes the guys managed to get almost all the big stuff up against a wall. There are still boxes everywhere, but at least you can see from one room to another.

Leaning to my left, I open the drawer and pull out the massive bag of green, orange, and yellow candies. Parker never let's go or even loosens his hold. The way Kaylan's weight keeps shifting, I think he feels like he's about to get jumped. Kaylan can fight, like fight-fight, but Drew and Parker are massive. They've got a good four inches on Kaylan, and they're built like semi trucks. He doesn't stand a chance against both at the same time. "Here." I hand him the bag.

He stays completely still and entirely silent while he stares. With a hard swallow he reaches forward and takes it. He laughs without humor sifting through the bag. "I still won't eat the pink ones." He gives me a small smile.

"I wouldn't recommend eating those. They're nine or ten years old at this point. Drew thought I should give it to you."

"Metaphoric nut shot." Drew pipes in.

Kaylan nods looking at the bag.

"How does it feel to know she held onto that because she was waiting for your ass to come back?" Drew asks, leaning against the half-wall to the kitchen.

"Like shit."

"You fucked up." Parker's voice runs over my shoulder, and I stiffen. "She doesn't need saving anymore."

"I know."

"But you will if you ever hurt her again." I smile inward. Jesus, knight in shining armor much? I'm not even mad that they think I'm this weak, little girl in need of big, bad body guards, I kinda like it.

"That's my baby sister in your arms." He points to me, "The center of my whole fucking world, despite popular belief. I'll take that ass beating willingly if I hurt her. I just want to get to know her."

"That's not up to us. We got a problem if Hales has a problem. If she's cool with you, we're cool with you."

"Meaning he's cool with you," Parker says dryly. "You did damage, and I don't take lightly to people breaking what's mine." He just called me his, and I kinda wanna squeal, but I also kinda want to bust him in the balls though too. I'm not a piece of property. Still, I let him have his pissing contest, I can yell at him later. "She's too good for that and life has been entirely too hard on her. If you're sticking around to remind her of y'all's past then you can forget it. Here to give her a grim warning and prophet shit-" He lets go of my waist to point to the door before dropping back onto my hip, "There's the door. She's got a family here. Roots. And you're not fucking that up for her. I protect what's mine. I don't care how big or how bad that something is if it comes knocking it's me who it'll be standing toe to toe with. Not to mention the others standing behind me."

I'm pretty sure this is why he's always so quiet. Anytime he speaks it's always this beautiful monologue. He uses the silence to create hypothetical bitch slaps.

"How much do you know?"

"Kaylan," I warn with a shake of my head.

"You haven't told them anything, have you?" His face is pained, and I hate that it makes me feel guilty.

"They know enough. No one needs the details."

"Someone should." He shrugs.

"Kaylan," I give an exasperated sigh, "Even you don't know everything. You were gone for ten years, remember? If you're here to pressure me into talking you can leave. I didn't invite you over for group therapy. You want to hug it out and share your feelings, go talk to mommy dearest."

"She dipped out after that thing at the bar." He shrugs.

I laugh without humor, "Got paid and split. Damn, if that doesn't sound familiar."

"She wanted me to talk to Joey. I said no. She got pissed and left."

My heart slams into the floor. "What?"

"Don't worry. She's not dumb enough to say anything."

"You sure about that?!" I fume, "He's deep in the devil's pocket. We're both fucked if she opens her mouth."

"She won't as long as you're near me. If he left we'd have to follow him around to make sure he- well, you know."

"Is that why it took you so long to approach me?"

"No. I actually didn't know where you were. I knew you got on a bus, but Mom had the guy following you, not me. She thought you were in with him because of how easy it was for you to leave. No one followed, no one went looking. She knew I'd come in guns blazing when I found you, so she kept it a secret to protect me. She wasn't wrong when I found out I came straight here. She followed a couple of weeks later. Ten years was a fucking death sentence, Ry. Once you were free, I had to see you. You may hate me, but I'd rather you hate me then be stuck back there. I know what happened when I was gone. Caroline's got a big mouth when offered enough money."

"What do you do for a living?" Drew asks from his spot against the wall.

"Everything. I do odd jobs wherever I'm at."

"How did you afford to give Hales over a grand and pay that girl to keep her mouth shut about it?"

"Hey, Ry, got a wad of bills tucked away?"

I nod. Duh, of course, I do. He's the one who taught me how to hustle. How to hide money and hide it well.

"Good girl." He nods at me before turning to Drew, "That's how."

"Kaylan's a hustler," I announce.

He nods.

"Pool?" Drew asks.

"Pool, cards," He shrugs. A slow smile climbs up his face, "You still hustle?"

I shrug.

"Did you hustle them?" He nods to each Hayes in turn.

"Maybe."

He laughs and then tries to cover it. "How much?"

"I won Drew's eight back."

"Damn, not bad. It was better when she was little. Not one person believed an eight-year-old could beat a grown ass man at pool. She made out like a bandit." Kaylan's eyes shine with pride. "Ever get good at cards?"

I shrug. "Depends."

"Poker?" He raises his eyebrows. I swear to God, Kaylan could go pro. I've never, ever seen him lose. He's scary good at poker.

"Shit player," I admit.

"Jack?" His brows raise, I can't help it, I smile. "I don't know how you do it." He shakes his head at me before addressing the brothers, "This girl can count cards like no other."

"Stop selling me out." I scold. "You're taking the mystery out."

"Not even close." Drew huffs with a smile. "You gonna teach me?"

"Fuck no. You got hustled- twice. You wanna win some money; you come to me."

"I'll teach you." Kaylan volunteers.

"You will not." I shriek.

"Sorry, Ken Doll. Mama says no."

Drew snorts, "Please."

I send him a glare, and he winks at me with a smile. Enraging man.

CHAPTER THIRTY-THREE

Kaylan stayed for about an hour before making his retreat. Parker and Drew have been helping me find places for the random shit Josh got.

"Hales, what's your favorite thing so far?"

Looking around at my new apartment it's tough to pinpoint one specific thing. My eyes fall on the three black and white photos above the mounted T.V.

"Probably the Ferris wheel." I nod to the center photo.

"Really? You got a fucking laptop, dude." He stares at me like I grew a second head.

"Shut up. I happen to love them."

"Really?" He says with an exasperated sigh.

"Yes, really. They're gorgeous." I huff back, but my annoyance wore off almost immediately as Parker's arms wrap around my waist. His lips drag against my throat, his breath causes goosebumps to race down my arms.

"Ew. God-" Drew exclaims, "Can't Y'all do that nasty shit when I'm not around?"

"You're always around," Parker mumbles against my neck making me giggle.

"It's almost three. I'm gonna head out before I witness shit I can't unsee." He says grabbing his riding jacket off the couch. "Place looks good, Hales."

"Thanks." I smile looking around.

It does. I know I protested, but I'm happy Parker got me to agree because, this place? This place looks impressive; magazine worthy even. I love it.

"Don't make plans for Friday."

I pull away from Parker's mouth to look at Drew, "I'm working."

"No, you're not." He shrugs the thick leather up his broad shoulders, "It's my skin party."

"What the hell is a skin party?" Parker lays his forehead against my shoulder gently chuckling.

"My birthday party." He says with a smug smile, "and it's exactly what you're thinking. Lots of skin."

"You have a naked birthday party?" I ask in horror.

I didn't work his birthday last year and made up an excuse not to go, but I know they're wild. I just didn't realize they were this wild.

He barks out a heavy laugh, "Oh, man. I wish. No, Josh would never allow that, health code and all. But you wear the bare minimum. It's amazing."

"And people go?"

"You're like the only chick I know who is against showing skin, Hales. And guys? We love when a chick is half dressed and grinding against us."

"Yeah, I have to wash my hair on Friday," I tell him with a smile.

He points his thick ape finger at me, "You're going, you're my best friend. I expect skin and lots of it!"

"Put your gorilla finger down; I'll go."

"Good. And you better buy me a present." He stares down at me with all the authority he can manage, "A big present!"

Little does he know I have a blowup doll in the closet with his name on it- literally.

"We'll see." I wink at him before he lowers to peck my cheek.

"Later, Haley, Bailey."

"Bye."

He and Parker nod to one another before he disappears.

BROKEN

The second my fingers fold the deadbolt into place, strong arms spin me around. Before I can yelp, my body is airborne for a moment before I'm thrown over Parker's shoulder. He smacks my ass twice while carrying me down the hall.

CHAPTER THIRTY-FOUR

Drew runs down the sidewalk with me on his back like a freaking moron, making motor sounds. A laugh bubbles out of my throat as I take in the looks people are giving us. Going so far as snort laughing when he tells this old man "beep beep" as we pass.

"You're a fucking idiot." I laugh into his shoulder.

Slowing down, he drops my legs. "Yeah, but you love me anyways."

I smile, moving forward to pull the door open, "Yeah, yeah."

Not paying attention, the thick metal door shoots open catching my forearm in the process. I recoil my arm, stepping back to let the pissed off blonde move past me.

"Where's the fire, sweetheart?" Drew asks behind me.

"Go fuck yourself." She hisses.

I feel my eyebrows pull up as an angry heat spreads over my skin. Drew chuckles, "I'd rather fuck you instead. Might fix your mood there, Princess."

An angry smile creeps across her face, "Come find me when you've got your top rocker, Tiger." Turning away from us I catch the writing across the back of her leather vest, Property of The Bastards.

"What's her vest mean?" I ask Drew as he holds the door open for me, his eyes are glued to her ass.

"Biker Chick. Hot as hell, too."

I roll my eyes with a scoff, "She's a bitch."

He shrugs following me in, "So are you, and I'm not complaining."

"Jerk." Still, I smile and shove him with my shoulder.

"Fuck, dude. She was like seriously hot. Like... Haley hot."

"That's a thing now?"

He nods proudly. "Right though?" He takes another look over his shoulder, "Wonder what pissed her off."

As we move through the club to the employee break room I spot a large group of men all sporting the same leather vests; I nod with my chin. "Said she was a biker chick, right? Those look like bikers to me."

"No shit. With any luck, she'll come back, and I can get her number." He wiggles his eyebrows at me.

"You're such a whore."

"Hungry." He corrects, "I'm *hungry*. It's more polite."

"And misleading." I laugh, entering through the employee's only door.

Hungry whore, ha. I smile at my thought as I pull my dress out of my bag and enter the bathroom. Five hours and I can go home.

"Wave me down if you need anything else." Giving my table a friendly smile, I collect their glasses, placing them on my tray before pocketing the tip they left.

Turning around I catch sight of a man. He's no more than 5'11, thin arms and legs with a rounded belly hidden behind an ironed gray suit. Greasy strands of hair wisp across a growing bald spot. Brown eyes bore into mine.

The tray dips and falls, glass shattering across the floor. Tears fill my eyes immediately and cascade down my cheeks.

I can't breathe.

I can't move.

BROKEN

I can't look away.

I'm frozen in fear.

Faces blur past me as they move to avoid being cut. Eyes burn into me, and I can't run. I try to swallow, but my throat is squeezed shut.

"There's the birthday girl." He says with a smile the devil himself created.

My limbs move before my mind can catch up, I turn and run.

Halfway to Drew, I twist to see if he's following and slam into a chest made of bloody stone, knocking the air out of me.

Josh grunts, catching me. His eyes meet mine before they look over my shoulder to whatever I was running from. "Haley?"

"He found me," I whisper, feeling the tears drip off my chin.

"Who found you?" Josh asks while looking over my shoulder once again before remembering something; he turns me abruptly. I follow, not giving a damn that he's touching me. Pushing me forward to the VIP stairs, we ascend leaving the man and the club behind us.

Entering the VIP room, he reaches for the remote to close the blinds, blocking out our view of the club below. A couple sits on the couch, staring at him in ragged confusion.

He returns to my side, "See the bar for a refund."

Not waiting for their response, he pulls me across the room to his office door, unlocks it and ushers me inside.

His office is clean and surprisingly small. The far wall has four monitors set up with four videos playing on each one.

"Find him." He says nodding to the screens.

On shaky legs I approach, searching each feed for the devil in a flesh suit. There are so many people it's hard to get a good look, but once you've seen a monster, you can find it anywhere. I press my trembling finger to the screen, "There."

"Who is he?"

I shake my head trying to keep the sob inside.

"Haley. I know your private. I get that, but I need to know who he is."

"My father," I whisper, my voice breaks and a small cry follows my words.

"Stay here."

No! I step forward, reaching for him. I don't want to be left alone.

"Josh." It's not a question or word it's a plea.

BROKEN

Reaching forward he picks up a phone, presses two buttons and puts the receiver to his ear. "I've got a problem in VIP. Bring Parker or Drew with you when you come. No one in or out." He pauses a moment listening, nods and hangs up. "Simon's on his way." He looks over my shoulder at the screen, "Are you okay to be by yourself for a minute? I need to go down and do something, anything."

"He already knows." I choke out, remembering the awful words that fell from his lips. "He talked- he talked to me."

His face grows dangerous, "Stay here."

I nod even though I don't want to. With a sad smile that I'm sure was meant to be reassuring, he steps out of the office and leaves me alone. I quickly shut the door and move back to the screen. If I can see him, he can't sneak up on me. Fear chokes me when I can't find him.

Eventually, I catch sight of him by the bar with a beer in his hand. He has this air about him that screams money and sophistication. People are naturally drawn to his charisma and easy smile, but I know the truth. I know what those hands are capable of. I see the things he's responsible for and his line of work, I can count the bodies he's dropped with the snap of those fingers. I know about the blood money in his pocket.

I nearly scream when the VIP door opens. Checking the monitor, I see Simon enter, Parker right behind him.

Launching from the chair, I throw open the door and collide right into Parker's chest, throwing my arms around his neck, the sobs finally break free. His arms fall around me, putting that protective shield around me.

"What's happening?"

"He's here." I sob into his chest.

"Who's here?"

I couldn't talk through the tears, all I could do was squeeze him tighter and cry.

One arm becomes a vice around my waist, the other sweeps under my legs, lifting me into his arms, he carries me to the couch and takes a seat, pulling me into his lap. I curled around him like a small child while his finger comb through my hair. I heard the door open and close but couldn't mute myself long enough to know who had entered or left.

"Are you hurt?"

Not yet. I shake my head.

"Who's 'he', sweetheart?"

BROKEN

"My father," I whisper through the hiccups that rack my chest. Parker stiffens under me and not in a fun way.

"He's here, currently?"

I nod.

"Is that who you were running from?"

One of, I nod.

"You're okay. You're safe here." He coos. "I won't let him anywhere near you. I promise."

I squeeze him harder as fear pours from eyes and terror shakes my bones. The devil came. I expected the spawns, but not the devil himself. You know it's bad when he, himself comes to claim what's owed.

CHAPTER THIRTY-FIVE

I didn't want to go home. I was terrified my dad would be waiting for me, and I didn't want to go to Parker's for the same reason so when Josh offered me his spare room, I gladly accepted. Parker stayed with me if I woke him with my nightmares he was a gentleman and never commented. I managed to hide out at Josh's all of Thursday and most of today. It's Drew's birthday party in a few hours, and I promised I'd go. With the club being closed to the public, everyone assured me he wouldn't be able to get in- and if he did, Simon would stop him. It's a comfort to know they made everyone aware of my father's face and instructed he isn't allowed and to report any sight of him to Josh. I can't tell you the story he spun to make that happen, but I'm thankful nonetheless.

Pulling into our apartment complex was miserable. I put on a brave face when I waved off Parker's attempts to follow me inside my apartment, to my shock, he actually let me go.

Entering, I wanted nothing more than to run back outside and make him check if it was safe, but I know better. If my father is here, he'll kill him for being a witness, and I can't have that. Slowly, I snake my way through the apartment checking each room more than once. Color me confused when there's no one here, not even a death note ominously placed. My father's dramatics knows no bounds.

Not wanting jinx myself, I dress quickly in the outfit I wore to Thanksgiving. After all, Drew paid a bloody fortune for it. Stepping into the bathroom, I purposely leave the doors open so no one can sneak up on me while I quickly do my makeup. I chose a mostly black palette. I look like I did in Reno, but it's second nature at this point so I can accomplish it in record time. Spraying my hair with some sea-salt spray, I crimp it with my fingers to bring my natural waves forward just as a figure walks into my room. My heart stalled only for a moment before God's gift to women steps into view. Our eyes meet in the mirror as the right side of his mouth lifts. Not even the press of my thighs is enough to control the way my body begs for him, God; he's perfect. What's that saying about fear? Scared girls are horny girls? Whoever came up with that needs an award.

"How'd you get in?" Fuck, my voice is embarrassingly winded.

He pulls his hand from his pocket to show me a key.

"Not sure if I want to smile or call you a stalker," I admit, throwing my hair over my shoulder.

"You're painfully beautiful, do you know that?"

I roll my eyes, throwing my makeup in the bag, though internally my stomach flips at the compliment.

I feel him step into me; his hands slide against the curve of my waist as his lips press into my neck, "Go out with me."

Goosebumps rage along the trail his breath left. I meet his eyes in the mirror and offer him a sweet smile, "No."

His hands tighten against me, scrunching the fabric as he speaks, "If I bend you over this counter," His eyes lock with mine, "Will it change your mind?"

Pushing my ass back I grind against him, "Only one way to find out."

Without breaking eye contact, his thumbs trying to find the underwear I'm not wearing. His eyebrows lift as a sneaky grin graces my face, and he growls, palming my ass with one hand, the other gently pushes my shoulders forward.

We walk in, and the club is PACKED. Which usually wouldn't come as a shock but Josh closed HEAT for the event. And did I mention everyone is basically naked? I know, I know- Skin Party, but still. The club is full of barely dressed people bumping and grinding against one another. They're either really sweaty or someone is passing around a bottle of baby oil.

The strobe lights are beating in every corner mixed with swirling white and red lights that change with the tempo. Girls are stripping along the length of the bar, tables and even on the couches.

"It's like one big orgy," I yell over Parker's shoulder, which shakes with laughter as he nods forward, pulling me along behind him. I try to be okay when I get touched- you ever see that episode of Key & Peele when Jordan goes to his coworker's house, and they're all having sex on the bed with the coats? Yeah... I feel like him right now.

Breaking through to the other side of the dance floor we spot Drew; they've pulled the big leather couch onto the stage, and he's sitting shirtless, wearing a crown, with a busty blonde under each arm. He looks like a douchebag, and I love it.

"Hales!" The two blondes- who might actually be twins, glare at me.

"Happy Birthday!" I yell over the noise. He stands, throwing an arm over my shoulder, turning me in the process to overlook the crowd. "So, this is the notorious birthday party, huh?"

"Damn right!"

"Do you even know these people?"

"Some of them!"

"What about the blondes behind you?"

"I plan to know them biblically if you know what I mean." Of course, I know what he means, anyone with ears knows what he's saying.

Hands land then squeeze my hips. I lean back so I can look at Parker, but his eyes are set in a glare. I twist to get a better view and then I see her in all her platinum glory.

Drew is quick to my side, "Oh yeah, I invited Lacy, just so you know." I turn and glare at him, "It's my birthday! You're not allowed to get angry!"

"Why? You hate her!"

"Yeah, but I like rubbing you in her face!"

I roll my eyes feeling her approach. Ugh, I hate this bitch. I fall deeper into Parker's side as she closes the distance. She's in a teeny tiny red dress; again, the neckline falls to her belly button. How she manages to keep her rack from falling out is beyond me. White stilettos vine up her calves. She looks like a fucking model- again.

"Were you not informed this was a skin party?" Her eyes narrow at my sleeves, her face growing more disgusted as she takes in my whole outfit, "Didn't you wear that on Thanksgiving?"

This bitch. I hate her, have I mentioned that?

"Parker likes it for easy access." I shrug.

Her body stiffens in response, and a smug smile adorns my face- ha! Bitch.

A very tall, very muscular, very naked man in- a loin cloth? A leather crotch cover? I don't fucking know steps into Lacy. Neon rings adorn his neck, glowing lines of orange, green and pink slide to side smacking her in the cheekbone as he sways in time with the music, she bats them away in annoyance. "Parker have you met Jeffrey?"

His tongue runs between his lower lip and teeth as he smiles, but it doesn't seem at all friendly. "Parker Hayes." He offers his hand.

"Jeffrey Laken."

"Oh, I know."

"Parker is still a little sour over how we met." She coos with a smile I'm itching to smear across her face. That's the prick she cheated on Parker with? Seriously?

"Harley," Lacy turns to me, "This is my date, Jeffrey. Jeffrey, Hannah."

His brow furrows as he looks at us, he offers his hand, "I didn't catch your name."

"Haley."

His eyes fall from my cleavage to the straps of my Mary Janes.

"Fits." He smiles, and it puts me off my eggs real quick.

I nod and sink into Parker's ribs. Ew. Just ew. I feel like I need a shower and he didn't even do anything wrong. He has a greasy looking smile and the way his eyes drank me in felt like I wouldn't want to be alone in his presence. Not calling him a rapist, but the vibe I get from him is a little on the rapey side.

"Oh my God!" Lacy squeals, pulling me from my unnerving thoughts, "I love this song, Jeffrey!" Like a puppy on a leash, he falls into her as she gyrates her hips against his crotch- classy.

I lean back to catch Drew's attention; his eyebrows raise as he leans in, "This is one of Lacy's favorite songs." I yell into his ear.

He pulls back with a smile then makes a slashing motion across his throat to the DJ who promptly changes songs. I cover my mouth to hide my laugh when Lacy sends daggers at Drew. Draping an arm over my shoulder, he blows her a kiss. Her fury grows behind her eyes before she stomps her foot like a four-year-old and plops down onto the sofa, her greasy date continues to dance next to her like Terry Crews in White Chicks.

"Seriously?" Parker asks with a smile.

"It's my birthday, and I wanted to piss her off- sue me. Speaking of my birthday, it's a skin party, dude."

Parker looks down at his button up. It's rolled to his elbows, and the top three buttons are undone. It's sexy as hell, but you know what's sexier? Parker shirtless.

"Yeah, it's a skin party." I back up Drew with a smile. "Take it off."

He opens his arms as if in invitation. My smile turns wicked as I step into his space.

"No, no, no, no!" Drew pushes between us. "Y'all can do that nasty shit later."

Parker smile grows in challenge as we stare at each other. "Just think how pissed Lacy will be to watch me undress him."

He considers that before rolling his eyes and stepping back, "Fine. But at least let me get a good seat so I can watch her face. Twenty bucks says she storms off."

"Thirty says her tit pops out at least once tonight."

"Deal." He kisses my cheek and hurries back to his busty blondes that immediately curl into his side.

"I'm all yours, sweetheart." That half smile is going to get me arrested for indecent exposure one day.

"Mm, don't I know it." My fingers trail from his collar to his belt, his dark eyes stay fixed on mine, though his breathing tells me this is totally turning him on. Grabbing fistfuls of material, I pull it out of his pants. My fingers deftly pop each button as I work my way up.

His head tilts back, and he watches me through hooded eyes as I place my palms flat on his rock-hard body, trying not to smile as they slide over his contours, up and over his shoulders until the material falls away. Hot damn. He's still watching me...and I need walls.

To prolong both of our agonies my fingers stroke the length of this arms, running from his shoulders, down his biceps until I reach the rolled sleeves. With a little-added pressure, they slip down to his wrist. I bend forward kissing his chest as I pull the cloth from his body. I barely catch the discarded material when his hands dive into my hair, pulling my face into his. I need walls- fuck walls, I need a less populated area with any flat surface. His tongue invades my mouth and steals the moan from my throat. Pulling away he smiles at me, he knows.

I can't hear his voice, but I can read his lips, "Go out with me."

BROKEN

Those blue eyes bore into mine, I don't know if it's because my libido is through the effing roof at the moment or the fact that my brain is still trying to get oxygen, but I nod.

His face turns very serious, his eyes widen as he takes in my motion, "Did you just say, yes?"

Another nod and a huge smile transforms his face. He kisses me again, hooking his hands under my ass and lifts me off the ground. On instinct, I wrap my legs around him- oh, I'm not the only one in need a little privacy.

My hair falls over his shoulders, my hands resting on his cheeks. We're on the stage in front of a couple of hundred people making out like it's our job, pulling a lot of attention, I'm sure. But to be completely honest, I haven't a fuck to give because I'm wrapped around Parker, and he's the only thing that exists.

CHAPTER THIRTY-SIX

Helping an extremely intoxicated Drew into Josh's truck, I hop into the back seat with him while Parker and Josh take the front. Drew's head rolls towards me, and a smile graces his lips, "Hi, Haley, Bailey."

I giggle at his slurred speech, "Hi, Drew."

"Hey?"

"Yeah?"

"Ask me if I'm a tree."

I laugh hard for a second, "What?"

"Ask me if I'm a tree."

"Are you tree?"

"No, but I got some wood for you." He busts out laughing like it was the funniest thing he's ever said.

"I don't think Parker would appreciate that." I laugh with him.

"Pssssht." He throws his head back to take in Parker who is sitting in front of me.

His expression stays serious for all of five seconds before his head tilts to the side and deep thunders of laughter spring from his lips. It's hard not to join in. His drunk laugh is so different from his everyday laugh. It's thicker and more of a belly laugh. It's far too entertaining.

I'm in tears by the time we pull up to an expensive looking brick house. Josh pulls into the driveway and kills the engine while Parker and I slide out to help collect a still chortling Drew from the backseat.

"Haley," I look up at Josh who digs in his back pocket, "Unlock the door, please."

Accepting the keys, I run ahead. Throwing the door open I catch the dark living room. I've never been to Drew's house before. His furniture is all very dark like Parker's, with what appears to be lots of navy blue accents. Before I can soak in any more detail, Parker and Josh half drag, half carry Drew through the door. I close the front door and follow behind them as they maneuver around the furniture in the dark. I try to keep close but manage to take a side table to the thigh in my efforts.

We enter into a massive kitchen, the light above the stove is on showing the dark granite counter tops and rich dark wood cabinets. His house is awesome. Drew mumbles something that makes everyone crack up when we enter the hall and into a bedroom.

His room is neat like Parker's. A massive platform bed with a black leather headboard takes up the majority of the room. Apart from the dark grey bedspread and curtains, he has little decoration. A black dresser and a desk take up the opposite wall, the only give away that this is Drew's room is the glass bowl full of condoms next to his bed.

"No, really." He slurs while Parker strips down the bed.

"I don't know, man," Josh tells him.

I scrunch my brows together when Parker looks at me. "He wants to know where his blondes went." He clarifies for me.

I giggle, "They're coming." I lie. "Said they'd be right behind us. Come on now, get in bed." He seems to be happy with my lie because he stops fighting and climbs onto the mattress willingly. I grab the wastebasket next to his desk and place it on the floor near his head. "Just in case."

"How 'bout a birthday kiss, bestie?"

I laugh long and hard, "You're trashed, dude."

"It's my birthday."

Pouting Drew is adorable, "Technically it's the day after your birthday."

BROKEN

"I'm not pretty enough?"

"Awe, you're beautiful." I sing. His frown deepens, and I laugh, "You're ridiculous."

"I'd kiss you on your birthday."

"Oh, for heaven's sake." Leaning down, I grab both his cheeks and plant a loud kiss on his mouth. "There you go, you big baby."

His hands grab my hips before I can react my head and hands bounce off the mattress while my waist lays over his stomach. "Ha! Always knew you'd end up in my bed."

"You're such an idiot." I laugh, climbing off him to sit at the foot of the bed.

I look up when Josh enters carrying a bottle of Tylenol and a glass of water when he passes I catch Parker's face, and he doesn't look happy- at all. I frown at him, but he just looks away.

After coaxing Drew to take the Tylenol, we say our goodbyes.

"Is he going to be alright by himself?" I ask once we're back in the truck.

"He'll be fine. He's going to feel like shit tomorrow though." Josh laughs.

"He's trashed. I've never seen him this drunk before."

"He always swears off drinking the day after his birthday. In a couple of weeks, he'll pick it back up and behave himself until his next birthday."

I shake my head even though they can't see me in the back. Being drunk has never been appealing to me. I like to get fuzzy every now and again, but I have to be in control of myself. The thought of being so blind drunk and dependent on someone to keep you safe isn't my cup of tea. In Reno, when you got piss drunk you were on your own.

The ride back to HEAT is spent in silence, Josh pulls up behind Parker's Camaro and with a quick goodbye speeds off into the night.

Closing the Camaro's door behind myself, I quickly bend forward to collect my cigarettes off the floorboard. Stealing Parker's lighter from the center console I drag the flame into the tobacco until poison fills my lungs and calms my nerves.

"You okay?" I ask after the silence starts to get under my skin. All I get is a shrug, but he won't say anything or even look in my direction.

I tell myself I don't care if he's pissy, but guilt and dread settle into my stomach anyway. "Are you mad because I kissed Drew?"

I notice his jaw tick before he sniffs and hits the blinker leading to I10.

"Where are we going?"

Again nothing. I roll my eyes at him, "The silent treatment? Seriously?"

He shakes his head but again says nothing. Anger is quickly pushing every other emotion to the sidelines as I cross my arms like an irate teen and stare out the window.

BROKEN

He merges onto I10 but only stays for four or five exits before taking an off-ramp. I haven't been in this area, tall grass lines the street, no street lights, it's creepy.

He follows a deserted side road until we enter an open chain link gate. Looks like an airfield; abandoned metal buildings line one side of what I can only assume is a cement lot. Knee high dry grass grows between the cracks of concrete. He pulls into the lot and parks the car.

He kills the engine but leaves the headlights on. After unhooking my seatbelt for me, he climbs out. I take that as an invitation to follow, so I climb out after him.

He's standing at the front of the car with his hands in his pockets.

"What are we doing here?" I ask nervously.

This place is cold and empty; I don't like this at all. If this were anyone other than Parker I would assume I was here for rape, murder, or abandonment.

"Get on the hood."

I look around at our abandoned surroundings, "What?"

"Get on the hood." He nods to his car but doesn't take his eyes off me.

"I'm going to dent your car-" I try to reason, but he shakes his head and nods me forward. Feeling all kinds of weird, I try to gracefully climb up his car, all too aware I'm still not wearing underwear.

"Lie back."

"What are we doing?" I ask while obeying him. I don't know if I'm excited or terrified.

He moves forward, his hands grip my knees and pulls me towards him, then lowers my knees. I sit up abruptly, pressing my hands against the skirt of my dress to cover myself. If I hadn't all my bits would be hanging out. Apparently, that's his goal because he takes my wrists and pulls them from my lap, while gently pushing me to lie back down.

Embarrassment flushes my cheeks as he pushes my skirt higher. The chilly air bites at my exposed skin.

"What are you doing?" I mean to ask it with oomph but all that came out was a whisper.

"Reminding you." His fingers dance up and down my inner thigh.

"Of?"

He bends down, kissing the line of skin just below the skirt, his hands squeezing my thighs. A shiver of anticipation sinks its hooks into me. "Who you belong to."

Before I can get angry, he sinks two fingers inside me. My back arches off the warm hood and all words, thoughts, and emotions are lost when his chin dips lower, and all I can feel is the sensation of his mouth. My body starts to tighten, and he slows his rhythm until I lose it just to pick back up. Every time I'm near the edge, he pulls me away again. I'm needy and frustrated after the fourth failed orgasm. "Parker."

"Hmm?" His reply vibrates against my skin, almost sending me over.

"Fuck. Please." I try to move my hips to satisfy myself, but the hold he has on my hips doesn't allow me much. He pulls his mouth from my body to look at me. The cold air quickly assaults my wet skin.

"Please what, baby?"

"God, Parker. You know what. Why are you torturing me?" I moan as his fingers sink deeper. God, I'm so close.

"Is this torture?" The right side of his mouth curves up.

"You not letting me cum is torture." His free hand presses down on my lower stomach, making his torture downright cruel. "Parker-" I try to sit up, but he pushes me back down.

"Who do you belong to?"

I moan against the sensation, "No one."

He chuckles softly, but it's more sinister than ha, ha. "Wrong answer, sweetheart."

The pressure in my stomach grows, and I can feel it, right there- he removes his fingers.

"Son of a bitch!" I get up on my elbows and glare at him.

He licks his wet fingers while wearing a proud smirk. Asshole.

"Seriously?"

He watches me while his hands fall to his pants, popping the button. "Am I yours?" He asks slowly lowering the denim, showing off that V thing that I love.

"No." I breathe. I'm embarrassingly hot for this guy. Jesus Christ.

He leans into me until I'm once again, flat against the cooling hood. Licking a line from my collarbone to my ear before nipping my lobe, "Wrong."

In one swift move, he impales me causing me to arch into his chest; my fingers lock around his wrists for dear life. God damn. The coil is so tight I'm pretty sure it's going to cause physical damage.

"I am yours." His face buries into my neck as he moves. "Tell me you're mine."

His teeth dig into my flesh. Gripping his wrists tighter, I bite down against the scream that wants to escape.

"Tell me." His voice is husky and demanding and mother mercy, so fucking hot.

"No," I say between clenched teeth.

My head tilts back on its own accord, but Parker will have none of that. He shakes off my grip before his fingers burrow into my hair, twisting and pulling so he has control. "Tell. Me. You're. Mine."

I'm right fucking there, oh my God. "Don't stop. Please, don't stop."

BROKEN

"Then tell me, baby."

My grip is probably bruising at this point, fuck. "I'm yours." I moan,"God, I'm yours. Don't fucking stop."

"Fuck, say it again." He demands, his pounding rhythm becomes bone crushing.

The coil snaps just as the words start to leave my lips, I end up screaming, 'I'm yours' as the most intense orgasm literally rips out me. His body stops my legs from closing, his chest keeping me in place, there's no way to escape the intensity. His hand keeps my head in place as my body seizes and pulses around him. I hear him growl out a cuss against my skin. His hand leaves my hair to vice around my hip bone. After a moment, he shoots upright to claim my hips as he slams into me. The strength of his hard body pounding into mine will bruise I'm certain, but I can't seem to care, it all feels too damn good. The headlights reflect off the beads of sweat appearing on his chest. With one final thrust forward his fingers dig deeper as that sexy growl climbs out of his throat.

If I had any doubts about being in love with him before, they're definitely gone now. I can't picture ever wanting anyone the way I want him. I can't imagine anyone but him, period.

CHAPTER THIRTY-SEVEN

I woke up sore. My body took a beating last night, and I feel it today. I need a hot shower, pronto. Stretching my sore muscles, I look around to find the bathroom door slightly open with steam pouring through.

Climbing out of bed, I approach and give a small knock. "I'm running over to my apartment. I'm going to shower and stuff."

"You can always shower with me." I can hear the smile in his voice.

"Tempting." And it is. Incredibly tempting. If it wasn't for the deformed marks, I hide I totally would. "But all my stuff is over there."

BROKEN

"Watch yourself. Drew will be out for blood when he wakes up."

I laugh, "It's his own damn fault."

"He'll blame us."

"Want to hide at my apartment instead?"

"Sure. I'll head over in a bit."

"Kay." I smile to myself as I back away from the door.

It's stupid to be this happy that he wants to be around me, but fuck it. I'm soaking up as much happiness as I can while it's here. The stairs prove challenging, but each step is a delicious reminder of last night. Dominating, mad Parker is fucking hot, and I kinda hope I piss him off again so I can have that version return.

I cross the courtyard and unlock my door unable to wipe the stupid grin off my face. Throwing my keys on the table, I close the door before my world comes crashing down.

"About time."

A yelp escapes my throat as I spin around. I'm face to face with the Devil himself.

"How did you get in here?" Moving slightly, I put the table between us. Parker said he'd be over when he was done. Please, God, if you can hear me, don't let him come.

"Amazing how easily people believe a lie."

"Why are you here?" I'm pleased my voice stays strong even though I am anything but on the inside.

"Now, let's try using that head of yours, daughter of mine. Why am I here?"

"I haven't talked. No one knows anything." Parker stay away; for the love of God, stay away.

"I don't think you're dumb enough to talk, Ryan. I'm here to collect a debt."

"Debt?" I breathe, trying to think how I could possibly owe him.

"You're eighteen. You were approaching seventeen the last time I saw you."

No! No, I can't. Not again. Reaching into my bra, I pull out every bill on me and throw it on the table in front of him.

"Consider that my buyout."

An evil chuckle pours from his lips as he collects and counts the money. "Four grand." He whistles, "Looks like you're doing well, not nearly as well as Reno, but fair."

Pocketing the money, he takes a step closer, on instinct I step back, deeper into the apartment, opposite of where I want to be.

"I'll consider this penance for running, but you still owe a debt."

"How much?" I don't know how the hell I'll get more money, but I'll die trying if it keeps him away.

He shakes his balding head. "I have no need for more money, Ryan. I want what is owed. Half the blood in your veins is mine. I own it, and I'll spill it when I please."

BROKEN

"You don't do this to anyone else!" I stumble away from him; tears fall down my cheeks. "Why do I owe a debt and they don't?"

"My boys bring me pride. The only thing you're good for is spreading your knees and looking like that whore."

"That's why?" I breathe in disbelief. "Because I look like her? I didn't choose that! I've done everything you've ever wanted!"

"Wanted? You think I wanted you?"

"I didn't choose to be born! You're punishing me for something out my control!"

"Calm your hysterics; tears won't do anything but annoy me."

"Please." I stumble back, smacking against the wall. "Please. I'll legally change my name; I'll remove all traces to you. You won't ever have to think of me again! It'll be like I never existed."

He seems to take a moment to roll the idea over before chuckling, "No deal. You brought me a lot of money. I had a great deal of damage control to take care of when my underage child disappeared." His face turns deadly, "You created problems for me."

A rush of air falls from my chest. "So, you're here to punish me?"

He waves me off, looking around at my apartment. "I have little need to seek revenge; it's been two years. Instead, I'm here to claim what is mine. Whether it's your body or your life, that's entirely up to you."

"What do you mean?"

"You will either return to Reno and work for me, or you will return, and I'll take what is mine. Half the blood in your body is sure to kill you, so you have a choice to make. Your body or your life."

"If you don't want me, why do you want me back? I can disappear."

"Because you are a source of income. One I'm not willing to part with."

"But you don't want me."

"You're right; I don't. But I will not share you, either."

"I'll pay any price you want." I try to reason, "I'll do whatever you want to let me disappear. I'm not a threat to you."

"You're a greater threat than you give yourself credit for. Your friends are an even bigger threat. I also know that you're in contact with another one of my offspring." He must have caught the color leaving my face because he chuckles, "Oh, I know all about Kaylan and the whore he's hiding."

"Why haven't you acted on that knowledge?"

"He's not a threat to me." He picks at glass trinket on the shelve.

"But I am?"

BROKEN

"You've seen and been witness to far more than even your mother."

"I don't remember anything."

"Of course not. Doesn't change the fact that you are a threat and threats must be dealt with."

"But I'm not a threat. All I want is to disappear. I have a new name; I can get it legally changed, you'll never hear about me, see me, it'll be like I never existed. Please."

"I've already given you your options."

"There has to be another way. You're a businessman. There's always a way to keep everyone happy."

"Indeed." He nods in thought. "How's this? I'll grant you your freedom; I'll give you my word that you'll never hear from me again," My heart picks up, I'll do anything. "But you'll have to pay for that freedom with the blood of your new friends. The one who is playing daddy, the one on the bike and the one you spread your legs for." I gag on the fear in my throat. "Or you can spare their lives and come willingly."

"What about Kaylan?"

"What about him?"

"Is he included in that?"

"Sure." He nods curtly.

"If I come peacefully you'll give me your word that he's free?"

"I'll give you my word that as long as he remains a non-threat to me or my endeavors, he will have safe passage."

I bite my nail trying to wrap my head around everything that's happening.

"Aren't you going to try and strike a deal for the whore?"

"No," I answer a little too fast. "Do what you want with her."

His laugh fills the once safe walls of my home, "Maybe there is a little more of me inside you than I thought."

"I'm nothing like you."

"Maybe. So, what will it be?"

My mouth gapes like a fish as I struggle to process the options. Obviously, I'm not going to let him kill them, I'm desperately trying to think of another way, but I just can't seem to find a single option.

"Your answer, now."

"I'll come willingly," I whisper in defeat.

"A fine choice. Here's how this will go; you will leave town, I expect all ties to be severed by tomorrow at the latest. In the event these people decide to report you missing, I don't want anyone sniffing in my direction, so you will stay gone until the new year, I expect you at my door on the first with an answer, your life or your body. If you fail at these instructions, I will revoke my end of the deal."

"And my debt?"

BROKEN

"Will be claimed upon your arrival."

"I'll need help getting out of town." I take a shaky breath, "I'll need Kaylan."

"I told you. He and your friends will be protected as long as you hold up your end of the deal." Walking calmly to the door, he places his hand on the knob. "Oh, one more thing," I look up to meet his old, dead eyes. "If you fail to arrive or tell anyone of our arrangement, I will kill everyone who you have ever befriended in front of you, and while you watch the life leave their eyes, I will slit your throat, so you bleed out slowly knowing you were the reason everyone you've ever loved was dead. The brother is my warning."

CHAPTER THIRTY-EIGHT

The door closes behind him as my knees break against the weight of my body. Forcing myself forward, I pull out my phone, speed dialing Drew. His phone answers on the second ring,

"Are you okay?" I sob into the phone.

I gag into the phone as Derek's voice slithers through the line. "Ask him again in about half an hour. I'll text you where to pick up the body." His laugh turns my chest to ice.

"Derek! Don't touch him! Please!"

"Looking forward to seeing you, little sister. I'll be claiming your debt when you return."

BROKEN

The line goes dead as sobs rock me. I force myself to my feet and flying out of the apartment. I race across the courtyard and up the steps to Parker's apartment. Beating against the door with everything I've got. "Parker!" I scream, "Parker, please!"

A second later, the door flies open. Parker's hair drips, and he has a towel loosely around his waist. "They have Drew!" I shove the phone at him, trying not to puke.

"Who has Drew?!"

"My brothers!" I bend over, trying to pull air into my lungs.

"What? How do you know?" He asks, holding my phone to his ear. "Hey, call me back."

He hangs up and then redials. "Haley. Words. How do you know?"

"My dad came back." I rush out; his eyes bore into mine. "Told me I had a debt to pay. Said if I didn't follow through he'd kill everyone. Drew was his warning." I suck in a breath, "Then I called Drew, and my brother answered. Said he'd text me in half an hour telling me where to pick him up."

He stares at me before hanging up and redialing. "When?"

"Right now!"

Hanging up, he scrolls through my phone before holding it back up to his ear. "Is Drew with you?... FUCK." He runs his hands through his hair. "I don't know. I'll call you back." He hangs up, scrolling through the contacts once again, "He's not with Josh. Said he was heading to HEAT, left about an hour ago." He pushes a button and holds the phone up once again. "Hey, Alice. Is Drew there?" His eyes squeeze shut to whatever is being said. "Okay, thanks."

Hanging up he squeezes the phone in his hand, the other threading through his hair. "He left the club ten minutes ago."

My heart slams against my chest. My knees are shaking, and I don't know how I'm managing to stand without assistance. I take my phone from him, scrolling through the contacts looking for a specific number of someone I don't want to talk to.

"What are you doing?"

Finding the number, I press the talk button. "Calling my mom."

His eyebrows pinch together. I think I forgot to mention Kaylan added her number to my burner along with his- oh, well.

"Ryan?" Sounds like she just woke up. It's three in the afternoon! Fucking junkies.

"They have Drew." I try to steady my voice, but it still shakes.

"Who has Drew?"

"Your fucking offspring, who do you think!? I need you to call off the dogs."

"Ryan..." Her voice is full of remorse. "Honey, I can't."

BROKEN

"For once in your goddamn life, do the right thing!"

"Baby, I can't. They won't listen to anything I say."

"That's a lie!" My voice cracks and stays in a high-pitched squeal. "I know you talk to Joey!"

"If they have your friend, your father is close behind..."

"He's already been here," I whisper, squeezing my eyes shut. "Please, Mom."

"Your father is here-?" She trails off in a panicked squeak. "I have to get out of here. I can't be near him. I have to go." I hear her say away from the phone.

"Yeah, save your own ass! AGAIN!" I scream into the phone. "You have a fucking shot at redemption, and you fucking abandon me- AGAIN! My best friend is at the mercy of your god damn kids, and you don't do a damn thing to stop it? How?! How can you be such a waste of life?!"

"Ryan. You don't understand, if he gets me- he'll-"

"He'll what? Beat me for your crimes against him? I'm sorry, I didn't realize you were selflessly sacrificing my best friend to save your own ass. By all means! What the fuck does his life matter anyways, right?"

"It's him or me, Ryan." She snaps back.

"HIM!" I scream into the receiver. "I choose HIM!"

"I have to go."

"Coward."

"I don't see you throwing yourself in front of a bus for the boy."

"I AM! Point me to the fucking bus, mom! Just call!" The silence on the other end is going to kill me. "I swallowed twelve bullets and countless blades because of you. The least you could do is make a fucking phone call!"

She sighs and then the line goes dead. I scream between my teeth and almost throw my phone. My knees finally break, and I slide down Parker's threshold.

"What debt?" Parker asks as he paces the living room, he must have gone down the hall because he's no longer in a towel. He's thrown on his basketball shorts while holding his cellphone to his ear.

I shake my head trying to keep my sobs silent.

"Haley." His voice is clipped and angry. He should be mad; I'm the reason his brother is going through whatever those demented assholes are doing. "What debt?"

"I'm not the person you need to be worried over right now, Parker."

"Dammit, Haley! For once just fucking trust me!"

"I do trust you!" I yell back. "I trust you more than I've ever trusted anyone!"

"Apparently not! My brother is missing and you still won't fucking talk to me!"

"The debt has nothing to do with Drew!"

His eyes widen as his neck flushes with anger. "Then what the fuck does it have to do with?"

"It's punishment for running!" I scream back. "I ran! And Drew is going through- God knows what, because of me! Not my debt- me! If you're going to hate me, hate me for that!"

I squeeze my eyes shut as my chest constricts so tight my nails bite into the floor.

"I don't hate you, Haley. I'm scared for you; I'm scared for my brother. All I want to know is what you agreed to because I know you. You may pretend I don't, but I do. You wouldn't let this shit happen, meaning you agreed to something."

"I didn't know." I choke, "It was the last thing he said before he left. I didn't have time to cut a deal."

"What the hell are you guys screaming about? I can hear you from the parking lot." I gasp and fall forward. Parker rushes past me.

"Jesus Christ!" Drew grunts as Parker almost tackles him. "Um, calm down." He pats Parker's shoulder awkwardly, "I've been gone for like nine hours, and you guys are at each other's throats? Figured you'd be down each other's pants."

BROKEN

The sobs break free as I curl into myself against the door.

"Jeez, dude. Harsh much?" Drew asks approaching me, "Hey, Hales." He kneels down trying to catch my eyes. Without warning, I wrapped my arms around his neck, losing his balance he falls into me, knocking us both to our sides. "Fuck dude. What the hell happened?" His arms fall around my waist. Pulling me on top of him as he rolls over onto his back.

"I thought they had you." I cry into his shirt.

"Who?"

"What happened to answering your phone?" I hear Parker ask over my shoulder.

"What?" Shifting me to the side, he reaches into his back pocket, pulling out a black cell phone. "Weird." I look up to see him twisting the device in his fingers, "That's not my phone."

Parker walks over and swipes the phone out of his hand. Sitting up, I watch as he sits down, "There's a text notification at the top of the screen, but it's locked."

"What the hell is going on?" Drew asks, also sitting up.

Parker grows frustrated trying to unlock it.

"Can I see?" I ask, for the first time I'm on the receiving end of Parker's glare. I lower my hand. "The password's 'whore,'" I say quietly. It has to be. Why else would Drew have a random phone if not meant for me?

BROKEN

"What? How do you know the-" The phone makes an audible click as it opens, silencing Drew. "How did you know the password?"

Parker glares at the phone then hands it to me. Without speaking, he stands up and walks outside. Looking down, I read the words that should strike fear into me. Instead, I breathe a sigh of relief.

We had the option to take mercy on him or you. See you soon. XOXO

"Will someone please explain to me what the fuck is happening?"

Parker comes back in, slamming the door behind him. Snatching the phone from my hands, he points to the couch. "Sit."

His face tells me there is absolutely no going against him. Drew and I climb to our feet and sit on the couch like chastised children. "Start talking." He stares me down. I turn a little to Drew as I start to explain,

"My dad showed up. Said I had a debt; if I didn't hold up my end, he would kill everyone. Said you were the warning. When I called your phone, my brother answered. Told me he'd text me where to pick you up. We thought they took you."

Parker is shaking his head in anger, while Drew's face screws up in confusion.

"You thought your brother got the jump on me? Pssht, please."

"They swapped your phone without you noticing. They can hurt you without touching you." I say quietly. "I thought they took out your bike."

Parker waves the phone at me, "Not that." He seethes. "This. Start talking about this."

"What about it?" I know what he wants to know but with him being so angry I'm counting on him storming away, and I can sneak out while he calms down.

"You knew the password."

I nod.

"The message was for you."

I shrug.

"Don't pull that bullshit, Haley! I know that was for you. Start talking! What's it about?"

Sealing my lips, I study the palm of my hand.

"I'm lost. What did it say?"

Without looking at him, I see Parker throw the phone into his lap from the corner of my eye.

"Haley, I'm not kidding. What is it about?"

After a moment Drew turns the phone off and looks to me for a response, "Hales?"

I don't answer. I keep looking down at my hands. I've had years of practice to master the art of silence.

BROKEN

"Haley?" He repeats. He puts his hand on my knee, and I close my eyes. Turning off my emotions, I sit there completely silent and as still as a statue; a good defense I learned from Kaylan.

"Fuck this." Parker seethes. "Drew, hand me my phone, I'm calling the cops."

I take a deep breath and stand. I can feel their eyes on me as I walk around the table, going for the door. Sensing my motives, Parker steps in front of me, putting his hand flat against the door while the other raises the phone to his ear.

"If you want my heart to continue beating you'll hang up the phone," I say in a flat monotone. "Your choice."

Some of the anger fades as he lowers the phone, ending the call. "What's that supposed to mean?"

"Please move."

"I'm not moving until you talk to me."

"There's nothing to talk about."

"There's a lot to talk about, Haley. Like what debt you agreed to pay, what that text was about, why my brother was singled out, and why you had me hang up on the cops. Just to name a few."

"I would like to leave."

"No."

"You're holding me against my will?"

"No, I'm protecting you against your will, there's a difference."

"I can protect myself."

"That asshole was in your locked apartment! I'm not letting you out of my sight! Do you want to go? Tell me what's going on! Just fucking talk to me." His last words were a plea that threatened to break my mask.

"I made a deal. Complete my end of it, pay my debt, and all is well."

"What's your end of the deal?" He grows more impatient the longer my silence draws on, "What debt are you paying?"

"Let me go."

"The debt, Haley." He says slowly.

"Will be paid, Parker." I give back in the same tone. "Now, let me go."

"No."

"Parker-" Drew starts.

"She took the heat for you, Drew! Did you not read the text? What are they planning to do that they won't be taking mercy on you for?"

"You're not letting me leave?"

He shakes his head slowly.

"Fine." Walking away from him, I turn down the hall and into his bedroom. I'd lock myself in the bathroom if I didn't think he'd knock the door off its hinges to make sure I didn't slit my wrists. Stepping out of my shoes, I climb into his bed. Sure, he can keep me here, but I don't have to stand there and have him ask a bunch of questions that I won't answer.

Go fucking figure I don't get left alone. The door cracks open, but I keep my eyes shut.

"Hey, Hales?" Drew's voice is gentle like I've got a headache and he's asking what I want for dinner.

"What?"

"Does this have anything to do with glass windows?"

I sniff pushing my face deeper into the pillow. "Yes."

CHAPTER THIRTY-NINE

Drew shut the door and left me alone after that. I lay awake in Parker's bed until the sun started to set. I've been laying here for almost three hours before the door opens. Parker and Drew both come in with Josh.

"Hey, Haley. You okay?" Josh asks. I nod, not taking my eyes away from the Arizona sunset. Reds and golds swipe across the sky turning the clouds an ochre color. "I don't know what's happening apart from you're in trouble, and you owe someone a debt. Someone who threatened not only your life but both my nephews as well. Name the price, and I'll have the cash to you by the end of the day."

I chuckle without humor, "He doesn't want money."

"Okay. Then, tell me what it is, and I'll get it."

"Money can't buy what he wants." I sigh. "I'm in possession of something he owns half of. I give him his half, and we're done."

"It's that easy?"

"It's that easy." Just half the blood in my veins, no problem, right?

"What are you in possession of?" Parker asks. The gentleness of his tone catches me off guard. My eyes break from the window, flashing to his briefly before returning to the darkening sky. The pain in his eyes is almost too much.

"Something that's been passed through the generations. I didn't know he wanted it until today or I would have given it to him a long time ago."

"Why not just take it today?" Drew speaks behind the other two.

"I have to complete my end of the deal first. It's my collateral." Collateral, the thing that keeps my heart beating- same thing.

"It's not that simple." Parker's voice is pinched. He's hurting, and it's killing me to know I caused that heartache. Josh steps forward, clasping Parker's shoulder. He whispers something to him, offers me a small smile and exits the bedroom. His visit was pointless, but I'm glad he didn't feel the need to hover, unlike my babysitters.

After a deep breath Parker continues, "The text said they could have mercy on you or him, they chose him. Haley-" The bed dips as he crawls over to me, placing his hands on either side of my face, "Baby, whatever you agreed to I need to know what it is." His eyes search mine before he dips down and kisses me, it's not gentle or possessive, it's desperate, a plea and my heart can't handle it. I try to pull away, but he holds my face to him, "Please."

"I've never been shown mercy before, and I'm still breathing."

"Did you agree to install glass windows?" Drew's voice is low when he asks. I squeeze my eyes shut as Parker pulls back to look at me.

"What?"

Dammit, Drew. I roll my eyes, "Nothing, Drew's an idiot."

"No, not nothing." He shifts into a seated position, turning to his brother. "What are you talking about?"

"Hales?" He asks, ignoring his brother. "I'm not going to say anything if it is, we're just trying to understand."

"What about glass windows?" Parker asks again. He scrubs his face with his hands when we don't answer, cursing into his palms, "Glass windows, bullets, blades, any other code words you want to throw around? I assume you know what they mean." He nods angrily to Drew who shakes his head.

"I only know about glass windows."

"Jesus!" Parker stands, "Am I that untrustworthy? That my brother knows something about you that I don't? That my brother doesn't trust me enough to tell me?"

"It's not like that, Parker. I have an educated guess on something that somehow got called 'glass windows' along the way, but she hasn't validated nor denied my guess."

Parker throws his hands, "Educated guess on what?"

He's just not going to give this up, is he? I exhale a heavy sigh, "My arm."

Parker freezes, slowly turning to me. "What about your arm?"

"Her mom brought a picture in. She fell through a sliding glass door; I thought it was something else-"

Parker holds his hand out, effectively silencing him. He turns to me expectantly.

"I ran through a glass door when I was seven. I have a few scars."

"Why would running through a door when you were a kid have anything to do with the current situation?"

"It doesn't. That's why I said he was an idiot."

"I'm not asking for your life story, Haley. I respect your walls and your limits, I don't push, and I don't demand. So why the hell won't you tell me anything?"

I blink the burn in my eyes away, turning back to the opened window as a distraction from the pain etched into his beautiful face,

"Because I'm protecting you." Because I love you.

"From what?" He asks defeated.

"The truth." I take a deep breath straining to see the last bit of purple slip away from the sky. "And from the consequences of knowing it."

"Baby, you gotta give me something. Every answer you give is more cryptic than the last, and I just want to help you."

I don't answer and he huffs before sliding the blinds closed, demanding my attention and destroying the last bit of patience and calm I had.

I shove myself up to sitting position as my volume grows, "If you want to help me then stop asking questions! Bad shit happens to me when people ask questions! If you want to protect me, then trust me when I don't answer! Understand that there is a reason behind it!" Bastard tears slip down my face, and I quickly brush them away.

Parker swallows hard, never breaking eye contact, making it known he's not backing down.

"What's glass windows?" I don't answer and his fist slams against the top of his dresser, "Fucking trust me, Haley!"

Furious adrenaline coats my skin and blinds rational thought. I whip the sweater over my shoulders and throw it across the room, revealing my damaged arm. Purple craters and red jagged lines run at odd angles, shoulder to wrist across burned skin.

"That's glass windows!" I hold my arm up, twisting so he can get the whole 360-degree experience of the scars that can only be described as looking like raw hamburger meat. "There's your fucking trust!"

Adrenaline caused me to act without thinking. Now I'm sitting on his bed in my bra with my disgusting past glowing like a fucking lighthouse in front of the two people I wanted to hide it from the most. I come to and immediately start to panic. Clawing at the sheets, I try to pull them out from under me to hide my shame but my hands are shaking too bad, and the tears are blinding. He left me when he saw; Parker's going to leave too. I pull harder as a sob escapes my throat. I can't; I can't hide it. I fold my arm in my lap, and I bend over to conceal it as shame washes over me. It seeps out of my skin, pours from my eyes and wails out of my throat.

Hands are on me, and I try to shove them off, but they're too strong, I'm opened, and something warm falls over my head, dropping over my arms before I'm lifted, covers are pulled over my head before a hand cups my cheek, pressing me against a muscular chest.

I know it's Parker, and I try to push him away, but he holds me to him. His fingers thread through my hair, his other pressing my shoulders down. Planting my knees, I try to pull away, but he rolls over, so he rests on top of me, using his body weight to calm my thrashing.

"Stop fighting." He whispers, kissing my hair. "I love you, stop fighting." He buries his face into my neck. "Baby, please. I love you."

Like this wasn't bad enough as it is. I cough out another sob, trying to cover my face but his body is too heavy, and my arms are tangled in whatever is around me. My hair is in my mouth and plastered to my tear-streaked cheeks as my heart breaks open, spilling its contents across his sheets. There's nothing inside me to love, and I can't stomach the thought of him figuring that out.

"You don't mean it." I buck against him. "Please, you don't mean it." It's going to hurt so much worse when I leave.

"The world doesn't rest solely on your shoulders anymore." He whispers into my ear, softly kissing my wet cheek, "You've got an entire family ready to fight for you. You just have to let us."

I try to pull away. Away from him, away from his words, away from the shattered pieces of myself. But he holds me in place, his body pressing me deeper as his hand wiggles from under me, brushing the hair out of my face so I can see him.

BROKEN

I work an arm free, setting it onto his chest, trying to push him off, but his mouth falls on mine, stilling my efforts. My head pounds painfully against my closed eyes, and my ears are ringing, though none of that holds a candle to the hole he just punched into my chest. He can't love me; he can't. I have to leave. He can't love me.

"You can't," I cry against his lips. "Please, don't love me."

"Too late." He whispers back, before sealing my mouth with his.

I can feel myself splitting open from the inside, and I can't stomach it. He wasn't supposed to love me.

CHAPTER FORTY

Once Parker's breathing evens out, I go through the agonizing process of inching out of his hold and off the bed. Tip-toeing to the door, I scoop my shirt off the floor and silently exit his room, leaving his bedroom door cracked. Half walking, half jogging down his hall I come face to face with the damn chain lock. I cringe with every tap the chain makes against the door.

I know when I close the door he's going to wake up, but if I can get a locked door between us, I might have enough time to book it across the courtyard before he can reach me- at least that's my hope in all of this anyway. Holding my breath, I steady the chain against the wall and move to the deadbolt. Despite my intentions, the lock slams against the fitting. DAMN IT. Covers rustle in the bedroom as I stand cringing, my finger still on the little golden knob, moving lower I twist the little dial and unlock the handle.

"Haley?" He voice is thick with sleep, but I can hear the awareness in his tone.

FUCK. I yank the door open, locking the handle and slam it shut behind me as I lunge for the stairs, I have like five seconds before he gets out here. I'm taking two, sometimes three steps at a time as I plunge down to the ground floor. Hitting the cement walkway, I break into a run and sprint across the courtyard, Parker calls after me, but I don't stop until I nearly knock myself over, hitting the pillar in front of my door. Jamming the key into the door, I twist the deadbolt.

"Haley, wait!"

Oye, he's a lot faster than I am. I get the handle next and throw myself inside. Slamming the door behind me. The deadbolt slides into place a millisecond before I hear Parker's fist against the door.

"Baby, open the door."

My lip trembles as I stare at the white painted door. It'll sink in. The disgusting deformity of my arm will sink in, and Parker will leave- just like him. It's better to leave, I tell myself. I can't bear to be witness to that again; I can't go through that pain again. I may not have loved him, but that didn't make him leaving hurt any less, I can't even fathom the damage it'll do if I see that look on Parker's face. I let myself get too deep with him and then he had to go and say those damn words out loud. It's better to leave before I'm left.

"Haley. Please, just open the door."

I shake my head as the tears start to slide down my cheeks. I don't want to leave.

"Talk to me, sweetheart."

I bite my lip to cover the whimpering.

"I'm not going anywhere so you might as well open the door."

Because apparently, I'm a glutton for punishment, I slide down the door. Sitting on the floor, I pull my knees to my chest as Parker beats on the door behind me. Pain climbs out of my throat, and I bury my face in my lap. I love you, I'm sorry.

"Baby, open the door."

"I can't." I cry to myself. "I can't."

"Yes, you can, sweetheart." I jerk at his voice; I didn't think he could hear me. "I'm not leaving until you open the door."

I swallow the tears, forcing my voice as stern as I can, "Go home, Parker."

"After you open the door."

"I don't want you here."

"Yes, you do. That's why you're running."

"I'm not running; I came home." Just go away. The pain is clawing canyons into my chest in search of an escape.

"No, you literally ran. My guess is because you love me and it scared you."

I bite my lip to the point of pain; my eyes fixed on the ceiling as I try to slow the steady stream of tears. "I don't love you."

"It's not polite to talk with a mouthful of lies, sweetheart."

"I don't." My voice cracks giving me away.

"You love me, and it scares you. You'd rather pretend not to feel anything than to admit it and get burned."

"Please, just go home." My voice is reaching octaves only dogs can understand.

A long silence falls, and I don't know if it hurts more or less that he listened. Reaching into my pocket, I pull out my phone to text Kaylan.

"Someone broke you," I jump at the sound of his voice. "and I'll admit that I don't know how to fix that. But if you'll trust me, I'll protect all of those pieces. I won't hurt you, and I know words mean little to you because life has taught you not to trust anyone but I swear to you, I won't let you down. I don't want anything from you; I don't expect anything in return, just let me love you."

I don't think tears are the appropriate term for the constant stream pouring down my face; I wasn't even aware pain could drain out of your eyes this way. I sit still at as a statue, fearing the slightest movement and my body will shatter across the wooden floor.

"I'm not a perfect man, Haley. I'll piss you off, and I'll say stupid shit and make stupid decisions, but despite all that, you'll never find someone who loves you more than I do."

I bite down on my lip once again to quiet the sob that is using hiccups as it's way of escape.

"I've never met anyone as brave or as strong as you. I've never met someone so beautiful that it actually hurts to look at them. You don't open yourself up, but when you do, you love with every fiber of your being. I watched hell freeze over when you called your mom for help. I watched you strip yourself bare to protect those you love. You can think you're not worth it all you want, but I'll spend the rest of my days on this earth proving you wrong because I love you."

The grief cracks my throat as it forces its way out. I shake my head as the pain rocks my body. How am I supposed to leave? I have to. I have to save him.

"You're already my favorite thing to fight for, Haley. I didn't need to know your history because I was already prepared to take on the world for you. I didn't need to see your scars to know someone hurt you. I don't care if I get burned in the process. So, you can continue to hide in there, and I'll sit out here and fight those demons for you. Because baby, I'm going to fight for you like crazy."

Laying down on the floor, I curl into myself. I can't do this, I'm breaking, and I have no way to put myself back together again. I'm begging anyone who will listen, let this all be a dream. I just need to have been born into a different life, one where he could put his arms around me, kiss me, and tell me he loves me and I would be worthy of it, I could do it without fear. But this life of mine is so deep with baggage and bullshit he'll drown before he can reach me and I can't let him go through that. I can't watch him die for someone who isn't worthy of him. Someone so flawed and disgusting a John wasn't even willing to stay for.

I'm alone, and I'm scared, and I'm breaking. Can't you hear me breaking? Can't you see I'm falling apart and losing all the pieces? Can't you see I'm not strong enough for this life? I don't know what to do, and I'm lost. God, I'm so lost.

I hold my hands to my mouth, trying to suffocate the agony as it leaks from my lungs as every fiber of my body tears and my soul shatters. The tiny specks float down around me as despair breaks every bone in my body one by one until I'm nothing but a pile of ash with a beating heart.

CHAPTER FORTY-ONE

    I don't question that Parker is still sitting against my door. He's probably sitting there listening to me shatter. Reaching blindly to the floor I feel around until my fingers close around the cold plastic. Unlocking my phone, I open a new message. The only way for me to break further is to see the look on Parker's face, and I just can't confront that.
    I'm a coward... and what do cowards do?
    They avoid. They run.
    Me: I need you.
    Almost immediately three dots line the bottom of the screen.

BROKEN

Big Brother: OMW
Me: Bedroom window.
Big Brother: Be there in five.

I lock my phone before lifting myself up into a seated position. My head feels like it's full of cement and my eyes sting as fresh tears slide down. I don't want to do this. I just want to be happy. I don't want any of this shit to be happening, and I can't do a damn thing to stop it, to make it go back, to be happy. I force myself up and put one foot in front of the other down the hall and into my bedroom, throwing my phone on the bed, I strip out of Parker's shirt and change into jeans and hoodie. Pushing my phone into my pocket, I open the hallway closet to retrieve my duffel and quickly fill it with toiletries and clothes. My butt vibrates, and I pull it out to see an incoming text from Kaylan.

Big Brother: At the light.

I open my contacts and select the Hayes men.

Me: I promised I'd stay as long as I could. I'm sorry. xxHaley.

Dots line the bottom, but I lock the phone and set it down on the table before I can read what it says. Walking towards my room, I hear

BROKEN

Drew's ringtone go off and then a pounding against the front door. I swear to God himself that my heart is pouring out of my eyes. It's abandoning me, and I can feel it. I'm not mad, I understand. They have my heart, and it should stay where it belongs.

Three taps ring against the window, and I see a hooded figure peering down the walkway making sure no one is around. I flip the latch and push the window open. Kaylan takes my bag and swings it over his shoulder as I squeeze through the opening.

"Careful." He whispers, holding one hand out as if I might fall.

"I've got it," I tell him under my breath, flipping my hood over my head. "Parker's out front. We need to get out of here without him seeing us."

"Yep." Without another word, he leads me down the path and towards an old car that's still running where a shadowed figure resides in the driver's seat. The trunk pops open before we even reach it, so I assume this is our ride.

"Who's the driver?"

"Hired help." He says, dumping the bag. "Come on."

BROKEN

He opens my door; my left foot touches the carpeted floor before I hear Parker call out my name. I look up without meaning to, and my eyes lock with his.

"Haley!" He yells again. "Don't!"

Kaylan's hand falls on my lower back bringing me back.

"Make a decision, Ry. Staying or leaving?"

I glance back at Parker who's reached my window at this point. The last of my heart drips off my chin as I slide into the car. Parker takes off towards the car, and I mentally urge Kaylan to move faster, but he's a pro at this shit and is in the seat beside me before Parker even reaches the walkway. Driver dude zips forward, throwing me back as we race through the parking lot and out into Phoenix.

"Where to?" Driver dude asks as we drive through a red light.

"We're not running from the cops, asshole. You can drive like a human being." I snap grabbing the oh shit handle.

"Where you picked me up is fine, Carl."

In less than a minute we pull into a child's park. The playground is deserted and creepy as hell. Carl doesn't turn around or cut the engine; he simply holds out his hand as Kaylan places a few folded bills into his palm. I follow Kaylan out as he grabs my duffel from the trunk.

"This way, kitten." I walk behind him across the eerie, horror movie playground to a waist-high, bowed chain link fence. Kaylan opens the loudest gate in the history of the world and nods me through. An overgrown yard leads to a sliding glass door covered in brown paper, looks like a damn drug house. Kaylan produces a key and unlocks the door before flipping on a light and waving me inside. I take a tentative step forward and enter into a kitchen.

The house is a little outdated but surprisingly clean. The kitchen opens to a living room, and I can see the beginning of a hallway to the right.

"Where are we?" I ask as he passes me and places my duffel on the counter.

"My house."

I stare at him waiting for the 'just kidding' or the owner to step out, gun loaded.

"You have a house?"

"Don't act so shocked." He laughs, "I rent month to month."

"Nice." Cause what else are you supposed to say?

"What's the plan?"

BROKEN

I swallow hard and try to form the words I don't want to say, admit the action that I don't want to take. "Dad found me." I start, Kaylan straightens, all humor escapes his features. "I need to get out of town. I threw all my cash at him to postpone, but he says I still owe a debt. He's sending the spawns to collect."

He nods, clearly in thought. "Okay. We'll crash here tonight. I'll pull some of my contacts together and get us out of here tomorrow night, Tuesday at the latest. No one knows my name or where I live except mom, so you're safe here."

Oh joy, I forgot about mommy dearest. "And will she be blessing me with her presence anytime soon?"

He shakes his head, "Nah. She cashed those checks and was out of here. She pops in every now and again when she needs something, but I doubt it'll be anytime soon if Dad's here."

Without a response, I offer him a patent Hayes brother head nod.

"Didn't tell the boyfriend you were leaving, huh?"

"Not your business, douchebag. Bathroom?"

"Rawr. Down the hall, first door on your right."

"Thanks."

Upon exiting, Kaylan has folded out his couch to a bed and is putting a sheet across the surface.

"Not much but it'll get you through the night."

"Up until a couple of months ago, I was sleeping on the floor. This is perfect." I tell him, grabbing the other side of the sheet and helping him dress the bed.

"Blanket's clean but the pillow's from my room so you'll have to ignore the man stink on it."

"Man stink. Charming."

"Hey- you okay?"

I look up from the worn blanket to his pained face. "Yeah, why?"

"I know this isn't easy for you." He shrugs, "You got attached, and I want to make sure you were okay."

"I'm fine," I say with more oomph in my tone.

"Does that ever work?"

"Does what work?" I ask in annoyance. I'm not actually annoyed it's just my defense against his questions and the mention of what I'm leaving behind.

"Saying you're fine when you're not."

"Yes."

"Nah. Anyone who knows you knows that's a load of bullshit. They're just letting you get away with it."

"And how would you know that?" I scoff, whipping the blanket with more force than necessary over the mattress. "You haven't been around for ten years. You don't know me."

"Exactly. I don't know you and I can tell that line is BS."

"Fuck off."

"Just saying."

"Well don't. I said I'm fine so, I'm fine. Got me?"

He surrenders his hands with a small smile. "Sure. But if you suddenly become un-fine, I'm here."

I give a firm nod as I kick off my shoes. "It's late. I'm gonna crash."

"Okay. I'm down the hall. Last door on the left."

"Kay." I slip under the blanket, turning my back to his somber face. I don't want his fucking sympathy.

BROKEN

"Night, Ry. Love ya."

I hear him shuffle across the floor towards the hall. "Hey, Kaylan?" I roll over to look at him when he turns to face me. "Thank you."

He nods, and the smallest of smiles crosses his face. "Anytime."

Our gazes hold a moment too long, and I roll back over to break the sibling bonding moment between us. I manage to keep my shit together long enough for his door to shut before burying my head into my pillow and unleashing all those feelings of 'fine' until my throat, eyes, and mind can tolerate no more.

CHAPTER FORTY-TWO

I wake up empty and completely emotionally drained. A dull ache permanently resides in my chest, guilt consumes my stomach, and all thoughts seem to be wrapped around Parker and the look on his face as he ran after the car. I squeeze my eyes shut to try and keep the tears from escaping. I've had my fill of tears over self-inflicted pain. I knew this shit was going to happen, can't blame anyone but myself for the way I feel.

Slipping out of bed, I shiver when my feet hit the freezing tile floor. I tiptoe over to my bag, throwing it over my shoulder and carry it into the bathroom for a much-needed hot shower. I dress quickly, doing my very best to avoid my reflection. That bitch in the mirror makes me want to break things, and with my luck, I just might break myself instead. I throw my red chucks on to protect my feet before exiting the bathroom, throwing my duffel haphazardly to the unmade bed.

"Kaylan?" I call behind me. "Hey? You here?"

After a moment the silence chills my bones and a sense of abandonment clouds over me once again. Did he leave in the middle of the night after he learned the Devil was here? Would he really do that twice? Who am I kidding? She looks out for number one, and I'm sure that was the logic he was brought up with too.

Slipping down the hall I knock on his bedroom door, giving it a moment- I open the door slowly, just in case he sleeps naked or something. Sure, I grew up with a house full of men, seeing more than my fair share of brother dick but trust me- that's not ever something a sister wants to see. I keep my gaze high just in case, but they fall onto an empty bed. Folded clothes lay in rows across the dark comforter. Odds and ends lay in groups next to two opened backpacks. The closet door is open, showing its bare hangers and empty shelves.

BROKEN

There's a desk next to an acoustic guitar with a laptop lying on the surface. The cord has been unplugged and wrapped around the machine. Posters line the walls, DVDs clutter the top of an empty dresser next to a flat screen television. If I didn't know better, I'd say he made himself a home here. All his shit is laid on the bed, so I feel a little less worried that he left without me, doesn't kill the dread completely, but it numbed it a bit at least.

Turning back around, I shut his door and take up exploring to kill time. The next door is to my right which houses a water heater, the door across from it is a linen closet. The following door leads to a second bedroom, boxes line the far wall, while a box spring rests on its side against the adjacent wall. Walking back towards the living room I pull my hair over my shoulder and absently braid and unbraid it while pacing the space.

There isn't anything to do; I don't even know where I am or what time it is.

It feels like an eternity passes before I hear keys fall into the front door's lock. A second later, Kaylan enters with grocery bags lining his forearms. His hair is pulled back under a red ball cap, nearly jumping out of his skin when he sees me.

"Fuck, Ryan!" He laughs, "Scared the hell out of me!"

"Probably deserved it," I tell him, leaning against the archway.

He laughs while dumping the bags onto the bed. "Probably."

"Where'd you go?"

"Had to get some stuff. Didn't want to rely on finding everything while on the road. Here-" He holds out a phone and phone card, "You're going to have to activate it here. If you need a computer, I've got one down the hall."

"Thanks." I reach forward and take the little green box.

"Any preferences to where we're going?" He asks as I gut the box and start assembling the little black device.

"Nope."

"Cool, that'll make traveling easier. Anywhere you're against?"

Snapping the back of the phone in place, I hold the power button down until it turns on. "Nevada."

"Damn. Really had my heart set on Reno." He says in the same flat tone I gave him.

"Well, alright- if your heart's really set on it. Think we should invite the spawns out for drinks? Maybe catch a movie while we're there?"

"Before they kill us?" He pauses for a moment in mock thought, then shrugs, "Sure. Would be nice to catch up for a bit."

My mouth curves up on the right, the tiniest bit as I punch in the activation number from the card. I jump when something little pegs my shoulder, immediately followed by another to my stomach, looking down I see two pink Mike & Ikes spinning against the tile.

"You used to call them, 'Ike and Ikes.'" He chuckles.

"Still do and stop wasting the pink ones, dammit."

He chuckles again before disappearing down the hall. I finish activating the phone by powering it off then back on again. Kaylan enters with both backpacks slung over his shoulder while carrying the laptop and a black tote bag as I plug the charger into the wall.

"Alright, baby sister. I've contacted a few people and here are your options, we've got Arlington- half hour or so away from Dallas.

Savannah, or a little town outside of Kansas City."

"Who's people?"

"People I've meet along the way." He shrugs, "They don't know anything- don't worry. Each one's willing to house us for a week or two until we figure out where we're going next."

I nod, letting that soak in. It's hard to trust, harder to trust someone I've never met who's an associate of someone I barely know. I take a deep breath. "Savannah? That's Georgia, right?"

"Yeah, cool dude. Owns a bar on this kick-ass street next to the water."

"Furthest away from Nevada." I say more to myself, "I'll take it."

"Deal. I'll let him know we're coming. The second question- we driving or flying?"

"I threw everything I had at-"

"Don't worry about money. I got you. Which do you want?"

I give him a shrug. "Guess it doesn't matter. Whatever will get us out of here faster I guess."

"Cool. I'll check flights and Greyhound see what we're dealing with. Oh, hey- put your number on my phone." He tossed me his phone before opening the laptop.

Unlocking his phone, it immediately opens to messages, before I could back out I notice there is an unread message from, KITTEN, only I didn't send him anything. The last text I sent was telling him to get me from the bedroom window. Pressing the conversation, my breath catches in my throat.

KITTEN: I need to talk to Haley. Answer the phone.

KITTEN: Answer the fucking phone before I remove every limb from your body and feed them to my brother. That's my best friend, dick sauce and I'm not gonna stop until I know she's okay. My brother may come off as a nice guy and shit, but if he finds you, he's gonna make you his very own fist puppet. Now for the last fucking time, answer the goddamn phone.

ME: She's safe, bro. Let me get her out of here, and I'll see if she wants to talk to you after we get where we're going.

KITTEN: Fuck that. You can't be trusted to take care of her, BRO. Now answer the fucking phone, so I can talk to Haley.

ME: Look- I'm sorry but have to do this for her. I don't know what you do and don't know about her past, but this place isn't safe for her anymore. It doesn't matter how good your intentions are; you can't fight what's coming, you can't stop it. This is her choice, and I'm not going to try and talk her out of it. I've already fucked up my relationship with her- I won't be making that mistake again. When she wants to reach out, you'll be the first to know, but until then just trust that I'll keep her safe.

KITTEN: Parker told Hales he loved her then she split and called you to come pick her up. She's not in danger, bro. She's in love.

ME: I have no doubt she loves him but you don't know the whole story, and it's not my place to tell you. He found her, and she needs to leave if she wants any chance. I'll keep you updated, I promise. Let her be for a while; she's a big girl. She'll reach out when she's ready.

KITTEN: Kaylan- I'm being real fucking cool with you right now, but you are sincerely pushing your fucking luck. I want to talk to Haley.

KITTEN: Parker just walked in. Let her talk to Parker.

ME: She's asleep. It's late; she's scared, she's heartbroken, let her be.

KITTEN: Wake her ass up, or I swear to God I'll start sending nudes of your baby sister.

ME: Let her be. She's safe.

BROKEN

KITTEN: FUCK THAT. I do NOT trust you! Especially when it comes to her!

ME: Goodnight, Drew. Tell Parker his girl's okay.

KITTEN: Calvary's out now. Better stay indoors, your ass is ours when we find you. Parker knows you're only a couple of minutes away, only a matter of time before we find you.

KITTEN: Hey, it's Parker. Nothing bad's going to happen to you. I just want to talk to her; I just need to know she's okay.

ME: She's okay. I already told Drew she's safe.

KITTEN: I get you think this is your shot at redemption with her, but look at the bigger picture. Look at her life. Was she ever happy before Phoenix? Did she ever smile or joke or live without fear? You take her away you're putting her back there, I'm not going to force her to stay or talk her out of whatever she needs to do, I just need proof she's okay. Your brothers swapped phones with Drew and in it was a text to her saying they had the option to take mercy on my brother or her and they chose him. I'm going out of my mind, man. I saw her arm, so I know whatever's coming is bad and like I said- I just need proof she's okay.

KITTEN: Keep her safe. Anything happens to her, and I'll do the same to you tenfold, you got me?

ME: Understood.

Unread KITTEN: How is she?

I stare at the conversation a little longer before programming my new number into it before tossing it next to Kaylan on the bed.

"New text. Parker wants to know how I am."

"What'd you tell him?"

"Nothing. You're clearly capable of texting him on my behalf anyways." There isn't nearly as much anger in my tone as I want there to be. Instead, I just sound sad and small, and I hate it.

"You were a fucking mess last night, dude. I could hear you crying from my room when you finally fell asleep I didn't have the heart to wake you and ask, figured you ask for my phone if you wanted to talk to anyone. Plus, I didn't know if you guys got in a fight or something."

"So, what happened?"

He looks up from the screen, meeting my eyes, "What do you mean?"

"He wrote you at like four something, and then there was a big time-gap, and then he wrote telling you to take care of me. What happened in between?"

"I answered the phone."

"Oh." Dumb response, I'm well aware, but I don't know how to ask. I want to know what was said but at the same time, I don't.

"I talked, he threatened, we parted ways." He answers my unspoken question.

"That's it?"

"That's it."

"And he's fine with it?"

His gaze turns glare, "Did you not get the part where he threatened? No, dude- he's far from being fine with the idea, but he didn't have a whole lot of options seeing as he can't find us."

"Probably for the best."

"Is it?"

I look up with my own glare, "Yeah. It is. What? Did you change your mind? It's safe being here, especially with Dad claiming it's collection day?"

"For the love of everything, you gotta believe me when I say that you are the last person I want to piss off. I want to be the knight in shiny armor for once in my pathetic life, but I have to ask..." He takes a deep breath, and I can already tell this is definitely going to piss me off, "Are you running because Dad found you or because you fell for Parker?"

Yep. Pissed me right off.

"Fuck you, Kaylan! I didn't fall for anyone, and the second he remembers what he saw he'll realize he doesn't love me, he just loved easy access down my pants. As for Dad- are you fucking kidding me?!" I'm standing at this point, growing angrier by the second, "I wouldn't lie about that shit! Those god damn spawns threatened Drew! Then that old bastard showed up at HEAT, and then he was in my apartment! I threw every cent I had at him and cut a deal. But I have to disappear cause he's got two birthdays and two anniversary's he wants to cash in."

Kaylan raises his hands in surrender, "Okay, okay. Down, Kitty. I just needed to make sure you were doing this for the right reasons."

"Right reasons? What do you care?"

"What the fuck is that supposed to mean, Ryan?"

"That's not my name!"

"Yes, it is!" He yells back, standing up, "You're either Ryan running from the devil or Haley running from love! Pick one!"

BROKEN

"Fuck you! You don't get to say shit like that! It's none of your fucking business!"

"You're my business, Haley. Your happiness is my business! The dude on the phone last night was willing to drop everything and leave with you! So don't act like I'm the bad guy for asking!"

"Fuck off with that! He ain't willing to leave, especially for me. There's plenty of pussy in this town; he doesn't need to travel across the country for it."

"Jesus, dude! Do you hear yourself? Oh my God." He looks disgusted as he shakes his head at me, "Does that actually work? Does it hurt less thinking of yourself like that?"

"Like what? Free pussy? Cause that's exactly what I am."

"What the fuck, dude!" His hands fall to his hair as he takes an incredulous breath, "That's not true, and you know it!"

"Oh, right. I forgot you left before I hit puberty. You weren't privy to Dads new side business."

His face morphs into panic slash horror, "Whoa, whoa, whoa, no." He's staring at me, and I fear his eye might twitch right out of his skull, "He didn't sell...he didn't- like, you weren't a-" He cuts himself off to rub his face roughly with the pads of his hands, "Fuck, I can't even say it."

"A prostitute? Lady of the night? Hooker? Free pussy? Sure did. Hit fifteen and had my first John."

"Jesus Christ! Stop, I don't want to hear this."

"You don't want to hear what? That I lost my virginity to someone, who paid for it? Or the fact that he was an okay guy?"

He stares at me in what I think is anger or maybe sympathy, hell I don't even know. I see red, and I've got far too much on my chest to hold back.

"Yep. The first John that picked me up, I cried so hard he returned me, didn't want to get popped for rape, so the spawns lit me on fire. Held me down and lit my arm on fucking fire. Told me if I ever cost them money again they'd burn every limb inch by inch. Next dude who came was a half decent dude. Had me rub his shoulders and shit, said he enjoyed my company. He paid in advance, said he didn't want me roughed up or to have any other dudes except him. Dad got cash, so he agreed. He was nice, never pushed for anything more than a massage, gave him my virginity willingly after a couple of months, thought I loved him. That was until he saw me without a shirt on, told me I was disgusting, and he couldn't believe he let me touch him with that. Dad just loved learning I lost a returning John, loved it so much I couldn't leave the house for over a month to make sure I was presentable for the public. After that, I did what I had to do to keep their hands full of money and off me."

"Please." His voice breaks as he eyes roam over everything except me, "I can't hear this, Haley."

"So, I'm Haley now? Ryan too big of a whore for your liking?"

"Jesus! Stop! You're not a whore! You didn't choose that life! Why the fuck didn't you run?"

And there went the fuse. "BECAUSE MY BIG BROTHER LEFT ME THERE!"

"When you were EIGHT!"

"And the beating I got when I was eight still hurts to this day! The bones that didn't set properly still hurt! The scars on my arm still hurt! I was too fucking scared to leave! Everyone knew me! Everyone was paid to keep their eyes on me! The only reason I got away when I did was because Derek was the only one not passed out and that fucking house bunny was dropping to her knees!"

"How bad is it?"

"What part?! Cause the whole fucking thing is bad!"

"Your arm. How bad is it?"

"Bad."

His eyes skirt over my sleeve. "Parker said he saw it."

And my heart sank right to the floor. I wish I could stomp on it and make it stop hurting. "Lost my cool," I whisper through my shame.

"He still wants to be with you."

"No, he doesn't and stop trying to change the subject."

"Maybe you should get that verified first."

"Maybe you should fuck off. If I want to get laid, I'll find someone in Savannah." His mouth opened but I glare until he shuts it. "Not up for conversation. We're getting the fuck outta here, end of story. My life is my business, my problem, my choice. You don't get a say. Book the travel so we can leave this fucking place behind us." He opens his mouth once again, but I cut him off, "I've got a lot more stories if you want to continue this heart to heart. If not, shut your cake hole and book the fucking tickets."

BROKEN

He lets out a heavy sigh and goes back to typing on his laptop.

I sit there tapping my foot in anger for close to forty minutes before he finally breaks the silence saying he booked us a flight for this evening. He wants to wait until the last possible moment to leave the house to avoid spending any unnecessary time out in the open. The plane was probably smarter; I have no doubt Drew spent last night and all of today at the Greyhound station.

No friends in Savannah this time. Nope, not one. I've experienced enough heartbreak to want to avoid any human interaction for the rest of my life at this point. It's my own doing; I'm well aware, I just wish I would have followed my own advice the first time, and I wouldn't be walking- well running- from a best friend, a man I'm in love with, and a real family.

But I'm a Hale. A coward, a runner.

And so, we run.

BROKEN

CHAPTER FORTY-THREE

I feel like I'm in one of those movies where the happy little airplane flies over the main character's 'New Beginning' only without the upbeat music and promises of a happy life.

The sun is bright and warm through the plane window, Kaylan has headphones on with his head tipped back against the seat next to me, and everything below me is green. It's almost unreal how green everything is for December; I figured there would be snow. We only have a few minutes before we land and I still don't feel like there's enough distance, I wonder what Kaylan would think about leaving the country. I might have a blinding fear of the ocean, so Canada sounds nice.

BROKEN

I'm not sure if I'm in denial or if I'm truly just incapable of understanding that I'm never going back to Phoenix or that I'll never see Parker, Drew or Josh again because this doesn't feel real. It seems almost hazy like it was all just a dream. I'm terrified, but I'm not. I don't know how to explain it but yeah, doesn't seem real. The seat belt light chimes and the captain talks through the speakers telling us we're getting ready to land.

I nudge Kaylan awake, "Seat belt. We're about to land."

This is the part I've been one-hundred percent dreading, take off was absolutely horrible. I've never been on a plane before, and landing seems even worse because you know- we're in a metal container falling towards the earth. We start to go down, and I can feel it. Fuck, this is awful. I plant my feet and squeeze the armrest. Oh fuck. I close my eyes, taking deep breaths when I feel Kaylan cover my hand with his.

Is he a prick? Yes. Am I still mad at him? Mhm. Do I need my big brother because secretly I'm a still a scared little girl? Yep. I let go and squeeze his hand, avoiding the window at all costs.

"Breathe, Kitten."

"Bite me."

He chuckles, squeezing my hand. "It's almost over. You can see cars and people."

"Not helping, jackass."

"Sure it is if we crash there's a higher chance of survival."

"I'm going to break this arm off and beat you to death with it."

He let out a real laugh with that. It's not funny; I'm going to do it.

"Brace yourself; it's going to get a little bumpy as the wheels touch down."

"Fuck." I draw the word out as the plane does exactly what he said it would. We bounce for a second then all goes calm, and my eyes slowly peel open.

"Safe and sound, darlin'."

"Ew. Don't call me that."

He chuckles as I release his hand and nervously glance out the window at Hilton Head International Airport. At least I'm on the ground now.

"Why can't I call you that?"

"Cause that's what you used to call those girls at the pool hall."

He laughs again, "Good point. Now come on, let's get off this tin can."

"You're such an ass."

"Oh, come on, it wasn't that bad."

"The middle part didn't suck so bad, it's the takeoff and landing that I hated."

"Meh, you get used to it." He hands me our luggage, seeing as it was just my duffel and his backpack we were able to bring them as carry-ons. I was already packed and ready, so we didn't need his second backpack. He left some cash and a note to mommy dearest in it instead, telling her we needed to split and that he would be in contact. With any luck, that bitch will stay gone.

Kaylan and I made our way through the airport and into a cab where we took a twenty-minute journey to a pub on River Street.

I walk behind Kaylan as we enter the four-story brick building, I understand why it's called River Street, not only does it smell like a river but the street runs along side of the Savannah River, which is just grand with my disdain for large bodies of water and all, especially since I'm entering a building that I'm fairly certain has blood smeared across the wall outside. Perfect body drop location if you ask me.

We enter into the dark pub, which is surprisingly nice if you ignore the broken table and glass shards everywhere.

"KD!!" A very large man holding the dustpan yells at us.

"Hoyt, you sexy son of a bitch! How are you?" Kaylan locks hands and does that bro hug thing with him.

"Right as rain, man. Yous missed the excitement."

"I can see that," Kaylan tells him surveying the floor around us. "Hoyt, this is my girlfriend Rae, Rae this is Hoyt." GIRLFRIEND?! Um...ew.

"Nice ta' meet you, darlin'." Double ew.

I give a smile and a side glare at Kaylan.

"I've still got that apartment upstairs. Yous can have it for as long as needed." He tells Kaylan while still looking me up and down.

"How much do I owe you?"

"Nah, nah, none of that. Kick me somethin' now and then if yous want, but it ain't required."

"Well, let me throw my shit upstairs, and we can throw one back, cool?"

"Yeah, o'course. Keys are under tha' bar, same as always."

Kaylan nods me forward, and I follow, feeling Hoyt's eyes on me the entire time. We walk up the stairs to the third floor, when Kaylan stops in front of a door and unlocks it.

"Girlfriend?" I ask in hushed grossness, "Really?"

"Hoyt's a cool dude, but he would spend every last breath trying to get in your pants if he knew you were my sister. This way, he knows you're off limits and not in a bro-code, don't fuck my family kinda way."

I make a face, and he chuckles. "You don't have to act like we're dating or anything."

"Well, that's a plus and takes most of the ew factor out of it, at least."

I watch him walk over and throw our bags onto the sofa allowing me to take in the little apartment. We entered the kitchen, or kitchenette I think is more accurate, which opens up into a little living room with an outdated yellow plaid couch, lounge and box television. An alcove leads to the three doors, directly in the center is the bathroom with a stand-in shower, toilet, and sink. A stacked washer and dryer sit in the corner of the bathroom.

"So, KD what's the plan?"

"I don't know, Rae. You want to do anything?"

"I need to get a job first and foremost."

His forehead crinkles as he turns to me, "No you don't. I've got plenty of cash, and I usually help Hoyt downstairs when I'm here."

"How often do you come here?"

"I used to come up here for a few months during the tourist season and help out. Free housing, crazy cash, and an endless supply of willing ladies."

"Jeez, you're as bad as Drew." I chuckle before the pain in my chest burns the noise away.

"You can call him." He sing-songs while pulling fresh clothes out of this backpack.

"Fuck off." I sing back. "Hoyt need a bartender? I'm twenty-two after all."

"No." He twists so fast I'm surprised he didn't give himself whiplash, "Please, Haley. Not here. If you want to bartend, cool, just not here. This place sees a lot of fights and the regulars?

Shit, I wouldn't trust them with a dead fish let alone you. The nicer bars and businesses are further up the street. If you want a job, get one there. This isn't me playing protector, so get that defiant look off your face- this is me laying shit out bare for you."

"If it's not safe, why was this even an option then?"

He blows out a frustrated breath, "It is safe, but it's not working safe, nah mean?"

"No, gangster-boy, I don't nah mean."

"Hard-headed brat." He chuckles, "Please? For me? Go down the street. That's where the tourists go. This is a dive that only brings in the strays. Just trust me."

"Fine. Am I allowed to travel alone or am I going to get murdered in an alley along the way?"

"Once Hoyt and I put the fear of God into these drunks tonight, you'll be as safe as they come."

"Hoyt gives me the creeps; I can feel his eyes on me." I shiver at the memory.

"Yeah, but he's harmless, he won't fuck with you or step outta line. He's an old pervert, but he respects women. Never seen him mistreat one yet and there have been many."

"Really?" I ask and sound a little too much like Ace Ventura.

"He's a big dude, but he's got game."

"Yeah, I don't want to come off like that person, but he's a big boy." I whisper 'big boy' like he'll hear me three stories down.

"Georgia girls like them big it seems."

I mock gag, "I'm your sister!"

"Not like that!" He laughs, "Though, that too."

I mock gag again, "I'm surrounded by a bunch of man-whores? Cool." I nod.

"Come on; it's not like that-"

"Doesn't bother me, Kaylan. Drew's the biggest whore I've ever met. Actually, the term he uses is 'hungry,' I'm used to it. I don't care if big dude downstairs is a whore and I don't care if you're a whore either. Don't care if you bring them here-" I wave around the space, "I just don't want to hear you because that would be super awkward and make sure they're gone before I get up cause I'm not going to be your post-fuck break-up wingman."

"Why not? Could be fun. You throwing shit at them telling them to 'fuck off'."

"I have a little more class than that, thank you."

"Oh, I'm sorry, you'd make breakfast and explain I'm just not ready for a commitment?"

I laugh, plopping down on the recliner. "I'd tell them to fuck off, sure. But I wouldn't throw shit at them."

"No?" He smiles, pulling his shirt off and throwing it on the floor. He turns to grab his clean shirt off the back of the couch, and my response gets caught in my throat.

I'm not the only one who was left with scars it appears. His entire back is covered with white and purple welts. The top of his shoulders all the way down to his pant line. I guess he isn't the monster I painted him out to be after all. He had his reasons for leaving- without a doubt he did.

"I may never understand why you didn't take me with you." I say softly, "But I understand why you had to leave." He throws his shirt over his head and meets me with remorse filled eyes while adjusting the material around his neck. "He might have killed you if you stayed."

He nods. "You'll never know how sorry I am, that I didn't take you with me. It's guilt I've lived with since the moment I kissed you goodbye."

"You told me goodbye?" I blink hard to avoid being a little crybaby- once again.

"I think I secretly wanted you to wake up so I could take you with me. I could claim I didn't have a choice, but you stayed asleep, and I left."

"How'd you do it?" I ask to break the hurt trying to escape through my eyes. "All the doors and windows were locked. Dad thought I let you out and locked up afterward." I shrug, "So how'd you do it?"

"Derek."

BROKEN

I gape, totally and completely taken off guard. "No fucking way."

He nods, "I crawled out of his window, and he locked it behind me."

"Wh- How- wait, WHAT?" I didn't mean to yell, honestly.

"Derek and I were at each other's throats constantly. He was pissed a sixteen-year-old could kick his twenty-two-year-old ass and wanted me gone. Dad would beat him every time I won and wanted me gone, so I gave him a couple of grand, and he let me go."

"That piece of shit watched as I was thrown around like a god damn rag doll for hours and said nothing!"

"Did you really think he would speak up?"

"Did he know I was leaving too?"

He shakes his head, almost violently. "No, neither did Caroline. I gave her hush money and told her to give you the envelope."

"How much did it cost you to keep her quiet? That girl's lips are as loose as her knees."

"Don't-" He cut me a glare. "She's a good girl, but a lot like you she was put up against a wall. You were strong enough to resist, but she turned to something to numb her life at the time."

I scoff and give him a hardy eye roll. "Did it numb her when she dropped to her knees for every male in that house?"

His face turns to disgusted anger. "Stop. I'm not kidding."

"Why are you so sensitive over a house bunny?"

He growls, running his hand through his hair. "She's not a fucking house bunny, now stop!"

My eyes grow in defensive anger, "Don't fucking yell at me over some whore!"

"She's the mother of my son, Ryan! Now stop!" My jaw hits the floor as I stare at him. "Fuck!"

"Whoa, whoa, whoa!" I run after him as he makes a beeline for the front door. "You can't just say that and then leave."

"There's nothing more to say. I shouldn't have even told you, dude."

"I'm an aunt?"

This stops him, slowly closing the door, he looks over my face, "You're not going to give me shit?"

My brows pull together, "What? Why would I? I didn't know she was anything to you or I would never have said anything, to begin with."

He sighs, taking his hand off the knob. "Yes, you're an aunt."

"How old is he?"

"He'll be two in November."

"Don't get mad." I raise my hands in surrender, "You're sure he's yours? Hey now!" I point at him when fury fills his gray eyes, "Don't get mad! I just don't want to get attached unless it's certain."

"We lived together for over a year. Yes, he's mine."

"Do you have a picture? What's his name?"

He pulls his phone out of his pocket, stares at me for a moment then sighs and unlocks the device. "His name's Elliot."

He tells me turning the phone, so I can see a photo of Kaylan kneeling down, holding the ribs of a chubby baby in a onesie.

"Look at those legs!" I squeal taking the phone from him, "He looks like the Michelin man! You've never been this cute, you sure he's yours?"

"Shut up, asshole. Yes, he's mine."

"I'm just teasing! God, Kaylan. You're so happy." I look up and see how much pain is on his face, "What happened?"

"Don't worry about it."

"Well, no. Since you've allowed yourself a voice in the Parker-Drew topic, I can dabble here. Why aren't you there?"

"Cause she doesn't want me there." He sighs, reaching for the phone. "I can see him twice a year on the dates of her choosing."

"That's bullshit; he's your son!"

"Don't." He points a finger at me, snatching the phone back. "You don't have all the facts."

"So, enlighten me. What makes it okay to not allow you near your kid."

BROKEN

"I lost my shit one night, tore the house apart. Scared the hell out of her and she told me to leave and never come back. I'm lucky she lets me see him when she does."

"So, you broke a couple of dishes, so what?"

"It's more than that. Just- let it lie."

"That's not fair. I'm probably not going to meet the greatest little human on the planet, and I'm supposed to leave it?"

"I almost hit her, Ry."

I felt myself withdraw, "How could you do that?"

"I didn't know it was her behind me."

"Does she know that?"

"Of course she knows. Didn't stop it from scaring the hell out of her anyway. On top of having her own demons, she knows who dad is. Doesn't want that lifestyle for our son, so I got the ax. I get it; you don't have to."

"That just seems so extreme."

"If you had a kid with Parker and he almost hit you, would you not do the same damn thing?"

"A- leave him out of this. B-that's different."

"How?"

"Parker wouldn't hit me. Would it scare me? Definitely. Would I make him leave? Absolutely. But not permanently, once I calmed down and he explained what happened, I'd let him come back."

He shrugs. "Well, she didn't."

"When did all of this go down?"

"Right after Mom signed those papers."

"What?! That was only a couple months ago!" He shrugs again. "Stop shrugging and talk to her, you idiot!"

"You don't get it."

"No, you don't get it, dumbass! You scared her and then when she told you to go- you left! You're supposed to fight for her!"

"I tried!"

"Apparently not!"

"You don't know shit. You ran from the only good thing you had so don't preach to me about fighting! You got a lot of talk for someone who is doing the exact same thing!"

"FUCK YOU! I didn't run from him! I ran cause the devil threatened to make good on his promise! I value living, so I left! Stop pretending to know how I feel about Parker or Drew or any of them cause you don't know shit about me or my problems!" God, I wish I could just come clean about the deal. This would make everything so much easier.

He mock-laughs through his glare, "Yeah, just like you don't know shit about me or my problems."

"I got a pussy, don't I?! I know how women work, and I'm telling you, you're fucking up by walking away! Walking away is admitting her fears are right! That you are like them and you're not!"

"Fuck this. I'm admitting her fears?" I give him a defiant nod, "Then what the fuck are you admitting?"

"What? That doesn't even make se-"

"It makes perfect sense. You're scared to be loved. You're scared to be protected and you're admitting it by running with me and not him."

"HE DOESN'T WANT ME, KAYLAN!"

"FUCK! Yes, he does! I was the one who talked to him! Why is that? Because you're too big of a coward to do it yourself! You know I'm right! That's why you had me get you from the window! You know he wants you, and you're terrified that if you hear it from him that it makes it real! That skip in your chest, that sense of safety- that it's real and you're petrified if you allow yourself to feel it, it will all be ripped away!"

"IT ALREADY HAS!" My voice cracks, but I refuse to cry. "My world will *never* be whole! You're proof of that! You had everything! The house, the girl, the kid, and you pissed it all away over the fear that she may not want you. So, don't you dare point fingers! If I'm a coward then so are you!"

"Fuck this." He steps out of the door, slamming it behind him.

I scream through my teeth, desperately wanting to throw and break something. Fucking enraging men! The lot of them! I'm not a fucking coward by avoiding Parker. I already know what he has to say, and I have absolutely no interest in having my heart broken over a fucking text message.

CHAPTER FORTY-FOUR

I'm pathetic in case you were wondering. I've been staring at my screen for over an hour, being the exact thing I claimed I wasn't: a fucking coward.

ME: I'm safe.

That's what it says. Two fucking words and I can't seem to send it. Fuck Kaylan and fuck him for being right.

"Fine." I mumble under my breath, "I'm in love with Parker Hayes. Truly, wholly, completely, and undeniably in love with him." There. I admitted it out loud.

Looking around the dark bedroom I'm currently sitting in, I wait for some grand display or some sign from above, but nothing happens.

Looking at the phone in my hand I still can't seem to hit send. "This is stupid."

"Try saying what it is you actually want to say." I jump at Kaylan's slurred speech. I didn't hear him come in.

"Fuck off. I'm still mad at you." I tell him pulling my ankles under me to get more comfortable.

"Still mad at you, too. Doesn't change the fact that I'm right. Say what you want to say, it'll be easier to send." He shakes his phone at me. "I should know."

"You text Caroline?"

He nods.

"And?"

"Again, I was right. Looks like having a pussy doesn't make you the all-knowing."

"She's baiting you. You're just too drunk and stupid to listen to me."

"Probably, but you should still text him."

"Fuck off." I sing-song at him.

"I'm sorry I yelled at you, even if you deserved it."

"Apologize to me when you're sober. Doesn't count when you're drunk."

He chuckles without humor with backing up into the living room, "Maybe you are the all-knowing. That's exactly what she said."

I don't say it out loud, but just for the record- told you so.

BROKEN

Looking back at the phone, I watch the cursor blink waiting for the courage to write the words I can't seem to say. With a deep breath, I erase the message and start again.

ME: I was too much of a coward to say goodbye to anyone because I knew you would make me stay and by me staying you were going to get mixed up in a life you know nothing about, and I'd be putting you all in danger. You were right, I agreed to something awful, and I had to leave. I know I hurt you, and I know I hurt Drew, Josh and everyone else and there are no words to describe how sorry I am for that but it was necessary for me to leave. My life before Phoenix is complicated and runs much deeper than calling the police or getting a restraining order. I know I'm an idiot and a horrible daughter. I know I'm selfish and the worst best friend there is, and for you, Parker. I know all we were doing was fucking around and I'm not your girlfriend, but I guess the best way for me to put this is that I'm the worst person you could ever fall for. I'm sorry. This started off with a simple, I'm safe but has turned into a novel, so I'll end with this, I'm sorry. Please forgive me.

Before I could second guess myself, I hit the send icon and stared in horror as the sent receipt appeared at the bottom. Then my fingers immediately started typing again,

BROKEN

ME: Please don't respond, I don't think I can handle what you've got to say. We were never together, so you're free to go on with your life. I don't deserve any kindness from any of you, but please, please don't respond. xxHaley.

I press send then promptly hold down the power button in case he ignores my request and decides to respond. Rolling sideways, I bury my face in the pillow and let the sobs out. Fuck, this hurts so bad. I'm crying so hard I barely feel the bed dip as Kaylan scoots in next to me, pulling me into his side.

"It's okay." The stink of tequila slides across my cheek as he slowly rocks me back and forth. "I'm sorry this is happening. I wish I could take it away."

I can't do much more than cry, so that's what I do. I cry until the tears turn to salt and the burning in my eyes and the pounding in my head is loud enough to drown out the heartbreak as it lulls me to sleep.

I wake up to the smell of coffee and something sizzling. Sitting upright I can feel how swollen my eyes are and the cement slosh around my skull from my night of crying.

Sitting on the nightstand is a bottle of ibuprofen and a cup of steaming coffee. Kaylan may be a dick, but at least he's thoughtful. I pop two ibuprofen and wash them down with the coffee, careful not to scorch my tongue in the process. Setting the cup down I notice my phone is not only plugged in but also on. Three notifications are listed across the screen, two from my old phone number, one from Kaylan. I open the phone, refusing to acknowledge the ones from Parker and open Kaylan's.

BIG BROTHER: Going out for groceries. Be back soon.

My phones miraculous ability to turn on and plug itself in finally makes sense. I was ready to be super pissed if he was trying to force me to read Parker's messages, especially first thing in the morning.

Throwing the blanket off, I slip into the living room where I can see Kaylan flipping bacon over in a pan, his phone tucked under his ear. Not wanting to eavesdrop, I quickly grab my duffel off the couch and hide in the bathroom.

Taking an extra long shower, I try to give him as much time as possible on the phone in the event it's his baby mama, so I dress slowly and spend extra time putting my hair up and brushing my teeth. I chase off any thoughts of that chubby baby, I've got enough heartbreak. I obviously don't have the skills to maintain a relationship with anyone at this point so getting attached to a baby I'm not allowed to meet is a super bad idea.

BROKEN

Exiting the bathroom, Kaylan is leaning against the counter eating bacon straight from the pan.

"Mornin'." He says with a mouthful.

"Morning." I nod to the phone on the counter, "You good?"

"Yep."

"Good." I take the plate he hands me and sit in the recliner, watching as he walks over with his own plate. "We good or do we need to have words?"

"Nah." He smiles at me. "We're good."

I nod and shovel a mouthful of scrambled eggs into my mouth while he continues, "We're too similar. We both want to help the other fix their shit without looking at our own mess. It's easier giving advice than taking it. We're a couple of hardheaded pussies. Neither of us wants to hear the other one say it."

"As long as you remember I'm the all-knowing, that's all that matters."

He coughs out a laugh, using the back of his hand to wipe his mouth. "Bullshit. I got read the riot act this morning. You're not the all the knowing; you're the ultimate shit starter. I'm pretty sure she's angrier now than she ever was."

"You can't say that and still smile."

His smile grows, "I may be in trouble, but at least she's talking to me. How'd you turn out? Saw the messages come in when I turned on your phone- didn't read them, but I know they're there."

"I don't know. Didn't read them."

"Why not?"

"I don't need a heavy dose of emotional bullshit this early."

"Early? Girl, it's almost one."

"We're two hours ahead here so technically it's almost eleven."

"Whatever. You only get that logic for another week before I start calling you lazy."

Picking up a piece of egg, I throw it at him. "Fuck off."

Chuckling he picks the egg off his shirt and pops it into his mouth, "So you gonna read them or puss out?"

"Probably puss out. Why? What's it to you?"

She shakes his head, "Just asking."

"Rather not have another night like last night, which I appreciate never being talked about, please and thank you."

"You got it. But why put it off? If it's bad, which it isn't, you can distract yourself with the town, if it's good, which it is, you won't have to walk around all day with that stress on your shoulders."

"What do you know?" I ask placing my dishes in the sink.

"A lot actually. Older and wiser." He taps his temple.

BROKEN

"Yeah, right. Just cause you have two heads doesn't mean you're wiser."

"Nope. You're my baby sister; there'll be no dick references, thank you."

"Oh, whatever you big baby."

"You're diverting. Go read the messages."

"Fuck off. No."

"Pussy." He whispers before walking into the kitchen, remote in hand.

"I'm not a pussy."

"Prove it, pussy. Go read the messages."

"No. I don't need to read the messages. I said my peace. I'm done."

His response? He decided to cluck 'pussy' like a chicken until I clocked him in the head with the dirty spatula.

"Ow. Fuck- good aim."

"I hate you," I grumble as I stalk past the television and into the room I slept in last night. Kaylan's dumb. I don't need to read the stupid texts. Good or bad they're going to hurt and I'm going to cry, and I am so sick of crying.

Ignoring my internal dialog, I sit down and stare at my phone. Seconds turn into minutes which turns into almost an hour before I slide the bar across the bottom to unlock the device, I open messages, and god knows how long staring at my old phone number before opening the message.

MESSAGE ONE: One, RUDE. Two, not true, well kinda not true. You ARE the world's worst best friend but you're MY best friend so that immediately cancels that out cause I'm fucking awesome. Three, I don't hate you, I'm super pissed at you, but I don't hate you. Never could, sunshine. I love you, and I swear to God, just cause you left you better fucking text and call me or I'll find you and ring your hot little neck. I love you, Hales.

Yep. Tears. Lots of them. I don't deserve him. I copy his phone number and paste it into my contacts. I know the long message is from Parker, and yes, I am avoiding it. I make Drew a profile and text him.

ME: I'm glad you don't hate me. Now send me a picture of your big dumb head for your profile pic, also cause I miss you more than you know and want to see you.

Backing out I'm unable to read Parker's text because Drew immediately responds with a picture of him, shirt off, open mouth screaming with his middle finger extending to the camera.

DREW: I'm a fucking stud, I already know. Your turn, topless if you're taking suggestions. Oh, by the way- still mad at you.

Tilting the phone up, I try to take a presentable image, picking the one that sucks the least, I send it to him.

ME: Incoming.

ME: I know you're mad. I don't know how to apologize other than telling you how sorry I am.

DREW: Fuck, sunshine. You look like shit. I'm more sad than mad. Please tell me I wasn't the one who made your face look like that.

ME: Jeez, asshole. I've had a rough couple of nights, okay. Way to soften the blow though.

DREW: Was it Parker's text? He wouldn't let me read it. I get that he's hurting alongside the rest of us, but if he was mean to you, I swear I'll pop him in the balls.

ME: I haven't read it yet. I'm a pussy.

DREW: Read it and text him back. He knows I'm texting you.

ME: Jesus, do you guys like radio my whereabouts back and forth or something?

DREW: No, smart ass. I crashed at his place last night. He's sitting right next to me.

ME: Does he hate me?

DREW: IDK, doubt it. Y'all hump like a couple of rabbits. I think he's just hurting a bit. The only way to find out is to read the message.

ME: Gimme a sec.

Backing out of the conversation I open the one with Parker's message. Fuck, this is long.

MESSAGE TWO: You don't get to say all of this and then ask that I don't reply. You are a coward; you left through a window after running out of my apartment like you were taking the walk of shame- on the same night I told you that I LOVED YOU. I know you can't say it back, I wasn't asking you to. I was asking for you to trust me. I don't know how to make you see that your demons are my demons. That I don't care that you agreed to do something, I care that you agreed and won't tell me what it is because I don't want you to face it alone. And of course I'd try to make you stay- I LOVE YOU.

Without knowing what it is that you're up against, I can't protect you. I don't know what's a real threat and what's childhood fear choking you so, I don't know how to handle it.

Baby, if you told me the truth and needed to run, I'd run with you. I'd go anywhere as long as I had you. Yes, I'm hurt. Yes, Drew, Josh, YOUR FAMILY is hurt. We're all scared to death and we want to help you but we can't when you run off with the brother you hate in the middle of the night. I'm terrified because whatever you agreed to is so bad that you think we can't protect you from it, something so bad that we can't stand by you and help you with. Terrified because you won't let me even try to protect you. You're so determined to watch my six that you've got nobody to watch yours. While you're out protecting all of us, who's protecting you?

And Jesus, Haley- if you compare yourself to a fuck buddy one more time I'm gonna lose my mind. No, despite all of my efforts you're not my girlfriend, but you're MINE. I don't care what titles you're scared of wearing; I don't care what you are and aren't okay with being called. You are MINE. You don't get to send a text and say that I'm free to go on with my life when my life literally jumped out of a window and ran off. I'm in love with you, Haley. That hasn't changed. I've been in love with you since you told me you weren't worth it.

You don't want me to love you? Fine. But first, you're going to have to give back what you took from me in person. I won't accept anything through a text or phone because it's easy to hide behind a screen. If you come back, look me in the eyes, and tell me you don't want me, that you don't love me, and mean it? I'll stop. But as I said, you're already my favorite thing to fight for and let me tell ya- you've got one hell of a fight coming, sweetheart.

I sniff, wiping my nose with the back of my hand in the most unladylike manner before texting him my response.

ME: I don't have words for how sorry I am. I'm sorry for leaving, I'm sorry for hurting you, I'm sorry for hurting your family, but most of all- I'm sorry for making you think you could trust me. Give it a day or so, when the memory starts to come back you'll be repulsed and thankful I left, it'll make getting rid of me that much easier. You don't have to be the asshole, Parker. I managed to do that part for you.

I throw the phone to the mattress as tears slip from my eyes. I don't want to be a dick, but I have to protect myself somehow, and this is the only way I know how. My phone chimes next to me and I'm actually scared to look at it.

Scared my attempts to push him away are working.

PARKER: Drew gets the 'I miss you,' and I get the cold, withdrawn bullshit?

PARKER: And it's not MY family, it's OUR family or did you forget that part?

DREW: Seriously? There's no makeup sex when you guys piss each other off unless that weasel brother of yours was lying and you're still here.

ME: I'm a very long way away from Phoenix. Not in the same time zone, let alone zipcode.

DREW: And what zipcode would that be?

ME: Nice try. And I need Parker mad. Makes shit easier if he hates me. The longer he holds out hope I'm coming back, the longer he's going to be hurting. Once reality hits him of what y'all saw, he'll reconsider. I'm just putting a little distance up in the meantime.

DREW: You're in a different time zone. I think you took the distance thing a little too literal, sunshine.

PARKER: I'm not going anywhere, sweetheart. Piss me off, fine. I'll just make the next time I see you that much more interesting. Never angry fucked before.

ME: Drew, get off Parker's phone, asshole.

PARKER: Not Drew. You piss me off; I'll turn you on. Seems like a fair trade to me.

BROKEN

ME: Turn me on, I'll get laid here. You're going to realize soon enough that I'm not worth it.

I won't. There's only Parker, but if he believes me it could be the final straw, he could let go, and I wouldn't have to worry about him when I'm in Reno.

PARKER: Stop acting like a couple of threats are going to scare me away. You showed me, Haley. I saw them, and then I covered you when you freaked out, and I told you I loved you. Your arm doesn't change who are you as a person. Let that sink in while I take a shower. Don't worry. I'll send pictures.

ME: What's Parker doing?

DREW: IDK. Headed off to his room, why? You and hubs having a fight?

ME: I don't know. I'm really confused. I'm waiting for him to freak out or tell me to go fuck myself but instead, he's telling me he's gonna seduce me for payback.

DREW: EW. One, rude. Two, that's my brother you're talking about. Three- is that a real thing? Wait, no- I don't want to know.

ME: I don't know if it's real. But I'm nervous. Can I ask you a question?

DREW: Yep.

ME: You see my arm?

DREW: Nope.

ME: Are you lying?

DREW: Yep.

ME: Parker says he doesn't care. Just- mentally prepare me, is he about to get revenge or does he really not care?

DREW: I think he cares the same way I care, so I don't know what you mean by getting revenge.

ME: Last guy that saw them ran off but not before telling me just what he thought of me before doing it.

DREW: What a dick! What's his name? I'm gonna track him down and beat him with his own dick.

DREW: You can't see it, but I'm snapping my fingers at you.

ME: He was a John, so I don't know.

DREW: Jesus, there's like a million John's, it's like the most popular name ever.

ME: His name wasn't John he WAS a John.

DREW: What like a guy who buys hookers?

ME: Ding ding ding. Feel free to stop responding when you figure it out.

DREW: Not ignoring the fact you just admitted to being a prostitute but Parker just came down the hall in only a towel with a shit eating grin on his face.

DREW: So, you're a hooker, huh?

ME: Jesus. No, I am not a hooker. Thanks though, your confidence in me just makes me soar.

DREW: Good, I try. I'm gonna want names of every asshole involved. I've got some errands to run, might as well eat the miles in Josh's truck while I've got it.

 PARKER: [attachment]
 PARKER: [attachment]
 PARKER: [attachment]
 Oh fuck. Nervously, I tap each icon and watch as the little download bar progresses.
 DREW: Growing old here. Names, Hales. Now.
 ME: John, John, and maybe a Johnny? I don't fucking know. They don't give their names. They paid my dad and off I went. I'm super regretting telling you by the way.
 My phone chimes as each photo loads, opening the messages I really, really, really, wish I never clicked them. The first, he's gloriously naked in the reflection, but the counter hides the goods. The second, he's in the shower, his face isn't in it, but it's shot from above him peering down, showing his hand wrapped around a certain part of his gorgeous body. The third, oh fuck the third... well the third isn't a photo at all- It's a video.
 Starts on his beautiful face as beads of water slide over his features and slowly pans down, the faucet must be hitting his shoulder because water is rushing down his bronzed body, he goes over his abs, and I'm definitely hating my life at the moment. His hand is moving, I can see just enough to know what he's doing before the camera lifts back up,

"God, after being with you it's kinda hard pretending. Though thinking of you pressed up against this shower, completely naked, scars and all," He groans a second, "Wrapped around me, screaming for me to fuck you harder as your nails dig down my chest." His shoulder tenses and the screen drops lower, showing his hand before abruptly panning to his face, "Too bad you're not here to see how this ends."

The video ends, and I swipe my finger back and forth trying to find the rest of the video but no dice. Fuck me that was mean. That was so unbelievably mean. Jumping up, I open the door, my eyes looking for Kaylan.

"Kaylan? You here?"

Nothing. Walking out I check the bathroom and the other room- all empty. The front door is locked, and the keys aren't on the hook. Perfect. Running back to my room, I shut and lock the door. If he wants to play dirty, I'll play dirty. I'm not going to be the only one frustrated. Fuck that.

Stripping off my clothes- all of my clothes, I lay on my stomach, using my left arm to hold the phone, I fan my hair to cover the available skin and take a photo showing just how very naked I am and send it to him.

ME: Is this what you were imagining?

PARKER: You're facing the wrong way, sweetheart.

BROKEN

Rolling over I once again fan my hair to cover the hideous marks and drop my right hand between my legs, rolling my head to the side I close my eyes aiming for that sexy, I'm-about-to-cum face that no woman actually has and send it to him.

ME: Like that, sweetheart?

PARKER: Jesus Christ.

I smile at the phone. That's right. See, two can play this game.

PARKER: Not that that isn't sexy, but I'm pretty sure I'm the one supposed to be between your legs.

ME: You're not here so I thought I'd pretend.

PARKER: You're gonna need more than two fingers to play pretend.

His video mixed with his text have me breathing heavy already, not wanting to stop and lose momentum I turn it to a video, taking extra care to avoid all possibilities of my arm being in the shot.

"Not if you were going down on me." I pant. "If your head was between my legs, you'd have two fingers right," I pan down to show my hand, just I push two fingers inside myself. "Here, and you'd curve them like this." My breath catches as I speak "Your mouth would be here," My thumb hits my myself and I move it to mimic his tongue.

My stomach starts to tighten. "Ugh, and you'd be looking up at me." My toes curl into the mattress as I ride the wave with thoughts of him and I don't realize I've started crying until I come down. Quickly turning off the video, I wipe my face.

Fuck, I miss him. I miss him, and he's clear across the country. I can't exactly send him a video of me crying, so I lean over and pull the phone into my hands to delete it, but to my horror, I realize the fucking thing is already sent. Quickly clicking the video, I fast forward through the embarrassing parts and stop when the camera hits my face- fuck, fuck, fuck. I don't know if you can tell without knowing but as I stare, I see a tear slide down my cheek and then when I opened my eyes you can tell. Dammit. Not only is the video slightly embarrassing but then I'm crying. Just peachy.

Three dots appear, and I swear it's like a train wreck, I want to look away but I can't.

PARKER: God damn, you're perfect.
PARKER: If I call you, will you answer?
ME: No, probably not.
PARKER: If I call, will you listen?
ME: No, probably not.

Before I know it, his name appears on my screen, and because I apparently love heartbreak- I answer.

"Hi, sweetheart." His voice is husky and deep and goddamn this was a bad idea. I cover my mouth trying to hide the cry. "Oh, baby- don't cry. Please, don't cry."

I try super hard to stop, promise I do.

"God, I miss you. You don't have to talk. I just want- I don't know...to feel like I'm near you, I guess. To try and make you feel like you're not alone." I sniff and stare at the ceiling trying to dry my eyes a bit while he talks. "Two things, one; if I was between your legs you would come a lot faster and a lot harder." I give a breathy laugh as I fight the tears, "Two, I wouldn't have made you cry."

He's quiet for so long I have to look at the screen to see if the call is still connected. When he speaks again his voice is raw and defeated, "God, I miss you, Haley. I know you're not here, but I keep getting up like if I knock on your door, you'll be there. I keep rolling over in bed, expecting you to be there and you're not. I got out of the shower knowing you weren't here but I still felt disappointed when I opened the door, and you weren't sprawled across my bed. Everything smells like you...my sheets, my pillows, my couch. What am I supposed to do when that fades? Because I'm terrified you're not coming back."

I choke on my cry, pulling the phone away from my face.

"I can't." I cry to myself, unable to control the heaves, I force a deep breath before picking up the phone, "I have to go."

BROKEN

I know he's talking, but I can't hear his words as I end the call. Throwing the covers over my head, I cry into my pillow. Ignoring the text ringer, ignoring the front door I hear open and close, ignoring the knocks, I ignore it all and cry. I'm in love with someone who might actually want me, and I can't have him.

If I go back, the devil will kill me, but if I stay away, this heartache might kill me just the same.

CHAPTER FORTY-FIVE

After the worst of my heartbreak passes I pull my phone over, ignoring any and all texts and start writing Parker the things I know will push him away, things that I've never told anyone. I'm not coming back, and I can't string him along, I can't be selfish.

ME: I was a prostitute, had my first John when I was fifteen. The man I lost my virginity to paid for it... you're the only guy I've ever slept with that hasn't given me money. I've fought, hustled, stole, and fucked for money.

We need to cut ties altogether. This number won't be valid in few minutes so responding is pointless. I'm not a good person, Parker. It's time you realized that. You think you love me, but the truth is, you don't know me. You're claiming to be in love with a junkie hooker who happens to be the daughter of one of the most powerful men in Nevada. You don't love me; you loved the girl I pretended to be.

Granted most of this a manipulation of the truth. Was I a whore willing? No. Am I a junkie? Absolutely not, the truth is I was drugged to forget, but I leave that part out, I also leave out the part where every birthday he carves a line into my arm and uses me as an ashtray every year on the anniversary of my mom's disappearance because that's how whores are treated. I don't mention that I've been beaten to the point I thought he ruptured a lung and I prayed that he did because suffocating to death was more comforting than living. Fortunately, for him, he had a side bitch that was once a doctor or some shit before she started shoving shit up her nose and was more than happy keeping me alive for a free high. I also leave out the part about the guy who was murdered and the first time I had to scrub blood out of the carpet. Dad likes drugs and control, he's made friends with a lot of very bad people, and if any of us talk we're dead, so I take all of that out and hope like hell it's enough to finally push him away.

I send the message and immediately open up the conversation to Drew-

BROKEN

ME: My phone is being deactivated. I'll call you tonight.

Once the chime of the sent receipt sounds, I pop the battery out and remove the SIM card, perk of leaving my iPhone back in Phoenix. Laying them flat on the table next to the bed, I tug clothing on, throw my hair up and pop my hood before exiting the room.

Kaylan is sprawled out on the couch, remote in hand. "Hey, you okay?"

"I'm going out."

"Out where?"

"Outside."

He stands, running to catch up with me as I walk through the door. "You got your phone?"

"Nope."

Descending the stairs, I can hear Kaylan trotting behind me, "You need your phone in case anything happens."

"Nothing's going to happen."

"You got money for a cab?"

"Nope."

"Fuck, Ryan. Wait!"

I ignore him, entering the back of the bar where Hoyt is serving a heavier crowd than I expect for five o'clock on a Monday. Being small it's easier for me to weasel my way through everyone than it is for Kaylan. I push through the door and swing a right when I exit the mouth of the alley. Apparently, the 'safe area' is this way.

BROKEN

Within maybe two minutes I walk through an underpass, oddly enough there are even shops here, exiting onto the other side the street is flooded with people. Some walk in a hurry where others stop and look at the last of what the street vendors are offering. Mostly holiday-themed items, like snow globes, wreaths, and handmade items. I pass a guy selling live trees with a sign saying all profits go to the local Boys and Girls Club.

With the last of the sun setting- at five in the evening which is crazy to me too, the street lights are turning on, painting the town in yellow and red light, it's surprisingly beautiful, and the cold is absolutely horrible in case you were wondering. Phoenix lows were maybe sixties. That's this places' highs and let me tell you- not a fan of the cold.

I snuggle deeper into my hoodie and press forward not ready to face reality yet. I pass Riverfront Plaza where this kick ass, old school looking riverboat with huge holiday wreaths decorate the sides, is loading passengers for a night tour. I people watch for a minute as I slowly stroll down the street, letting the sounds and sights dull the ache in my chest.

Stopping abruptly when a couple of little kids run in front of me. I watch them run down the stairs to climb into a play boat named, TINKERBELL. The little girl has on a little sailor hat and claims she's the Captain because of it.

Not wanting to seem like a creep I continue my journey to nowhere.

The sidewalk opens up to a pavilion, and I step inside to give myself a break and trying not to get run over by tourists. Taking the steps, I sit halfway down and watch as the massive cranes across the river move side to side. A few pavilions down they're setting up a community tree taller than the two-story building across the street. The town is coming to life, music is coming from all different directions, people are laughing, clearly starting to drink- which seems odd for a Monday, but what the hell do I know.

A man in a suit passes me thumping a pack of cigarettes on his palm, fumbles and drops them at my feet. Bending down I pick them up and hand them to him.

He nods and takes them from my hand, making it a bit awkward when he sits down beside me and lights one, before offering me the opened pack.

"Thanks," I say, pulling one from the pack and placing the filter between my lips. Extending his hand out to me he lights my cigarette, then places the lighter in his chest pocket, looking across the water.

"Beautiful night." He says.

I nod, pulling the addicting poison into my throat.

"Business or pleasure?" he asks when I don't move the conversation along.

"Haven't decided yet."

"Well, I hope you find what you're looking for, looks like a good night for figuring it out."

I look up at him for a moment trying to understand his words. I know he's speaking English, but I'm a little slow at the moment. He doesn't continue or elaborate, just stares out across the water, so we end up smoking in peaceful silence before he stamps his cigarette out and stands. "Thank you for that. It's been a long time since I was able to just sit with a person and think."

Not sure what to do, I blow out the last of the smoke and crush the cherry under my foot, noticing his pack still sitting on the step, I pick up before calling after him.

He turns but continues up the steps. "You forgot your smokes."

"Keep them. I think you've still got some things to work out." With a small smile, he disappears into the crowd.

Man, Savannah is weird. With the chill numbing my fingers I decided to man up and call Drew, then I can walk back up to the room and hopefully sleep until the pain is gone.

Walking up I find a payphone and drop in a few quarters, dialing Drew's number, making sure to star-six-seven the number, I wait as the dial tone rings out.

"Hello?"

"Hey, it's me."

"Hales?"

"Yeah."

"What the fuck, dude. Are you okay? That douchebag didn't fucking leave you in the middle of nowhere, did he?"

"No, I'm about to board my bus. I just wanted to call you before we left. I don't know the next time I'll be able to, so..." I trail off, not knowing what to say.

"What's up with your phone? Do you need me to send you money?"

I laugh a little at his sweetness, "No. I'm fine."

"So, what happened?"

"I can't come back, Drew." He takes a breath like he's about to say something, but I keep talking, "I can't. I want to, you'll never understand just how bad I want to, but I can't."

"Where are you headed? Parker and I can come to you, Hales."

"He knows who you are and he knows he can use you to find me, so the best way to protect everyone is to keep you out of this."

"Not if we're smart about it."

"It won't work. Kaylan and I are going to have to split ways soon because the risk is higher when we're together. It won't work, I wish it could- but it can't."

"Then tell me what to do, Hales. I don't care what it is if we have to rent a fucking private jet and move to Bora Bora, we will. You just have to tell us what to do."

"I'm sorry," My voice is giving me away, and I don't think I can do this. "I have to go."

"Haley- please don't. Not yet."

"Drew, I have to."

"When does your bus leave?"

"It's boarding."

"Liar."

"No."

"Yes, you are. You just don't want to sound weak on the phone cause you're crying. Cry, dude. Cry if you're sad, but don't stop talking to me just because of it."

"I really do have to go."

"You haven't even asked about what happened with that biker chick."

"What biker chick?"

"Remember that one that ran you over at HEAT?"

"Oh, yeah the bitchy one."

"Yeah, her. Got her number, yesterday."

"Congratulations, when's the wedding?"

"We decided to skip the ceremony and go straight to the honeymoon. Taking her out tonight."

"Don't wear that flannel shirt."

"What? That's my lucky shirt, of course, I'm going to wear it."

BROKEN

I giggle at the memory of the deeds performed while wearing that shirt. "Trust me. Wear the grey one. Makes you look hotter."

"DAW, you think I'm hot. I knew it! Still wearing the flannel though."

I laugh through the tears, "Ask Parker if you should wear the flannel, then when he laughs ask him why."

"EEEEEWWWWWW. NO, YOU DIDN'T!! I'm wearing it right now you, jackass!" I laugh again, wiping the tears away, the phone alerts me my time is running out.

"I'm out of quarters. I gotta go."

"Get a phone, Hales. Please. Not only because I'll have the opportunity to chew your ass out about bumping uglies in my shirt but because I'll know you're safe if you have one. I'm really not cool with you traveling without one."

"I have a phone; it's just... not in use at the moment."

"Why? For real, do you need money?"

"I can't talk to Parker, Drew. I just can't. This is hard enough, and after what I said to him earlier, I don't think I can handle hearing what he has to say."

"Parker was pissed earlier, but not at you. He tried tracing your phone but couldn't do it without knowing your phone's info and shit-"

"Hey, Drew. The phone's gonna die and I have to say goodbye this time."

BROKEN

"No- Haley! Goodbye means I'm not seeing or hearing from you again!"

"You're my best friend."

"Haley- fuck. Please, don't."

"Bye, Drew." I start to put the receiver down when I hear him yelling, "What?"

"I said, I love you, and this sure as shit isn't goodbye. You call me when you can."

"Bye."

"Later, sunshine."

Placing the receiver down, I open the pack of cigarettes and pop one in between my lips, walking over to a group who's smoking I speak to the girl who first makes eye contact, "Lost my lighter, can I bum yours for a sec?"

A guy next to her pulls a red zippo from his pocket and hands it to me. I light it fast and hand it back, "Thanks."

The walk back feels far longer than coming in, probably because I'm freezing my ass off. After walking through the underpass, it got a little tricky seeing as this is more or less all bars on this side. Going too far and knowing it, I swing back around and back track until I start to recognize things, with a few creepy glances inside bars, I finally find Hoyts and walk up the alley to the side entrance.

Hoyt is pulling a case of liquor from the shelves to my left, "Yer old man's pissed."

I assume he's talking about Kaylan, "Why?"

"Yous rushed outta here, and he couldn't find ya'. He said to tell yous to get yer little ass upstairs and call him immediately."

"Yeah, well he can take his request and shove it up his ass." Nodding to the packed bar I ask, "You need help? I've got lots of experience."

"Little too rough for yous, darlin'. But thanks."

"That ain't rough."

He laughs, shaking his head. "KD'll cut off my balls and feed 'em to me."

"KD can suck it. If he was here minding his own damn business, you wouldn't need my help."

He laughs, scrubbing the stubble along his jaw. "Alright, darlin'. If that's the way, yous wanna play this, grab one of 'em shirt outta that box and meet me up front."

He walks to the front while I grab the first shirt I touch and throw it on over my hoodie.

Approaching the bar, I nod at the man who's currently tapping his fingers impatiently against the bar.

"Shots."

"Of?"

"You, if your offering."

"I'm not, so pick your poison or get the fuck out."

BROKEN

He laughs a greasy sounding laugh and points to the Maker's behind me. "Gimme four."

Fishing out his glasses, I fill them and turn to Hoyt. "Maker's-four." Looking back at the impatient man I nod toward Hoyt, "Pay the man."

"What you want?" I nod to the barely-there dressed blonde; Drew would lose his mind over this one. "Six shots of tequila, six chasers."

"We don't serve pussies; I can get you water."

"Ugh, sure."

I nod grabbing a tray, filling her order and slide it to Hoyt. "Six- speed rail tequila, six water backs." He nods ringing it up.

This method is how we carried out the evening. Around one thirty Kaylan came in, if he was angry while looking for me, he certainly wasn't happy with me serving. He attempted to remove me by grabbing my elbow until I twisted and kneed him in the balls threatening to rip them off next time he grabbed me. I carried on as nothing happened, even helped Hoyt close up, all the while Kaylan sat glaring from the steps.

"Looks like yous got some shit ta' talk through," Hoyt tells me when we're finished. "Try not to bust up my bar too bad, if yous wanna get hot and heavy- do it upstairs 'less yous want to be recorded." He nods to the security camera before climbing the stairs leaving Kaylan and me alone.

"I tell you to bring your phone- you don't. I tell you to call me when you come back- you don't. I tell you not to work in this bar, and you do it anyway. What the fuck, Ryan?" He says with barely confined anger.

"Perhaps next time you won't tell me to do shit. And if you were here and not chasing after me like I was a child, he wouldn't have needed the help."

"I didn't know where the fuck you were! How the hell am I supposed to protect you?"

"Jesus, Kaylan! Stop with the protecting bullshit! I don't need protection. I walked around; I came back. I'm not seven anymore; I don't need my boo-boos kissed and shit. I worked behind the bar and made two hundred bucks, all without your protection."

"Then why the fuck am I even here?"

"If you don't want to be here, leave. It's what you're good at after all. No one's making you stay. Got along in Phoenix just fine."

"Until you got attached. Until you stupidly let your guard down and got caught. Until you needed me to pull your ass out 'cause you couldn't!"

"Fuck you! I'm running *for* you, you arrogant bastard! I'm running to protect you and Parker, Drew, Josh, all of them!"

"What the fuck is that supposed to mean?"

"It means I cut a fucking deal and I'm running with it!"

"What deal?"

"It's done, it doesn't matter."

"Dammit, Ryan! WHAT DEAL?"

"You sound just like Parker. A deal, a bargain, an agreement between two people-"

"Jesus, I'm not a fucking idiot I know what a deal is, what was the deal?"

"One that saved your life. So, do me a favor and lay off. I got this shit under control."

"Jesus Christ." He breaths, wide-eyed. "What did you do?"

"What was necessary. Because *yes,* I did get attached, I fell in love and let someone else love me. *Yes,* I did let my guard down, I let myself be part of a family, and *yes,* that was stupid, but for a brief moment, I got to *live.* Are you telling me that living with a woman and having a kid you didn't let your guard down? You didn't fuck up so you could selfishly enjoy one goddamn moment of happiness? And I didn't need you to pull my ass out; I needed my fucking brother so I wasn't completely alone again! I did what was necessary to protect the only fucking people that matter to me. So, you can take that stance, that face, and that tone and shove them right up the ass I just saved."

Shoulder checking him, I pound up the stairs, jumping out of my skin when I run right into Hoyt who was smoking on the stairs. Double fuck.

"Didn't wanna to miss the epic fight tha' was brewing, was hoping you'd break up with him." He laughs, "But it appears either yous lyin', or you's a couple of freaks."

"You repeat anything you just heard, and it'll be the last thing you ever hear. Got me?"

He whistles, staring at his cigarette. "Yous a feisty one. Whas' tha' deal, runnin' from the law?" Kaylan, clearly hearing us talking, approaches behind me slowly.

"I wish. Pissed off the wrong people at a young age." He says.

Hoyt looks from him to me and back. "Yous lying, KD?"

"Nope."

"If I report you's, am I gonna hear different?"

"No," I growl.

"Wha's your name, KD?"

"Kaylan Hale."

"Idiot," I mumble.

"Wha's yer's, darlin'?"

"None of your goddamn business."

"Ryan."

"Jesus, Kaylan. When was the last time you were knocked the fuck out cause I'm about to pound you seven ways from Sunday."

"Why hide who we are if there's nothing to hide?"

"I got a lot I'm trying to hide, fuckwad. He runs those names; they land in Reno. Guess who's the first to find out? Daddy dearest that's who and we're both dead."

Hoyt whistles again with an apologetic smile. "I gonna need proof, darlin'. I ain't riskin' jail time ov'a few words."

"Fucking fantastic." I growl, "Give me your phone." I tell Kaylan who curiously hands it to me. "This is just fucking perfect." Dialing my old number, I wait until a beautiful voice answers.

"Hey."

"Hey, it's me."

"Fuck, Haley. Are you okay?"

"Not exactly. I need you talk to someone. Just answer whatever questions he asks, please. And truthfully."

"Um, sure. Okay. But are you okay."

"I'll let you know."

Handing the phone over, Hoyt looks at it a moment then puts it his ear.

"Hello?...Who's I talkin' to?... Alright, Parker. Do yous know the woman who called you?... Do you know the guys she with?... Wha's their names?.." He laughs once and looks at me, "Wha's their relation?. Okay, well her brother said her name's, Ryan." He chuckles again. "Ah, I see that's the oth'a I.D. Here's ma' problem, I overheard some shit, and I need'a know if them is running from the law... She said sometin' like that. How old are they?.." He chuckles again.

"Again, didn't get no I.D, so how's 'bout you give me which ever is true?...Damn. She makes a kick ass bartender... Yeah, o'course... Oh, I don't know 'bout that." He looks up at us, "He wan's to know where yous are."

"Of course, he does." I huff, "The only thing he needs to know is if we're safe or not. Whether you're running our names or taking his word for it. Whether we've got a place to crash or not."

He thinks for a moment before answering me, "I trust wha's been said, yous free to stay as long as needed."

"Then tell him we're safe. It's all he needs to know."

He nods, taking the phone off his shoulder and back to his ear, "Sorry man. Yer girl says the only thing yous need to know is she's safe...yeah, brother. Here she is-" He extends the phone to me, taking it, I offer Kaylan a glare and move past Nosy Rosy and go up to our floor.

"Hey."

"What was that about?"

"Kaylan was an angry bastard, and that dude over heard. Threatened to run our names but that will lead my Dad right to us, so I called you."

"I'm glad you did. How was the trip to wherever you are?"

"Fine. Look, I gotta go."

"Haley. Please, don't go. Just let me talk to you."

"We don't have anything to talk about."

"Maybe you don't, but I do."

"I know you do, but I can't handle what it is you have to say. I'm not coming back, Parker."

"I know, but that doesn't mean I can't talk to you."

"Yes, it does."

"I have to fly out in a couple of days to check a few HEAT locations; I'll be hopping place to place, I can come to where you are, and no one would blink an eye."

"He'll know to follow you. That's a risk I can't take."

"He's going to follow me to three different states while I'm having meetings all day? There's also a paper trail that has these trips planned for the last six months. It'll work, I just need to know where to meet you."

"Parker," My voice threatened to break, so I gave myself a second to recover. "We can't be doing this. All it's doing is twisting us up more than we already are. You had to have known I wasn't a forever thing. Can't we just say goodbye and be done?"

"No, we can't. The second you kissed me outside of HEAT you were a forever thing. Do you remember what I told you after Thanksgiving? I want you today. I want you tomorrow, I want you a week, a month, a year from now because you're worth it-"

"A whore is worth it, Parker? Do you want to know how many times I've been passed around? Too many to fucking count, so many they don't have faces. I'm not worth it, I've never been worth it but I'm selfish, and I wanted to know what it would feel like if I was born into a different life and it fucking destroyed me. So, for the love of God, Parker, just let me go before I destroy you too."

Without letting him respond, I hang up and twist to the stairwell. "I know you're fucking there, Kaylan. Open the goddamn door."

Without speaking or looking at me, he comes around the corner, slides the key from above the light and unlocks the apartment.

"That's a stupid place to hide a key." I grumble as I pushed past him and into my 'bedroom,' slamming the door behind me, but not before throwing his ringing phone onto the couch.

Pacing the room, I finally decide on the floor next to the window. Who knew a beetle walking across the railing of a fire escape could be so interesting. I stare at that stupid bug for what has to be close to an hour before Kaylan blesses me with his presence.

"What are you doing?" He growls from the door he entered without knocking. "You're fucking up the one good thing you've ever had."

"Yeah, what the fuck do you know?"

"I know how much this life sucks when you give that shit up! I know how lonely it is! I know that this decision is going to kill you! You may be breathing, but it will kill anything good still inside you."

"There wasn't anything good to start with."

"How can you be this stupid? He doesn't care! All that truth you laid out to push him away? He doesn't fucking care! He's literally willing to leave everything for you! You're so swept up in your self-pity bullshit because one guy was grossed out. One and he didn't even matter! The one who actually matters knows, knows your history, knows you're a self-hating coward, and still he wants to save you. Jesus, Ryan, just let him save you, take a fucking chance."

Taking the remote off the stand next to me, I throw it at him. "You don't think I want to?!" I scream back. "Jesus, if it were that easy I would gladly go! The deal was I leave and never come back! My happiness was the first thing he made damn sure to destroy! I keep in contact, and they're dead, Kaylan! I told you I made a deal to protect everyone!"

"Who the fuck's protecting you?!"

"I AM! Like I always have!"

"Look at your fucking arm and say that again." Picking up whatever this x-shaped luggage holder thing is, I throw that at him too.

BROKEN

"FUCK YOU, KAYLAN! Look at my arm and tell me again why you didn't have the balls to take me with you! I'm breathing aren't I?! I protected myself a hell of a lot better than you ever did! Dad tracked *Mom* to Phoenix! He found me through the both of you! I got my ass kicked because of you, yearly scars because of that gash and then when I was finally happy it was all ripped away because of the both of you! *THEN*, I save your ass, and all you can do is throw names at me and remind me of everything I was forced to leave behind! So fuck you, Kaylan!"

"I didn't ask for you to save me!"

"And I didn't ask for you to find me!"

We both stand our ground, glaring holes through one another while our chests heave.

When he speaks, it's calm despite his breathing, "Negate the deal."

"You don't negate a deal with the fucking devil, Kaylan! You know that!" I, however, am not as calm as him.

"Then offer him a new deal. Me for you."

"You don't have anything he wants."

"He wants me dead."

"Still not a better offer."

"What the fuck are you giving him then? Can't be money so what is it?"

"I have two options."

With a heavy sigh, I watch him try to reign in his temper, "And they are?"

"Return to Reno or -"

"Fuck no, you're not going back to Reno. What's the second option?"

"Half the blood in my body." I look up at him, watching as my words sink in.

"Half the blood-? That will kill you."

"Pretty sure that's the idea."

"And this is all due when?"

"Don't worry about it."

"Fuck that. When?"

"January First."

"That's in a couple of weeks, Ryan!"

"Three."

"Jesus, were you ever going to tell me?"

"No, probably not."

"And how does that work?"

"I dip out. Leave a note, spin a lie that leaves you blissfully ignorant."

"So, you're going back?"

I give him a shrug. "Don't know yet."

"Jesus, you can't seriously be weighing these as viable options."

I nod, "Have to. Keeps him away from you and everyone in Phoenix."

"For how long, til he gets bored?"

"He gave his word, Kaylan."

"Fuck his word!"

"Other than his right hook, it's the only thing you can depend on from him!"

"You're dead either way!"

"That's not your decision!"

BROKEN

"Jesus Christ." His hands tangle in his hair, "I don't know how to get you out of this other than running."

"I can't run. Parker and Drew are the first people he'll go after."

"They're willing to come with you!"

"What about Josh?! And Maria, Vinny, Jules?!" I count on my fingers, "What about them?!"

He stares at me, chest heaving. "I can't let you do this."

"You can and you will. I made the deal. I made peace with the deal."

"Fuck no; you haven't! Or you'd have found another way!"

"There is no other way!"

"FUCK! Ryan!"

"WHAT?! What would you have done if he offered me, Caroline and your son protection for life? Would you have found another way or would you have dropped to your knees and kissed his shoes?! Cause I chose the one that keeps the people, I love, safe!"

"That's different!"

"HOW! How is that different?!"

"Because I can defend myself! I stand a chance! You'll pay for every day you spent away, pay for every smile, every laugh, everything."

"And it'll be worth it because everyone will be safe. You're not changing my mind, and there is literally nothing you can do to stop it."

"Goddammit, Ryan." He runs his hands through his hair once again, looks at me and turns for the living room, "Apparently, there's a HEAT here in Savannah. Parker will be here Tuesday. Thought you'd want to know."

With that he stepped out of the room, entering the one next door and shutting the door like nothing was just said, nothing laid bare, like it was a Monday night and he was simply going to bed.

CHAPTER FORTY-SIX

After Kaylan and I's little blow out he has very little say when he's around, and he's not around much. Over the next week, Hoyt allowed me to help open and close, but I haven't been allowed back behind the bar, so I've had a lot of time to myself. I mostly just walk up and down River Street, hang out at the plaza and watch the riverboats, oh- and try to find HEAT.

Found it on Saturday, turns out it's not on River Street. Not sure why I assumed just because it was in Savannah it would be on the same street as me. It's a twenty-minute walk from Riverfront Plaza. Using my fake I.D, I wandered through, which proved to be a terrible idea. It's a carbon copy of the Phoenix location, just with different furniture in the lounge areas. I was quick to leave after that and haven't returned.

Parker apparently arrives at some point tomorrow, and I'm having the internal war from hell. I desperately want to see him, but I know if I do, I'll lose all self-control and barrel into him in a fuck-the-consequences sort of way. Wouldn't do well for my week-long sobriety of all things Hayes. No Parker, no Drew, crickets.

I feel like I'm already losing this battle as I stare at the SIM card that's still laying on top of my phone from last week. Afraid seeing it will lead to temptation, I open the draw and swipe everything inside, slamming it shut.

I had nails an hour ago, I desperately tried to forget what day of the week it was so I could avoid his visit but Kaylan, in all his fucking glory, decided to pop his head in my door and announce it before retreating to his bedroom when he came back home. Bastard's up to something, I know it. No way he would let this lie. I'm a fucking idiot for letting anger bring out the truth.

Staring at the drawer, I yank it open, grabbing the pieces to the phone, I pop them into their designated spots and turn it on. Hey now- I never claimed to be a smart girl. With its resurrection, the screen lights up with texts and missed calls. It appears my week-long sobriety was one-sided.

BROKEN

Most of the texts start with 'Don't know if you're getting this," "Don't know if you've read," all from Drew and Parker. Also from Parker was a handy little itinerary with the locations, time arriving and time departing, hotel information, all staring me right in the fucking face.

SAVANNAH, GA Tuesday, 3:25 pm. Flying out Atlanta, Thursday, 7 pm.

FUCK. No, I can't. I throw the phone in the drawer and stare at it. That lasts all of two minutes before I pull it back out and send a message to Drew, because yes, I'm that stupid.

ME: At a motel up North. I'm safe. Going off the grid again, just wanted to check in. Hope things with Biker chick went well.

Staring at the message, I blow out a breath and deleted it. I can't. I'm disappearing in two weeks, better to start now. If I check in, they'll expect it. I can't.

Locking the phone back in the drawer I lay down and try to force sleep, which as you know- never happens when you do that. I toss and turn with that internal battle. My head is going one way, my heart in the other and I can't steady my body long enough to make a decision.

Blinding light wakes me, incredibly too early, I might add. The stupid thing was rising when I finally fell asleep, but at least I made a decision. I've decided that I will under no circumstances talk or make Parker aware of my presence, but I will give my selfish side a little nibble and more or less stalk him. Do not look at me like that, I'm running off of like two hours of sleep, and it's the best I could come up with.

Pulling myself up, I go to get out of bed but then remember the phone can tell me what time it is faster than the stove can. Pulling it out of the drawer I nearly audibly gasp, 3:54 PM. Fuck! Jumping out of bed, I quickly dress, throw my hair up, brush my teeth and basically run out of the apartment, turning back around to grab my phone.

Kaylan smiles at me from the couch, "For stalking purposes, not to contact him, thank you very much."

"Mhm, let me know where you're sleeping tonight."

"I'm sleeping here. Alone. Because I'm not telling him I'm here."

"Okay! Have fun. Use protection!" He yells after me.

"Fuck off!"

I don't know if he heard me, but I wasn't about to wait and find out.

I run like a bat out of hell out of the bar, using fancy shortcuts I've found over the last week, I cut through alleys to HEAT.

BROKEN

I'm sweaty, out of breath and any weakness I had at approaching Parker basically vanishes when I catch a glimpse of myself in a shop window. I'm a hot mess, less on the hot, heavy on the mess. My skin is flushed from running and the cold, mixed with the wayward hairs sticking to the beads of sweat dotting my forehead- it's not cute. Pushing the strands of hair back, I sit in my little stalker post across the street and like the unpracticed stalker that I am, I fucking stare.

He's gotta show up at some point, right?

FOUR HOURS later, I'm a fucking popsicle.

To prove my, 'I look like hell' case, the shopkeeper brought me soup for free, because I apparently look homeless.

Fuck it; I've waited long enough, pulling out my phone to check the time, I see a message from Kaylan.

BIG BROTHER: You said your mind was made up, right? There's no changing the deal? If that's true, give yourself this. Spend a couple of days with him. Say a proper goodbye, leave with no regrets. You'll have something to focus on when shit goes bad. I love you.

DAMNIT, Kaylan! Stop waving temptation. Fuck. No, the dumb bastard's right, fuck it.

BROKEN

Opening up my texts, this is a mistake, I can feel it, I open a new message, big fat fucking mistake.

ME: You're in Savannah?

Ten agonizing minutes later I get a response,

PARKER: Yes, until Thursday evening. Is your phone on for good?

Ignoring the phone comment,

ME: I was there last week. There's this place called the River-something plaza. It has these really cool riverboats there. I sat under the pavilion and watched them for hours. Probably my favorite place there.

God, I'm an idiot.

ME: I don't know why I'm telling you this. I'm sorry. Ignore me.

PARKER: I know it. Drew and I grew up here, we've been on those boats more times than I can count. Which pavilion?

Grew up here! OH, MY GOD, I'm such a fucking idiot!! Parker used to live here! I knew this! The day we went swimming a Josh's he told me he had just moved back from Savannah after getting a new HEAT up and running. IDIOT.

ME: I didn't realize there were more than one. It was more of an overhang, a ton of steps; there was an event there one day, they were setting up a giant Christmas tree.

PARKER: I know where you were. Is this the first time your phone's been on?

BROKEN

ME: Yes. We're crashing in a motel tonight, thought I'd let you guys know I was okay. Saw your text and went off in some stupid memory when I should have left you alone. I shouldn't have texted you, I'm sorry.

This was a mistake. I stand up, trying to get my frozen fingers to pocket the phone when it starts vibrating, Parker.

Of course, he's calling me. Fuck. I swipe to ignore, but he calls again, staring at the screen, movement across the street catches my attention. Holy Christmas balls, Batman. Parker steps out the front entrance wearing slacks with a button up shirt, rolled to his elbows. Oh, my God. Because I'm a fucking masochist, I answer while I drink every delicious inch of him in- I've never seen him dressed up

Hobo speaking, I swear that's almost what I answered with instead I go straight the apology, "I'm sorry. I shouldn't have-"

"Shut up." This causes me to stop everything. He's never told me to shut up before. "I'm walking down to the water. Just humor me, will you?"

"Um... okay."

Stalker mode, engaged.

Keeping to the other side of the road and a healthy distance behind I follow him. He's taking the twenty-minute version, so this will be agonizing, at least I have a great view of his ass in those slacks.

"You okay?" he asks after an awkward silence falls over the line.

"Yeah. Just never heard you tell me to shut up before."

"I'm sorry about that but if I didn't get your attention I was going to lose you again, and I can't go another week with silence."

"I have to save my minutes."

"Can't bullshit me, sweetheart. I've seen you hustle and seen the wad of cash shoved down your bra. I know you can cover minutes."

"Nest egg goes fast when you're constantly moving."

"I can help if you'll let me."

"Parker, if we're going there then I'm hanging up."

"Don't hang up. What are you doing right now?"

"Sitting outside my motel room."

"How's that going?"

"Peachy. Beats sleeping on a bus plus I can smoke whenever I want. What about you? I mean I know you're going to the river but what else are you doing?"

"Just walking. Now that you talked about smoking, I'm about to have one. Been cooped up inside HEAT for a couple of hours."

Oh, I'm well aware. Four to be exact.

"I'll smoke with you," I say.

"Yeah?"

"Yeah. It'll be like were smoking together, walking down the streets of Savannah."

I pull my pack out and light one, all while keeping my eyes on Parker, which is hard seeing as it's freezing outside and my fingers are numb. "Where are you right now?" I ask around my cigarette.

"Halfway there. Deb's Deli is coming up on my right."

In a split, and dumb fucking decision, I just start talking, "Deb's Deli? Purple awning? If that's right cross the street and take that alley. There's this mural down there."

No there's not. What am I doing?

"Between the bead shop and vendors?"

"That's the one. Now, I was only there a couple of days so forgive me if I get you turned around."

He chuckles, and it's the best sound on the face of this planet. "I've got until Thursday, sweetheart."

"With my memory, you might never make it out again. Those alleys were confusing as hell."

"Grew up here, I know them pretty well. Okay, I'm in the alley."

"Okay turn right and go down to the next turn."

"Okay... there."

"I think it's a left?"

He chuckles again, "Okay, left it is." I'm one turn behind him in this maze, and I'm pretty happy with my stalker skills so far. "Now where, sweetheart."

"What's in front of you?"

"I can go straight or turn right."

"Right and then a left, you should end up with the street you came from behind you."

"Okay. Hey, your memory is proving to be pretty good."

"I went there a lot." LIE. I have NO IDEA where I'm leading him right now.

"Alright, sweetheart. Where to now?"

"I think another left?"

"No left, I can go straight or right."

"Right."

"I'm at a fork. Right goes back up to the street; left has a dead end."

"That's where you're headed then."

"Okay."

Oh fuck, what am I doing? My fingers pull my bun painfully while I try to figure out what the hell I'm doing.

"Hey, Parker?"

"Yeah, baby?"

GOD, swoon. "If you could have anything, what would it be?"

"You."

Stepping up against the wall, I can hear him walking behind me. "God, that was a good answer."

His footsteps grow further, and I know he's going to realize there's nothing down there soon. "If you got your wish, how would w goodbye?"

"I don't know if I could, but fuck would I make good use of our time."

I smile at his tone, "Like what?"

"Anything, everything. I'd take you on a fucking date for starters." I stifle my laugh, resting my head against the brick wall. "There's no mural, sweetheart."

"Are you sure? On your right-hand side?"

"Nope. Just brick."

"Okay, don't laugh."

"Why would I-"

"Shush I wish I was with Parker." I'm such a moron. "Fuck. Nope, still a shitty motel. You try."

"Okay." I hear his half smile in his voice, and I'm weak. His footsteps grow closer, Jesus, my heart is beating so fast. "I wish I was with you, Haley."

Okay. Biggest mistake of my life in 3.. 2.. 1.

Stepping around the corner, I drop the phone to my hip, "Yeah?" he stops dead in his tracks, oye, he was a lot closer than I thought, tears immediately surface, and I swallow the emotion, "How bad?"

"Jesus Christ."

No words, not really, for what happens next. He lunges forward, hands sliding into my hair, threading, pulling, his mouth immediately crashes against mine. My hands are everywhere; I can't seem to pick a spot on his body.

His hand leaves my hair to grab my hips, pulling me against him before walking me back into the wall.

"Is this real?" He pulls away enough to look at me before giving in and taking control of my mouth once again, "God damn, I've missed you." He says between kisses.

I love you, is what I don't say. Instead, I take the Debbie Downer route, "This is a mistake,"

"I don't care. God, how long have you been here?"

"The entire time."

He pulls his face up, so we're eye level as his hand's cup my cheeks, then push the hair out of my face, his thumbs brush against my lips, my cheekbone, anything that involves touching me as he speaks, "What?"

"We got on a plane and flew here. I've been here the whole time."

"Here? In Savannah?"

I nod, kissing him chastely.

"Where?"

"A safe house Kaylan has."

"That idiot did something right," He takes my bottom lip as his arms wrap around my middle.

"What do you mean?" I ask when we come up for air.

"Baby, that's really not what's important right now." He bites down my neck, and a moan makes its way out of my throat as my fingers dig into his triceps. "Whose place is closer? Your's or mine?"

"I'm twenty minutes, west."

"I'm five in a cab." He says, grabbing my hand and pulls me beside him, kissing my knuckles as he masterfully works his way out of the alley.

"Parker- wait. If you were followed, we can't be seen together."

"If I were followed they would have appeared by now. I went into an alley, and you followed." He pulls me against him once more, kissing me senseless before dragging me to curb. Doesn't take him long to hail and cab and give them the address to his hotel.

Seats and public decency apparently don't apply to Parker and me seeing as he pulled me into his lap and we've been sucking face the entire ride. He throws some bills at cabby, pulls me into his side and rushes me forward. Elevator etiquette also does not apply to us; he has my legs wrapped around his waist as his hands climb under my shirt.

"Fuck, when does this elevator end?" I whine.

With those magic words, the elevator stops, chimes and opens up to a group of people waiting to board, see public decency above to know what happened with that.

    Carrying me down the hall, he stops momentarily in front of two double doors, throws a key card from his pocket into the door, it chirps and in we go.

CHAPTER FORTY-SEVEN

Hands, mouths, we're no longer human. My ass hits the TV stand, and I'm only there long enough for me to unhook his belt and for him to pull my hoodie over my head before his arms pull me back into him and onto the bed.

I bounce twice as he pulls his shirt over his head as I unsnap my jeans. His hands find the waist of my pants and starts pulling them down as I toe my chucks off. His mouth hits my thigh, and I'm already a moaning, groaning mess. He pulls off my pants without taking his mouth off me.

BROKEN

Working his way back up, I'm unbuttoning my flannel top, but my fingers are still numb, despite how boiling my blood is. My libido is through the effing roof, I need his hands on me, giving up trying to undo the buttons, I just start tugging, popping buttons along the way. Parker notices and decides to partake in the fun, grabbing the collar with both hands, he gives one good tug and buttons flying in every direction as the fabric hits my ribs. Grabbing for his waist, I pull the slide button and unzip. The groan I earn when I palm him through his pants vibrates across my chest, and I just need his pants off.

"Fuck. Parker." I've stooped to begging, and I don't fucking care, I need them off. With his help, his pants and boxers slide down his thighs, using my feet I push them off while his fingers snake around the little black lace that's doing a poor job of hiding just how turned on I am.

He pulls them down, replacing lace for his mouth. I arch forward, my fingers threading through his hair as I gasp. Moaning, I rock against his mouth; he uses one hand to untangle my panties off my ankle, the other slides under his jaw. His fingers are as cold as mine adding a very new sensation as he slips two fingers inside, curving them up, he rocks his hand to sync with his tongue.

Jesus, I'm not going to last. "Parker. Parker- I'm gonna-" I break off when an involuntary moan climbs out of my throat. My stomach is tightening, my toes are curling, "I'm gonna cum. Fuck. I want you- Oh God. Fuck- Parker, I want-"

Jesus, he's fucking me stupid- literally.

"Fuck me. Please, fuck me." He shakes his head 'no,' and his restraint breaks, his fingers pound into me at an almost painful speed and the coil inside me explodes.

I scream, my body folding up and into itself. His free hand vises around my hips so I can't scoot away. He holds me to him, forcing me to ride out the orgasm, giving me no room to come down from it alone. His mouth and fingers slow but he's still not releasing me.

"Fuck me. Please. I want you to fuck me." My fingers knot in his hair as I force the words out.

"Baby, I'm just getting started." He wipes his chin with the palm of his hand before putting the two fingers he was just fucking me with into his mouth. Jesus Christ, he's sexy. Grabbing his jaw, I crush my lips against his. He groans against my mouth as he crawls up my body, reaching between us, I wrap my hand around him. He lets out a hiss before sucking on my shoulder. Reaching down, he gently removes my hand, pinning it above my head.

"I've been fantasizing what I would do to your body for the last ten days. Spoiler, it all evolves you screaming my name, not me blowing my load in the first fifteen minutes."

"What are your fantasies?" I ask, trying to grind against him.

Looking between my legs, he smiles, "That was one of them. Ever since you sent me that video that's all I've wanted to do. Drove me crazy." He grinds his erection into my thigh. "Been living with a permanent hard-on ever since."

"Let me fix that for you." I wiggle my wrist that still pinned above my head. "You're not the only one with fantasies."

He groans, taking my bottom lip between his teeth, "Pray, tell." His hands roam down my stomach.

"Riding you." I moan, as his fingers fall lower, "Turning that little video you sent me into a reality. God Parker, you better fuck me and real soon cause I'm dying."

"Are you?" The hand not pinning me to bed pushes against the fabric on my shoulder,

"Parker-" My voice goes from sultry to panic in a nanosecond.

"Not the left." He says as he leans over, kissing my shoulder, fuck, that's a first, and I like it. "Parker, why won't you fuck me?" I whine.

"I've got to calm down first. I want to make you cum again, but I can't do that if I'm this close already."

"You can fuck me again, later. Please."

"You've never begged before, and it's not helping me calm down."

I breathe, as he continues to slowly peel my sleeve down.

He squeezes my hip as I moan, "Jesus, you're gonna kill me, woman."

He lets go off my arm so he can get the sleeve past my elbow. Sitting up, I let him roll the sleeve off, watching as he kisses down the path of exposed skin, running my fingers down his chest, I lean into him. "Let me ride you. We'll work fantasy to fantasy."

Kissing along his jaw, he draws my knee around his waist. Finally.

BROKEN

Slowly, laying back he lets me straddle him, I grab the sleeve and start to put my arm back into it when he stops me. "Leave it."

"I don't want it to fall off."

"Let it." He sits up, so we're nose to nose, I can feel him between my legs, and I'm about to explode. "I want to see all of you, as much as you'll let me."

"I can't," I whisper against his mouth. "I'll be terrified of it falling off the entire time."

Without words, he grabs the collar and helps me cover up once again, taking the loose ends of the shirt he ties them behind my back, so more of my chest and stomach are exposed. Palming my chest with one hand, his other guides me to raise up on my knees, we both inhale at the same time while I lower onto him.

His hand finds my hip as I claw his sides, trying to drown my cry against his shoulder. Fuck, I miss this, this is where I belong, throwing caution to the wind and reverting back to the animalistic behavior I arrived with, I sit up and slam back onto him.

His fingers dig deeper as he grunts against my neck, sucking and biting from my left to my right. "You should know, I plan on turning your neck, so purple, every man within a hundred miles knows you're taken."

"Fine with me."

He meets me thrust for thrust, setting a bone breaking speed between us. We're a clawing, grunting mess as we lose ourselves in each other. His abs harden, and I can feel his breathing change.

"God, yes." I moan, he turns almost savage everytime he cums, and it's my favorite part. I crave it.

Feeling his fight against it, I rock harder, take him deeper, his hands run from my hips up to my back and into my hair before abruptly, flipping me over and pulling out.

"Nooo!" I whine, "Why'd you pull out?"

"Cause I'm not ready for this to be over." Grabbing my hips, he slides me to the end of the bed, then picks me up, I wrap my legs around his waist, devouring his mouth with mine as he walks us into the wall.

He slams into me, and I tighten my hold around his neck. "You're beautiful." He thrusts into me, "I'm in love with-" Slam. "every inch of you." Pound. "If you let me," Thrust. "I'll prove just how true that is." Slam. "I love you." He picks up speed until my insides tighten. "God." He groans against my shoulder.

His hand moves down to my hip as he pistons himself harder and I can't hold out, "Parker-"

"Cum, baby."

"Fuck-" Oh my God, I'm building, and I can't slow it down, a surge of adrenaline races under my skin creating goosebumps to surface, "Parker...Parker...-" FUCK! My body detonates around him so powerfully; my head falls back involuntarily; every limb tightens and digs deeper into his muscles.

"Ah, Jesus-" He buries his face into my neck, biting as his hand closes painfully around my hip- fuck, this is what I wanted.

Throwing my ass down I let him sink deeper as he roars against my throat. His fingers are sure to bruise, and I still crave his grip be tighter. After his breath slows, he pulls out, lowering me to the floor, he takes my jaw in both his hands and kisses me with so much love and longing, I break.

Holding my arms close to my chest, I fall into him, hiding my face against his pecs and I cry while his arms wrap protectively around my shoulders, his hand comes up to rest at the back of my neck, holding me tighter against him.

"I love you, Haley. If I could take whatever it is you're running from away, I would. I'll go anywhere with you, if you wanted to leave the country, I could have you on a plane in an hour. Just tell me how to help you. Please, baby, because it's killing me knowing at any moment you could disappear, and I may never see you again."

His fingers tilt my head up so he can kiss me, he holds me against the wall, pouring his heart into this kiss and it actually might be killing me.

Feeling like the pain will cause physical damage.

"I need a minute," I tell him pulling away to enter the bathroom.

Splashing my face with cold water, I decide to dress in the robe hanging off the back of the door- you know, easy access. Exiting the bathroom, I crawl up onto the bed and sit cross-legged, watching the muscles in his back ripple as he puts his pants back on.

"Do you have smokes?" I ask.

"Of course." He gives me a wicked smile before pulling a pack out of his pants pocket, sticking two in his mouth, he lights both before handing me one.

"I don't know what it is about that- but I love it."

"What? Lighting both?"

I nod, he smiles. "Are we allowed to smoke in here?"

He gives me a shrug and unwraps a plastic cup, making me giggle.

He stills, "God, do that again."

"Do what?" I ask around a lung full of smoke.

"Laugh. I think that might actually be my favorite sound in the world."

I give him a sad smile, "I miss you."

"Miss you doesn't fit." He says, climbing up the bed with the little cup for us to ash in, sitting with his back against the headboard, he pulls me between his legs, letting me rest my head against his chest. "I'm miserable without you, sounds a little more accurate."

He rests his chin against my hair as a tear slides down my cheek, "This was a mistake, wasn't it?"

"No." He says quickly. "It'll make leaving so much harder- but no, being with you is never a mistake."

BROKEN

"The shit I've done though. How can you still want me?" Tears slip unchecked as I wait for his response.

"Because that's not you. Maybe at one time, but nothing you've said sounded like it was your choice. Everything sounded like you did what you had to do to survive."

Absently he collects my left hand and runs his thumb over my- mostly unblemished wrist. I pull it away and hide it in my lap.

"Why do you hide?" He whispers gently against my hair.

"Because they're disgusting and something I never want you to see. Something I never want to see."

"Nothing on you is disgusting." He kisses my hair, using his fingers to put out the cherry of his cigarette, I watch as the little red ember falls to the bottom of the container.

"They'll scare you away, and as much as I need you to leave, I'm terrified of it actually happening." I put my cigarette out on the side of the cup and then place it on the side table.

"I told you once that unless you've got a dick, it'll take a lot to scare me away." I give him a little smile before leaning back into his chest.

BROKEN

"I knew this guy; he was the first guy I was- well, that part doesn't matter." I whisper, "He was nice, didn't force me into anything, paid in advance, so I didn't have to do that kind of work because he knew I didn't want to. Thought I was falling in love, so I gave him my virginity. I was so nervous he let me keep the lights off, but once the lights came on, he was so repulsed that he said a lot of nasty things and left me in the motel room and never came back."

"He didn't deserve you," He gently lifts my left arm, even though I fight it, he slowly lifts it until he can kiss my forearm through the fabric, "How do I make you see that I'm not him?"

I turn to study his face; there's no hurt or anger there, just general wonderment. "I don't think you're him."

"How do I prove to you that I think you're beautiful, that a couple of marks don't bother me?"

"It's a lot more than a couple and if the shit it triggers whenever I'm touched isn't bad enough-" I trail off and try again, "When I took off my sweater in your room, I haven't felt fear like that since Nevada. I don't ever want to feel that way again. Being face to face with my dad was less scary than having my biggest flaw out in the open to the two people I wanted to hide it from the most."

"Drew never mentioned it and the only time I remember is when it's brought up."

"You always say such pretty things."

"I always mean them too." He kisses my hair once again before leaning over and collecting a spiral bound book off the side table.

"What are you doing?"

"Changing the subject," Wrapping his arms around me he opens the book to reveal the room service menu, "If I plan to make good use of my time with you, we both need to keep up our strength."

Using my hand, I pull his face into mine and kiss him, 'thank you' doesn't really cover it, so I hope this does. Pulling away he smiles, leans in and kisses me chastely once more before flipping through to find the dinner menu.

CHAPTER FORTY-EIGHT

Parker orders us food that we enjoy wrapped around each other in bed. I don't think we're making the conscious decision of constantly being in contact with one another; it's just happening.

"Do you hear that?" I ask. We both lean forward, listening. "Shit. It's probably my phone. Kaylan's probably pissed." I lay on my stomach, reaching over the edge of the bed to get my phone out of my jeans, well aware that my ass is hanging out.

Parker is aware too; his hands fall to the back of my knees as he rubs up my thighs.

BROKEN

Finding my phone, I see the screen is clear of all notifications. "Not my phone. Is it yours?"

"Don't care." He admits, crawling up my legs so he can kiss my inner thigh.

Searching the floor, I find his discarded slacks and pull his vibrating phone out of the pocket. "It's Drew."

I reach behind me and hand him the phone, which he then takes and tosses it on the bed beside him. "He can wait. I've got more important things to tend to." He pushes the robe up my back, kissing a line up my spine as the phone starts to vibrate again.

"That's like the fourth time." I tell him, he answers with a 'Mhm' but doesn't stop, "Could be an emergency."

His mouth stills a minute, then pulls me back into him and grabs his phone, placing it on speaker, "Hey, Brother."

"Holy shit, asshole. We've been freaking out!"

"Why? What's going on?"

"You never told anyone you landed. You've been MIA for like seven hours."

"Oh shit, I'm sorry. I went straight to HEAT and then I kinda got..." He looks down at me and smiles, "distracted."

BROKEN

"What the fuck could be more distracting than letting us know you're safe, man." Drew sighs, almost angrily.

"Hey man, you're on speaker, and I'm not alone."

Before I can say anything, Drew's rage blares through the speaker, "No, you fucking didn't! What about Haley, dude?! Her life ain't hard enough without you nailing some gash in Georgia?! What the hell is wrong with you?" I start laughing, and Parker leans down to kiss me.

"I'm not here," I whisper against his mouth, he gives me a questioning look but doesn't say anything.

"Seriously?! Your side bitch is laughing? For fucking real man?" Starting at Parker's neck, I kiss a line south. "Parker's fucking some skank in Georgia while we're all out breaking our necks trying to find Haley." He yells into the background while I continue down Parker's body.

His chest is rising and falling rapidly as I pull his zipper down. He's already hard as he ignores Drew's rant and watches me while I wrap one hand around him and start pumping in long, slow strokes, he takes a deep breath and then holds it, eyes closed, head tilted back.

Smiling to myself, I leaned forward, wrapping my lips around him and slide him to the back of my throat.

"Gah- fuck!" He gasps, grabbing a fist full of my hair.

"What, dude?" Drew asks in annoyance.

"Fuck." He breaths, his fingers tangling in my hair as I continue, "Stubbed my toe."

"Boo-hoo. What the fuck, Parker?"

"What?"

"Jesus Christ. If you're getting nasty with that bitch, I'm gonna lose my mind."

"Let's not call her a bitch, alright? You're still on speaker."

Bobbing my head, his hips start to move. Without mercy, I let go of him and slam down, taking all of him, swallowing as he pushes past my throat.

"Jesus Christ! Drew, I'll call you back."

"God dammit, Parker! You're a piece of shit!"

Without responding, Parker hangs up and tosses the phone to the side, using both hands to cradle my head. The noises Parker's

BROKEN

producing are nothing shy of animalistic, "Fuck, I'm gonna cum."

"Mmmm."

"Jesus! Baby- Gah. Shit..." I hum against him again, swallowing in rapid succession until his body jerks forward, "Fuck! Now-" His fingers tightening further. Pulling him out enough to take a breath, I swallow once more as he loses himself.

"Holy shit." He rests his head against the headboard, while his shoulders rock with heavy breathing.

Smiling, I wipe my mouth and reach for his phone.

"You're in trouble."

"I know. He thinks I'm cheating on you." He says tucking himself away.

My smile fades as he takes the phone to call Drew back. "It wouldn't be cheating."

Pressing a button and audible ring comes through the speaker, "You're mine, Haley."

Before I can say, anything Drew answers the phone, "No- I don't want to fucking talk to you right now!"

"DREW!" I yell into the phone, "Calm your tits!"

"No fucking way." He whispers, "Hales?"

"Awe, my knight in shining armor!"
"What the fuck?! You're in Georgia?"
"Since last week."
"I told you to come with me," Parker adds.
"Josh, Mama Mia- Hales is in Georgia. She's the skank Parker's nailing in the hotel." I can hear Josh and Maria in the background; their voices growing louder as they approach.
"Drew!" I hiss, "You can't be telling people! I'm safe here, but I don't want to leave before Parker has to. If you announce to the world where I am, I'll have to leave again!"
"Wait- did Y'all know you were meeting up?"
"Way to ignore me, asshole."
"No," Parker cuts in, "I sent Kaylan and Haley my itinerary, she showed up when I left HEAT."
"I'm confused. I thought you've been on a bus traveling the damn country?"
"Nope. Been freezing my ass off in Savannah." I smile against Parker's chest as his hand wraps around my waist.
"Is that really, Haley?" I hear Josh ask in the background, "She okay?"
"Yeah, she's with Parker in Savannah."
"Did Parker know she was there?"

"Nah, sent his flight details to her brother and she showed up."

"Thank God." Maria sighs, "Is she coming home with him?"

My heart sinks, and I find myself close to tears once more.

"Let's just take this one day at a time, alright?" Parker steps in for me.

"Are we on speaker?" Josh asks, and someone must have answered because he continues, "Haley, Parker has your phone. Use. It. Don't feed me any of that 'I can't' bullshit either. I'm telling you to use it, so use it."

I shake my head. "My brothers have that phone number; it's traceable."

"All phones are traceable. This way you're guaranteed a phone with everyone's numbers."

Looking up at Parker, I shake my head, "I can't" I whisper.

"Humor him." He mouths.

"Okay. I'll take it." The lie tastes bitter in my mouth, but I take comfort in the reassuring squeeze I get from Parker.

"Thank you." Josh sighs, "Do you need anything? Money, plane ticket?"

"No, I'm alright."

BROKEN

"If I ask what's going on, are you going to answer me?"

"No, probably not."

"Will you call me if you need help?"

"No, probably not." I laugh.

"Stubborn child. I swear."

"HA!" Drew barks, "I'm not the problem child anymore!"

A loud popping sound followed by Drew's shriek makes Parker, and I laugh.

"Are you eating?" Maria's motherly tone takes over the line.

I laugh, "Yes, I'm eating."

"Parker, did you feed her?"

"His dick." Drew laughs, then yells for Josh not to hit him.

Parker smiles down at me, "Yeah, I fed her."

"Good. Are you warm enough?"

"I'm fine. We've got everything we need; I'm okay."

She sighs sadly, "Okay. Well, I'm going to give you back to Drew before Josh kills him. We love you, Haley."

My chest seizes, and I can't force the words out.

BROKEN

"I know. Thank you." I bang my head against Parker's chest for my weakness, and he hugs me in response.

"Damn, I wish I would have come with." Drew whines.

"You can come next time." I lie. There won't be a next time, but I say it to help alleviate some of the hurt in his tone.

"Yeah. Definitely. You're there till when? Thursday?"

"I fly out of Atlanta at seven. I'll be in Phoenix around ten, I've got a layover in Dallas."

"Alright, what's y'all's plan? Well, other than gettin' freaky."

"It's after eleven, probably get some sleep." Parker mouths, 'no' to me and I smile up at him.

"Well, wrap it before you tap it. Don't need Haley running around the country with little Parker Jr swimming in there."

My face scrunches up, and its apparently pretty good cause Parker starts to laugh so hard, he tilts his face away from the phone and covers his mouth. "You should have seen Haley's face right now!"

"I wish I could; I haven't seen it in like a month!"

BROKEN

"It's been ten days, Drew."

"Fuck you, it feels like a lifetime!"

Rolling my eyes, I scoop my phone off the comforter and turn the camera towards us, holding the center of the robe closed, I stick my tongue out and snap a picture and send it to Drew's phone. "Incoming."

"Awe, look at you, all just fucked and everything."

"Shut up." I laugh, but I know he's right. My hair's a mess, I never put on makeup, and my neck is bruising.

"Jesus, Parker. The girl is supposed to have the mouth like a vacuum, not you."

"Fuck off." I tell him, "He's making sure every guy in- what a hundred?" I look up at Parker and he nods, "in a hundred miles knows I'm taken. My other option was to be peed on, and I'm just not into that sorta thing."

Drew barks out a loud, "Yeah, me neither. I guess I would have taken the brand too. What about you, Hales? You gonna mark your territory?"

"No, I'm just gonna fuck him so good I ruin him for all women."

"Ew. Just fucking- ew. That's my brother."

"You're just jealous."

BROKEN

"Love you, Hales, but you're not my type."

"I'm a big chested blonde." I laugh.

"You do have a great rack, but you're a brunette, dumbass."

"I'm a natural blonde."

"Oh shit. Well, stay brunette, and I won't try to steal you away from Parker."

Parker laughs, brushing the hair off my shoulder, "Good luck, brother."

"Don't think I won't win. How 'bout it, Hales? Two for one special?"

"Nah," I twist my fingers into Parker's, thick hair. "I've got a thing for brunettes."

"Well, damn. Bet if I dyed my hair you couldn't tell us apart."

"Parker's hotter, and you've got a fat head- I'd know."

Parker laughs as Drew scoff laughs, "One- rude. Two- not true. Three- mean."

"Speaking of mean, how'd biker chick go?"

"Fuck man. Just add insult to injury why don't you."

"Couldn't seal the deal?"

"Fuck you. I'll get there."

"Don't stalk her you creep."

"Don't tell me how to live my life."

BROKEN

We laughed and carry on like it was just another night at the apartment until almost one.

Settling under the covers, I curl up against Parker's side while unlocking my phone,

ME: I'm safe. Check in with you later.

"Kaylan?"

"Yeah, I'm letting him know, I'm okay."

My phone buzzes in my hand, drawing my attention,

BIG BROTHER: Am I locking the door?

"He wants to know if I'm coming back tonight."

"No." He answers quickly, wrapping his arms around me. "You're staying here."

Folding my lips in to hide my smile, I reply.

ME: Yeah. I'll be back tomorrow to change.

BIG BROTHER: Use protection. Sweet dreams. Love you.

I scoff audibly and set my phone on the side table before falling back into Parker. His fingers hook under my knee and draw it over his waist, while his fingers slide up and down my legs.

"Hey, sweetheart?"

"Yeah?" I ask closing my eyes, drowning in the happiness I feel being against him.

"Go out with me?"

BROKEN

I chuckle and snuggle in closer to him, "No."

He sighs, kissing my head, I can feel sleep start to pull me.

"Stay with me." It's the last thing I hear before I fall into the best sleep I've had since Phoenix.

CHAPTER FORTY-NINE

I wake up to lips against my neck and an erection against my hip. Easy to say this makes top three best wake up calls. Post morning sex, I lay on my stomach, resting my chin on my folded arms, watching Parker rifle through his suitcase. Every part of him becomes my favorite whenever I see him, but his back always remains high on my list. The way the light bounces off his sun-kissed skin, the way the shadows hide in the craters of muscle. Those panty dropping dimples. Jesus.

"Enjoying the show, sweetheart?"

"Mmm. I think that's an understatement."

He gives me that half smile of his laying his clothes next to me. Picking up a folded shirt, I roll onto my back to play with the fabric. "You're so organized."

He shrugs as he pulls on his jeans- commando. I raise an eyebrow at him, and he gives me a knowing smile.

"That's just mean."

"How so?" He pulls my ankles, so my legs fall flat and crawls up my body. One hand supports his weight while the other pulls the robe open, "I think you should just wear this- all day, every day." Kissing the valley between my chest, he rocks against me.

"Better behave, or you'll never get to work," I tell him, secretly hoping he chooses to stay in.

"Fine by me. Playing hooky anyway." His thumb pulls my lower lip down, and he catches it between his teeth. "Spending the day with my girl, today."

I smile against his mouth and groan when he pulls away, grabbing his shirt off the bed.

"I can't go out like this." I look down at my nakedness.

"I mean-" He shrugs, "If you really wanted to, I won't stop you, but it'll be hard to wake you like I did this morning if I'm sitting behind bars for murdering half the town."

I blow out an incredulous breath. "I'd be in the cell next to you. All those girls throwing themselves at you while you exert your male dominance? I'd have to kill a few to set an example."

He nods, "Fair point. So, maybe we don't wear the robe?"

"Guess not." Standing up I collect my jeans from the floor and dress quickly while throwing my chucks on my bare feet.

Parker smiles at me, "No panties or socks. Trying to one-up me?"

"I already wore both of those; I can't." I shudder, "Ew." Grabbing my hoodie, I step into the bathroom. After discarding my robe, I pull my hoodie over my head. "Jesus. I look like a hobo." I try to smooth my hair, but it's useless.

"A very beautiful," Parker walks in behind me, "very sexy, hobo." His hands climb under my hoodie and palm my chest. I rest my head against his shoulder, "I want to fuck you like this later, I want to watch you come apart."

I meet his hooded eyes in the mirror and smile at him. "Am I spending the night again?"

He nods, pulling his hands out from under my shirt, he catches my belt loop and pulls me from the bathroom. "Am I coming with you to change, or are we meeting up?"

"Are you going to try and kill Kaylan?"

"No. He did what he said he'd do; he's safe."

"What?"

He pockets his phone, wallet, and key card before linking our fingers together, "Ready?"

"Yeah, but what are you talking about?"

He gives me a smile, kissing me quickly and pulls me from the room. What the hell did Kaylan do?

Parker, being all about conveniences, hailed a cab that made the journey to Hoyt's a hell of a lot faster. Stepping out, he links his fingers with mine and allows me to lead him to the side entrance.

Hoyt's eyebrows shot up when he took in my appearance and then narrowed at the sight of our hands. "Not a brothel."

"Not a whore." I shrugged, trying to divert his attention away from Parker.

His eyebrows lift as if questioning that statement and Parker takes a step forward.

"Hoyt, Parker. Parker, Hoyt." Kaylan says quickly, stepping in between the two.

"Ah, tha' fella from the phone," Hoyt says with a huff as he lowered the case of booze. "Don't make waves in ma establishment."

Kaylan sends a nasty glare in my direction. "That's her boyfriend, Hoyt. The real one."

I roll my eyes, trying to step towards the stairs but Parker doesn't move with me, so I more or less stop abruptly since he still has my hand. "Parker?"

"We gots a problem?" Hoyt asks.

"Jesus, Hoyt. Knock it off. He'll hit you so hard you'll wake up three months from now, nine months pregnant, maybe even paraplegic, who knows." Hoyt turns to glare at me, and I offer him a shrug. "What? Were you hoping I'd make my way into your bed? Like I said, not a whore."

"Just think it's fucked up yer man lets you go off on your own when yous was in trouble is all."

"Sounds like you don't have all the facts, friend." Parker takes another step towards him. "Also, doesn't give you a right to call her a whore, so yeah, I got a problem."

Turning to me, Hoyt gives me a once over, "He treat yous right?"

"God, what are you? You got no right playing white knight; I don't fucking know you."

"Yous always in sleeves and yer neck is mighty purple. Makin' sure he ain't using yous as a punching bag is all."

"It's fucking freezing here and my necks purple because I was up all night taking that dick."

"God, Ryan. Not what I want to hear."

"Why are you here?" I ask my annoying ass brother.

"Making sure we don't end up on the street cause these two can't play nice."

"Long as he ain't slappin' her round, I'm good."

"And the whore comment?" Parker asks, "Cause that's my issue."

"Di'nt say she was one. Said this wasn't a brothel."

"Implying what?"

"Implying that girl's been awful sad since she came here, makin' sure she don't go round makin' bad choices."

"Kay. Well, now that, that's settled- Parker." He gently shakes his head, still looking at Hoyt. I let out an exasperated sigh. "You leave tomorrow. It'll be god-knows how long until we can see each other again. You really wanna spend that time having a stare down with this guy? Or would you rather nail me against my bedroom wall? Cause this-" I point between them, "Is fucking pointless." Letting go of his hand, I move towards the stairs, "Let me know what you decide."

I made it to the second floor before Parker came up after me. "Good choice."

"No-" he snakes my wrist, turning me back to face him, "Don't be mad." He dips his face into my neck, his breath is hot and goosebumps race across my skin. "He pissed me off. Had one of those internal wars, just took me a second."

"War with what? Not pissing me off vs pissing me off?"

"No." He places a kiss to my bruised skin, "Knocking him the fuck out or not. I realized if you got kicked to the curb Kaylan would be coming with and I'm just not down fucking his sister in front of him."

A loud throat clears, making us both jump apart.

"Much appreciated. So maybe the stairwell isn't the best place for that either."

I giggle as Parker slaps him on the shoulder, "If you don't want to see or hear it, not sure why you followed us."

"I've got the keys." He dangles the piece of metal in front of him, "Also, Ryan, a word?"

"A sentence."

He sighs angrily, passing me up to our floor, I roll my eyes and follow. Parker takes my hand as we wait for Kaylan to unlock the door. "Alone, Ryan."

"For fuck's sake. Both you guys are truly determined to waste my time aren't you. Make it quick, and I mean quick."

"Just get inside."

I turn towards Parker, stepping up onto my tiptoes to kiss him. "He gets one minute. Come in anytime after that."

"Ryan."

I drop down and glare at him. "Kaylan," I say in the same angry parental tone.

Waving me through, he closes the door behind him.

"Make it fast, Sparky, I got shit to do. Well, actually I've got Parker to do-"

"What the fuck, Ryan?"

"What?"

"Why would you bring him here?!"

"Well originally I was just gonna suck him off in the cab, but then I realized just how annoyed you'd be if I did it in my bedroom, so I brought him here instead."

"UGH!" He shudders, "Ew, stop it."

I shrug, hopping off the counter and towards my bedroom. "Don't ask questions you don't want the answers to."

"Goddammit, Ryan. You realize we have to leave now, right?"

I spin at the foot of my bed. "Why?"

"Because he knows where you are."

"Ugh... slept in his bed last night, Kaylan. Pretty sure he already knew."

"What happened to just stalking?"

"I got a text that said I might as well enjoy what little time I have left. It's the damnedest thing. I can't seem to remember who it was that said that."

"Drop the shit! You should have met up with him later, not brought him to the damn safe house for a quick fuck! You didn't learn how to do that shit outside? Surely, being a whore taught you something!"

NO, HE FUCKING DID NOT.

Picking up that weird luggage thing again, I throw it at him. He ducks and it smacks into the wall, caving the drywall as it falls. Kaylan stares at the hole for a minute and then stares at me in silent rage.

"FUCK YOU!" I scream, pointing at him.

"Fuck me? If that had hit me, I could have needed a hospital!"

"How dare you bring up that shit!" Grabbing a frame off the wall, I throw that at him too, "And use it against me!" He back pedals into the living room while clutching his bleeding forearm. "GET OUT!" I yell at Kaylan, "FUCKING LEAVE."

The door swings open and Parker steps through, clearly hearing me scream at Kaylan.

He looks me over before taking in Kaylan and the rest of the apartment.

"You're making a mistake here, and you fucking know it."

"I said, get out."

"Have your shit packed and ready to go. The second his family gets on a plane to get you we're both fucked. But sure, spread your knees before all that goes down."

Raising his finger to Kaylan, Parker steps forward. "Watch your mouth."

"Or what, Prom King?"

"Or I'll beat some fucking manners into you. I don't care how you to talk to me or to other women, but you will not talk to her like that. And her family isn't coming either so don't go making demands about packing any bags."

"Fuck this." Kaylan shakes his head, "If this shit comes crashing down, it's on you, Ryan." With those last words, he slams the door closed behind him.

BROKEN

Parker and I just kinda stare at each other while my breathing calms. He's the first to break the silence, "Go out with me?"

I smile at his clear deflection of the situation.

"No."

Stepping back into my room he follows and leans against the doorway. Seeing the hole in the wall, he looks down and toes that weird wooden thing. "Remind me not to piss you off."

"Don't bring up my past and I promise not to throw things at you."

He whistles before moving to lay down on my bed. "Do you own a skirt?"

I outright laugh, "No, no I don't."

"A dress?"

"Not currently."

"Hmmm, we need to pick you up one, I think."

"Why's that?" I ask straddling his hips.

"Just had a thought is all." his hands run up and down my thighs.

"You're up to no good." I tell him leaning down to kiss him, "I like it."

Pulling myself upright I grab a clean change of clothes and move towards the door, "I need ten minutes."

He groans then pouts, let me just say this- Parker pouting? Super hot.

BROKEN

"You want to watch me shower?" He sits up, a half smile on his beautiful face. I hold out my hand, and he takes it. "This way."

I make him turn around as I undress, not letting him look until after I'm behind the frosted door.

"Funny." He says with absolutely no humor.

I giggle, grabbing the loofah off the hook. "You can kinda see me, I'm sure."

"This is rabbit-eared cable compared to the full HD I was expecting."

Lathering soap onto my arms I notice the weak spray keeps my arms sudsy and my scars aren't noticeable...nope, that's a dumb idea. I don't need to see his reaction. His room was pretty dark the night he saw my arm, and this is a well-lit bathroom. Shoving the thought away, I quickly rinse and wash my hair.

Ringing the water from hair that stupid thought resurfaces.

"Hey, Parker?"

"Yeah, baby?"

I go silent weighing this decision. I want to, but I don't at the same time.

"Sweetheart?"

"Yeah. Sorry. Um... I was just thinking-" I take a deep breath, looking down at my Frankenstein's arm. "Did you mean what you said last night? About not caring? About my arm, I mean."

"Of course, I meant it."

"If I asked you to come in here and you saw it? What would happen if it was worse than you remember? What if I let you in and everything I said was right, that it completely grossed you out, would you still want to be with me?"

I catch his silhouette stand from the counter, "Nothing on this earth could change my mind about you. Scars, no scars. Living in Phoenix, on the run across the United States. There isn't anything you can say, do, or show me that's going to change that."

I nod, even though he can't see me.

Using the loofah, I apply another thick layer of lather before opening the stall door, "Then you can watch, or you can join."

The second that sentence left my lips, he reached behind his neck and pulled his shirt off, dropping it on the counter behind him, his eyes never leaving mine. He toes off his boots while popping the button on his jeans. I step in deeper into the shower with a speedy heart, looking down to make sure the worst of my arm is covered just as he steps in, closing the door behind him.

I don't move, I just kinda stand out of the way of the spray as he stalks towards me, his fingers diving through my wet hair, he pulls my mouth to his in a kiss so sweet I want to cry. He reaches blindly to my hands and wraps both of them around his neck, slowly stepping backward to pull me under the water. My heart picks up as the water slides the thick foam down my arm. Without breaking eye contact, he holds my left hand in place and kisses the inside of my wrist. His thumbs rub in idle circles against the back of my hands while he slowly kisses lower on my arm, my skin is like one of those raised maps with all the bumps and craters on it, so I know he can feel the difference. My eyes tear up when he doesn't let me pull away.

"You're beautiful." He says softly. "Inside and out, top to bottom."

I stare at him, trying to see any disgust or regret in his eyes...nothing. I see none of it, just the same kind, blue eyes as he's always had.

"What?" He asks gently, searching my eyes.

I shake my head a moment, while my fingers trace his jaw, "Nothing."

I kiss him again before side stepping to exit the shower.

Swiping the towel off the hook, I wrap it around me before grabbing one out of the closet for him.

Not knowing what to do, I grab my brush off the counter and pull it through the tangles while he washes in the shower.

After my tangles are free and my teeth are brushed he comes up behind, sliding his hands against my waist before leaning into my damaged arm and kissing my shoulder. "Thank you."

BROKEN

I look at him through the foggy mirror, "For what?"
"Trusting me."
"I've always trusted you."
"This is a different kind of trust."
"I was just scared," I whisper back.
"And are you still scared?"
"Terrified."

After dressing in clean clothes and grabbing a few things to get me through the night, we were back in a cab. After dropping my stuff off with the hotel clerk, Parker took me out to an early lunch, then down to check out the historical landmarks, past the cemetery where his parents are buried, he didn't want to stop, and I understood. I knew they died when Drew and him were kids, but I never realized they died here.

We ate dinner at a cafe and then despite my fear of large bodies of water, we walked down to Riverfront Plaza and took a riverboat tour. Through the events of today, I learned Savannah must be thoroughly haunted because everywhere you look there are advertisements for ghost tours.

BROKEN

Returning to his hotel, we ordered up dessert and threaded our bodies together under the covers. I had an amazing day, one of the best days I've ever had; I'm still laying here trying not wake Parker with my tears.

Wednesday's gone. Tomorrow will be our last day together before he leaves. One more day of happiness with Parker then thirteen days of misery until I hand my soul over to the Devil.

I don't want this to end. It's physically painful knowing that my happiness is about to come crashing down around me and I don't know how to stop loving him enough to survive it.

CHAPTER FIFTY

With Parker flying out of Atlanta tonight, I decided to go with him and get a bus back, it's not the smartest plan but Atlanta is just under four hours away, and that would mean he'd be leaving me at two-thirty. Making the decision this morning, I only got about three hours of sleep before my body refused to give me anymore. Parker woke up around five and agreed to my idea. He kissed away my tears, laid me down and showed me just how much he's going to miss me.

I thought being in a cab for four hours would feel like forever, giving the illusion that today was longer, but that didn't happen, we were there before I knew it. It was already close to noon, and my stomach was in aching knots as we pulled up in front of the airport, a painful reminder that in six hours I'll be saying goodbye.

I follow Parker into the terminal to a bored clerk behind a computer. I hold Parker's hand, playing with his fingers while he makes arrangements to ship his luggage ahead of time. He pays the lady, hands over his suitcase and pulls me outside. Atlanta is actually very pretty, but my mood is so sour I'm not able to enjoy any of it.

"Hey." He whispers, pulling me into him. "It's okay."

Not wanting to cry, all I can do is shake my head. Because it's not okay, this is last time I'll ever see him. In exactly two weeks I'll be dead, either physically or mentally. So, no it's not okay.

With the smallest of smiles he dips his face and kisses me so gently I can feel my heart break and mend under the pressure of his lips. I'm in love with him. Wholly and completely in love with him. He starts to pull away, but I'm not ready, I don't want him to see the change in my eyes, so I thread my fingers through his hair, pulling him back into me.

His face falls to my neck, "Come with me?"

Anywhere, I nod.

BROKEN

Taking my hand, we approach the curb where Parker hails a taxi. We load in, and Parker tells the driver to take us to Skyview- whatever that is.

Twenty minutes later we pull up outside a massive Ferris wheel that's just sitting in the middle of Atlanta. Parker pauses at a little street vendor while I stare up at the white beast, this thing has to be like two hundred feet tall, my goodness. It's beautiful.

The entire thing is white with the exception of one black cabin. The American flag is painted across its center circle with the word, SKYVIEW in the middle. After a moment, Parker returns to my side and leads me to a booth where he gets us tickets.

Not five minutes later we're boarded into a white cabin. I sit across from him on the black leather seats and absently play with the A/C controls above my head.

"I've never ridden on a Ferris wheel before," I admit as the massive wheel starts to rise. In a matter of seconds, I'm basically glued to the window. "Holy crap." I end up muttering out loud. I can see everything up here.

"That's the CNN center, behind you." I turn to look at the massive building. "That's Centennial Olympic Park." I follow his gaze to, what looked like a small park from the ground, to a massive square park with fountains in the center.

"This is so cool."

We continue to rise and then the cabin stills. Fingers close around my hand as Parker pulls my hand to his chest, flipping it, so it's palm up, he wraps a chain around my wrist and closes the clasp. Turning my hand over, he shows me the front of the bracelet, KISS ME AT THE TOP is written across a silver bar with a little Ferris wheel charm dangling off the right-hand side.

I smile, running my fingers over the engraved surface, "We're at the top." I smile.

Without responding, his hand falls behind my neck and kisses me- igniting those flames in my chest. It's long and scorching, almost pleading.

Pressing his forehead against mine, he whispers, "Leave with me." against my mouth.

I pull away enough to look at him. "I can't."

"We can go anywhere, Haley. I don't care where, just-" He searches my eyes, while his thumb brushes my cheek, "Just stay with me."

I feel the burn behind my eyes as the tears scorch my throat. "That's not how this works." He pulls his hands away from me, and I choke on the hurt as he withdraws, closing my eyes I attempt to will the tears away. "I want to. But I can't."

"Do you love me?"

BROKEN

Opening my eyes, I met his hurt gaze. Crushing my teeth together, I try to distract myself from the pain in my chest.

"Please, don't do this," I whisper. It's too early; I still have time. This wasn't supposed to happen until later. Not now, please, not now.

"Yes or no, Haley."

"It's not that simple."

"Yes, it is. Either you do or don't."

"I can't answer that."

"Can't or won't?"

"I don't want to hurt you." I still have time; it's not six yet. Please, please, not now.

"So, no?"

The first tear falls, and I wipe it away quickly.

Pulling in my lips, I try to force my voice steady, "No." I lie through clenched teeth. "I don't love you."

Silence fills the cabin as it passes the ground once more. My body is trembling, and I'm trying to keep myself together, but I just want to run away. Away from my choices, my obligations, my lies. I just want to run until I can't anymore. Run until my legs buckle, until my lungs collapse, until my heart gives out. I just want to run.

"So that's it?" He asks near the top.

I take a deep breath. "I don't know what you want me to say."

"I want you to tell me the truth."

"I am."

"No, you're not. I can tell by the way you look, the way you're trying to mask your emotions, that you're lying. You're hurting."

"You asked me a question, I answered it. I'm sorry it wasn't the answer you wanted to hear, but now you have it."

"Bullshit." He shakes his head. "Why are you lying to push me away?"

"I'm not."

"If you didn't love me you wouldn't have met me back in Savannah. You wouldn't have risked getting caught if you didn't. You wouldn't cry yourself to sleep knowing this was our last day together if you didn't, so why lie?"

"Maybe I just wanted a good fuck while I could get it."

He laughs without humor, "And following me up here?"

I shrug. "Free entertainment."

He purses his lips and nods, looking out the window. "So, I'm to believe that through everything, through all the time we've spent together, I was simply someone who could get you off? That there's no depth to the emotions, you feel for me other than convenience?"

At this rate, my heart is just going to kill itself to spare itself the pain of this conversation, "That's right."

BROKEN

The cabin stops and Parker stays silent as the doors open. He doesn't make eye contact, just stares out the window towards the street,

"I'm sorry," I whisper, standing up. "I really am."

Side stepping his knee, I take the stairs off the exit and pull my sleeves into my palms, squeezing the little charm as I walk down the street, leaving Parker and my heart in a cabin of the Skyview.

CHAPTER FIFTY-ONE

"Haley!" I hear him call behind me, but I don't stop.

Using my sleeve, I desperately try to dry my face as his footsteps close in on me. Hands wrap around my shoulders, and I'm spun and backed into a brick wall. I have no time react before his lips crush against mine. He's not just kissing me; he's branding me, owning my body and soul.

Taking his wrists in my hands, I struggle with the urge to kiss him until he knows I was lying and forcing him away to keep him safe. It damn near destroys me when I lower them and step around him. I can't do this. He's going to see the truth, and then he'll never stop looking for me, he'll never give up, and I don't want that for him. Not when there isn't a chance of us being together.

"Dammit, Haley," He calls after me, "Why kiss back?"

I ignore him and continue walking. To where? No fucking idea. I was supposed to get on a bus at the airport, but that's not happening now, so until I figure it out- I'm just walking. Maybe I'll get lucky and rather than riding a bus; I'll get hit by one instead. Could be fun.

"Jesus! Would you stop running for two fucking minutes and just be here!" I continue to ignore him but being the persistent fucker he is, he follows. "I've got six hours until I leave. I can continue to follow you to wherever it is you think you're going, or you can talk to me. Your choice."

"There's nothing to say," I tell him, still walking. "Go home, Parker. Enjoy your life, get married, have kids. Just go. The sooner you leave, the sooner you can get back to your life before I came in and fucked everything up." I slow and face him, Jesus Christ he's beautiful. "After tonight I'll leave Savannah, and you'll never have to see me again. I won't waltz back into your life and fuck anything else up. I won't call, I won't text, I won't come back. You told me you wouldn't accept anything over the phone or in text because it's easy to hide behind a screen," I swallow hard, pulling the mask tighter around my face, I meet his gorgeous blue eyes filled with hurt and anger, "I don't want to be with you because I don't love you."

Before a flicker of emotion has time to cross my face I turn and run across the street. Once on the safety of the sidewalk, I push forward, refusing to look back, refuse to hold hope he'll spin me around again and prove just how full of lies my mouth is.

My belt loops are tugged, and something slides into my back pocket.

"You're a shit liar," he whispers angrily into my hair, "and I don't like liars. You want me to give up? Let go and forget about you? Fine by me. Don't text, don't call, don't come back. Keep your word, and I'll keep mine." His fingers leave my jeans and feel him pull away.

My chest constricts so tight my breath comes in shallow, and my legs don't move for a moment. Any breath after that is a sob. Forcing one foot in front of the other I move until I come to an alley. Slipping inside, I pull the contents out of my jeans and slide to the cold concrete.

A wad of cash and my old phone sit in my hands. Rolling my phone over between my fingers the screen comes to life, showing the photo of Parker and me in my apartment, snuggled close together with brilliant smiles filled with young love and promises of a future I should have known I'd never have.

BROKEN

The dam breaks and I start to ugly cry; knees pulled tight into my chest as wave after wave of regret, heartbreak, and sheer pain explode from my lungs, pour from eyes, and drip off my chin.

I sit alone in an alley, in a town I've never been to and shatter. Leaving pieces of myself everywhere that I have no intention of collecting. The world can take whatever the fuck it wants from me now, I'm done with this shitty hand I've been dealt, and I'm done pretending like I have a say in what happens to me. I have nothing left to offer but the air in my lungs and the blood in veins, so take them. My heart just left to board a plane back to Phoenix; I have no use for them now.

The four-hour trip back turned into almost seven. I was able to find a bus station, but I had to take eight thousand different ones to finally land me back in Savannah, another hour to sulk in a corner booth at Hoyt's before going upstairs to the apartment.

Opening the door, I noticed Kaylan's backpack and laptop sitting on the counter. Rounding the corner, he stops dead in his tracks.

"Jesus. What are you doing here?"

BROKEN

Not able to take my eyes off the bags, I force my emotions down and look up at him. "You're leaving." It's not a question.

"You're supposed to be on a plane right now."

I open my arms in a grand 'What the fuck' expression. "Why would you think that?"

"Why are you here?"

Did I literally cry my brains out? Because this makes no sense. "What's happening? Why wouldn't I be here?"

He rubs his neck, "You're an idiot." There's no anger in his tone; he seems... sad. "You were supposed to leave with him. You were supposed to choose *him*, Ryan."

"You're speaking English, right? Cause I don't understand any of this."

"Seeing him was supposed to knock some sense into you!" He yells, but again there's no anger. "You were supposed to be selfish!"

"I can't be selfish, Kaylan. You know that."

He shakes his head. "You're still going to Reno?"

"I don't know what I'm going to do."

He shakes his head more aggressively, "This isn't how it was supposed to happen. None of this is going the way it was supposed to."

"What are you talking about?" Agitation is thick in my words. What the actual fuck is happening right now?

"He called me!" He yells, rubbing his neck. "Back in Phoenix. Told me to bring you to Georgia or Texas. Bring you somewhere he would have to travel to so he could convince you to leave with him." His glassy eyes met mine, "I told him, dude. I told him you loved him. How you were crying yourself to sleep, how if he could prove he'd be there for you, you'd leave with him."

"Did you tell him about the deal?" I ask, hurt boiling into rage.

He shakes his head, "Not in any detail. I was worried he'd call the cops and get you killed. I figured you'd tell him and he'd force you to reconsider. I just said you couldn't stay here, that he had to take you with him. You were supposed to leave with him, Ryan. Why are you here?"

"Because this isn't some fairy tale where true love conquers all. This is real life, and my life doesn't allow me to run away without consequences. People *die* if I don't hold up my end of the deal."

"You'll die if you do!"

"Yeah, but you'll be alive. Parker with be alive, Drew, Josh, Maria- all of them will be alive."

His fingers tighten in his hair as he twists away from me, then twists back, "Do any of us get a choice? If you told them, I bet every single one would choose a life of looking over their shoulder over a life without you."

"We live that life every single day, do you really wish that on anyone?"

"I do if you're still breathing at the end of the night! I'd wish it on everyone if it meant your heart was still beating! Jesus, just be selfish! *Please!*"

"I can't."

He lets go of his hair and crashes into me. His arms vice around my shoulders and panic rises in my throat. "I love you, Ryan. Do you get that? Love." He lets go of my shoulders, taking my face between his thick hands, "I love you. I don't care if you hate me, I don't care if we fight, if we kick and scream at each other, I don't care. But I care about *you*. Please, I'm *begging* you- don't do this."

How the fuck is my heart still beating? This is a legitimate question to the universe right now. How can it take so much abuse and pain and still beat?

His eyes burn into mine, "Kaylan." I whisper, trying to keep the trembling away, "I have to."

His eyes squeeze shut before he kisses the side of my head roughly. "I'm not going to watch you die." He whispers against my hair, "I can't."

He kisses me roughly once more before grabbing his computer and throwing his bag over his shoulder, "I love you, Ryan."

BROKEN

With that he steps out of the apartment, leaving me totally and completely alone. Again.

CHAPTER FIFTY-TWO

"Jesus, kid." Hoyt's voice trails into my bedroom. Throwing the covers down I jump back into the wall. "Whoa, calm down." He surrenders his hands, taking a step back. "Haven't seen yous in almost four days. Making sure yous still alive is all." He looks around the destroyed bedroom, "KD told me to watch after yous."

"I'm fine." I croak.

"Think yer lyin'. What you eat last? Hell, when's the last time the shower was turned on?"

"It's been a minute," I admit. My heart's still racing when he turns around.

"Shower. I'll bring up some vittles."

My first thought was, 'I hope that's not a sex thing.' my second thought was, 'When did I turn into Drew?'.

"What's that?" I ask.

"Vittles? Grub, food. Shit yous eat."

Oh. "I'm not hungry."

"Don't gimme any of that, I'm bringing something up, and yous gonna eat it."

"I don't do well with orders."

"Yous don't do well on your own, either. Least this way, yer mad but got a full belly. Be back in a few, if yous ain't out of the john, I'll leave it on the stove. Eat. I'll be back to check."

I scoff but find myself walking into the bathroom anyways. Dumb. I really do need to shower though. My face is stiff with salt, and my hair is in desperate need of some TLC.

Stripping off my clothes, I enter the stall and avoid the corner I spent with Parker. The hot water burns as it slides across my raw knuckles. Perhaps losing my mind wasn't the brightest idea, I'm fairly certain Kaylan won't be welcome here after Hoyt does inventory of the damage I've caused to his place. I scrub and shave, leaving the conditioner in my hair for as long as possible before rinsing and stepping out.

I hear the door open and heavy feet step inside. Hoyt seems nice, he really does, but I don't want to be naked with only a thin board door separating us, so I throw my clothes on quickly and open the door.

BROKEN

JESUS, MARY, AND JOSEPH.

I shriek and slam the door shut, throwing the lock into the wall, I press myself on the opposite wall. OH FUCK.

"Oh, Ryan!" A deep voice sings. Fuck, fuck, fuck.

"I made a deal!" I yell through the wall, "He knows! I made a deal!"

"We know." Go away, go away, go away. "We just need to talk to you for a sec."

"So talk! I can hear you just fine in here."

He laughs, and I swear to God, I might pee a little. "Oh, come on, baby sister. It's been so long, I've forgotten what you look like."

"You'll see me in eleven days, Derek. I'm listening, say what you have to say."

"So, what you're saying is, you don't want to come out here and give me a big-ole-hug?"

"Let's save that for the reunion, huh? What're eleven more days? Distance makes the heart grow fonder and all that jazz."

He chuckles again, and I swear my heart stops beating, the door flies off the hinges, sending splinters of wood in every direction. I scream, holding my arms up to protect my face as he steps over the wood, wrapping his hands into my knotted hair, he drags me out of the bathroom, tossing me onto the living room floor. My body makes impact, and I'm almost immediately up and backing away from them,

BROKEN

Joe and Evan flank Derek as he stalks towards me.

Fuck, I forgot how big they are. Each one is roughly the same height as Drew, Derek has one of those prison-bodies where he's muscular but in a daunting kind of way. Evan is the 'chubby' one of the group, but he packs one hell of a punch. Last is Joey, who's the shortest and thinnest, on his own he's not that intimidating but standing next to the torture twins my blood still runs cold.

"Look at you." Derek smiles, "All grown up and shit."

"I have eleven days to come back. He told me nothing would happen in between."

"I know." He looks around, "So, uh. Where's that other little bitch? Heard you took him with you."

"He dipped out."

"Is that so?" His lips curve into that smile I hate, the one that says pain is about to be inflicted. "Joe- go search the rooms. If I find out you're lying, Ryan. I'm gonna have to remind you what happens when you lie."

"He's not here." I say quickly, "He left. Packed his shit and dipped out Thursday."

"Speaking of Thursday, a little birdie told me you had a visitor. One you were specifically told not to see."

No, no, no, no.

BROKEN

I can't speak, I just stare as my throat fills with bile, and my head goes warm.

"See, I heard that a certain boyfriend came to visit. Heard he stayed in a hotel not far from here and- oh yeah, had a female with him during his stay. You wouldn't know anything about that, would you?"

"I didn't know he was coming."

"Of course not." He says it as if he believes me though I know him and I know he's playing with me. Just like I know he's got a steel zippo in the pocket he's fumbling with. "Didn't think you did because the Old Man told you not to see him and we know you're not dumb enough to go against him, are you?"

"I saw him." I admit, "But I didn't know he was coming. Not until the day he showed up."

"And where is this supreme stalker now?"

"Left. I sent him away. I cut ties; I did everything Dad asked me to. He just didn't listen the first time. But I ended it- I swear." Tears start to pour out as he moves in on me, "I swear!"

Grabbing my wrist, he twists it down while the back of his hand bounces off my cheekbone. "The deal was you end it, and you end it then, not later." He hisses down at me, still holding my wrist. He adds more pressure, and I swear he's going to snap it.

"This is what happens when you don't do as you're told." He bends it back until my legs give, then his knee makes impact with my ribs. That gasp was the last full intake of air I was able to take before white flashed behind my eyes and everything started to hurt. I can't tell you what was making an impact where after that. It all happened too fast to register.

Getting me on my back, he straddled my lap; I tried pushing him off, bucking violently and trying to get my wrist free as I screamed between my teeth.

"Get her arms."

"NO!" I scream, "No! PLEASE, I didn't know!" Evan takes my only defense as Derek's ham-sized hands start to collide with my face, two cracks are all I remember.

I come back to with Derek still sitting on me laughing. My hands are free and laying limply above my head; I draw them up to protect my throbbing face, he laughs harder and slaps them down.

"Derek, too much and she'll draw attention," Joe says above my head.

"Fuck off, little boy."

"Old Man's gonna lose his shit if you bust up her face, you know that."

"Shut the fuck up!" He points his blood-streaked hand to our brother; the sight of the blood makes my stomach turn.

BROKEN

The adrenaline keeps most of the pain at bay, but it doesn't do shit to my fear. "I'm done when I decide to be done. Got me?"

Joe surrenders like he always fucking does, "Just looking out for you, man."

"Well, don't." He growls, turning back to me. "She ain't too bad. Shit will barely be noticeable by the time she comes back." Looking down at me he smiles, "Learn your lesson yet?" Unable to speak, I nod. "Good. Anybody asks you got mugged, got me?"

I nod again, but he raises his hand, "Yes." I squeak painfully, "I got you."

"Good." He pushes off the floor, toeing me with his foot and laughs when I flinch away from him. "Missed you baby sister." He steps away, eyeing the cash Kaylan left on the counter, "This is mine now." He pockets the money, eyeing his brothers, "Let's go."

Derek and Evan step out before Joe turns around and approaches me, I flinch and try to pull away from him, but everything hurts too bad to get very far.

His hands slide under my armpits and lifts me before leaning me against the counter, "Deal's still in effect." He rushes out, watching the door. His gray eyes, my eyes, met mine and I notice the yellow bruise faded around his eye. "Just do what you're told."

Without another look he steps out of the apartment, closing the door behind him. With their absence, the fear breaks free through my throat as the pain settles in. I feel like my body has been thrown into a garbage disposal, everything hurts.

The four feet to the dining table is almost unbearable as my knee buckles. Limping, I catch the back of the chair and sit down, I don't think anything is broken, but Jesus Christ it hurts.

I have no fucking clue how much time passes before a key slips into the unlocked door and opens to reveal Hoyt. His face turns murderous as he takes in my appearance. Apparently, it's as bad as it feels.

"What the fuck happened?!" He drops to the floor in front of me taking note of my injuries.

"Got mugged." I lie.

"Yous need a hospital, kid."

I try to shake my head but flinch, "No, I don't." He reaches into his pocket withdrawing his phone; I lay my hand on the screen. "Don't."

"Yous need a doctor."

"Nothing's broken." Hopefully, that's true. "Just- hand me my smokes, will you?"

"What happened?" He asks again while pulling a cigarette out of the pack and handing to me. "I only been piddlin' about for an hour or so."

"Told you. Got mugged."

"Not here yous didn't, and I don't reckon yous was outside and climbed up all them steps neither."

Taking the lighter, I try to get it to catch, but my fingers aren't working right through the shaking. Noticing my struggle, Hoyt sighs and snatches the lighter out of my hand.

"Let me see that thing." He flicks it once, and the fire ignites from the tip, I draw in the deepest breath I can and light it.

"I'm fine, Hoyt."

"Was this-" He waves across my face, "That thing yous was runnin' from? You and KD?"

"Wasn't running and no. Like I said, I got mugged."

"Why are yous lyin' to me, kid?" His eyes shoot up to the hall, "We alone here?"

"Yeah," I say with a rush of smoke.

"Ima take a look, hope yous don't mind."

"Not at all." I draw in another shallow breath as he stands and disappears from view.

After a minute Hoyt returns, taking the other chair, he sits down in front of me. "I ain't talk pretty, but I know a thing or two about taking care of brawler marks. If I leave for a sec, yous gonna be in one piece when I come back?"

Who the fuck knows, "Yeah."

"Don't go try moving 'round. Not till I have a look 'atcha."

"Kay."

BROKEN

He stares at me for a long moment then disappears down the hall, leaving the door open. Couldn't have been more than four minutes before he walked back in with a large first aid box.

Opening it up, he starts removing shelves and packs of things. "KD says yous gotta thing about being touched." I nod- well kinda. "Yous gonna freak out if I patch up yer face?"

"No. You're good."

"Alright then. Try to hold still."

Pretty sure the clean up is worse than the beating. After disinfecting, he added some butterfly stitches to my cheek and eyebrow; the rest is apparently just swollen or bruised. After the millionth time, he asked where else I was hurt, I finally gave up and told him my ribs and knee. He lifted me with ease and helped support me while he poked and prodded my side until he was convinced nothing was broken. My knee, on the other hand, had him worried. After asking if I was attached to my jeans, he used medical scissors and cut ankle to thigh. I wish I would have understood what he was asking before I answered. He added an instant ice pack and wrapped it with an ace wrap before carrying me to the bed where I'm currently residing.

He goes so far as to bring me the remote, my phone, plus my cigarettes, lighter and an ashtray.

"I'll be in and out to check on yous. Change yer mind about what happened?"

"Nope."

He shakes his head while his eyes look over my face. "Anything I can do? Call yer people?"

"My people?"

"Yer kin. Family, friends, yer people." He shrugs.

"No, thank you though. For patching me up and stuff,"

"No problem, kid. Hit the hay, as I said, I'll be in and out to check on yous. Gonna crash on the sofa, make sure no one returns. If yous hear someone movin' round, it's just me."

"Kay. Thank you."

He looks over my face once more before sighing and closing the bedroom door.

If this was Darling Dad's reminder, I can't wait to see what's in store for my home coming party.

BROKEN

CHAPTER FIFTY-THREE

Hoyt stayed annoyingly true to his word. Felt like every hour on the hour he was waking me up by fiddling with something. Apparently, he was concerned that I had a concussion, but if memory serves me right- you're not supposed to go to sleep with a concussion. The silver lining, I'm alive and not in a coma, so I'm assuming I didn't have one.

"Biscuits 'n gravy. Eat 'em while they're hot." He tells me setting the plate on my lap.

"Thank you; you don't have to do this, you know."

"Girl gets beat up under ma' roof, and I don't gotta care fer her? Not how I work, kid."

"You're calling me kid a lot." I eye him over my glass of milk.

BROKEN

"Found out yer barely legal. Yous still a kid."

I smile as much as my cheek will allow me before digging in.

Hoyt pulled one of the dining room chairs into the bedroom where we watched reruns of F.R.I.E.N.D.S all day. Hoyt is a big fan of 'Crazy Eddie', thinks he's the best part of the show, I don't have the heart to tell him he's only in the one season.

By the end of the day I was able to walk to and from the bathroom. My knee is a little tweaked, but it gets easier to walk on every time I get up. Hoyt gets pissy, but I'll be damned if I let someone carry me to and from the bathroom. Nope- not happening. My ribs hurt like a bitch, but those also seem to be fine, I can take breaths without coughing up blood and extend my arms out without doubling over in pain- so that's good. The bruise on the outside hurts a lot worse than anything on the inside; I'm counting my blessings on this one. I've refused to look in the mirror, so I'm not completely sure what that looks like.

Hoyt apologized for the fact my cheek will probably scar when he changed my dressings, and I almost laughed. If only he knew what was hidden under my sleeve, he would know that a tiny mark is nothing compared to the shit I've got under there.

He kept the bar closed tonight, against my protests and 'hissy fit' as he called it. He kicked

BROKEN

back in my room watching TV, apart from little quips about the episode every now and again; we sat in comfortable silence. He crashed on the couch again to make sure my 'muggers' didn't return. I like Hoyt quite a bit; he doesn't push. He knows I'm lying, and he makes it obvious that he knows, but he doesn't push, he doesn't ask questions, like me- he just exists.

Day three post attack or Wednesday as I'm calling it, I woke up alone and to be completely honest, I'm a little disappointed he didn't cook anything cause that man can cook, Maria would love him. I've successfully avoided all contact with every human being- apart from Hoyt, obviously. Probably because both phones are turned off and on the bedside table, but who cares- I'm counting it as a personal win. Out of sight, out of mind- kind of.

Pulling myself to my feet, I shuffle into the bathroom, pleased that my knee barely hurts. You know when you whack it on the corner of something, and the next day you're like, 'Oh crap, I got myself good.'? Well, that's how it feels. My ribs are tender, but mobility is mostly just stiff rather than painful.

Stripping off my clothes, I step into the shower, careful not to get my face wet, and scrub quickly. Killing the water, I wrap a towel around myself and risk a glance in the mirror.

Oye Vey. I'm. Well- I look like I got my ass kicked.

BROKEN

I'm bruised, that's for sure. My right cheekbone is purple; the bruise travels along the bag under my eye and changes from purple to an ugly yellow and green as it surrounds my orbital bone. My lip is busted, but already scabbed and healing. Pulling the stitch off my eyebrow, a little knick rests underneath it- nothing crazy, so I decided to ditch the stitch, see what I did there? Laughed at my own expense, high-five to me.

The black eye underneath it, however, is impressive, it's so purple it's almost black. Hoyt has been doing something he calls 'lancing' the last couple of days to drain the 'bad blood' underneath. I didn't ask for details.

For pulling his punches he sure got me good, bruises travel my jaw and hairline as well, but those are mostly just red and shadowed, probably be gone in another two days or so. I got beat up, and there's no denying it, though if we're comparing my current injuries, I'd say I was definitely lucky. Derek was right; everything will be mostly faded before I get to Reno. My cheek and shiner will be sticking around for awhile, I imagine.

Not wanting to look at myself anymore, I turn my back to the mirror and change.

Hoyt is sitting on the couch when I exit, jumping at his sudden appearance, I flinch at the jolt of pain through my ribs.

BROKEN

"Easy, kid. Sorry, I thought yous heard me come in."

I shake my head with a small grimace as I walk over to sit in the recliner across from him.

"Someone dropped something off fer yous. Seeing as I been taking care of yous and yous being on the run and all, I wasn't exactly trustin' of what I was handed, so I opened it. I hope yous don't mind too much. Just didn't want you receiving threats or somethin'."

He hands me an opened envelope. Pulling out the paper, I read over the messy handwriting;

I was pained to hear about the mugging that took place in Georgia. I hope you are healing well and your injuries aren't too terribly bad. I wasn't happy to hear the extent of the event and wanted to offer you my sincere apologies. With that, I would like to extend an olive branch of sorts. After all, it will be Christmas on Thursday; perhaps you would like to see your friends in sunny, Arizona?

In fact, I insist on it. I still expect to see you come the first, but with recent events, I felt you could use the support of your comrades while you heal.

Eagerly awaiting your return.
    Dad.

My hands shake as I fold the letter and try to deposit it back into the envelope. This is a trap. The paper repeatedly catches on something, and my preexisting fear turns to frustration before peering inside to see a plane ticket. My heart stalls, this has to be a trap. Pulling it out, I see I have a flight this evening boarding out of Atlanta at 4:10 PM. Destination, Phoenix.

"You lookin' as nervous as a long-tailed cat in a room full of rocking chairs; I imagine that there letter ain't as innocent as it looks."

I shake my head, "Just excited about my flight home, is all." I blatantly lie.

"What you plan on doing with it?"

"I've been invited home. It would be rude to deny such a generous gift, don't you think?" I paste a fake smile on my face and replace the contents.

His brow pulls together, "I ain't gonna pretend to get what kinda thing yous got going on." He points to the letter, "But that don't seem right."

"It's a generous gift from my father. It looks like we're parting ways a little earlier than expected."

"I don't think yous should be leaving. Not when yous getting mugged and all."

"I'll be fine." I hope. "I should probably make some arrangements."

He nods and watches me while I, less than gracefully, climb out of the recliner and enter my room. Trying to keep as nonchalant as possible, I leave the door open to look less suspicious, highly doubt this is working but whatever, I'm trying.

Pulling out my phone, I try to unlock it quickly to avoid the picture of Parker and me before scrolling down to find Drew's number and press talk.

"For the love of God, please don't hate me," I whisper while it rings.

"Baby sister, how are you feeling?" My stomach falls to the floor.

"Never better." Why the fuck does Derek have Drew's phone?!

"What do I owe this pleasure?" He asks while I scroll through my burner, oh thank god. Drew has a different number. Trying to steady my voice I pretend this was all intentional.

"I received a letter from Dad today. Was just wondering if he was around? I wanted to thank him."

"You got company?"

"Yes."

"What kind?"

"Just hanging out with my neighbor, he brought my mail up, and we're probably going to watch some TV before my flight."

"Hold on." There are some shuffling and muffled voices before the devil himself answers.

"Ryan."

"Hi, Dad. I just wanted to call and thank you for the letter I received today."

"You have safe passage."

"Just wanted to make sure it was from you," I whisper.

"Nine days until I expect an answer from you. I want you to use this time to spend with your friends, at the end of your stay you will give them a believable story and return home where you will give me your answer. We will move forward accordingly."

"Nine days. I'm excited to see you."

"I expect you here before noon." The line goes dead. I can feel Hoyt's eyes on me, so I continue talking to a dead line.

"Thank you, again. I'll let you get back to work. Love you." Pretending to hear I response, I hang up.

"Yer leavin'?"

"I'll call a cab to take me to Atlanta."

He nods. "If yous leavin', I better make you a farewell meal."

I smile despite the fear choking me. This is a trap, right? Why would he give a damn about me? Problem is- I don't know what the trap is or who it's for.

"Yous gettin' a ride from the airport?" He calls in from the kitchen.

"Gonna call my friend and ask him to pick me up."

He doesn't respond, that or he did and just didn't hear him. Picking up my burner, I transfer

Drew's correct number into my old phone and call him.

The longer it rings, the more I convince myself he hates me for what I did to Parker. My eyes burn, and I'm about to hang up when he answers, "Hales?!"

"Hey."

"What the hell, sweetheart? Where the fuck have you been?"

"There, uh-" I can't find words.

"Haley?"

"Yeah?"

"You okay? You're talking weird."

Far from okay, Drew. Far from it. "Yeah. I'm uh, I'm coming home for Christmas."

"Wait, what?"

"My dad bought me a plane ticket home. Wants me to see you guys."

"Wait- hold on. Your dad bought you a plane ticket home?"

"Yeah. I fly out of Savannah at four. I was wondering if- well-" Jesus, I'm a moron. "I don't know. If you don't hate me, I was wondering if you maybe wanted to see me...?"

There's a silence, and it cuts deep. "Drew?" I look at the screen showing the call is still connected and hold it back to my swollen face. How I'm going to explain this away is beyond me. "I'm sorry I called, never mind."

"Wait! Haley! No- don't go. I'm a piece of shit, yes, of course, I want to see you. I'm just trying to understand what's happening. Are you really coming home?"

"Yeah. It's a four-hour flight. With the time difference, I think I land around five thirty."

"Sky Harbor, right?"

"Yeah. Look- please don't tell anyone I'm coming. I'll be home around six-thirty or seven. Maybe you can come to my apartment or something."

"Why don't you want people knowing you're coming home? We've been worried sick, sunshine."

"Have you talked to Parker since he got back?"

Another long pause, "Yeah." His tone is sad, and I hate it.

"That's why."

"But if you're allowed to come home, your good right?"

"Not exactly, I'll be leaving New Year's Eve."

"What? To where?"

"I'll fill you in tonight if you're able to come over."

"Of course, I'll be over. I haven't seen you in almost a month. Kaylan coming with you?"

Now it's my time to struggle with an answer, "Kaylan, uh. He kind of split."

"What the fuck?! No, he didn't!"

"Yeah, he had shit to do. Left the same day as Parker. Don't worry though, I've got a friend here, and he's been keeping me company." Hoyt harrumphs in the kitchen, eavesdropper.

"Friend?! I swear to God, if you're cheating on me I'll kill them. Unless she's hot, if she's hot, bring her with."

"Well now that you mention it... Hoyt's actually-"

"Hoyt? You made friends with another dude?! Now that's just fucked up."

"He means nothing, you know you're my one and only!" I mock swoon into the phone.

"I fucking better be."

"Look, I've got to pack and stuff. So, I'm going to let you go, but I'll see you tonight."

"Fuck yes you will."

"I mean it, Drew. This stays between you and me. I invoke the best friend card."

"Fuck. For how long?" He whines

"I don't know. But just- don't tell anyone."

"Can it be like a surprise?"

"What? I don't know- sure?"

"Sweet! I'll see you in-" He draws out the n while he thinks, "seven hours."

"No, I land in seven hours."

"I know. Love ya!" The line ends.

SHIT. How the fuck am I supposed to keep my face a secret or talk him down from rage in the middle of a damn airport?! I groan loudly, resting my face gently in my hands.

"What's wrong with yous?" I start when Hoyt speaks from my door.

BROKEN

"Jesus! Warn people when you approach!"

"I'm leanin' close to four hundred pounds, darlin'. Reckon you can hear me moving round."

"Oh. I'm 'darlin' again." I smile at him.

He smiles a little then presses on, "What's all this ruckus 'bout?"

"Wanted my friend to meet me at my apartment to avoid the freak out he's going to have over my face, but he's meeting me at the airport."

"Don't yous got makeup? Bet my whiskers it'll cover up most of that."

"Your whiskers, huh?" I give his beard a pointed look.

"Mhm. I'm pretty attached to these, too." He gives it a good tug.

"Yeah, I'll give it a try."

"You like fish?"

"If you're cooking, I reckon I'll love it."

"That southern twang sounds good on yous." He smiles, turning back to the kitchen.

I take a deep breath, looking around the room I once hated. What the fuck, Haley? You swore you wouldn't make friends. I roll my eyes at myself and lay back on the bed. What an idiot I turned out to be, huh?

Half an hour later, my bruises are sort of hidden. You can't exactly hide my black eye and the abrasions, but the bruises are fairly hidden, you can see the shadows resting below, but hopefully, it will be enough to avoid a complete meltdown in the middle of the terminal.

I was absolutely right about the fish; it was fan-fucking-tastic. 'Fat as a tick' is apparently the correct term for stuffing yourself stupid on food.

I tried not to get emotional, but saying goodbye to Hoyt was rough. He hugged me- despite my panic, and put me in the cab, telling me I always had a place above his bar and wished me a "Lord willing and the Creek don't rise," whatever the hell that means. I ended up twisting in my seat to wave at him from the rear window like I was starring in some cheesy movie.

Arriving at the airport, I kept my duffel as a carry-on like I did with Kaylan and waited to board the plane. I'm on an emotional roller coaster. I'm thrilled to see Drew but terrified to see Parker. I'm so excited to be going back to Phoenix I want to puke, but I also know this is a trap of sorts and that makes me want to hurl. I'm so happy I want to cry, but I'm also so nervous I'm on the verge of tears. I'm up one second, down another.

Taking my seat on the plane, I remember how terrifying takeoff and landing is, that and how Kaylan isn't here. We can't seem to hold a conversation without screaming at each other but I miss the asshole, and I really wish he didn't leave as he did. Having these feelings still hasn't allowed my pride to wave the white flag and reply to his messages, but they exist nonetheless.

The plane straightens as my stomach drops. Gripping the armrest, I squeeze my eyes shut as we pick up speed. I really, really, hate airplanes. I feel the change as we leave the earth and breath a sigh of relief when we don't die.

Leaving Phoenix I was heartbroken and scared, returning I'm still both of those things, but this time my heart knows where we're going and for a few moments, it doesn't hurt so bad. Trap or not, I'm going home.

BROKEN

CHAPTER FIFTY-FOUR

Landing barely fazed me, I saw Sky Harbor and was even pro crash landing if it got me to Drew faster. My face is a mess- I don't even care. I bounce impatiently in my seat as I wait for them to allow us to stand.

"Finally!" I yell, getting to my feet.

You always hear about that one asshole on the plane- today that title belongs to me. My fucks are back in Savannah as I use elbows, knees, anything to get around people and into the airport.

My eyes searched over people as I pushed past the less enthused. There- with his blue cap twisted backward, is the second most beautiful face I've ever seen. "Hey, sweetheart."

With a loud squeal, I throw my bag down and literally jump into his arms. There might have been words but I'm so fucking happy at the moment I can't hear anything. Strong, muscular arms wrap around my ribs, and a cry escapes my throat.

"Fuck." He set me down, looking over my middle, "Did I hurt y-" His voice fades as he looks up at my face.

His mouth opens and closes like a fish before I shake my head at him and wrap my arms around his neck, "You're allowed to hug me. Take advantage."

He's hands fall loosely around my shoulders, my darkness can fuck-all at the moment.

"What happened?" He whispers.

"Not important. Jesus Christ, I've missed you." I say through the happy tears.

"Missed you more."

"Liar."

"Pssht, please."

"I want to go home, but I don't want to let go."

He chuckles against my head then sighs, "You're going to explain why your face looks like that, right?"

"Later. It's not important right now."

"I've got an idea." He lets go, leans down and collects my discarded bag from the floor. Walking up to a bench he holds his hands out, and I smile. "Best of both words?"

Taking his hand, I stand on the metal seat as he turns, giving me his back. Throwing my arms around his tree trunk of a neck I give a little hop, wrapping my legs around him. His hands hook under my knees and starts forward my ribs protest, but as I said, I left my fucks in Savannah.

"Does Josh ever get to drive his own truck?" I ask as we approach the massive silver, Dodge.

"Sometimes."

"Why don't you just get yourself a truck?" I ask as he throws my bag into the backseat.

"Cause then I couldn't borrow his."

Sliding off his back, I wince a little at the pain but try to cover it. Drew notices, he doesn't say anything, but the crease between his brows and the way he's chewing on his lip tells me he wants to.

Opening my door for me, he helps me into the cab. I could get in myself, but it hurts less letting him assist.

"You didn't have to come and get me," I tell him once we hit the main road leading home.

"Whatever, I'm not going to sit around twiddling my thumbs for two hours when I know you're here."

"Did you tell anyone I was home?"

"No, ma'am. I've basically ignored everyone since you called to avoid it slipping."

I chuckle, "I'll probably go to HEAT after Christmas and see Josh for a little while."

"What about Parker?"

Pain slices through me, "He doesn't want to see me. We uh- we made a deal of sorts. I'm breaking part of that deal being here, but if I don't make waves and let him know I'm here, I'm hoping he'll still keep his end."

"What was the deal?"

"He'll accept things the way they are as long as I don't call, text, or come back."

"What do you mean, accept things?"

"Accept that we'll never be together. Accept that I won't be coming back."

"But you're here now."

"But only for a week. This is my chance to say a proper goodbye."

His hand clenches the wheel harder as his jaw works, "And why aren't you coming back?"

"Because I've been offered a job and I'm taking it."

"A job." He pulls back in disgust, "What the fuck? You can't stay here because it's 'not safe' but you can take a job?"

"The job is to his standard. I take it- everything goes away. No more running."

"So, you and Parker can't be together, because?"

"Because it's not in Arizona."

"So? Parker can live anywhere, dude. He's not tied down here."

"Yes, he is. His family is here."

"Yeah, it's called holidays and a plane ticket." He shrugs, "Don't see the issue here."

"The issue is that I don't want to be with him, Drew. So drop it."

"BULL. Shit. You guys hump like rabbits. You'd still be with him if you're Dad didn't scare you out of town. Speaking of your dad- what the fuck is up with him getting you a plane ticket?"

"It was an apology."

"An apology for what?"

"I uh, I got mugged in Savannah. That's why I look like this."

"You got mugged?" I nod. "In Savannah?" Another nod. "Yeah right. Muggers don't wait around and beat you up. They snatch and run. What actually happened?"

"I was mugged. He was upset to hear the extent of my injuries, so he flew me home for Christmas to give me the opportunity to say a proper goodbye." The truth is right there; you just have to decipher it.

"You sound like a fucking robot, dude. Don't take up acting; it's not your strong suit."

"Oh, don't get snippy, please? I'm only here for a couple of days. You're the last person I want to fight with."

BROKEN

"I'm not fighting you, Hales. I'm trying to figure out what the fuck's happening. You up and leave in the middle of the night with Kaylan of all people, he whisks you away, and I barely hear from you, and when I do, you're heartbroken, scared, and desperate to push everyone away. Then you spend a couple of days with Parker, and you're back to being happy Haley, then something happens, and you and Parker are on the outs, I go a week without hearing from you and all of sudden you're coming home after telling us you weren't safe here. Come to find out, the dude you're running from paid for the flight. And to top it all off- you show up with a busted face and whatever else is wrong with you and you're saying you're leaving for a job in another state that your Dad approves of, so I'm sorry if I'm frustrated that my best friend is lying to me."

"I don't want to lie to you."

"Then why do it?"

"Because I was told to."

"By who? You're dad?"

"I can't talk about it, okay? He knew where Kaylan and I were, he knew Parker came to see me, he knows shit, and I don't know how he's figuring it out, but I just need you to go along with it. Please? For me?"

He blows out a lungful of air and shakes his head, "You've got to give me something, Hales."

"I already have. You just haven't figured it out yet."

"Why are you so cryptic? You're not going to like off yourself, or something are you?"

I laugh, because well, in a way I kind of am. "No. I'll be boarding a bus."

"What's the job?"

I shake my head; I hadn't gotten that far yet. He sighs, resting his head against his hand.

"You're so pretty." I smile at him. He looks at me through the corner of his eye.

"You're a pain in my ass."

"I'm serious!" I shove his leg over the console. "Even when you're pissed and mopey you're still pretty."

"Thought Parker was hotter." He said hotter in his best whiny girl voice.

"He is." I smile and dodge the hand the snakes out to tickle me. Then flinch, grabbing my rib.

"You alright?"

"Yeah. Just a little sore."

"Where are you hurt?"

"Got kneed in the ribs."

I can tell he's doing his best to control his temper, "Broken?"

"No."

"See a doctor?"

"No."

"Dammit, Haley!"

"Don't be mad, please?"

"I am mad!" His eyes blaze as they scan my face, he glances at the road while his arm shoots over to my side and pulls the visor down, "Look at your face! How am I not supposed to be angry?"

I don't look, I already know what it looks like, I'm just glad I'm wearing makeup, hate to think of his reaction if I arrived without it.

We continue in silence until we approach VIN's and he kicks the blinker on. "Drew, what are doing?"

"Grabbing us food."

"I don't want anyone knowing I'm here."

"I'm not gonna walk in and announce it. Just stay in the truck." With an epic eye roll, I unbuckle my seatbelt and crawl painfully to the floor. Drew starts to laugh, "What the hell are you doing?"

"I don't need someone recognizing the truck, asshole."

"Why can't Vinny and Jules know?"

"Did you see my face?" I scold, "The second they see me they're gonna call Josh and who is Josh going to call?"

"Me?"

"Parker. And then he'll know I'm here."

"And remind me why that's not on your to-do list?"

"Because it isn't. Now go inside before people notice you're talking to the floor."

"You're a weird chick." He laughs, opening the door.

The door shuts, and my heart begins to beat out of control.

"Hi, love." I hear Jules; she must be smoking. "Who were you talking to?"

"Hales." YOU ASSHOLE.

"Is she okay? Do you know where she's at?"

"Yeah, she's okay. I know where she's at, but she's being a moron and doesn't want anyone to know."

"Where is she?"

Don't you dare!

"Closer than you think."

"What?" I can imagine her face as she slowly puts this together.

"Don't worry about it. You'll know soon enough. Here to grab food. Think Dillon's up for making a cheese steak and a turkey club, no pickles, extra tomatoes?"

You bastard! I scream in my head.

"Andrew." Her voice goes stern. "Are you messing with me? If you're messing with me-" She trails off.

"I'm not messing around. Think he's up for it?"

"Where is she?"

"I told you. Closer than you think and being a fucking moron." He said the last part so loud; I'm positive she's going to come looking through the windows.

"Is she here?"

"Dunno, I'm gonna go see if Dillon's free."

I hear her call after him, but I can't tell if she followed him inside or if she's still standing outside. Carefully rearranging my feet, I sink deeper into the footwell. I'm gonna fucking kill him.

Thank the stars above she didn't come peaking into the windows. Drew climbs back into the truck, setting the food down on the center console with a shit eating grin on his face. He fights a laugh, but it eventually breaks free.

"You're dead to me," I tell him climbing back into the seat. "What the fuck was that?"

"What? I didn't tell her you were here."

"Yes, you did!

"No. I said I didn't know."

"After you basically pointed a neon sign to the truck! She knows, and now she's going to tell Vinny, and in about twenty minutes everyone's going to know!"

"No, they won't." He sighs, "I told her I was messing with her."

I glare at him until I'm convinced he's telling the truth. "You're such an asshole."

The trip to my apartment was short, and words can't describe how excited I am to be home. "How are you going to explain the truck?" I ask as he pulls into a spot in guest parking.

"To who?"

"To Parker, you big dummy. He'll see the truck and know you're here."

"Then he'll call."

"And you'll say what? Parked the truck and decided to walk around?"

He chuckles, "He ain't gonna notice, and if he does, I'll tell him I saw a nice piece of ass and got distracted." He wiggles his eyebrows at me.

I sock him in the arm, "I am not a piece of ass."

He laughs harder, rubbing his arm, "You hit hard for a chick."

"Keep up with your shenanigans, and I'll hit you like I mean it."

He surrenders his hands, laughing. "Okay, okay!"

Exiting the truck, I take the back way to my apartment, ignoring Drew's huffing and puffing. Approaching the corner, I lean forward, checking his balcony to make sure he's not out smoking when Drew, being the supreme asshole he is, jerks his fingers into my back, "BOO." I jump, wince at the shock of pain, and then sock him the arm.

"Ow! Fuck!"

"Warned you."

"What are you worried about?" He asks, rubbing his shoulder.

"I'm worried he'll come out to smoke and see us going into my apartment."

"He's not gonna see. Come on, 007."

"I'm not kidding, Drew."

Seeing the seriousness in my face, he reaches into his pocket and pulls out his phone. After pressing a few buttons, he holds the phone up to his ear.

"Hey, brother. Is my lucky shirt at your place? You sure? I think I left it in your hall bathroom." He nods me forward, and I rush down the sidewalk, fishing my keys out of my pocket. "Damn. Alright. Hey, what are you doing tonight?" I shove the key into the lock and quickly enter, ushering him inside.

The smell hits me first, home.

Closing the door behind him, I lock it and twist to see the barely lit apartment. Everything is exactly as I left it. I smile taking in my little piece heaven as Drew continues talking on the phone, "Care if I come by later? Cool. Hey, have you heard from Haley...Damn, well I'll probably see you in a bit... Alright, later."

He looks up at me and smiles a beautiful Hayes family smile while tucking his phone into his pocket. "Damn dude, I was scared I'd never see you in here again."

"Me too," I admit looking around. "I missed it here."

He sets my duffel on the table before moving to sit on the couch with our food. "I bet. So, tell me what you've been up to."

I sit down and have to take a moment to enjoy the pure bliss that is my couch. "Give me a minute. I've missed my couch so much."

He chuckles, pulling our sandwiches out and handing me mine. Sitting up, I unwrap the sub and take a very unladylike bite. "Oermoigerd!"

"Was that English?"

I laugh and try not to choke on the overwhelming amount of food in my mouth. "I said, Oh my God! This is like my favorite thing of all time."

"Apart from my brother's dick."

I choke and start coughing into my hand while he laughs, taking a bite of his own sub.

After I'm able to inhale without coughing, I kicked him playfully. "Why are you such a dick?"

"Part of my charm, sunshine. So really, what have you been doing?"

We eat in the growing darkness as I go over my time in Savannah. Telling him about Kaylan and I being at each other's throat, him leaving, Hoyt patching me up after I was 'mugged.' Told him about what I did around town and then went into long, exaggerated detail about the blonde I served shots to.

Close to one in the morning, Drew decided we needed donuts and chocolate milk and might die if we didn't get some. Sending him on

BROKEN

the donut run, I decided I'd shower and set up the movie in the bedroom, too scared the light would be visible through the blinds.

Stepping into my bag I catch sight of the Christmas tree, was it really only a month ago we strung up those lights? It feels so much longer, a lifetime or more since I did anything without feeling pain or having the urge to cry at the drop of a hat. Scary how long those weeks felt without having those I love most around, Reno is going to be hell.

Not wanting to fall into a depressing downfall, I snatch up my bag and walk down the hall. Flipping on my bedroom light, I refused to look too closely at the bed I've only ever slept in with Parker. I grab my toiletry bag and hide in the bathroom before thoughts of Parker can destroy my homecoming high.

Stepping out of the shower, I use the towel to wipe a section of fog off the mirror. Jesus, I look like I got hit by a car. Not seeing my face without makeup in hours, it's startling. I should probably put some foundation on before Drew gets back. He barely held himself together seeing me with the worst hidden; I don't think I could keep him from losing his mind if he saw me like this.

Opening the door, I step out to grab my makeup bag when I catch sight of a figure leaning against the bedpost. I scream, jumping back, and try to shut the door, but a hand stops it. That's when I notice the boots and then his scent invades my senses...

    Parker's here.

BROKEN

CHAPTER FIFTY-FIVE

Turning quickly, I let my hair fall over my face as I pull the towel tighter around me, trying to keep my arm and face away from his line of sight.

"Haley?"

Oh god, that voice.

"You scared me," I admit, stepping back away from him.

"Look at me." His tone is urgent and cold.

I shake my head, "You should go."

"No." He takes a step forward, and I put my hand on his shredded stomach to stop his motion. Just touching him sends shivers of electricity through me. Keeping my head down, I push against his frame harder, twisting my head to avoid his hand. "You should go."

"DAMMIT, HALEY. Look. At. Me." I've never heard him so angry before.

Unable to look at him or fight the emotion in my throat, whispering is all I seem to be capable of, "I can't."

His hand catches my neck, and I try to back away, but the counter stops me as his other hand pushes the hair out of my face. His hands let go, and he steps back as if I shot him. Refusing the meet his eyes, I stare at my feet.

"Haley." His voice is a plea like he might die if I don't answer.

"I know I said I wouldn't come back-" I tell him, still looking at my feet but my voice breaks and I let the sentence die off. Rolling my lips between my teeth, I wait for him to say or do something but he doesn't. He just stands there.

Risking a glance, I peak between the wet locks of my hair, and he's still staring at me. His chest heaves as his fists open and close at his sides. A hiccup of a cry pushes past my lips, and I swallow the pain. His hand scrubs angrily across his face, as he stares at me.

"I'm sorry," I whisper, trying to hide the thick emotion currently choking me.

"What happened?"

"I know I said I wouldn't come back-" My sentence dies as he moves in on me, instincts kick in and I cover my face, stepping back, only I trip, and the corner of the counter catches my bruised ribs, I cry out, grabbing my side.

"Jesus." His voice is thick and hurt as I pull myself as upright as I can, "I'm not going to hurt you, sweetheart."

Moving very slowly, he approaches me. I watch him through the curtain of hair as he moves, standing close enough I can feel his body warmth, his hands follow my jawline as he gently tilts my head back, he holds me still with one hand as the other pushes the strands away from my face. He works his jaw as he looks over my face, his thumb gently running the length of my swollen cheek bone.

His eyes travel lower to where my hand is still cupped around my throbbing injury. "How bad?" He asks, gently.

"It's not." He meets my eyes, but I can't bare to see the anger behind them, so I look away. "Nothing's broken."

"What happened?"

BROKEN

"Got mugged."

His body tenses against my lie. "Kaylan?"

I look at him, and his eyes tell me he actually thinks Kaylan might have done this, "God, no. He left the same day you did."

"That big guy? The bar owner?"

"No, Hoyt's the one who patched me up. I don't know who, it happened fast."

His fingers brush over my ribs, and I can't stand it, I shy away, and his hand falls to my hip while the other pushes the flap to the side.

"Parker." I whisper, trying to move but the wall and his hand keep me in place, "Please, don't. It's not that bad."

He ignores me and peels the towel up, my hand tightens around my ribs, "Let me see."

I don't like this Parker. Cold, unattached, with a harsh tone and anger resting behind those his eyes. I know I'm the one who put all of these things into effect, but it doesn't change the hurt I feel experiencing it.

Slowly moving my hand, I hold the towel to my chest as he uncovers my black and purple ribs. "Jesus Christ." He whispers, dropping the towel. "Not that bad?" His voice starts to raise, "It's not that bad? Have you looked in the fucking mirror?" He twists away, rubbing his hand through his hair, "Who?"

"I don't know." I lie, and he knows it.

"You can't possibly think that by consistently lying to me that I could trust that, do you?"

"I don't know who it was, Parker, so just..." I swallow hard, "Just go."

"Tell me who did this and maybe I'll consider it."

Willing my voice stern, I meet his angry eyes with my defiant ones, "This is still my apartment, and I'm asking you to leave."

We stand there, staring each other down.

"Haley, Baley! I'm back! Why the fuck is the door unlocked?" I close my eyes against Drew's grand entrance. "If I didn't make it obvious earlier, you're a moron."

I open my eyes and see Parker's are blazing. So much anger is rippling off him, I take a step back and shake my head.

"I made him promise not to tell you." I plea, "Threatened not to come if he did. He wanted to tell you, but I wouldn't let him. Don't be mad at him, be mad at me."

"Oh." His laugh is hollow, "I'm definitely mad at you." He takes a step into my bedroom and stares at the open door when footsteps sound. "What the fuck, brother?"

"Shit," Drew says slowly.

"Parker, I made him keep it a secret. Please, please don't be mad at him." I beg, stepping towards him, feeling beyond hurt and rejected as he steps away from me like I'm revolting. "It's not his fault," I say a little more defeated than I wanted.

"You knew?" He drops the base in his words as he glares at his brother.

"Only for a couple of hours."

"Look at her fucking face!" Parker roars, pointing at me. "You didn't think to fucking tell me someone beat the shit out of her?!"

"I've been trying to get her to tell people she's here-"

"Look at her face, Drew!"

"She's a little roughed up, but I-"

"Roughed up?!"

"I made him, Parker!" I say in Drew's defense. "He's been trying to get me to tell someone else I was here all night, I was the one that made him stay quiet."

"So, what if she told you not to!" He yells at Drew, completely ignoring me, "I'm your fucking brother! If anything happened to Emma, I

BROKEN

would tell you! I wouldn't care what she threatened!"

Emma? Who the hell is, Emma?! Not important, Haley.

"Parker!" I yell, trying to pull his attention.

He points an angry finger at me, rage spilling out of his pores, "Don't."

"Fuck that! Put your goddamn finger down. If you're going to yell at someone, yell at me! I'm the one who forced him not to say anything; I'm the one you're pissed at. Take that shit out on me, not him!"

"Stop." He growls in warning.

"Or what?" I step forward. "You gonna put hands on me too?"

His eyes shine with hate, "What happened to no texting, no calling, no returning?"

"I got my ass kicked, what's your excuse?"

"Saw your bedroom light was on." His chest heaves as he looks me over, without another word he grabs something off the bed and throws it at me. Snatching it midair, I see it's a massive zip-up hoodie. Realization smacks me in the face, and I quickly shove my arm into the sleeve, covering myself up. Thank god, Drew's not in the bedroom to see.

"I get why you came back, what I don't get is how you kept it a secret." He turns back to Drew.

"One of us would have told you. Probably not tonight, but tomorrow at some point."

"How long?"

"She called me earlier today. Said she was flying in."

"Did you know she was hurt before that?"

"Fuck no. I didn't know until I saw her at the airport and she was just a little swollen around her eyes, didn't think to bring out the cavalry over that."

Parker steps back and looks at me. "A little swollen around her eyes? Are you out of your goddamn mind?"

Drew steps into view and I quickly look away, "Jesus Christ!"

"Yeah, Jesus Christ. And you thought it was fine?"

"She didn't look like that when I left- I swear."

Parker turns to me and scoffs.

"I had makeup on," I say to the floor. "A lot of makeup on. I was coming out to get it when I saw you."

"When?"

BROKEN

"Right now-"

"No," He interrupts me with a frustrated sigh, "When did it happen?"

"Oh. A couple of days ago."

"Don't fucking lie to me, Haley."

"I'm not lying! You left, Kaylan left, I was alone and bam!" I clap my hands for emphasis, "It happened. Hoyt found me and patched me up. Stayed on the couch to make sure no one returned."

"What happened?"

"I got 'mugged.'" I tell him using my fingers as quotation marks. "My Dad heard about it and bought me a plane ticket home. Said he was unhappy to hear the extent of my injuries and thought I'd heal better if I were surrounded by friends."

He stares at me for what feels like forever before he exhales loudly. "How did he hear?"

"Same way he knew where to deliver the ticket." I shrug. "Just did."

He nods as his jaw works, then looks at Drew, who has been surprisingly silent. "I'm still pissed you didn't tell me she was here."

"I know."

Parker rubs his hands through his hair looking at Drew and then to me. "I get that you had to come back." He starts, "Doesn't mean shits good between us. I understand you're gonna be around to see the family and that's fine, but unless it's a family thing I don't want you coming around-"

"Whoa, Parker-" Drew cuts in but Parker speaks over him, his tone growing in volume, his anger rolls off his tongue coating every word in disdain.

"I don't want you calling, texting, or coming over to my place. You wanted distance; you got it." With those departing words he storms past Drew as the first sob rocks out of my throat.

"Real nice, asshole!" Drew yells down the hall before wrapping his arms around me. Pain rips me open, and I can't seem to pull in enough air as the hurt from his words blast holes through my chest.

I hear the front door slam and everything breaks.

Drew's arms vice tighter as I break in his arms, "I love him." I sob into his shirt, intake of air is painful as my chest bucks, "I'm in love with him."

"I know, sweetheart." He coos into my hair. "I know."

CHAPTER FIFTY-SIX

Drew spent the night with me. Not sure when it happened, but I ended up curling around him on the bed and crying myself to sleep. I remember him getting up at one point but I know he came back because he handed me my shorts and had me change into them before passing out next to me.

Getting out of bed, I shuffle down the hall finding him sprawled out on my couch watching some sort of show with an obstacle course. Without speaking, he lifts his legs allowing me to sit down then lowers them over my lap.

Looking at him, I see the shadow forming across his jaw. "What happened?"

"Parker and I had words."

"Looks like you had more than words."

"You're not wrong."

"Because of me?"

"Don't worry about it."

"I am worried about it," I tell him twisting my bracelet around my wrist. Haven't even been here a full twenty-four hours and I've already gone and fucked everything up.

"I'm worried about your face, but I don't see you talking about that."

"Touche'."

We sit in silence for a while before he speaks again, "I'm not mad at you, by the way. In case you were over there thinking I was- I'm not. I'm pissed my brother's a dick."

"He's not a dick." I defend, "I said some pretty fucked up things in Savannah. I had it coming."

"And he knows it was all bullshit, so the fact he's pulling this makes him a dick."

I sigh not wanting to start a fight and watch as some guy jumps rope to rope like a monkey on the television.

"It's Christmas Eve." He says out of nowhere.

"Merry Christmas?"

He chuckles lightly, "No. It's our ugly sweater party tonight; you're my plus one.

BROKEN

Wear something nice; we'll stop by the mall before we go."

"What about Emma?" I gently elbow his leg.

"She's got plans with her family. I'll see her Thursday."

"You gonna fill me in or..." I trail off.

"Nothing to really fill in. Remember biker chick?" Sitting up, I stare at him, mouth wide open and he chuckles before shoving me with his foot.

"No way!" I laugh, "Biker Chick? Are you guys dating?"

"I don't know." He groans, scrubbing his face with his hand.

"You don't know if y'all are dating?"

"It's not that simple, Hales. Emma's...Emma." He shrugs.

"Do I get to meet her?"

His eyes narrow at me, "I don't know yet. It depends if you're going to be nice or not."

I slap at his leg, "Of course I'll be nice!"

"I'll think about it."

"How long have you been a thing?"

"Couple weeks I guess."

"Awe." I smile, sitting back into the couch and stare at him.

"What are you staring at?" He huffs, moving a pillow to block my line of vision.

"Nothing. Just thinking how sweet it is that you found yourself a girl. You know if she hurts you I'll break her in half right?"

BROKEN

"Yeah, sweetheart."

"Good, as long as you know."

"You should start getting ready soon, probably gonna take you a while to hide all that shit on your face."

I let out a sigh and smack his ankle, "Alright, get off me before your girlfriend gets jealous."

"Shut up," he whines, lifting his feet.

Apparently, he's not worried about that seeing as he slaps me on the ass hard enough to leave a handprint when I walk past him.

Using half a bottle of foundation, a tube of concealer and evening it out with powder, I still look like I was hit by a car, but at least it looks like it was a sedan rather than a semi. Trying to draw attention away from the puffiness and bruising, I apply red and brown eye shadow, sweeping a tiny bit of green along my lower lashes.

Looking at myself, I'm not sure the eye shadow helped or just highlighted the red under the five pounds of foundation. Either way, it's there now. I line my lower and upper lids with thicker, longer strokes to darken and redefine my eyes, again in hopes to draw attention away from the elephant in the room. Lastly, I throw on enough mascara I can literally feel myself blink and step out to get Drew's approval. Lazybones is still in the same place I left him.

"How's it look?"

BROKEN

He glances up, and his gaze roams my face, "Looks like you got beat up." He sighs, "But at least it doesn't look like we need to take you to the ER anymore."

"A win's a win." I quote Parker, and I don't even try to hide the hurt that brings.

"That what you're wearing?"

I look down at my outfit, red fitted long sleeve, black skater skirt, black pumps. "Yeah."

"Cool. Let's roll then."

I grab my keys and Parker's hoodie and meet him at the door. He walks straight to the truck without looking at Parker's place. Despite the fact I desperately want to look, I fight the urge and follow Drew. He opens the truck and helps me in again before walking around the front and getting in on the driver's side. Pulling out into traffic he gives another sigh and rests his head against his folded arm.

"Is there anything I can do?"

He shakes his head, "Nah, I'll get over it."

"So, what does this party- that I didn't fight you on, by the way, consist of?"

"We wear ugly sweaters and hangout mostly. Mama Mia will cook something, and we'll binge corny Christmas movies until we fall asleep. In the morning we open presents."

"Wait, we're spending the night?"

"Nah, I usually would, but I don't feel like being around Parker that long so you're my ticket home."

"Deal." Noticing his fresh clothes, I take a longer look at him and notice he looks bathed too, what the hell? When did that happen? "When did you shower and change?"

"After I left Parker's last night I grabbed shit from my place. Showered in your spare this morning."

"Oh..." Noticing the tick in his jaw, I can tell he's thinking about whatever went down between them. "How come you're not wearing an ugly sweater?"

"Gotta pick one up."

"And where does one find an ugly sweater?"

"Mall. I prefer the inappropriate ones."

I laugh, "No." I gasp, "Really? You?"

He gives me a smirk, hitting the blinker that will take us into the mall parking lot.

"What did you wear last year?"

"Wore one that had Jesus in a party hat, under his face, it said, 'Birthday Boy.'"

I actually snort, "That's amazing. Why not wear that again?"

"I like to keep them guessing."

"Right. Well, how about a game then?"

"Yeah?" He glances at me from the corner of his eye, "What kind of game?"

"One where we compete against each other."

"I do like the sound of that...proceed."

"We have to find the ugliest sweater we can, but here's the catch- it has to fit the other's personality."

"Interesting. Where did you learn about this game?"

"I didn't. I'm making it up as I go."

He laughs a little, "Alright game master, how do we pick the winner?"

"Who ever laughs first?"

"What happens when I win?"

"When I win, you have to wear the sweater of my choosing."

"So, when you laugh at my perfect sweater, I can put you in a neon pink one covered in unicorns and glitter, and you have wear it?"

"It has to be Christmas related, but yes, that's the idea."

"Okay, then. I accept."

"Good, you're gonna be wearing a chick's shirt, two sizes too small by the end of this." I smile wickedly as he puts the truck in park.

"You're going down." He gives me the stare down.

"Pretty sure that's the dude's job."

"HAYOU!" He yells, wide-eyed. "Haley Rae Carter! Who taught you to talk like that!"

"I don't know what you're talking about. I speak with nothing but class."

I jump out of the cab and meet him in front the truck. Walking through the mall, the stares of passerby's don't go unnoticed.

"I bet you twenty bucks they think I got one good hit in before you beat my ass seven ways from Sunday."

"I'm not wasting my money on that bet." He says, dropping an arm over my shoulder, he ignores it when I go stiff and steers me into a store.

Dildos.

Dildos everywhere.

"Drew, where the fuck did you bring me?" I look around, and I'm horrified, I don't know what ninety percent of this shit is or where it goes.

"Calm down, you prude." He smiles down at me while an associate approaches us. She's got one of those piercing between her nose and upper lip, and it's gaged to the point I can see gums.

"Do you need help finding anything?"

"Where can I find the ugliest Christmas sweaters you've ever seen?"

She smiles, and all I can do is stare at that huge hole in her face.

Leading us to the back she stops in front of a wall made up entirely of Christmas items. "What you see is what you get."

"Cool. Thanks, sweetheart."

I glare at him, and he smiles at me. We rifle through the clothing until I have two items I'm in love with.

BROKEN

I put them behind my back, "I'm ready to show you my choice. Well, choices. I couldn't decide which one I liked more."

"Good, because I've got three."

"Cheater." I chuckle, "Since you have three, you go first."

"Okay, Door number one," He holds a green sweater with a chimney and Santa's bare ass hanging out of it. Below the image, it says, 'Santa loves to go down'.

I bit my cheeks to try and fight the smile, "Fitting." I nod.

"I thought so, too. Your turn."

"Okay," I pull one of my arms forward to show a black sweater, reindeer and candy cane's run the collar and hem, except they're not just any ordinary designs, they are formed with tiny penises. In big letters, it says, 'Jingle my balls.' with two huge ornaments hanging off the letters, also made up of penises.

Drew smiles at me, clearly proud of himself. "The devil is in the details," I tell him pointing to the millions of dicks on the shirt.

This time he chuckles and tries to hide it, "My turn."

He twists a red sweater with mittens over the boobs that say, 'Tits the Season'.

"The hearts on the gloves are a nice touch," I say. "Not as funny as the first one, but it's good."

Without waiting, I twist my last shirt and enjoy watching his cheeks pink, "I thought this one was super fitting."

I hold a black sweater decorated with red and green designs, with the words, "Kiss me under the mistletoe." A huge arrow points down at his crotch where an image of mistletoe resides.

"Fuck, that's good." He looks at it again and nods, "That's super good, actually. But I have the golden ticket. You're perfect sweater in three...two... one-"

He twists a simple green sweater decorated in sweet little designs but the best part, the best part is the center. In white letters, it says, "Merry Fucking Christmas, Bitches."

I smile, and I can feel my dimples pull into my throat. "That's good." I will not laugh, I will not laugh.

"Damn!" He says, and laughs, "I lost, didn't I?"

I nod. "You chuckled at the little dicks."

"Fuck." He turns and sets his choices on the shelf. "What's the damage?"

I shrug, "What size do you wear again?"

"Three XL." He lies and smiles.

"Liar," I whisper handing him the mistletoe one.

"I'm not going to argue. Not, even a little." He takes it and folds it over his arm. "Your turn."

"Gimme that Merry Fucking Christmas one."

"Not Tit's the Season?"

"No, I'm tempted to wear that Santa one, but this is more me." I hold the sweater up to me and check the length of the sleeves.

"Haley." He deadpans, looking down. I follow his gaze to a red skirt with snowmen, Santas, reindeer and penises in Santa hats, all flipping the bird.

"Oh my god, That's fantastic! How much is that?"

He flips the tag over, "Twenty bucks."

That's like four times more than I'm willing to spend on clothing, but- not like I'll need money when this week is over. "Grab a small and let's go."

"Yes! This is going to be great!"

After paying for our clothes, I stepped into the bathroom to change while Drew, being Drew, took his shirt off right there in the middle of the mall. I giggle when I walk out and give Drew a twirl.

He laughs and nods. "You're the greatest human being on the face of the planet."

We walk back to the truck, and he giggles again, "You're wearing a skirt with dicks on it to a family Christmas party."

"You just don't pass up this kind of opportunity. How long do you think it will take for someone to realize?"

He thinks a moment before answering, "Twenty bucks. Maria notices first- within half an hour."

I nod. "Okay. I say, Josh in the first twenty minutes."

"You're on."

The drive to Josh's was painfully long as always, didn't help my anxiety level went through the roof. Not only was Parker going to be there but no one else knows I'm here. I'm a surprise.

Parking the truck, Drew makes sure no one's outside before ushering me forward. He opens the front door, looks around and pulls me in behind him. Walking on my tiptoes to avoid my heels from calling attention, I followed him and hide in the laundry room next to the kitchen while he goes deeper into the house.

"Mama Mia!"

"Merry Christmas, my boy." A moment passes, and I stand awkwardly against the door trying to listen.

"Don't worry about it. Hey, can I ask a huge favor? I've got a pretty big surprise, and I need everyone in the living room."

"I think everyone's already in there."

"Vinny and Jules here already?"

"Yep. They brought Dillon, what's the surprise?"

He scoffs playfully, "Like I'm going to tell you. I know you're cooking, do you have a couple of minutes? It'll be fast."

"Sure."

A second later I hear footsteps approach and move, so I don't get whacked by the door.

His head pops in, "It's showtime."

"I'm nervous," I admit.

"Don't be." He smiles, holding out his hand, "This is going to be great."

I take his offered hand and walk with him until only a wall separates me from everyone else. I can hear voices as they talk over one another, laughter rings and then Drew clears his throat loudly.

"Merry Christmas-" He starts, the room echoes back, "I have a surprise that just couldn't wait another day. Does anyone want to take a guess at what that is?" He asks rubbing his hands together like a junkie about to get his fix.

"Does it have anything to do with why both my boys are busted up?" Josh asks, and I smile.

"Well..." Drew chuckles, "Kind of."

With that, his grip tightens and yanks me into the archway.

Wide eyes, gasps, cheers and my name all happen at once, but I don't hear any of that cause my eyes are pinned on Parker.

BROKEN

He sits in a recliner wearing a black t-shirt that says, 'This is my ugly sweater' in white letters, but that's not what makes my heart drop out of my stomach as the air rushes out of my lungs. No, what does that is the perfect blonde leech currently sprawled across his lap, licking his neck as his hand rests on the high part of her thigh.

His eyes meet mine, and the corner of his lip smirks in the ugliest expression he could ever wear. It's the expression that says he knows he just hurt me and that was the plan all along.

CHAPTER FIFTY-SEVEN

Forcing my eyes away I try to focus on all the faces currently crowding me. Maria reaches me first, wrapping her arms around my shoulders and kissing my cheek. I pull my left arm tighter around my body when she lets go, and Josh takes her place. His arm wraps around me in an awkward hug; then he pats my back with a smile.

Vinny smiles and grabs my cheeks, "Good to see you, my dear."

I smile and let Jules take my hand; she gives it a squeeze before letting go. All eyes are on me, and I know everyone is talking to me, but there are too many questions, too many voices to put anything together. Hands close around my shoulders and gently slide me back, instincts cause me to recoil.

"Hales." I realize it's Drew and let him steer me back while he talks over everyone. "Hold on- hold up, hold on- Guys, wait a minute." He starts laughing, "You guys!"

Once the room starts to calm Josh is the first to grab my attention. "Why the hell are all of my kids black and blue?"

I didn't notice anything on Parker when I saw him, but yet again I didn't exactly have time to check for injuries while I watched that leech lick up his neck.

"Hales got mugged. She's fine."

Chants of 'I'm sorry.', 'Are you okay?', 'Did they catch the attacker?' ring out.

"I'm fine. It happened fast."

"I'm so glad you're back," Maria says taking my hand in hers, almost like she was proving to herself that I was really here.

"Just for the week." I clarify, "But I'm really glad to be home."

"What happens at the end of the week?" Josh asks.

"Don't know why you're asking that," Parker says as he approaches the group, his arm around Lacy's shoulders. Her fingers play with his belt loop as she smirks at me. "Not like she'll tell you the truth anyway."

"Parker." Maria glares at him. Who would have thought such a sweet woman would be capable of having a deadly mom face- but she's got one, and it's in full effect at the moment.

He shrugs and looks me, "Ain't that right?"

I glare at him and then decided that if he's going to hurt me anyway then there's no point in trying to protect myself, "I leave for Reno on the thirty first." I don't break eye contact. "He's got a job for me, and I accepted. He bought my plane ticket here after I got my ass kicked."

"Your dad? The one who showed up at HEAT?" Josh is pissed, well that wasn't thought through, was it?

"Yeah, he wants me to come home." I shrug, "So, I'll only be here for a week."

"I don't understand," Josh admits, looking at Drew and then to Parker as if they have the answers.

"He found me and offered me an out. So, I took it"

"Alright, little miss honesty," Parker says, stepping closer in challenge. "What's the deal?"

I laugh and give the arm around Lacy a pointed look, "Lose the leech."

Lacy glares but remains silent. That same cruel smile touches his lips as his thumb rubs absently against her shoulder.

"Stop being a fucking asshole," Drew speaks up.

"Stay out of it, Drew," Parker growls back.

"Fuck that! Like she doesn't have enough shit to deal with?"

"Drew." I shake my head at him. "Let it be."

He ignores me and continues, "You gotta bring that trash in here and rub it in her face?"

"Who are you calling trash?" Lacy shrieks, taking an aggressive step towards Drew.

Before she reaches him, I step between them, so Lacy and I are now nose to nose. "Back the fuck up."

Voices everywhere.

The room explodes, everyone talking over one another. One half of the room is trying to separate Drew and Parker who are throwing hands at one another; the other half is trying to put distance between Lacy and me.

"It's fine," Lacy says, allowing Vinny to pull her back a step. "You and your bestie can think whatever you want about me. I know who'll be warming my bed tonight."

"He's all yours, sweetheart." I sing back in the same calm tone, "Just know that the next time he puts his mouth on you that it was branding me just a few hours ago." I pull the neck of my sweater down to reveal the collar of hickies he left back in Savannah. I know I'm lying, but the look on her face is worth it. "I just hope I left him in good enough shape for you." I shrug, and she seethes, trying to close the distance between us.

"You fucking whore!" Lacy shouts, "You were nothing but an easy fuck, he said so

BROKEN

himself." And then the hands that were resting on my stomach lift, giving me the green light.

I smile and step into her. My hand falls into her hair as my heel hooks the back of her stiletto wrapped ankle, with the pull of my leg and the twist of my arm she hits the tile floor with a sickening crunch before she knew what was happening.

Dropping to the ground, I straddle her and smear that perfect face sideways as my knuckles make impact. She tries to pull away, clawing and scratching as she screams bloody murder. My vision is red. No way Parker would tell her I was a whore, he's pissed sure, but he's not cruel. For whatever reason, my heart and my head aren't in sync, and I end up taking my anger and hurt out on her face.

A thick arm wraps around my ribs, and I cry out as fingers dig into my bruise. I'm lifted off the ground and off the bleeding parasite who's doing her best to pretend like I killed her.

"Put me down!" I scream trying to get free, my shrill tone echoes off the entry room ceiling, circling back down to me. It's one of the Hayes men, I'm sure of it, I just don't know which one yet. "You fucking asshole! Put me down!" Steps come into view before I'm dragged backward to the second floor. "Goddammit! LET ME GO!"

A door opens and closes before I'm finally released. Grabbing my ribs, I stand to my full height and spin on the bastard that carted me up here.

I laugh and then stare back into the rage-filled eyes of the man who drove me to this point in the first place.

"What the fuck is wrong you?" He yells.

"You are!" Taking both my hands I slam into his chest. Doing nothing but making him step back, "You fucking asshole!" He keeps his hands raised as I continuously push him, "You fucking promised!" I know I'm crying, but I'm so angry I can't seem to find a single reason why I care. "You promised you'd never hurt me!" I pound on his chest with everything I have, despite the blinding pain in my side, "You promised!" My strength leaves my body as I start to collapse, his arms wrap around me, and for a split second I feel the real Parker, I feel the protective shield as it closes around me, but it's tainted now, I shove his arms off me, "Don't fucking touch me!" I back up and wipe my face furiously, "You swore you wouldn't hurt me! Being lit on fire hurt less than this! I'm sorry! I'm sorry I can't tell you what you want to hear! I'm sorry I can't be who you want! I'm sorry that I hurt you, but I don't have a choice!" His eye's watch me as I pull in painful breaths through my sobs, watches as I clutch my side. "You used her to hurt me." I say, reigning in my temper, "Her, Parker."

He says nothing as he stares at me. I sniff and move towards the door, "Way to point out every fucking flaw I have."

"I'm just a convenience, remember? You don't want me cause you don't love me. Those are your words."

"Yeah, and I'm a shit liar," I say opening the door. "Those were yours."

I make it two steps before my arm is snatched and I'm pushed against the wall, his hand sliding up my bare thigh, as his breath heats my neck, "Does this feel convenient?"

His hand pushes under my skirt, and my breathing picks up, "Is that what you're feeling?" His fingers slide under my panties rubbing his palm against me as he slips two fingers inside of me. I gasp, clutching his biceps. "Answer me, sweetheart."

"What are you doing?" I moan, as his fingers work deeper.

"Just showing you how convenient I am." His teeth graze my neck, and it's like all the fog clears from my head at once. A hot tear slides down my cheek, and I lose it.

Bringing my knee up, I aim for his goods but miss and get his thigh. He grunts and steps back, my right hook comes up, but he grabs my wrist before I make impact, shoving me against the wall. His hands hold both of mine above my head, "Wanna try that shit again, sweetheart?"

"Fuck you."

"Yeah, fuck me." He sighs looking at me, resting his gaze on my mouth. "I'm not the one who's spilling lies like it was my job. Denying shit because I'm too much of a coward to admit it."

"You go from kissing and rubbing up on Barbie to fucking with me without even washing her stink off you first," I growl.

"I never kissed her." His hands slide my wrists from above my head to my shoulders.

"Now who's the liar?"

"Still you."

"Name one thing I've lied about since I walked through those doors." He doesn't answer, "Exactly."

"Why'd you hit Lacy?"

"She called me a whore and told me you said I was nothing but an easy fuck."

"And you believed her?"

"Seeing as her spit hasn't even dried on your neck while your hand was down my pants I'm going to go ahead and say, yes."

I feel the anger flow through him as he readjusts his feet, his erection pushing into my stomach. "You honestly think I would say that about you?"

"I think you'd say it if you knew you could dig the knife deeper."

"If you don't care about me, how is there a knife in the first place?" I scoff and try to pull away from him, "No, ma'am." He readjusts to keep me in place. "No more running."

"You've made it abundantly clear that you don't want me anymore. Go peel your girlfriend off the floor and leave me the hell alone."

"There it is." He smiles, "That's two lies."

"Let me go, or I'm going to scream bloody murder and let Drew throw your ass off that balcony."

He shakes his head slowly, "I don't think you will. I think you like this, being pressed up against the wall. All pissed off and sexy."

"Last chance."

"Do it, then." He whispers against my throat, "You can scream and keep running or you can admit how you feel and I'll pull you into that bedroom and give you something to scream about."

"The only thing I'm willing to admit is that if you touch me with another body part that was up against that bitch, I'll rip it off and make it a permanent part of your rectum. Ya got me?"

He chuckles, "If that's all that's holding you back, sweetheart, I can just as easily make you scream in the shower."

"You're a bastard."

"At the moment." He nods.

"Let me go, Parker. Anything you wanted to hear died the second you pulled the trigger and put your hands on her."

His grip loosens but doesn't let go, "What was it that I wanted to hear?"

"You wanted me to admit that I loved you." His eyes search mine, his brow furrowing, "The one person I trusted not to hurt me was the one who fucking destroyed me. That bullet not only went through me it went through any hope you had of ever hearing it. Now, let me go."

His fingers tick against my wrist a second before he uncurls his fingers, releasing my arms. I step around him, fixing my skirt as I step down the hall and down the stairs.

Maria and Drew sit on the bottom step, they both turn to look at me as they come down.

Drew stands quickly, "Everything okay?"

I shake my head, looking at Maria, "I'm so sorry. I should never have disrespected you like th-"

Maria waves me off before looking up the stairs, "What happened?"

"We yelled."

She smiles, "And did that get you anywhere?"

"Got me downstairs."

She folds her lips in and smiles.

"She still here?" I ask to no one in particular.

Maria nods as Drew answers, "In Josh's study."

"How mad is he?"

"He's pretending to be mad," Maria says. "He'll be over it once she leaves."

"You mean he's pretending to be mad at Hales," Drew says.

"Right."

Sitting down on the step behind Maria I put my head in my lap and wrap my arms around my knees. How much damage can one person make in twenty-four hours?

"You done being a dick?" Drew asks.

I pull my head up to see Drew looking up the stairs behind me. I didn't hear Parker speak, but I knew when he was behind me. "You're lucky Hales went after that gash and not you."

"She took a swing or two," Parker says as he passes me.

"I hope she knocked your ass out."

"Pretty sure she tried."

"Good for you," Drew tells me as he sits down next to me.

"Lacy's in the office with Josh," Maria tells Parker, disappointment heavy in her tone. "You should probably take her home now."

I don't look up, but I hear him walk away.

"You knocked him out, didn't you?" Drew nudges me. "That's why it took him so long to come back down?"

"No."

"Shame. He would have fucking deserved it."

"Andrew."

BROKEN

"Maria."

She glares at him, "He's your brother."

"And he's an asshole."

"It's my fault." I say, "None of this would have happened if it weren't for me."

"It's not your fault," Drew says, almost angry.

"You don't know the whole story."

Before either can press further Josh steps into the foyer. His hands on his hips, face flushed, "Family meeting. My office. Right now."

Drew and Maria both stand and start forward. "Haley, that means you, let's go." My brow furrows as I look up at him, "Now."

"I thought you said-"

"Office." He turns and disappears down the hall as I stand and walk forward just as Vinny and Jules come out with a blonde mess between them. Lacy's hair is a rat's nest as she presses an ice pack into her face. I can't see if I did any good damage as they pass, but I certainly hope I did. Vinny opens the front door for them before I turn down the hall and into Josh's office.

CHAPTER FIFTY-EIGHT

Josh leans back on his desk while Maria sits in the chair behind him. He points to the empty chair between Parker and Drew. "Park it." I sit and lean away from Parker as my palms start to sweat and my heart begins to race.

"What. The. Fuck. You guys?" He starts. "All three of you show up looking like you stepped into the ring and no one's willing to talk about it, and then you all lose your minds. You boys start throwing hands at each other while you, my newest child, starts pounding that girl into the ground. So, someone better start talking."

The three of us remain silent, and Josh grows angrier.

"Parker, care to tell me how you went from being with Haley in Georgia to bringing Lacy tonight? Or Drew, might want to shed some light on why you took a swing at Parker? Or maybe Haley would like to start by telling me literally anything because I have no idea what's going on with you." He looks at each of us in turn.

"Took a swing at Parker for being a dick."

I raise my hand slightly, "I also swung at him for the same reason."

Josh looks at me, and I swear to god he almost smiled before scrubbing his face, "That's just fantastic. Care to elaborate?"

His eyes fall on me, and I take a nervous breath. When his eyes don't waver, I speak. "After letting that bleached skank grind against him, he thought it was wise to make a move on me." He makes a face like he doesn't understand but doesn't really want to ask for me to clarify, "I wasn't feeling it, so I swung at him."

Josh's eyes touch Parker, "Didn't connect." Parker tells him, out of the corner of my eye I see his wave to his jaw, "That's Drew's right."

"And that happened before you showed up?" Nods happen, "Why?"

"I picked Hales up from the airport yesterday. We didn't tell Parker, he found out and told Haley to stay away from him. After seeing her reaction, I went over to have words."

"Words don't leave marks. What happened that lead to hands being thrown?"

"I sort of opened with that."

BROKEN

Josh closes his eyes and takes a deep breath. "Drew, from the beginning- go."

"Apparently Haley told him shit in Georgia that pissed him off, then he came over to her place and saw her face and told her to stay away from him, Hales was a fucking mess, and instead of manning the fuck up and taking care of his girl, he left. I went over to tell him to stop being a cock sucker when I lost my mind thinking about what he did, went in swinging. We both took a couple of hits, then I left. Crashed at Hales' place and came here to find him with that gash on his lap when he knew she was going to be here tonight. Then he fucking smiled when he saw it bothered Hales and again- I lost it. Took a swing." He shrugs. "That's all of it."

Josh looks at the three of us, searching for holes in his story before turning his attention to me, "Haley, from the beginning- go."

"She called me a whore, so I beat her ass. The end."

"You're missing the Parker parts of that story."

"His main source of pussy was currently lying on your kitchen floor so he thought he could borrow me for a round. I took a swing."

Josh pinches the bridge of his nose, "I'm really hoping that's not the whole truth. Parker, from the beginning- go."

"Took a swing at Drew cause he failed to tell me not only that she was back, but that it looked like someone took a bat to her face. Have Haley take that makeup off, and you'll understand why I was so pissed." He takes a breath and pushes it out, "I brought Lacy to piss Haley off and get her to admit she's in love with me. After she beat the shit out of her I pulled her upstairs, and she was all pissed off and hot, I made a move, she took a swing, so I pinned her against the wall. She can say she wasn't having any of it, but she's got a complex with admitting how she feels."

"Fuck you." I pipe in, "I do not have a complex with admitting how I feel. "

"No?"

"Was my right hook too subtle for you?"

"I don't know, sweetheart. Does it count after you've already let me put my hand down your pants?"

OH, MY GOD. Everyone just heard him say that. "What the fuck is wrong with you?"

"I'm in love with a girl who refuses to let me love her. What's your excuse?"

"I believed you when you made promises and then watched as you broke every. Single. One. Of them."

"Alright!" Josh steps in. "Jesus."

"I asked you to come with me!" Parker yells, ignoring him.

"And I told you I couldn't!" I scream back.

"Why?!"

I shake my head and curl further away from him. Josh looks between the two of us and sighs. "Haley, if I ask you to talk about why you left, why you came back and why you're returning to Nevada, are you going to answer?"

"No, probably not."

"Okay. Is there any part of it that you are willing to talk about?"

"Not if you expect the truth." Parker cuts me off, "She'll give you a few lies, I'm sure."

"Fuck off, Parker."

"Am I wrong?"

"I lie because it protects people."

"Bullshit. You lie to protect yourself."

"Is that right?" I stand up, "Maybe you didn't get a good enough look at what happens when people ask questions."

"Let us protect you!" He yells, standing up to meet me.

"You can't!"

"How would you know? You haven't given us a chance!"

"Because I already know!"

"Whoa, you guys are getting too heated," Josh says stepping forward.

"Fuck that. That's the only way you can get anything out of her." Parker tells him without taking his eyes off mine.

I scoff, "Fuck you, that's not true."

"No? Would I know what you hide under your sleeves if you weren't pissed?"

I glance at Josh and Maria who watch us with questions written all over their faces, "Stop."

"No. Answer me. Would you have ever told me?"

"No. Now, shut up!"

"You hide, and you run, and you lie, and then you wonder why people leave?"

I take a step back as his words smack me in the face. He knows he went too far; his expressions softens, "I didn't mean for it to come out like that."

"Yes, you did, man of few words. You don't let your mouth run off, everything you say is said with purpose. You want to know why I lie? I lie because the truth is painful and the truth is haunting, and I'm choosing to spare you of that knowledge. Here, I'll give you an example. Remember when you told Kaylan where to take me? Remember when I said it was dangerous and you needed to stay away from me? Ask me what happened to my face."

He stares at me as dread crosses his face, "Go ahead, Parker. Ask."

When he doesn't speak, I continue, "My dad found out you visited me so he sent my brothers in. After he kicked down the bathroom door he dragged me out by my hair and threw me into the living room where he proceeded to slap me around, after kneeing me in the stomach he had them hold me down so he could sit on top of me and I had to watch as his fists came down knowing there wasn't a damn thing I could do about it."

I heave and watch his face fall as my account of the 'mugging' sinks in.

"There you go, Parker. There's the fucking truth. Now, what would you prefer? Knowing that because you ignored my warning I got my ass kicked or accepting the lie, I fed you?"

I watch as he takes a step back, then looks at his family and back at me.

"I'm sorry, was that painful to hear? Let me guess, that feeling in your chest isn't anger anymore- it's guilt. The truth hurts. Anything else you want to know while I'm dishing it out?"

"I have one," Drew starts, readjusting in his chair next to me. "What's the job in Reno?"

"He didn't give me the specifics." Shut up; it was kind of the truth.

"Is it-" He looks at Josh and Maria and then shakes his head, "Nah, nevermind. I don't want to know."

"Were you going to ask if history was going to repeat itself?" He looks at me and gives the smallest nod, "That would be my guess."

I raise my eyebrows to Parker. "What about you, Parker? Anything you want to ask? You've been full of questions lately. Let's hear them."

"Why don't you go to the cops?" Josh asks.

"Because I'll be dead before they can respond, he has everyone in his pocket, cops, lawyers, judges; you name it. Nothing happens that he doesn't know about, nothing can be done once he makes a decision, and nothing can protect you once you betray him." I shrug, "Cops have been around before, they can't touch him."

"Why didn't you leave with me?" Parker finally speaks.

"Because I couldn't."

"Why?"

"Because I was told not to." I wave over my face, "This is what happens for seeing you. Can you imagine the damage if I left with you? I told you before; there's a reason behind why I do things, behind the lies, trust me when I say or do things."

"And you want to go back to that?" He asks, the anger is apparently making a trip back for round two.

"I don't want to, but it's better than the alternative."

"And what alternative is that?"

"Having my wrists slit and being left for dead or watching him kill people and get away with it."

"And you think we-" He points in a large circle around the room, "won't protect you from that?"

"You can't, Parker. It's not that you won't try, it's that-"

"You have no trust?" He finishes for me.

"No, asshole. It's that he'll take out Drew while he's on his bike. You in some alley while you're away, Josh in a burglary gone wrong. It's that he will kill you to get to me."

He throws his arms out, "Will he? Or is that what you're afraid will happen? Cause I have a feeling you're so used to running, it's easier for you to do that than to stay and try. Face your fears, sweetheart."

"This isn't going into the ocean, Parker! This is death. And no, it isn't just a fear, this shit was my life. And that was for people who owed him money or pissed him off. Not his second highest income taking off in broad daylight. He wants blood, Parker! And I'll gladly spill all of mine before I spill yours."

"Do we get a say in any of this?"

"No," I say with finality.

"And why not?"

"Because you have no self-preservation! You'll go toe to toe with the Devil, thinking your hot shit and get yourself killed!"

"You're damn right I'd go toe to toe with him!" He yells, taking a step towards me, "Because I love you! We love you."

"And that alone will get you killed. Think with the head that has a brain for once. I'm a piece of ass, Parker; they'll be plenty more like me to come around."

"I swear to God, Haley." He fumes, "Stop fucking saying that! You are not some piece of ass! You're the woman I want to fucking marry some day! The woman I want to have kids with, a future!" Stunned into silence, I lose all words, all my anger as they slide down my throat clogging my airways. "There's your declaration of love."

Drew whistles next to me, I look over and see him smiling broadly at both of us like a child on Christmas. "Awe, the big idiot's kind of romantic."

"Shut up, Drew," I whisper, staring at Parker. What the fuck do you say to that?

Parker stares back, slightly shaking his head as hurt falls over eyes, "Still nothing?"

"What do you want me to say?"

"I want you to fucking say it back, Haley! You can tell everyone else how you feel, but you refuse to tell me!"

"If I were to admit anything, you'd never give up! You'd waste your life trying to find me, and I don't want that for you! I. Am. Not. Worth. It. Get it through your thick skull!"

His laugh is hollow and empty as he looks around the room, rubbing his mouth he points to Josh, "He adopted you so that you could be a permanent part of this family." He points to Maria, "She has never allowed anyone but my mom to cook with her, until you." He points to Drew behind me, "He risked his relationship with me and with this family, for you." He breaths heavy, shaking his head, "You think they're just going to give up? You think you can just walk away without them trying to stop you? Without them finding you? Without fighting for you?"

I look around and see no arguments on their faces; everyone is either nodding along or staring at us. "I'm not the only one willing to fight for you, Haley. Want to know why?" He doesn't give me the chance to answer before he continues, "Because you're worth it. Get that through your thick skull."

I shake my head; I don't know what to say or how to go back. Me and big mouth are to blame for this, but I don't want to take responsibility, I just want to get the hell out of here and pretend like this isn't true. Like they aren't stupid enough to follow me.

"I don't want you to fight for me. I just want you to let me go."

"Too bad." He shrugs, "We didn't get a say, neither do you."

"I'm protecting you!"

"I don't need to be protected!" He yells back. "They don't need to be protected!"

"Yes, you do! If you're dumb enough to risk not only your life but the lives of everyone else, then yes you do!"

"Who's protecting you?"

"Me." God, that sentence is in a loop or something, I swear.

"You? The girl who was beaten, burned, and forced into prostitution?"

"Jesus Christ, Parker!" I scream, "What the fuck is wrong with you!" I shove into his chest, and the asshole doesn't even blink, he's like a fucking brick wall. "God! Look around you, you fucking asshole! It's not just you and me in here!"

"No, but your family is. And not one person in here wants you to go back to that life."

"You don't get to decide that! It's my life! My body! My choice! So, fuck you! I can't believe you took something I told you in confidence and ran your mouth!"

He shrugs, shrugs. And I lose it, once again. Throwing myself forward, his arms come around me in a bear hug and lifts me off the ground, walking me behind Drew's chair, he presses me against the built-in shelves.

"Stop fighting." He whispers as I thrash in his arms. "Baby, stop fighting."

"Fuck you! Get off me!"

"Not until you stop fighting." He steps into me, and I can feel his erection.

"Jesus Christ, there's something seriously wrong with you!"

BROKEN

He smiles, smiles. Like he's fucking proud he got a woody from pissing me off. "Why'd you hit me, sweetheart?"

"Cause you're the bastard I fucking trusted to keep a goddamn secret, and you betrayed me in every way! Now, get the fuck off me." This manhandling bullshit is really starting to piss me off.

"And that bothers you because..."

"Because I put my trust in the wrong guy," I continue to thrash and buck against him. "Drew didn't run his mouth, and I didn't need to suck his dick to keep it shut."

"For being mad at who's listening, you sure are admitting to a lot." I start to run out of steam as I suck in air.

"You just told everyone I'm a whore, pretty sure they know I've had a dick in my mouth," I tell him, far quieter than before because he has a point. Not something I really want to advertise.

"You're not a whore; you were forced into a situation. There's a difference."

"You're a bastard."

"And you're a coward."

"Fuck you. Put me down."

"No."

"Damn it, Parker! Put me down!"

"Tell me you love me."

"No." I spit.

"Do you love me?"

"Fuck you; I'm not doing this."

"Because you're a coward."

"No. Because I don't get a happy ending, Parker! It's not in the cards for me! I fall for you more and more every goddamn day, but I end up hating myself more for it because I know we can never be together! I know in the end I will hurt you and you'll hate me because of it-"

His mouth seals over mine as his hands drop from around me to thread into my hair. I grab his shoulders to keep from falling as he presses his body deeper into mine reminding me how much I missed the fucking idiot.

Coming up for air, he smiles down at me, "That's all I wanted."

I push against his chest until he takes a step back, "And all I wanted was for you to wash that cunt's stink off you before fucking touching me."

"You can pretend to be mad all you want, sweetheart. Fact is, you kissed me back after admitting you loved me."

"I didn't admit to shit." I move around him, feeling embarrassed as everyone's eyes fall on us.

I sit next to Drew and pull my legs to my chest, crossing my heels to cover my ass. Drew sighs and pulls out his wallet, slapping a twenty into Josh's hand. I pull my brows together at the exchange.

"Bet twenty bucks you guys were going to forget we were here and start undressing each other."

I feel my face heat and immediately look away from both of them.

"So," Josh says abruptly. "Drew- you and Parker good now?"

"Yep."

"Parker- you good with your brother?" He doesn't answer- go figure. My monies on a head nod. "You finished with the Lacy bullshit...You done pushing Haley to the breaking point...Good. Haley?"

"Hmm?" I ask from under my arm.

"You good with Parker?"

"Are we done if I say, yes?"

"More or less."

"Fine. We're peachy."

"You good with Lacy?"

"FUCK no."

Chuckles happen around the room.

"Fair enough. Alright, children of mine. Stop fucking hitting each other! You're too old to punish- I get that. But we don't hit each other; it doesn't matter what the reason is. We're a family. We support each other even if we don't agree, if you're so upset that you feel the need to invoke violence, then come to Maria or me- let us mediate. Understood?"

We all mumble our agreement.

BROKEN

"It's Christmas Eve. Get out there so we can eat and pick up where we left off." We all start to stand, "Oh and Haley- I was going to mention it earlier, but all that shit went down-" I stop and look at him, "You've got a bunch of dicks on your skirt, kid." He goes to exit before I stop him,

"How long would you say before you noticed?"

"Too late," Drew says, but I ignore him and stare at Josh.

He shrugs, "Couple of minutes after I saw you, why?"

Drew huffs loudly, fishing out his wallet. I hold my hand out to him while he slaps a twenty into my palm. "No reason."

BROKEN

CHAPTER FIFTY-NINE

After an incredible ham dinner, we all moved into Josh's home theater and started to watch Christmas movies on his monster-sized television. Drew made it through four flicks before passing out on the floor. Maria was quick to follow after she folded herself under Josh's arm, I can't not stare, cause like seriously? Are they a couple? I've seen Josh with a ton of women at HEAT, so it's hard to guess. They're certainly snuggled up against each other like a couple. They've lived together for like ten years or something and raised the boys as a team, so I don't know if it's a familiarity that I'm seeing or if this is more. I'm barely paying attention to the Jim Carrey film that's currently on because my mind won't shut up. I really don't want to talk to Parker, but this is going to drive me crazy.

Leaning over the arm of the chair I pssht until Parker looks at me and nods- asshole. "Are Josh and Maria together?" He shrugs, "Helpful."

I curl back up against the arm of the couch and ignore him until he hits me on the shoulder with a pillow. "God!" I stage whisper, "What?!"

"Why do you ask?"

"Seriously?" I pick up the pillow and tuck it under my ankles, he smiles, "God, I hate you."

"Not what you said earlier."

"Fuck off, Parker. I didn't admit to shit; you heard what you wanted to."

He chuckles, and I glare at him. "Whatever you say, sweetheart."

"Don't call me that, you lost that privilege."

"What would you prefer? Baby?"

"Absolutely not."

"Darling? Love?"

"Shut up, Parker. Call me, Haley."

"Nah, I think I'll keep sweetheart."

"Why are you such an asshole?"

He shrugs, "You liked it until you admitted you loved me."

"Again, I didn't admit shit. I don't love you. In fact, I think I might actually hate you."

"Love and hate are two horns on the same goat."

"What?" I hiss over the arm of the chair.

"Love and hate are-"

"No- I heard you. What does that even mean?" He goes to open his mouth, but I cut him off, "You know what, I don't fucking care. Let's go back to not talking; I liked that better."

"I like this better."

"Don't care. Now, shut up before I shut you up." I hiss.

He chuckles, "By all means," He opens his arms in invitation, "I'm all yours, sweetheart.".

"Not how I would do it. Besides, that nasty bitch was all over you, Parker. I'm not coming anywhere near you."

The recliner shuts, and I turn to look at him. Meeting my eyes, he pulls this shirt over his head and pulls the right side of his mouth up when my eyes involuntarily travel down his chest. "How about now?"

"No. Go away. I'm trying to watch the movie."

"His heart grows three times, and he gets to carve the whobeast." He whispers loudly, earning a glare from Josh.

"Fuck. Off. I'm not interested, got me? If you want to get your dick wet, call Lacy."

Josh snorts softly, covering his mouth, his eyes don't avert from the TV.

"I used her to piss you off, not because I was interested. And if I wanted to, how'd you put that? Get my dick wet? Well, there's only one person I would want."

BROKEN

"Good. Go call her; I'm sure she needs her wounds licked anyway."

I catch him shaking his head out of the corner of my eye. "She's not the one I want to lick."

"Ugh, guys?" Josh says a low tone, so he doesn't disturb Drew or Maria, "I can totally hear everything you're saying."

"Like I said, not interested." I shrug. "Go call Malibu Barbie."

He walks towards me, and I glare at him. "Stop, Parker."

"Not doing anything, sweetheart." He sits down at my feet, so I draw my legs up under my butt to avoid contact. Sliding back, he drapes his arm over the back of the couch and smirks at the movie.

"You're such a child," I mumble, laying my head on my folded arms.

"You tired?"

"No."

"Want me to take you home?"

"No." I plan on kicking Drew awake and making him drive me after this movie ends.

"I can if you want. Just let me know."

I ignore him and continue to watch the film. Even though my eyes grow heavy, I force them to remain open. I just have to outlast Parker, and then I can wake up Drew.

BROKEN

I'm half dead when the movie ends; Parker sits up looking over the room before resting his eyes on me. "How are you holding up?"

"Peachy."

"Come on. Let me take you home."

"No, Parker."

"Everyone else is asleep, and I know you don't want to spend the night. Come on." I glance over and see Josh is passed out holding onto Maria's middle.

"No, Parker."

"You want to watch another one?" He asks like he already knows my answer is no.

"Sure."

"Really?"

"Either shut up and go home or put a movie in."

He sits up, grabbing a stack of movies from the end table, "What do you want?"

"I don't care."

"ELF or Christmas Vacation?"

"I don't care, whatever you want."

He nods, "Okay. Cousin Eddie, it is."

He changes the discs and returns to the couch, "You look miserable."

"My ribs hurt," I admit.

He looks me over for a moment before speaking, "Are you laying on them?" I nod, and he starts moving pillows around, "Come here, sweetheart, get off them. I'm sure with the fight and everything else the last thing you need is to be laying on them."

"I'm fine."

"No, you're not. Come on; I won't touch you- I promise."

"You've got a shit record with me on keeping promises."

"I don't want you in pain, please?"

"Parker you smell like that skank. No, thank you."

He sighs, rubbing his hand over his jaw. "Okay. Here-" He sits up, pushing the pillows against the arms of the chair, "Come lay on this side."

I glare at him but it's short-lived, I really do need to get off them. I try to sit up but gasp as the pain spikes across my middle. His hands are in front of me in an instant.

"I'm fine," I say quickly. "Just stiff."

"Can I touch you?" Fuck it all if I don't nod cause I'm a weak child who can't sit up properly.

He takes one hand, while his other rests under my arm, gently pulling me while my free arm helps push up. I hold my breath and shut my eyes against the pain as he helps me flip sides.

Once rotated, I finally let go of the breath I was holding, "Thanks." I whisper.

"Of course." His fingers gently brush my sides as he releases me, "I'll be back in a minute." He stands and presses play on the remote before disappearing into the kitchen.

It feels like forever when he returns. Shut up, I may be mad at him, but I still love the idiot. Clark finally got the lights to turn on, and that girl from Seinfeld is crying over her carpet when he kneels in front me holding a glass of water and two white pills.

"Here, baby, take these."

"Don't call me that." I flinch as I sit up enough to take the glass from him.

Throwing the pills back, I chase them down with water and try to set it on the table, but Parker takes it from me before I'm able to. That's when I noticed his hair's wet and he's wearing a pair of pajama shorts.

"Did you shower?" His gaze meets mine and nods, "Don't you usually shower in the morning?" Another nod. "God, you're so great at this conver-" His mouth slides over mine once, so gently I can barely feel it, then comes in with slightly more pressure.

Now, don't fucking look at me like that, my libido controls this aspect of my body, and it's hot-wired to him- so fuck off.

His fingers slide gently across my jaw and into my hair, very gently pulling me forward. It's so incredibly sweet and gentle I might cry. Pulling away, he rests his forehead against mine, "I'm sorry," His thumb brushes over the cut on my cheekbone, "Am I hurting you?"

"No." Not physically that is.

"I'm an asshole, and I handled this in the worst possible way imaginable. I didn't mess around with her, Haley. I put my hand on her leg, but that was it. She was over, and you showed up, she knew you weren't around. Drew came in, and I pulled her onto my lap to make you jealous, I didn't know she was going to go and lick me, that was all her, and I swear to you, there was absolutely no enjoyment in that for me. I just wanted you to get heated enough so I could prove you cared. I only want you." His lips brush mine again, very gently, "I'm sorry, hurting you was never my intention."

"What do you call last night?"

He shakes his head gently, skimming his thumb over my cheek and then across my jaw, "I was so angry that someone hurt you. And on top of that, you went to Drew and not me. I wanted you to choose me, and you didn't. I got childish and lashed out. I wanted you to come over, tell me the truth. I wanted you to want to tell me." His fingers trace my features while he speaks, "God, I love you."

"What about telling everyone I was a whore?"

"I was so determined to get through to you; I wasn't thinking. I just said it, and then it was too late."

BROKEN

"You're supposed to be the one who protects those pieces, remember? You were the one who wasn't supposed to hurt me."

"I know." He kisses me gently.

"I think the worst thing, in all of this, was what you did upstairs. Fingering me and then telling me you were a convenience while her spit was still drying on your neck. I've never felt more like a whore than I did there." A hot tear escapes, and he smooths it against my skin.

"How do I fix this?"

"I don't think you can."

His eyes are deep with remorse. Ugh, I'm so mad at him, but I can't stomach his eyes, I can't handle the hurt swimming inside them.

"Tell me what to do, and I'll do it."

"You can't go back in time, what's done is done." He watches his fingers as they glide across my skin, "All we can do is assess the damage and move on."

"When you say move on?"

"Work past it. If this is my family, then we have to get along for them." I look over and see the resting faces of those I love, "And despite everything, I don't want to lose you."

"You're not going to lose me. I know I did damage today, but I can promise you that."

"I don't want you to promise me."

"Because you don't trust what I say?"

"No, because you're going to lose me in a week and if I can't promise to stay, neither should you. If you want to promise me something, promise you won't hate me when I leave. Promise that in a few years you'll smile when you think of me, promise that when this is all over you'll respect my decision and know that what I do, is my choice, it's what I wanted."

"You want to go back to Reno?"

"No, but I have a choice of what happens to me there, and that's what I want you to know was my decision."

"Feels like you're saying goodbye." He whispers, still watching his fingers trail over my features.

"In a way, I am. I don't want to argue with you." Another tear falls, "I just want to use this week to be happy before I have to say goodbye."

"Then don't say goodbye," He kisses me again, "Just stay with me."

His lips press firmer as he leans into me. He doesn't give me time to respond as his lips turn from gentle to fierce, going from embers to full-blown flames.

My hands fall into his hair and against his jaw. Trying to avoid moaning, my throat ends up vibrating.

"If I don't stop now, I won't be able to." He tells me but falls against my mouth for a second round. Pulling away, I almost groan. "You're hurt." He says, moving to sit by my feet.

"Hold on." He looks up at me, his face full of question, "Help me up." He holds his hands out slowly and helps me to sitting position and then standing, "Lay down."

"What?" He looks at me like I've gonna insane. "No, sweetheart, lay back down."

"Shut up and listen to me, would you."

He stares at me a moment and then sits on the center cushion, laying back against the pillows. I pat his knee until he lifts both legs onto the couch, watching me in half annoyance, half curiosity.

Carefully, I put one knee between the cushion and the back of the couch at his hip and sit on his lap. His erection pushes against me and because I'm me- I 'accidentally' rock against him despite the protest in my ribs. His hands grab my hips, his fingers digging into my flesh. I slide against him once more on 'accident' before smiling and laying down, so my head rests against his chest.

He grabs the blanket off the floor and throws it over our legs, mainly to cover my ass I'm sure. One arm comes up to rest on my shoulder while his fingers thread into my hair, the other hand rests on my good ribs to keep me from falling off him.

Every few seconds I tilt my pelvis down so I create the tiniest bit of friction to 'get more comfortable,' each time his hands tighten.

"Behave." He whispers, though he still tilts his hips up to meet mine.

"Or what?"

"I'll fuck you right here on this couch."

"Whatever. Everyone's sleeping in here."

"So?"

This earns him an eye roll. No, he won't. "Whatever."

"It'd be easy; you're in a skirt. I'd just have to move that tiny piece of clothing to the side." He tilts against me again, "If you keep doing it, I'm not responsible for what I do next."

Knowing he won't fuck me in a room full of people, I rock against him again. Squeezing my hips, his free hand travels under the blankets to my ass, he gave it a good squeeze before moving around and sliding it between our bodies. His fingers smooth over my panties as he rubs against me, causing my body to jerk against him. Biting my lip, I bury my face in his chest, trying to avoid making any noise. My nails dig into his chest, he pulls his hand back a moment, just to slide it under my panties, teasing and rubbing as he goes.

"See how easy that is?"

Carefully pushing up into a straddling position, I smile down at him. He won't actually go through with it, we both make entirely too much noise for any of that.

Wiggling my ass down, the elastic band of his pants follows, undressing him as I move, my hand comes up to palm him. Closing his eyes, his hands rest against my thighs. Leaning on my knees, I lift myself, and his eyes shoot open. Sliding my panties further to the side, I take him and rub him against me, waiting for him to call it quits in this odd version of chicken we seem to be playing.

I line him up and rest the tip against me, making small bobs with my hips, he still doesn't stop me. Instead, he presses down on my hips, so I fall at a deliciously slow rate until my ass is firm against his thighs, his hands squeeze my hips as I stretch around him. Leaning forward, I take the blanket with me and lay back on his chest, taking his bottom lip in, I gently bite.

I succumb to his mouth and let him kiss me as his hips start to move, making short, slow thrusts. It's enough to make me dig my nails into the cushion and hold my breath. He stays at a leisurely pace before picking up speed, using his hands he holds my hips away from his body as he pulls out and sinks back into me. I press my teeth into his shoulder as I force myself to remain silent. We've never gone this slow before, and never have we have tried doing this quietly.

Needing more, I fuck him back and revel in the way his breathing increases and his hands tighten. I push back on him and then we both immediately still when Drew gets restless on the floor. I hide my smile against Parker's neck as I squeeze my muscles around him. Without mercy, he lifts my hips and slams once into me. A cry escapes my lips, and I bite my lip until it hurts to stifle it while I rack my nails down his chest.

"What the hell are you doing?" Drew's sleep thick voice asks.

"Moved wrong." I lie, "My ribs are killing me."

"Want me to take you home?"

"No, I'm alright. Sorry, I woke you up."

"You're good."

Within seconds, the soft hums return, and I chuckle against Parker's chest. Gently peeling myself off him, I stand to take his hand.

"Where are we going?" He smiles, tucking himself into his pants.

"I need Tylenol."

He makes a face at my lie but plays along. "Okay, this way."

I let him lead me down the hall and into the bathroom. The second the door shuts, we're all over each other. His hands are up my skirt while mine are down his pants, putting me against the counter, I twist as he folds my skirt up my back before pulling my panties down. I gasp and hold the sides of the sink for support when suddenly he's inside of me.

Apparently, he doesn't want me bent over because he pulls me, so my back is against his chest, his fingers grab the hem of my sweater, and he tugs it over my head. His hands slide up to grope my chest through my bra before pulling the cups down, so I spill over the top. He pulls back and buries himself deeper inside me. I grip his hip and the back of his neck as he sets a bone-crushing speed and within minutes my body is tightening, squeezing him as the coil grows tighter and tighter.

All fucks are gone about volume as the coil snaps and shatters, turning my body rigid as stars bloom behind my eyes.

I can taste sound and hear colors as he rocks harder into me before he too goes mad, his fingers digging into me as he growls against my neck, slamming into my body.

Jesus Christ, it's never dull, never enough. He kisses the growing mark on my neck and smiles at me in the mirror as he pulls out, slips his pajama pants up and tucks himself away.

I attempt to bend, but the throb in my side won't allow it. Parker doesn't comment, he simply drops low, seizing the tiny scraps of fabric and slides it up my body. Putting them in their proper place, he kisses my bruise with every ounce of tenderness as he rights my skirt.

Parker pulls my sweater over my head, once my arms are through he takes my hand and leads me back to the couch where I lay, once more, on his chest. Sated, happy and finally at peace. His heart sings me a lullaby, and before I know it, I'm out.

BROKEN

CHAPTER SIXTY

The scent of bacon, cinnamon rolls, and pine needles wake me, sounds like a weird combination but I'm pretty sure this is what heaven smells like. My senses wake, but I keep my eyes closed, all too aware that I'm still laying on Parker and I don't want to wake him if he's still sleeping.

"Jesus." Josh whispers, "When did it happen?"

"She said a couple of days ago." Drew whispers at my feet.

"Are you sure they're not broken?"

"No, but it's not like you're going to get her to go the hospital."

"I'm sure we can go along with the mugging story if it means she can get checked out."

"I'm sleeping." I mumble to them, "Stop staring and no, I'm not going to the hospital." Grabbing the blanket, I cover my exposed skin.

Parker moves slightly underneath me, "Good morning, gorgeous." His voice is alert, leading to the belief he's been awake for awhile, but my lazy ass has kept him on this couch- oh well.

"Morning." I keep my eyes closed but smile when he kisses my forehead.

"DAW. You guys are all made up." Drew coos.

"Fuck off."

"It's Christmas; you have to be nice to me. It's the law."

"It is not."

"You should see someone about that bruise, Haley," Josh says a little further away.

"It just looks bad," I mumble. "Nothing's broken."

"How would you know?"

"Cause they've been broken before. Trust me; they're not broken." He starts to inhale, so I cut him off, "Isn't it Christmas? Can't y'all lay off me and my life choices until tomorrow? I thought today was supposed to be like a day of magical unicorns and sparkles or some shit."

Parker chuckles under me. Someone nodded somewhere- I'm sure of it because all conversation died after that.

BROKEN

"You plan on climbing off my brother anytime soon?"

With my eyes still shut, I hold up my middle finger and wave it in the general direction of his voice. "Some of us were actually able to hang last night."

"It's almost nine."

I moan and turn my face into Parker's neck, "In the morning?" His arms tighten around me as he chuckles. "I don't want to get up."

"I know." He smooths my hair, "You can go back to sleep upstairs if you want."

"What are you going to do?"

"I need to shower."

Didn't he shower last night though? Oooooh, this is an invitation. "Hmm, that sounds nice."

"Gross," Drew adds.

I flip him the bird again. "I'm injured, I need strong hands to hold me up."

Drew makes gagging noises and my stone expression breaks.

Giggling, I open my eyes to see his horrified expression. "Whatever, like you've never showered with a chick before."

"Nope. Don't plan to either; I prefer my women already clean."

I laugh a little harder, "You're missing out."

"Ahhh! Stop talking!" He stands up from the floor, giving an exaggerated shudder. "I don't want to think about my best friend nailing my brother, thank you very much."

"Yet you go into graphic detail about your conquests?"

"That's different. It's me; I was there. I don't want to hear about you."

"Prude."

He scoffs at me, "Yeah right. I've got stories that'll make your kinkiest moment look juvenile."

"I don't know about that." I smile at him, "You're talking to a professional, remember?"

He shudders again, "Nope! Not allowed to make prostitution jokes, Hales!"

I shrug, pulling myself away from Parker's chest. "Just saying."

"Ah! No." He plugs his ears, leaving the room.

Parker chuckles under me, his fingers twisting in my hair, "Do you want to shower?"

"With you."

He smiles, patting my thigh in a silent gesture to get up.

Pulling off the couch, my ribs protest but I manage without flinching. "How are you feeling?"

"Fine." He gives me that smile that says he knows I'm lying but he's letting it go. "They're a little achy, but I'll live."

"Mhm." He claims my hand and leads me upstairs to, what I guess is his bedroom here, and into the attached bathroom.

"I don't have anything to change into. Drew said we weren't spending the night."

"You can get in; I'll grab something from Maria."

He leaves me, so I strip and step into the hot spray, careful not to get my face wet. Most of my makeup has worn off during the night, but there's enough to hide at least a little of the bruising.

I'm rinsing the shampoo out of my hair when he returns. I watch him through the glass as he undresses. That incredible man is mine, maybe not for long, but right now, at this moment- he's mine.

"What are you smiling about?" He pulls the door closed behind him and joins me under the water.

"Nothing."

"Something." Leaning down his lips press gently into mine.

"Just thinking."

"About what?"

"You."

"What about me?" He quirks his eyebrow.

I smile, stepping up on my tiptoes to kiss him again, resting my body against his.

Just as it starts to heat up, I pull away and smile. Grabbing the conditioner, I work it into my hair, resting my gross arm against the wall to watch him as he works body wash into a thick lather across his body. Jesus.

He watches me, taking a deep breath as his head tips back to stare back down me. Before I can ask, his hands gently slide across my neck, tilting my chin up, as he steps into me, kissing my throat, following up my jaw, and then his lips close over mine. It's not rushed, it's not heated, it's earth shattering and gentle.

He pulls back, his thumbs rubbing under my eyes, then over my eyebrows, he pulls in to kiss me again, slow and sweet. Not sure when, but my hands have ended up at his hips and I use him as an anchor as he kisses away the pain, the hurt feelings, the fear. Feeling that protective shield as it falls around me and brings me home.

"Stay with me." He whispers, resting his forehead against mine.

We both know I can't. Looking up into his eyes, I see the pain, the fear that resides there and I'd give anything to take it away. We're both aware I leave Wednesday, but I can offer him this lie. Something to take it all away, even if just for a short while.

Meeting his eyes, I give him a weak nod, "Okay." I whisper.

His eyes grow wide as he takes in my face, "What?"

BROKEN

"I said okay." I run my finger across his jaw, "Now, kiss me."

His face breaks out in an outrageous smile before his lips seal over mine, igniting my blood and stroking the flames inside me.

I love you; I tell his heart. You'll own me forever; I tell his soul. I'm yours, I whisper against his mouth.

After an incredible breakfast, I sat next to Parker and watched as everyone opened their gifts. Laughing and joking as the morning turned to late afternoon.

"Now, I know you said no one was allowed to get you gifts." Parker starts, causing my lighthearted smile to turn deadly. "But I never agreed to such a ridiculous thing." He smiles at me, and pulls a tower, yes, a tower, of stacked presents from beside the couch and sets it in front of me. "So, this is yours."

Maria 'awes' while Josh and Drew hold secrets smiles.

"What is it?" I ask tentatively as I stare at the gifts. All rectangle, same height, width, and length. Held together with ribbon.

"Open it and find out."

I give him another glare and pull the green twine free. Grabbing the first one, I give one last look around, "It's really weird to be stared at while I do this, guys."

It earns me a few chuckles, but no one looks away. Pressing my nail into the paper, I slide it across the lip and lift the corner of paper just to cover it instantly as I laugh nervously and look at Parker who's smiling like a boy on, well- Christmas.

"You got me chucks?" His smile grows. "Seriously?"

He tilts his chin to the gift, and I pull the paper off to reveal the brown and black converse box. Pulling the lid off, a pair of classic, high top All Stars stare back me. I bite my lip to hide my smile. "Thank you."

"Open the rest." Drew whines playfully, pushing the stack towards me. Picking up the next box, I pull the paper off to reveal another shoe box with red high tops. The next has a post-it note taped to the top; it reads; 'Not a gift. -Drew'

I laugh and open it to find a pair of blue high tops, and the last has another note, "This isn't a gift either. -Josh"

Pulling the lid, a pair of low top converse sit, they're covered in pink flowers.

I look at all my new shoes and smile, "Thank you."

"You've got one more," Maria says, sitting up. "I never agreed, either."

BROKEN

Oh, fuck. She hands me a long, white, rectangle box, unwrapped. In delicate handwriting, 'Love, your family.' is scripted across its surface.

Looking around, I see no one is wearing those secret smiles anymore, they all seem- nervous? Sad maybe?

Cautiously pulling the lid off the box, a necklace shines against a cotton lining. Taking the chain, I lift it from its prison and rest it against my palm. A compass hangs from the silver chain, upon closer inspection I notice an engraving on the outer circle,

So you can always find your way home.

The light catches and bounces off the diamond center, "It's beautiful."

Offering me a smile, she pulls her arm away from Josh's shoulder and takes the chain. I pull my hair off my shoulder and force the darkness away as she clasps the chain around my neck, allowing it rest against my chest. It's surprisingly heavy for being so simple and delicate, but I welcome the weight. Every time I feel it, I'll be reminded why I'm making this choice and who I'm protecting.

BROKEN

"No way!" Drew shouts, standing abruptly from the table were all currently eating dinner at. An enormous smile takes over his face as he stares at me.

I have no idea what's happening in case you were wondering. "Really?"

Looking around, I catch the eyes of everyone else who seems to be as clueless as I am.

"What?" I ask slowly.

"You're not fucking around? Like, definitely? A hundred percent? No, take backs, no false positives?" He looks at Parker and me.

"Wh-" I start, but Maria interrupts, "Oh my God, you're pregnant?"

"What?!" I shriek, "Fuck; I hope not."

I have one of those things shoved up my hoo-ha that's supposed to prevent that sort of thing from happening. I look back at Drew who's still smiling like an idiot.

"What the fuck are you talking about?"

"The secret!"

"What secret?"

Parker drops his head in his hand and groans. "Nothing."

"What?" Drew and I ask at the same time.

"Leave it alone, Drew." He sighs loudly before whispering into my ear, sending goosebumps as he speaks, "Drew was upset. I told him you said you'd stay. He wasn't supposed to say anything."

BROKEN

I pull back and stare at him in shocked horror, "No, you didn't."

"What's going on?" Josh asks.

"Haley's staying!" Drew basically screams.

I cover my face. FUCK. That was a lie to keep Parker happy, not raise everyone's expectations and then crush them when I leave.

Everyone seems to be talking over one another while I try to find my way out of this shit storm without ruining Christmas.

Parker squeezes my knee under the table, I peak at him, and he nods to ask, 'What's wrong?', I shake my head, "I didn't want people to know that I said that." I whisper back.

"Why not?"

"Because." I groan into my hand. You were supposed to know it was a lie.

"That's damn good news." Josh says from the head of the table, "Damn good news."

After the talking dies down, I can feel everyone's eyes on me.

"I didn't want to get everyone's hopes up." I glare at Parker and then at Drew, "I did tell Parker I would stay this morning-" Everyone starts to talk again, and I can't seem to find another place to interject before we hear a scream in the kitchen.

Everyone stands at once and moves towards the commotion.

"Mama Mia? You alright?" Drew calls as we herd ourselves into the kitchen.

BROKEN

Maria stands with one hand over her heart, the other over her mouth while staring into the chill drawer. Josh moves forward and takes something out, Maria's shocked eyes fall on him as he gets down on one knee.

"Oh fuck," I mumble, stepping back. This seems too personal, I shouldn't be here, but Parker's frame stops me.

"You've been by my side for the last twelve years. We've grieved together, laughed together, and fought together. I've yelled; you've thrown things. I've made mistakes; you've kicked me out of my own damn house for 'em." They both laugh before his face and tone turn very serious, "But God dammit if I don't love you more for it. I've loved you since I was sixteen and I'm done pretending that I haven't. I can't give you the world, but I can give you everything I am. I know I don't deserve you, no one deserves you, but I promise to spend every second of my life trying to be that man because I love you, Maria. I always have and I always will. So, for the love of God, woman- marry me."

Folding her trembling lips between her teeth, she smiles the most radiant smile I've ever seen and nods. Letting out a nervous laugh, he raises to his feet and slides the ring across her shaking hand. The room erupts in applause and cheers as Parker's arms wrap around my middle before resting his chin on my shoulder.

"Did you know?" I whisper, not taking my eyes off the romantic scene in front of me.

"Maybe." He whispers back, kissing my cheek.

I stare ahead, overjoyed for the happiness unfolding in front of me. Josh and Maria are getting married, Drew has a girlfriend even if he won't admit to it, and in this current moment, Parker seems happy to have me.

A small window of pain opens knowing I'll never have that moment. Having someone drop down in front of their family and friends while declaring their love, opening themselves up, trusting the other not to let them down as they lay themselves bare.

Squeezing Parker's wrists, I snuggle in deeper. In another life, it's easy to picture that being Parker and me. In another life where I don't trail pain and destruction, I can see us being that fairy tale couple that everyone envies. In another life, I can see children and tradition, love and family, I can see a happily ever after, and dammit if that doesn't break something inside me.

What if Kaylan's right? What if I told them the details and let them make the decision? What if he's right and they do choose me? Would that let me have this? Would I get to take this moment and make it my future? Could

BROKEN

I fold my hand and walk away from the table of my life? Or would the chips hit the table and everyone I ever loved be dead within the year? Is my chance at happiness worth the lives of those I love?

No. No, it's not.

Excusing myself to the restroom, I pull out my phone and open a text to Drew's old phone that is now in my brother's possession.

ME: I've made my choice.

NEW MESSAGE: That is?

With trembling fingers, I write the words that turn my stomach and damn my soul.

CHAPTER SIXTY-ONE

Thursday was spent in Parker's bed- literally. He set up the TV, and we binge-watched shows, ate takeout, the only time we wore clothes was the couple of hours that Drew was here.

He laid out at the foot of the bed before his shift at HEAT, the moment he was gone, so was our clothing. Friday was more or less the same, except we went to HEAT to keep Drew company where it was apparently decided I'm still an employee and was expected to work tonight. You can't see me, but I'm rolling my eyes. I leave in four days, working is not how I was planning to spend my time, but it means more time with Drew and Josh, so I accepted.

I instantly regret that decision when Parker exits the bathroom in a towel. Beads of water slide down his chest and between the valley of his abs. Pretty sure I'm drooling.

Noticing my gawking, the right side of his mouth lifts before he lets the towel pool around his feet. My mouth goes dry, and I am definitely regretting the decision to go back to work. He stalks towards me like a predator, and I'm all too willing to be devoured.

BROKEN

His hands slide around my waist as he walks me back against the door. He's barely touched me, and my breathing is a ragged mess. His fingers bunch the material of my dress at my hips until my panties are exposed. His thumbs hook around the tiny scrap of lace and start to slide them away from my body.

I shiver against him as he drops to his knees. I watch him through hooded eyes as he drags one leg over his shoulder. I'm a hot mess; my fingers run through his hair as greed takes over and guides him between my legs. I can't even tell you my name at this point, all I can focus on is his mouth and how shaky my legs are. The coil snaps almost immediately, doubling me over, he keeps me from falling without taking his mouth off me.

He drops my leg and stands; my arms lock around his neck as he lifts me, pressing my back against the bedroom door. His hands find my ass as he holds me in place against the door, I reach down wrapping my hand around him, and I lead him inside of me.

An animalistic groan escapes his throat at the same time a moan slips out of mine. His teeth latch onto my bottom lip as his hips start to move. Just as the coil begins tightening inside me once again, I hear the fucking front door open.

BROKEN

No. No, no, no, no, no. Parker must hear it too because he stills against me, turning his gaze to the door.

"Haley, Bailey! Let's go." I hear Drew call from the mouth of the hallway, growing closer. "Time to rock and roll."

"Go home, Drew," I yell breathless.

"Ugh! Can't y'all do that nasty shit later?"

"You have two options." I yell, still wrapped in Parker's arms, I hold his face to my neck, stifling a moan as he rocks his hips slowly, "Go home or listen to your brother fuck me against the door."

Parker chokes on his laugh, resting his forehead against my neck as his shoulders shake against my palms.

"Man, Y'all need Jesus." Drew calls from, what's sounds like the end of the hall, but a moment later the front door shuts and like nothing happened at all, Parker's mouth crashes down on mine and picks up his punishing rhythm that sends me over the edge once again, only this time I take him with me.

I fall back into work effortlessly, despite the extra business with the U of A being on winter break and the extra Christmas crowd. As annoying as it is, I'm kind of glad that one Hayes man is always around me, I feel protected and feel as though I can focus on the crowd and not needing to look over my shoulder every three seconds.

Though, needing anything in the back is a headache, it's hard enough getting what you need by yourself let alone with a man-tank standing behind you in the crowded space. After a fight broke out, Parker left me with Drew during my break to help Simon with the bouncing while Josh cleans up the mess those frat jackasses left.

"It's packed!" I yell over the music.

"Yeah, and it's almost unbearable being paired with Alice." He rolls his eyes while filling a series of shots. "When are you twenty-one, again?"

I gave him a laugh, watching as Alice, less than gracefully, attends to patrons.

They've never really gotten along, but Josh is convinced Drew would sleep with Danica if he paired them. Little does he know, they've already slept together- twice.

"Fuuuuck." Drew groaned before looking around. "Hey, new blood! Jake, right?"

I follow his gaze to the bartender I was introduced to last night. "Yeah?"

"You got a minute? I'm overflowing, dude." Drew nods to the trash bin at his hip.

"Uh, yeah. Gimme a sec." He drawls, I wonder where he's from, his twang is different from Drew and Parker's.

BROKEN

"Hales? Be a lamb and get me another drawer of cherries, please?"

With a nod, I hop off the stool, sidestepping Jake and entered the storage room.

Not more than a minute later, Jake shuffles in, carrying two trash bags.

"Nope." I stop him in his tracks. "You can't go through here, against the health code. You gotta use the alley door." I point down the hall.

"Crap. Sorry."

"It's alright. Hey- where are you from?"

"Abilene." When my face clearly states I have no idea where that is, he continues, "Texas. I'm a student at U of A."

"Oh! That's cool. What are you-" The music of the bar show kicks on cutting off my question?

"Shit!" He looks from the bags to the door, not sure what to do.

"Here, give me those. Go."

"Drew said you weren't to go anywhere without an escort."

"Drew's a drama queen. I was mugged on the other side of the country. I'll survive the ten feet to the dumpster." Twenty, but whatever.

His face scrunches with uncertainty while bouncing from one foot to the other.

"Seriously." I growl, "Danica needs you, or she can't do the show. Go!"

After another moment of hesitation, he hands the bags over and runs down the hall. I roll my eyes to no one in particular at Drew's stupid warning.

Stepping into the hall, I catch Jake drying his hands in record time before jumping up onto the bar to join Danica. She would have ripped him a new asshole if he cost her tips because of his absence.

Taking the opposite direction, I enter the utility room and pull the alley door open. Using my foot, I slide the heavy rock against the frame before exiting. When I first started here, I forgot to move the rock and ended up being locked out and had to walk all the way around the building to get back in. After the ribbing I got from Simon, it was a mistake I only ever made once.

My heels wobble against the uneven pavement of the alley as I scurry over to the dumpster. I've always been safe here, but alleyways have always given me the wiggins anyway.

Before I reach the dumpster, I hear the tell-tale sound of the heavy metal door closing and spin around just to have the air ripped from my lungs.

"Baby sister." He chuckles, rolling the rock I used to hold the door open between his meaty hands, "Tell me, have you missed me?"

Thick hands snaked around my middle, hauling me up and backwards before a car peels into the alley, coming to a screeching halt in front of me.

PANIC.

That's all I can feel.

Unaltered, raw, PANIC.

"I have safe passage!" I scream as Joe holds me back. "I have safe passage!"

Evan climbs out of the driver's seat while Derek crosses the alley to meet him.

"Old man got your message," Derek tells me, closing the door that Evan left open.

"I have until the first!" I try to reason when I notice he never killed the engine, "He gave me until the first, I have time!"

"Do you?" He unbuttons his cuffs, then proceeds to roll them up his tattooed forearms.

"Call him! I have time!"

"Who do you think sent us?" Evan adds in annoyance without looking at me.

"Derek, I have time!" I struggle against Joe, but the guy is like a brick house.

With a dark chuckle, Derek unsheathes a large hunting knife. At the sight of the blade, my body completely takes over as I struggle to get out of Joe's hold. "LET ME GO!"

"The Old man thought it was pointless to wait if you had already made up your mind."

"Not here!" I plead, "Please, not here!"

He looks to me like he's sincerely taken back. "This is my mercy, Ryan." He shrugs. "Seems Joey's gone soft." He and Evan share a sinister chuckle, "He said we should do it here. That way, when your precious family finds you, you might even be saved." He laughs outright this time before nodding to the hood of the car.

    He'll guarantee I won't survive. Joe moves forward, taking me with him and I let out an ear-piercing scream that leaves my throat as raw as my fear.

CHAPTER SIXTY-TWO

Grabbing my wrist, Joe twists it behind my back and lifts me clear off the ground.

"Derek! Stop! No, please!" Joe's body slams into me from behind, his knees dig into the back of mine, pressing me painfully into the side of the car.

"Stop!" I sob as Evan grabs my arm, pulling it taut over the hood, I can feel the heat of the engine as it pushes through my sleeve. I squirm and scream as hot tears roll down my cheeks.

"Stop!" Evan tries to pull my sleeve up, but grows impatient, motioning Derek forward, he uses the knife to the separate the fabric before grabbing the ends and ripping the sleeve up to my shoulder. I buck harder, trying to get something free, anything free. "Don't do this! Please, Derek!"

I'm crying so hard I'm gagging on the sobs.

BROKEN

"STOP!"

Joe grunts behind me, but his hold doesn't waver.

"The old man would have been gentler." Derek's lips curl as he approaches my exposed arm. "I'm supposed to make up for lost time before honoring your choice, as he put it. Now, let's take a look."

"STOP! NO! DEREK-" A mangled scream erupts from my throat as the blade pierces through the skin in one slow agonizing line. Heat races down my arm while the outer edges of my vision start to darken.

"There's one." He laughs, Evan grins. I'm flopping around like a fish out of water, but the bastard is too strong. Derek wipes the blood off the blade on the belly of his shirt.

"STOP! PLEASE. Joey! Please!" Derek laughs at my pleas, "PLEASE!"

"Oh, come on now. We're just having a little fun with you Ry."

"LET ME GO!"

"When we're done. Convenient to work at a nightclub, no one can hear you." He laughs again scanning my arm up and down. "Damn dude, I think you're out of room."

Flipping my arm over he scans the inside of my bicep. His lips purse as he tries to find an unblemished spot.

"Might have to start on the other arm," Evan suggests, also looking over my arm.

BROKEN

"Nah, Dad wants both birthdays on this arm. Watch your hand, Evan; you're going to get blood on you."

I shutter at the words, my brain registers the pain, but it's on overdrive, trying to process the panic and adrenaline that it doesn't fully sink in.

"Stop!" I cry in a defeated tone. He lets the tip of blade slide across the coarse surface of my skin, "PLEASE STOP! EVAN!"

"Shut up, Ryan." Derek whines, "The sooner I find a spot the sooner we're done."

Turning back to my arm he smiles. "Looks like I won the golden ticket." He laughs, "I get the wrist."

Jesus Christ. I throw myself around, catching Joe's chin with the back of my head. "Fuck!" He pulls his face back; I fall a fraction of an inch.

"HELP!" I scream until my throat rips in half.

"Shut her up!" Derek points to Joe with the blood-streaked blade.

"Sure, let me just grow another fucking arm for you."

"Let go of her shoulder and shut her up! We've got her arm."

Like the good soldier he is, he releases my shoulder and tries to cover my mouth.

"NO! HELP! PLEASE!"

His fingers dig painfully into my chin until my mouth is encased in his thick hands. The salt on his skin burns my lips. I try to pull free; I swear I try, it's just not enough. It's never enough.

"On the count of three." Derek chuckles, "One." I buck violently, screaming into Joe's palm. "Two." God, please stop this. Stop them. PLEASE. "Three." Fire races across my skin as the blade digs deeper; I swear to God I can feel my vein being opened.

"PLEASE!" My scream is muffled under the weight of his hand. "STOP!"

My cries go unanswered as Derek demands my other wrist. He's going to fucking kill me, oh my God.

My right hand is snagged and pulled across the hood with enough force that I end up smacking my face into the heated metal. The smell of copper and the thick movement of liquid against my cheek make me panic even more.

My hands are turned palm up and forced together, so they're resting side by side. Holding my wrists together, Evan moves to allow Derek more room.

"The decision was yours, Ryan. You could have come home; he wanted me to remind you of that. He also wanted me to assure you that we'll make sure you're found, if not tonight, then to deliver you to a certain boyfriend's house tomorrow." God, no. I sob against Joe's hand.

BROKEN

I'm not scared of dying; I'm terrified that they'll be the ones to find me. When I made the choice to die, I sincerely thought he'd slit my wrists in some motel and leave me there to be labeled a suicide, not dump my body on Parker's doorstep.

I didn't want them to be a constant pawn in his game with my life; I couldn't handle him going back on his word the next time I pissed him off- I couldn't. So, I choose death thinking I could protect them; I can't imagine how my death is going to affect them, especially if they're the ones to find me.

I feel the bite of the blade on my left wrist, just under the previous laceration and start screaming against the agony all over again as the knife travels across one wrist and begins to dig into the other.

I'm going to fucking die in this alley.

One second I'm screaming the next I'm shoved against the asphalt. The gravel bites into my skin as I slide across it. Ignoring the crimson stream racing down my arm, I pull it into my chest, pressing my thumb against my wrist to try and stop the blood gushing out of the incisions as I crawl away from them.

"Should have fucking known your bitch-ass wouldn't be far behind." Derek sneers.

"Ryan?" I hear Kaylan call out in a fury.

"Here!" I choke out, not even able to fully process how or why he's here.

"Get inside! Call the cops."

"She ain't gonna call the cops. She knows what happens to snitches, we don't have to be around for the consequences to reach her and she knows it."

"Haley! NOW."

I gag on the burn in my throat and try to stand, tripping and falling into the pile of trash collected against the dumpster. Half walking, half limping I follow the wall out of the alley with my shoulder to the access door. Beating it repeatedly with my fist, all the while shoving my wrist into my collarbone. Blood runs down my chest at a sickening rate.

Derek laughs from his spot next to the car, "You gonna snitch, Haley. How long before boy toy finds a better pussy, huh?" Car doors open, "He can't watch your back forever, and this little bitch is breathing on borrowed time."

I continue to smack the door while sobs rock my body. Even when I hear the engine fall into gear, I continue to beat on the door. "We'll be back, Haley. Keep your fucking mouth shut, or I'll make sure to find you last."

The last door falls closed before the sound of screeching tires echo off the alley walls around me.

"Do you need an ambulance?" I hear Kaylan ask behind me once the sound of the car disappears.

BROKEN

"No." I lie, my arm slowly giving up the fight against the door. "He barely started when you showed up."

I almost fly backward when the door is shoved against my face. "Jesus Christ!" a rough male voice

I fall into Josh's chest, not giving a damn that he might be uncomfortable. "What the fuck happened, are you okay?"

"Call the cops, Ryan." Kaylan's voice rings in warning behind me.

"Who the fuck are you?" Josh fumes at hearing my real name, Kaylan must still be in the shadows. Turning to me he asks in a dangerous tone, "Did he hurt you?"

"I'm not the bad guy."

"Did he hurt you?" Hiding my arm, I shake my head.

"Haley?" Drew pushes through pulling me away from the doorway. "Where the fuck did you go- Wow, are you okay?!"

"Get her to the hospital and make sure she talks to the cops," Kaylan says again, closer this time.

"Hospital? Hales, what happened?"

"Don't move," Josh warns with a pointed finger. That's when I notice the blood on his forearm, Josh notices at the same time, "Is she bleeding?"

BROKEN

Drew pulls away from me, his eyes narrowing around my bent arm and the hand holding the fabric closed.

"Are you bleeding?" I nod, unable to speak through the tears. "Alice! Call the cops and get Parker! It's an emergency!"

"Where the fuck are you going?" Josh yells out of the door. "The cops are going to need to talk to you!"

Drew squints into the night trying to see who Josh is talking to, "Is that Kaylan?" His tone turns dark, "Did he fucking hurt you? I swear to God I'll kill-"

"He saved me." I cut him off shaking my head. God, my voice sounds like sandpaper feels.

"Kaylan, I know you got a shit record with your sister. But, I swear to God you better get your ass in here and make sure she's alright."

"Her new daddy doesn't want me near her. Call the cops, Drew. They'll be back; they know where she is and didn't finish the job."

"Stay with Haley," Josh tells Drew before stepping outside. "Who will be back and what job?"

"Our brothers and-"

"Kaylan!" I cry out. Stop talking; please stop talking.

"What job?"

"Kaylan, don't!"

"Hales?" Drew shakes his head at me in confusion.

"I don't know how to protect you any other way!" His voice raises, and I can hear the raw emotion threaded between each syllable.

"Stop talking." I sob, losing the strength in my knees. Drew steadies me to the floor, his concern growing more by the second as he pulls me into his lap.

"Are you finally going to tell them?!" He demands, sounding much closer now. "Are you going to tell the truth? Cause if you don't then I don't have a choice!"

"You're dead if you talk." I don't know if anything out my mouth is intelligible through the slurred sob.

"You're dead if you don't!" He yells. "Don't you get it?"

"Haley?!" Parker's voice carries down the hall.

"She's here!" Drew calls back while Kaylan and I glare at each other.

"How many birthdays do you have left in you, Ryan? How many birthdays until your wrist is the only available space? How long do you have until they come back to finish the job that you agreed to!"

"Kaylan!"

"NO!"

BROKEN

"What the fuck is happening?" Parker enters the room, rushing to my side, eyes wide with concern. "Is that blood?"

"Dammit! Stop trying to protect me!" Kaylan screams over Josh's shoulder. "That's my job!" His fist pounds against his chest. "It's my job to protect you! Don't you get it?! I thought if I left, they'd run out of reasons to hurt you! I'd rather die than witness that shit again!" He points down the alley. "Do you hear me?! If you don't talk, then I will! I'll swallow the consequences if it means you'll still be breathing at the end of the day!"

Parker is kneeling next to me trying to get me to release my arm. Drew is still talking to him, but I can't hear the words, my attention is solely on my brother. Twisting away from Parker, I hold my arm closer to my chest so he can't see. My vision is becoming blurred as my body grows colder. The edges are tinted in white as Kaylan goes in and out of focus.

Kaylan's head stops shaking, his eyes widening in concern, "Ryan?" I blink harder trying to focus on his face before he shoves past Josh and kneels in front of me. "Give me your arm."

"Back off," Drew warns in a tone to make the toughest guy wither.

"You said they didn't do anything!" He panics, reaching once again for my arm. Without asking again, he grabs my wrist, and I scream when the pain shoots through my chilling body. "No! No, no, no, no, no." He repeats, trying harder to claim my arm. "I think he slit her wrists. Ryan, give me your fucking arm!" His voice cracks.

"I'm sorry," Parker whispers into my hair. "I'm so sorry."

For the second time tonight, I'm held against my will. "I love you, I'm sorry."

Strong arms wrap around my middle, claiming my right wrist and pinning it to my stomach.

"Don't!" I sob as Drew pulls the sleeve away from my arm and Kaylan grabs at my forearm, prying it away from my body and into his lap. "I need a towel or something!" His thumbs wipe the blood for a moment before his breath catches, "Call an ambulance!"

The arms holding me down let go and I lose the strength to fight back. My brain is screaming to pull my arm away, to protect them from knowing, but my body won't respond. A second later Parker is leaning over me, shirtless. If I weren't so out of it, I would have really enjoyed this part. He hands his shirt to Kaylan before standing and pulling a box down from the shelf. Blinking hard I catch a long white line in his hand before he ties it around my forearm so tight that I cry out.

"Ambulance is on its way." Someone, somewhere says.

BROKEN

Kaylan repeats his favorite four-letter word while everyone else starts talking over one another, but I can't catch enough words to form sentences.

Parker kneels by my head, before dragging me onto his lap. He grabs my left arm and holds my wrist to his shoulder. "Look at me, baby. Don't close your eyes."

That's a very unfair thing to say. I'm not consciously making the decision to do it; it's just happening.

"Haley." I try to focus on his eyes, the blue is gone they're just dark smears across a blurred face. I blink again; I get a short glimpse at his beautiful face etched with unshed agony before it blurs and distorts again.

I just want to take his pain away, but at the same time, I'd be okay if this was how I go. Being in Parker's arms, surrounded by the only people that have ever mattered to me. Yes, this would be a nice way to go. I love him, I do. I love all of them.

I hear Parker calling my name but he's too far away, he's too far to hear me, so I tell him the words that were never able to escape my lips, I love you, I love you more than anything.

The pain goes away, the worries fade, and all I feel is the love and happiness swelling in my chest as my heart slows. They never left me. I'm okay with this being the end...because yes, all good things end, but I don't have to die alone,

BROKEN

and that's the most comforting thought I could have as the last pulse of energy slips from my grasp.

CHAPTER SIXTY-THREE: HALEY'S FUNERAL

I feel cold.

My head feels disconnected from my body and an odd combination of heavy and weightless claims me.

I feel my chest rise; the air is stale and cold.

Was I holding my breath?

My chest expands again; chemicals burn my nostrils. I try to pull away from the burning, but my neck isn't in control of my head anymore.

Muffled noise slowly sinks into my ears.

Thump, Thump, Thump.

Am I underwater? No, I can't be. I'm not; I can breathe.

Very slowly an itchy sensation tingles down my right arm and like I was standing too close to a blast, my body all at once feel overly warm.

Thump, thump, thump.

BROKEN

My thoughts dance around my head, but they're moving too fast to hold on to anything.

A small tug on my hand morphs into pressure, grounding me in a way.

I can't seem to hold on to anything except the pressure.

It's the only thing that's constant.

I think I hear my name but the fear of losing the steady push and pull against my hand keeps me from following the sound.

The longer I focus, the more I notice, like the fact there is slight pulse dancing between my pointer and middle finger, and every so often heat tickles across my knuckles. Sometimes the pressure eases for a split second before returning stronger than it was before.

I keep trying to catch it in the palm of my hand, but it slips away.

I'm scared I'll lose it.

Thump, thump.

The calm is being tainted with frustration as I try to hold on to it.

With my last-ditch effort, I force myself to close my hand.

It closes.

The pressure is rough, terrified to lose it I hold it tighter.

The water ebbs from my head leaving a god-awful ticking in its wake.

Beep, tick, thump.

"Haley?"

BROKEN

I know that voice.

I know, I know it.

Beep, tick, thump.

My mind is a book with every other page missing, and the goddamn noise won't stop long enough for me to focus.

I can't focus.

Beep, tick, thump.

I can't seem to grasp anything until the fire kisses my wrist.

That single kiss lights my skin on fire, and an agonizing ripple engulfs my arm.

I gasp, letting go of the pressure to stamp out the flames.

It hurts.

It hurts so bad.

I can't put it out-

PANIC.

Panic vices around my throat cutting off my scream.

"Baby, calm down. You're alright."

"My arm!" I hear a voice come out of my throat that doesn't belong to me, it's shrill and terrified, and screaming. "It's on fire! Put it out! Please, put it out!"

"Give me your hand, baby. I'll put it out, just give me your hand."

I start to tingle.

My head, my chest, everything starts to tingle.

"I know you. I know, I know you."

BROKEN

"You're alright, baby."

"I want Parker."

The pressure returns to my palm as the flames calm; he put them out.

Beep, tick, thump.

"I just need to- I just need..." I need something. I need to do something.

Something cold races through my veins, plunging me head first back into the abyss.

I lost the pressure.

PANIC.

Panic seized me until something captures my hand again.

The pressure.

The fire in my arm is gone while something beeps next to me.

Beep, beep, beep.

It's steady, pulsing.

Beep, beep.

My eyes-

They're closed.

I need to open them.

I know I need to, but someone needs to let them know that because they're ignoring my efforts to open them.

Beep, beep, beep.

Where's Parker? He could help me.

Beep, beep.

"I need Parker."

"I'm right here, sweetheart."

"I need you."

BROKEN

"I'm here, baby." The pressure tightens around my hand, and I squeeze back.
"Don't let go."
"Never."
And then I'm falling.
Fast.
My head turns cold.
My nose burns.
Darkness come claim me,
I don't want to fight.

I open my eyes to a green room with wood paneling. What the hell? Rolling my head to the right, I see him, the most beautiful person in existence. The corners of my lips twitch. His elbows are propped up on the bed; my hand is buried under both of his while his forehead rests against his knuckles. He looks so uncomfortable in the hideous pea-soup colored chair. My heart clenches so tight I think it might break, I squeeze his hand to alleviate the pressure building in my chest. His head snaps up.

"Hey, good looking." My voice comes out hoarse.

BROKEN

"Oh my God." He jerks forward, sliding the chair closer with one hand, still holding mine with the other.

"Are you okay?"

He laughs not with humor but shock, his expression pained. "That's my line." He shakes his head; there's so much pain behind those remarkable eyes, "Are you okay?"

At that moment the events that lead to this moment crash into me. My eyes widen as I take in the room, the hospital room. That god-awful beeping is my pulse. My gaze shoots to my exposed arm. Thick white gauze covers my wrist, my left arm is in a weird spoon-like brace. I try to rip my hand free of Parker's to hide the hideous purple and red scars showing, but he squeezes tighter, holding me back.

"Don't." He whispers gently. "Don't hide, not from me."

"I don't want you to see," I whisper, afraid any louder and it would give away the emotion I'm desperately trying to hide. "I don't want to see."

My breathing turns ragged, and I try to blink the tears away. Derek tried to kill me, Joey held me down, Kaylan showed up, I thought I died.

BROKEN

His hand gently grazes my chin, turning my face, so I'm looking at him, "Then look at me."

My teeth are going to break from how hard I'm biting down to keep the sob from escaping.

His thumb catches a rogue tear, "Please, don't cry."

I try, but I can't seem to make them stop now that they've fallen. He's in danger now; they're all in danger now.

Standing up he leans over me, bringing his lips to mine, in a kiss so tender I feel my heart literally breaking in my chest. I can't stop it; the dam breaks and I cry harder. My right hand comes up to hide my face from his view.

Climbing onto the edge of the bed, he pulls me against him. Cooing soothing words into my hair.

"I'm so sorry."

"Don't apologize." He pulls my hand down. His face is gentle, but I can see the seriousness in his eyes, "There isn't a damn thing you need to be sorry for. No part of this was your fault." His hand claims my jaw, "Do you hear me?"

"He's going to come after you now, and it's all my fault." I don't know if he can understand me, but I still try to talk through it anyway, "He said it was you or me. It was supposed to be me, why didn't you let it be me? It was supposed to be me."

"Shh, baby. It's okay now. It's over, sweetheart."

"It's not. He's going to kill you, and it's all my fault."

"Baby, shhh. No, he won't, it's over."

"It's not." My chest is constricting so tight I start to gag. "It's not." That fucking tick and beep every second is driving me to the point of insanity. "Make that noise stop, please make it stop!"

"Baby, you gotta calm down." His hands hold my face, so I'm forced to meet his eyes, "Focus on me, sweetheart. Breathe, baby." I force myself to take measured breaths like him until the erratic beeping of the machine next to my bed calms. "You're okay. I'm okay. Drew, Josh, Maria, everyone's okay. We're all here. Even Kaylan and some blonde girl with a kid. We're all okay, just breathe."

I don't know how much time has passed when he rests his forehead against mine. My heartbeat has returned to normal, and the tears have slowed.

"I've never been so scared in my life," he whispers.

BROKEN

"I'm sor-"

"Don't apologize." I can feel his him shake his head. "Don't you dare apologize."

I go to apologize for apologizing, but his mouth seals over mine, silencing me.

"Fuck, I thought you died." He sucks in a sharp breath, "I thought the only girl I've ever loved died."

I shutter as a new wave of emotion climbs out of my throat, he was never supposed to find out, he wasn't supposed to know, I was supposed to bleed out eight hundred miles north of him, not in his arms.

"I love you, Haley."

Unable to speak, I pull his face back and crush my lips against his. This time when I pull away from his hand, he lets me go. Placing my hand on his jaw, I draw him closer. I need him to know how I feel even if I can't get the words out, so I show him instead. Pouring everything I have into him, I try to make him understand that I really do love him. I love him with every fiber of my being. Every breath I draw in, every beat of my heart, it's all for him.

CHAPTER SIXTY-FOUR

    I didn't look when the nurse changed my dressings; I'd already seen the bruises from where Joey held me down, I didn't need to see the evidence of my opened vein or the incision against my palm where they had to reattach my flexor tendon. It's all just a reminder that their plan was to leave me for dead where I would be found by someone I love.

    I didn't tell the cops anything, either. Apparently, Josh and Kaylan already pointed fingers. I claimed my memory was still too fuzzy, reciting a few minor details, I tried to make them believe that I was actually trying to help. The truth is, I was all too aware that

BROKEN

Parker was next to me, hanging on to every word I said. I didn't want to cause him additional pain knowing the details of what happened. I later found out from a not so hushed conversation outside of my door that a HEAT surveillance camera caught the majority of the attack, including the faces of my brothers and the license plate. That's what happens when you get too cozy with being untouchable; Reno police have no reach here.

My first visitor outside of Parker is Drew, who enters with his eyes downcast holding out a maroon sweater and chocolate, Parker leans forward to accept them while Drew immediately turns around. I almost fall into another crying outburst.

With a wobbly lower lip, Parker helps me cover myself, careful not to tangle the IV lines or get my brace caught in the sleeve.

"She's good," Parker says while sitting down, he immediately claims my hand once again.

"Hey, sunshine." Drew meets my eyes, and I can see his heartache.

I choke on my breath and reach for him. Parker let go so I can wrap my arms around Drew's neck. He falls into me willingly, with his thick arms clutching around my middle. I can't speak, I'm sure to lose all composure if I do. We hug for a minute in silence before he pulls back and kisses the side of my head. With the grace of a pregnant cow, he flops down against my knee.

"I don't want to ask if you're okay because I know you're not but- Fuck, are you okay?"

I nod, and he shakes his head, his gaze falls to Parker and then back to me. His hands come up to roughly rub the emotion away from his face before they drop heavily into his lap. "You scared the ever-loving crap out of me, Hales."

My eyes burn, "I'm sorr-"

"Stop apologizing." Parker chastises gently, taking my hand again, his lips trailing lightly across my exposed knuckles. "He's not saying that because it's your fault. He's saying it because he wants you to know he cares about you, and he's relieved you're okay."

I nod, trying to blink away the tears when a gentle knock raps against the door.

"Party city!" Drew calls out.

I don't know what that means and before I can ask Josh comes into the room, holding a little brown bear with a balloon tied around its

BROKEN

wrist. I clench my jaw shut until the pain chases away the tears.

"Heard you were up." He says approaching my side with Maria in tow. "Also heard that girls like gifts. So here ya go, kid. From me to you."

I bit my lip as my shaky hand reaches out for the little plush bear.

Tears blur my vision as I hold the soft little toy to my chest, "No one's ever given me a teddy bear before."

"Every girl should have Teddy," Maria says gently.

I nod to keep the tears from falling. Sensing my hesitation, Maria comes to my rescue, "Hospital food tastes like dirt, so I made you some things." She moves to the little side table beside my bed, opening a canvas tote and starts to pull out containers, "I've got a turkey club from VIN's if you've got an appetite, some soup if you don't, and some shortcake. There's also hard candy and some sodas in here."

"Thank you." I rasp.

"Jules is bringing you some toiletries and other little nick knacks. They should be here soon."

Swallowing the lump in my throat, I nod. Funny that I was always teasing Parker for the motion, yet it seems to be the only thing I'm capable of doing today.

"What's the appropriate length of time to wait in a situation like this before it's acceptable for me to start cracking jokes?" Drew asks from his spot at the foot of my bed.

A real honest laugh bubbles out of my chest, "For the love of everything holy, now. Start now."

A wide smile engulfs his face, "Remember when Haley confessed her undying love to Parker?"

My smile drops off my face, "What?"

He eases back onto his elbow, so his face is directly above my foot. "Yep. Right there, bleeding out on the floor at HEAT." He deadpans me,

I sucked in my lips and nervously look at Parker, he's staring at the mattress with my hand against his chin, a gentle smile rests on his beautiful face.

"You don't remember that?" Drew smiles.

I shake my head.

"Well, wasn't the most romantic setting but I mean," He shrugs, "You guys first slept together on Josh's desk- so whatever."

BROKEN

Lifting my foot, I kick him gently in the ear. "We did not sleep together!"

"OW!"

"Wuss."

Without mercy, he grabs my foot and starts tickling me through the thin hospital sheet. Squealing, I try to stop him, but Parker has my injured hand, and I have an IV in the other.

"Stop!" I laugh, "That's cheating! I'm plugged in and can't reach you!" I howl with laughter as I thrash in the little bed, everyone seems to be enjoying my torture, "Traitors!" I yell trying to pull away.

When he finally let's go the heaviness in the air has vanished, leaving love and the power of a family in its wake.

BROKEN

EPILOGUE

Correcting the sleeve of my gown for the umpteenth time, I give the mirror a heavy sigh. "I don't know if I can do this."

"Haley. Breathe." Kaylan takes my shoulders and forces me away from the mirror. "You put one foot in front of the other until you reach the end of the aisle. Easy, peasy."

"It's not that easy. Everyone's going to be staring at me."

"Mhm, that's kinda the point."

"I don't want to be stared at," I whine, fluffing the skirt of my dress, so it covers my feet.

"Then you shouldn't have said yes." He gives me an easy smile before gently kissing my forehead.

Kaylan and I have been doing really well. The last fight we had was the day before my

BROKEN

father's trial. I refused to go; I had already been forced to recount the attack in front of a jury after my brothers were pulled over and arrested while trying to flee the state. They were found guilty and sentenced to fifteen years in prison. And wouldn't you know, hearing that gavel smack into the podium made Derek sing like a bird. He gave up my dad, the corrupted officials, and countless other names that had my father in handcuffs by the end of the day. Kaylan wanted me to testify against him, but I refused, they have so much against him nothing I said was going to make a damn bit of difference. All I knew was that I wasn't the snitch and my father was rotting. I was free.

Parker took the liberty of moving my shit into his apartment one day, and I've been there ever since and Kaylan manned up and put a ring on Caroline's finger, so I gave him the key to my old apartment to keep them close, I wasn't willing to lose my nephew anymore than I was willing to give up Kaylan, though Caroline I could live without. Drew finally let me meet biker chick, yes, I am well aware she has a name, but I choose not use it, I enjoy pissing her off.

She's a cool chick when she's not a bitch; her cousin is the one who tattooed me- oh, right, you don't know about that.

Drew convinced me to get a permanent sleeve to cover my shame. Josh, Parker and

BROKEN

Drew kicked her cousin, Lynch- stupid name, I know, some money and he covered every available inch of skin, shoulder to wrist in a beautiful mural.

My shoulder is a stunning Arizona sunset; the sun is kissing the saddle of Camelback Mountain which blends into a desert that takes up my entire tricep. Following the spiral road from my elbow, you pass VIN'S Dive Bar, a motorcycle, and the entry to Basswood Apartments before it curves once again and travels down the inside of my forearm. HEAT takes up the majority of skin, its entrance butting up against the road that travels straight to my wrist where a devilishly handsome silhouette rests against a 1969 Camaro SS. The detail and amount of work that went into this is remarkable, the texture of my burns and raised edges of my scars make the whole thing appear photorealistic- it's incredible, but also terrifying. I have yet to reveal my arm to anyone, other than Parker since Lynch finished my wrist last week.

"Pink's a pretty color on you." I jump out of my skin and spin towards his voice.

Parker is leaning against the door; he's dressed in a perfectly tailored black suit. Mother mercy me, he is a steaming pile of yummy. He shaved the scruff off his jaw for the wedding, and I'm still pouting about it.

BROKEN

"You scared the hell out of me." I hiss, my hand still resting over my racing heart, "You're not allowed in here."

"No, the grooms not allowed in here." The right side of his mouth raises, and I melt a little. "What were you thinking about?"

"My tattoo," I start, moving to the little chair in the corner to put on my silver heels. "The fact my brothers and my dad are behind bars and that I'm finally free, then you popped out of nowhere and scared the hell out of me."

Parker chuckles while he approaches, holding his hand out to me so I can stand easier.

I accept and allow him to pull me against him. "Didn't you hear Kaylan? He said bye to you before I even spoke."

I look around the room, surprised that Kaylan really is gone. "I didn't realize he left."

Parker chuckles again, his nose sliding up my throat. "Are you ready?"

Nervous butterflies take over my stomach, and I grip his forearms for support, "No, I'm terrified."

"Don't be. I'll be there with you the whole way down, and by the time we get to the altar, Maria will be coming down, and no one will even remember you exist."

I laugh, and he gives me that panty dropping Hayes family smile, "You know, I'm going to marry you one day Haley Carter."

BROKEN

"I know." I kiss him gently, "I'm counting on it."

BROKEN

Drew's story is **available now**!

FAMISHED: PART ONE

Takes you back to the night Haley ran away from Phoenix with Kaylan. Giving you a behind the scenes look at what was happening while Haley was away and the hell trapped inside Drew's head.

LINK:
https://www.amazon.com/Famished-Broken-Ellie-Messe-ebook/dp/B07L2BRC5V/ref=cm_cr_arp_d_product_top?ie=UTF8

Part Two will be released May 2019.

BROKEN

You can talk more and stay updated with Broken characters in my reader's group on Facebook:

Ellie's Broken Bitches
https://www.facebook.com/groups/293842771137422/

JOIN AND YELL AT ME. ☺

You can also sign up for a non-monthly newsletter containing cover reveals, release dates, and day of releases here:
https://www.elliemesse.com/members

BROKEN

PLAYLIST

Mother - Danzig (cover by Lissie)
Take me to church- Hozier
Family - Noah Gundersen
Cherry Wine- Hozier
My Blood- Ellie Goulding
Dancing on my own- Calum Scott
Fight Song- Rachel Platten
Little Bird - Ed Sheeran

Parker's Song:
Love Me Now - John Legend

Haley's Song:
Too Good at Goodbyes - Sam Smith (Sofia Karlberg Cover)

BROKEN

ACKNOWLEDGEMENTS

I blame all of you.
Because of your nagging and endless support, I have a completed book ready for print and ebook release. *squeals*
If this book is a success, know that it wouldn't exist if it weren't for my sister. She was the one who encouraged all of this. On that same note, if this book sucks, she is the head of the complaint department because she told me it was good and it's all her fault.

To my amazing and incredible sister, Nae Nae,
For all of your encouragement, rage texts, and long conversations involving this book. I seriously could not have done this without you. I might have gone insane if it wasn't for your support. Thank you for putting up with me and humoring me when I go into two-hour long rants about something I didn't even put in the book.
You were the one who told me to write for the first time. You convinced me that everyone could kindly fuck off and I should write. Without you, I wouldn't be here. I love you twat-licker, you're my muse, my rock, my bestest friend. Oh... and for anyone who wants to oppose you, Nae already called dibs. #ParkerBelongsToNaeNae

Ian, thank you for all your support, helping me, and listening to my endless rants. ALSO, because I love you; *his engorged purple headed member pressed into my lush lady garden.* There, I put your suggestion in my book.

My amazing PA, BETA reader, and dear friend, Sam Knowlton - because you called me a pretty whore when we first met. <3
Your enthusiasm was the kick to my ass that I needed to stop dragging my feet and finish this book. Thank you for your support, quirky comments, and endless encouragement. #BookWife #ThugLife #DrewBelongsToSam

To those bangerangin' bitches in BANG and Mel Teo at Booksmacked for creating it. Thank you for making this process way less scary and showing interest and support in a nobody's work. Thank you! I love everyone of you peen loving hookers.

And last but not least, I would like to acknowledge that my spelling is glaring problem. It was there all along, starring me in the face until I was certain we would loose our minds. Hahaha.

BROKEN

MEET THE AUTHOR

My name is not actually Ellie Messe, I have a pseudonym so that I can feel like the Batman of the author world. I'm a fun-loving book dragon who has the ability to make sailors blush with colorful language and obscene gestures. I love reading, mostly young adult and new age romance. I'm a part of a BANGerangin' book club that is guaranteed to be better than yours. I like to spend my days wondering around department stores while reading erotica out loud, scaring the piss out of people, and playing "The floor is lava". (Adulting is lame.)

STAY CONNECTED ON SOCIAL MEDIA:

-Let's be friends on Facebook; https://www.facebook.com/ellie.messe.1

-My reader's group for exclusive excerpts, first looks, and sneak peeks; https://www.facebook.com/groups/293842771137422/

-Website: https://www.elliemesse.com

-Like Page: https://www.facebook.com/EllieMesseAuthor/

-Instagram for teasers; @EllieMesse.Author

Printed in Great Britain
by Amazon

68437342R00440